The Olcinium

THE AUTHOR

ANDREJ NIKOLAIDIS was born in 1974 to a mixed Montenegrin-Greek family and raised in Sarajevo, Bosnia. In 1992, following the breakout of ethnic strife in the country that soon erupted into an all-out war, Nikolaidis' family moved to Ulcinj, his father's hometown in Montenegro, where he still lives. He is an ardent supporter of Montenegrin independence, anti-war activist and promoter of human rights, especially minority rights. His books fiction work include *Mimesis* (2003) and *Sin* (*The Son*), 2006, for which he was awarded the EU Prize for Literature; *Mimesis i drugi skandali* (*Mimesis and Other Scandals*), 2008; *Dolazak* (*The Coming*); 2009; *Devet* (*Till Kingdom Come*), 2014, and most recently *Mađarska rečenica* (*The Hungarian Sentence*), 2017, which won him the Meša Selimović Prize. His non-fiction works are *Homo Sucker : Poetika Apokalipse*, 2010 and *Mala enciklopedija ludila* (*The Small Encyclopedia of Madness*), 2013. Nikolaidis still lives in Ulcinj and writes freelance for a number of regional newspapers and online portals, and has also written for the Guardian online.

THE TRANSLATOR

WILL FIRTH was born in 1965 in Newcastle, Australia. He studied German and Slavic languages in Canberra, Zagreb and Moscow. Since 1991 he has been living in Berlin, Germany, where he works as a translator of literature and the humanities (from Russian, Macedonian and all variants of Serbo-Croatian). His best-received translations of recent years have been Robert Perišić's *Our Man in Iraq*, Aleksandar Gatalica's *The Great War* and Faruk Šehić's *Quiet Flows the Una*, all published by Istros Books in London. See www.willfirth.de.

ANDREJ NIKOLAIDIS

THE OLCINIUM TRILOGY

Translated from the Montenegrin
by Will Firth

Foreword by Morelle Smith

istrosbooks

First published in 2019 by
Istros Books
London, United Kingdom
www.istrosbooks.com

Previously published in English in three editions by Istros Books:
The Coming (2012), *The Son* (2013) and *Till Kingdom Come* (2015)

This translation of The Olcinium Trilogy is published by arrangement with
Ampi Margini Literary Agency and with the authorization of Andrej Nikolaidis

Cover design and typesetting: Davor Pukljak | www.frontispis.hr

ISBN: 978-1-912545-99-5

Education and Culture DG

Culture Programme

This project has been funded with support from the European Commission. This publication
reflects the views only of the author, and the Commission cannot be held responsible for
any use which may be made of the information contained therein.

OFF THE MAP –
THE WHERE AND WHY OF
ANDREJ NIKOLAIDIS' FICTION

"Ulcinj was a place at the margin of old maps,
where you step off the edge of the flat earth."

So wrote Harry Hodgkinson, writer and journalist, in the 1930s. Hodgkinson was walking across Europe, and he was to discover there was more world beyond Ulcinj, even if there were no more maps.

That was almost a century ago, and today Ulcinj is a picturesque Montenegrin town of red roofed houses on the shimmering Adriatic coast, and a popular tourist resort in the summer months. Yet in Andrej Nikolaidis' novels, Ulcinj, however beautiful on the surface, hides a murky brew of neighbourly intrigues, resentments, prejudices, alcoholism, dastardly murders and despair. This small town even turns out to be the scene of apocalyptic weather conditions for which the term 'climate change' is much too tame: the pot of simmering antipathies overflows into severe floods, destroying fields and crops and farm animals, and then into conflagrations that annihilate olive groves, barns and houses, or even summer snowstorms that sow panic among the tourists.

Ulcinj's history swarms up to the surface in Nikolaidis' stories; a history of slave trade, piracy and fighting for survival and dominion – Venetian fleets, Turkish fleets, British gunboats: ships go up in flames, cannons are fired, populations suffer miserably. History spews up its past like volcanic eruptions, and the future too, arrives ahead of its time in its varied – though often watery – weather disguises and tricksy deluges.

Time is in fact one of the major themes that Nikolaidis addresses in his novels; his characters often suffering from a sense of time being split, fragmented and even dissolving into a morass of unidentifiable discrete episodes, which they struggle to force into relationship. Since time, memory and identity are all so linked together, the fragmentation accelerates. Because the main characters' vision sees through the sleepy domestic superficiality into other eras, as well as into the present, revealing seething desperations, they address – even attack in some cases – the political patina of ideals and goals, and delve instead into truth and its nature, as they are personally experienced, in contrast with the politicians' slick slogans.

Nikolaidis is a virtuoso of ideas, and multiple narratives. Yarn is both thread and story in the intrigues, mysteries, and conspiracies of his work: disbelief is here not just suspended but stretched and spun into multi-patterned cloaking fabrics. The reader is taken on a breath-taking, fast-moving examination of how people form their ideas, beliefs, opinions and prejudices.

"When has the non-existence of something ever been a reason not to live one's life by it and to kill in its name?" muses David in *Till Kingdom Come*. *"Things that don't exist, but which people believe in, produce consequences much more real than things that exist and no one believes in."*

On this tour through history (geographical, political, military, ideological) we are introduced to curious and influential figures from the past – religious, political, and literary – who are pulled into the flow, to act as witnesses to change, revolution and even, sometimes, inspiration.

This blend of narrative and ideas reflects the geography of this part of the world – rising steeply to dizzy heights like the mountains, and breaking up into fragments like the many islands off the Adriatic coastline, as stories interweave and link together. Stories of local inhabitants mingle with stories from the past, and with literary and philosophical references. People's motives too, can be clear and calm as the sea surface, or as raging and despairing as the storms battering the shore. The flood flotsam is mirrored in the waves of displaced people who have been stranded by war and despotic regimes in the past, along with present day tourists and refugees – stranded by economic, political or climate collapse.

In all of these novels there are puzzles to be solved – puzzles of personal identity, of meaning, of relationships, or the investigation into who perpetrated heinous acts. The metaphorical and the real intermingle gloriously, with actual tunnels leading out into light, and actual works of art - such as Dürer's *Melencholia I* - providing another (possible) clue in the protagonist's trajectory through time and geography in his quest for truth.

Time is explained in many ways - by both the learned and the uneducated - but one property it never possesses is the arrow-straight line of past to future. It circles and doubles back on itself, a multi-dimensional maze.

"For me today, the years don't pass: they fall like trees – not olive trees but the massive trunks of the northern forests… …They fall and it hurts. Maybe the logic is, the more we get battered, the better we can measure time."

Yet for all the serious themes, there is never a lack of humour, and Nikolaidis' humour is often dark and biting, his characters' misanthropic remarks side-stepping – or deliberately challenging – social and cultural taboos.

"A primitive person is unable to exist in quiet discretion: he always creates noise, unsightliness, and stench. He does everything he can to be noticed – he constantly emits his existence. His being is a blow to the senses and an insult to the intelligence."

However dark, the humour is genuinely funny, it cuts below the surface, revealing people's motives, pretences, and rock-solid prejudices. It runs like quicksilver through the philosophical and linguistic patterning of these extraordinarily inventive novels.

These translations by Will Firth catch so well the irony and the dark humour, the rapid changes of consciousness and scene, the different registers of the varied characters, with an idiomatic use of English that does justice to the quirky and the profound in these remarkable novels.

Morelle Smith, poet and author of The Tirana Papers

**The
Son**

I

Everything would have been different if I'd been able to control my repulsion, I realised.

The sun was still visible through the lowered blinds. It had lost all its force and now, unable to burn, it disappeared behind the green of the olive groves which extended all the way to the pebbly beach of Valdanos and on as far as Kruče and Utjeha; bays sardined with bathers determined to absorb every last carcinogenic ray before going back to their accommodation. There they would douse their burnt skin with imitations of expensive perfumes, don their most revealing attire and dash off to discos and terraces with *turbofolk* music, full of confidence that tonight they would go down on another body with third-degree burns; possessing and then forgetting another human being almost identical to themselves.

At first I'd resolved to stay in bed a bit longer, but I had to get up because the stench of sweat in the room was unbearable. The room is located on the western side of the house, and it's as hot as a foundry in there in the afternoons. The sun beats against the walls for hours and hours. Even when the bugger goes down, the walls still radiate the heat. They bombard me with it all night long. Ever since we moved into the house and I first lay in that bed, I've sweated. I wake at three in the morning and have to get out of bed because the pillow and the sheet are drenched with perspiration and start to stink. What's more, they stink dreadfully – it's simply unbearable. My own body drives me out of bed.

Making that room the bedroom was a catastrophic decision. We carried in the bed, wardrobe and bookshelves, and sealed the unhappy fate of our marriage, although we wouldn't realise it until later. Nothing could survive the night in that room, certainly nothing as fragile and bloodless as our marriage.

For two years I sweated, woke horrified by the reek of my own body and drank coffee on the balcony for hours. Shortly before dawn,

I would fall asleep again briefly on the couch in the living room. Worn out by insomnia and fatigue, I would go in and cuddle her when she woke. For two years I tried to grasp what was amiss and why everything seemed to go wrong for us. I strained my mind as best I could, exhausted by insomnia and the dissatisfaction which filled the house. For two years I wasn't even able to think. And then it was all over. She left. 'I can't take this anymore', she yelled, and was gone.

That same instant I threw myself onto the bed, where even just the night before we'd said 'I love you' to each other in our ritual of hypocrisy. I was asleep before I hit the pillow. I woke bathed in sweat, as usual. She really has gone – that was the first thing I thought when I opened my eyes. She wasn't there anymore, but the bed still stank of me.

I got up and almost fled from the bed. I closed the door behind me, determined that nothing would ever leave that room again. I plodded to the kitchen and put on some water for coffee. Then I ran back to the room and locked the door twice just to be sure.

I thought it would be good to read something, I said to myself. It really was high time. For two whole years I hadn't read anything except the crime column in the newspaper. The only things which still interested me were crime news and books about serial killers. It was as though only overt eruptions of evil could jolt me out of my indifference. I no longer had the energy for the hermeneutics of evil. That was behind me now. I could no longer stand searching for evil in the everyday actions of so-called 'ordinary people'. Instead, I chose vulgar manifestations of evil. If a man killed thirty people and buried them under his house, that still had a wow factor for me. But I'd lost the strength to deal with the everyday animosities, suppressed desires and cheap tricks of the people I met: those who treated me as if I was blind, convinced that they'd duped me into believing their good intentions and made a total fool of me, while I simply looked through them as if they didn't exist.

He Offered Himself for Dinner, the paper wrote that morning. The crime column reported on the cheerful story of Armin Meiwes, a cannibal from Germany, who had joined an online cannibal community. Humans are sociable beings: they come together when they're born, they flock together when they go off to do their military service and learn to kill other human beings, they come together to mate and to marry, and ultimately they also congregate when they want to eat one another. Meiwes had found a place where kindred souls gathered. He wanted to eat someone and confided this to his friends from the cannibal community. When he placed an announcement in the forum, replies came in from 400 people who wanted to be eaten. And so he chose one of them. It seems this fellow had particular demands: he requested that he and his benefactor celebrate a 'last supper' together and eat his penis before he be killed. Obliging Meiwes wanted to fulfil his wish, but after their initial enthusiasm they agreed that the meal was inedible. The paper then went on to explain how the 'volunteer' then felt sick and started saying the Lord's Prayer. Meiwes, whom doctors established to be quite normal, stated that he skipped the prayer because 'he couldn't decide who his father was – God or the Devil – so he didn't know whom he should be praying to'. In any case, Meiwes killed the fellow after the prayer, later ate him and filmed the whole business.

I went to the bookshelf and took down Eliot's *The Waste Land*, which a friend had given us in our first summer in the house. The November of that year was rainy and condemned us to stay at home since the continuous deluges made our walks through the olive grove impossible. That month we tried to achieve the idyll from B-movies, sitting in armchairs in *our* living room with a fire crackling in *our* fireplace. We sat and read Eliot. I read aloud and she listened. I loved her then, like I always loved her. Then I couldn't take it anymore, like I'd never been able to take it anymore. But I decided to go on after all, like I always decide I should go on. Things never fail *because of* me, nor do they go off well *thanks to* me. They always happen with me as a bystander. I just adapt to them.

As a child I imagined life as an enormous desert which I had to walk through while trying not to disturb a thing or to leave any trace. Not one footprint was to remain in the sand after I was gone, not one flake of ash from the fire I laid, not one bone of an animal I killed to eat, not one scrap of waste from the caravan I met, not one tree at the oasis whose bark I carved my initials in, not one woman in a village with a child of mine by her side. I was just passing through, and I took care that no one noticed and was able to say: he was here. That's how I thought back then, and that's how I still think today. But that's not what I did. I got married. I took a wife but continued travelling without a trace. In the end she declared 'I can't take this anymore!' and left. I could have said that too, but I didn't – she said it because she was stronger than me.

April is the cruellest month, according to Eliot. But he never lived on the Montenegrin riviera, and his fellow citizens didn't rake in wealth by renting out rooms. He never saw tourists arriving in his peaceful town like hordes of Huns and turning it into a giant, barbarian amusement park, and he never felt how it feels when your habitat shrinks to the boundaries of your courtyard, because simply leaving the house means having to forge your way through a seething mass of foreign bodies, all of whom are ugly, loud and possessed by the pursuit of pleasure. It is this that always forces me to rush back home in panic, constantly vigilant for the omnipresent, lurking danger: I return to the world of my own property, separated by a tall fence from the rest of the world which has been occupied by unknown and terrible people. August is the cruellest month, I say.

I think it was Al-Ghazali who wrote that *heaven is surrounded by suffering, whereas hell is surrounded by pleasures.* Seen from up on the forested hill where my house is, the town I live in looks like hell in the summertime. Tourism is a trade in pleasure, and people in a tourist town are indeed *surrounded by pleasures.* So Al-Ghazali was right: I am in hell because I am *surrounded by pleasures.* Sartre is also right when he says *hell is the others.* Their pleasure is my hell.

The phone rang. A friend was calling to tell me that a DVD edition of the film *Cannibal Holocaust* had just arrived from America.

'What's that?' I asked him.

'A film about an expedition of film-makers who come across a tribe of cannibals in the Amazon jungle,' he said.

'Sounds good for starters. What happens after that?'

'Nothing much – the rest of the film is about the cannibals eating them. The distributors I got it from are called Grindhouse and specialise in the obscurest, most shocking and most repulsive films of all time,' he explained, not without enthusiasm. 'Imagine what I've just seen in their catalogue: there's a whole range of films where people are put to the most terrible of tortures, raped, slashed open, quartered and eaten. There are also titles where it says *No animals suffered in the making of this film*. Get that?' he yelled into the receiver.

'I get it,' I answered through my teeth.

'They're worried that some lovers of cannibalism, who watch movies of people being disembowelled, might feel squeamish about violence towards animals,' he bellowed.

'I'm afraid I get it,' I said.

I realised I wouldn't be able to read any more after that. There's always something at the last instant which prevents me from reading. For reading and any kind of mental exertion I need leisure. If I never felt bored, I'd never write anything. And I was still bored now, as usual, but for some time I'd been unable to think why I should read or write at all and why it was important to 'develop my mind'. I gave up all thought of reading and turned on the computer.

I couldn't get onto the internet. The dial-up connection kept tossing me offline. The telephone exchange was overloaded due to the thousands of Kosovo-born tourists who were probably sending messages to their families in Western Europe. In the summertime, these *Gastarbeiters* like to show off the pittance they've earned by insisting on these two weeks of annual holiday which bring them only frustration: no matter how much they've strutted like peacocks and seduced young girls from Peć with their gold chains and ten-year-old Mercedes, the stench of the toilets they've cleaned and will go back to clean in Munich, Stockholm or Graz still sticks in their nostrils. Now they were back from the beach and frantically phoning and sending mails, driven by the need to communicate, despite being illiterates for whom every spoken word induced suffering like that of giving birth.

I was livid with contempt and antipathy, an abhorrence which flooded over me as completely and utterly as they say saints are suffused with love. I needed to see open space: the soothing emptiness of the sea; a blue unpolluted by people. I rushed out onto the balcony.

The first shades of night were falling. The sun was setting once more behind my great-uncle's olive grove, which is what we called the hill laden with rows of overgrown olive trees. In fact, it was fifty hectares of viper- and boar-infested scrub blocking our view of the sea. My father claimed he'd once seen 'something otherworldly' come down to land behind the hill. I never managed to convince him that it was just the sun. Evening after evening, we sat on the terrace waiting for darkness to fall. We watched in silence as the sun slowly disappeared behind the silhouette of the hill, which had always stood between me and the world. When the light was gone, my father would get up, state resolutely, 'No way, that wasn't the sun!' and disappear into the house. From then on, the only sign of his existence would be strains of Bach which escaped from the dark of the bedroom, where he lay paralysed by the depression which had abused him for two decades.

That evening the hill caught on fire. Instead of feeling a breeze from the sea, I was hit in the face by the heat of the burning forest. The fire would erase all my father's labours once more, I thought. After each blaze, the police scoured the terrain searching for evidence which would lead them to the culprit. Needless to say, they never found anything: not a single piece of broken glass or a match, let alone any trace of the firebug. 'They'll never find out who set fire to our hill, I tell you. How can they when the fire comes from another world?' my father repeated.

When the hill burned the first time, he saw it as a sign of God: 'My whole life passed by without me even taking a proper look at the olive grove my uncle left me. Now there's no olive grove left – just my obligation to the land,' my father spoke with the fatalism so typical of this crazy, blighted family.

He built a fence around the entire hill. He worked his way through the charred forest step by step, breaking stones and driving hawthorn-wood stakes into the rock, as if into the heart of a vampire. Then he tied barbed wire to the stakes, which tore into the flesh of his hands. For months he came home black from head to toe like a coal miner who had just emerged from the deepest pit. And that's what he was: a miner. He delved into the heart of his memories. He wasn't clearing the charcoaled forest but digging at what was inside him, breaking the boulder which oppressed him, shovelling away the scree which had buried him alive. He came home all wet and sooty for months, until one day he announced that his work was done. The property was fenced in and cleared. He had built new dry stone walls and planted olive saplings. He took me and my mother onto the terrace and showed us my great-uncle's olive grove for the umpteenth time. 'I've resurrected it from the flames,' my father pronounced.

When the hill burned the second time, he installed a new fence and planted the olive trees again. As if that was not enough work, he also built a barn. Then he brought in goats from Austria. His diligence went so far that he even minded them. That year he was a goatherd. During the day he would roam over the hill with the goats; in the early evening he would bring them back to the barn for the night. 'The pasture is excellent this year –,' he said, 'fresh growth is coming up from the scorched earth, and so the goats are eating the best food. Now they're fenced in, safe from the jackals, and have a nice dry place to sleep: like a five-star hotel,' he was fond of adding.

My mother thought she knew the root of my father's devotion to the goats. She claimed to remember from my grandmother's stories that my great-uncle had tuberculosis. 'He died of it in the end, too, but he owed the last years of his life to the goats,' my mother said. 'A goatkeeper came from Šestani and brought him milk. He lived on even after the doctors had written him off, thanks to that milk.

He had no wife or children, only your grandmother – the wife of his deceased brother – your father, and those goats up in Šestani. He lived with your grandmother and your father, and the goats helped him survive,' my mother told me.

Born in the coastal range of Crmnica, my great-uncle had left for America in his youth. He fled his impoverished village for New York, only to go hungry in the big city for the next three years. He slept in neglected warehouses and stole vegetables from the markets to feed himself. Occasionally he would kill a stray dog, and then he thanked the Lord for the skills with knife and stick he had learnt hunting birds on Lake Skadar. 'After the first week I knew I'd succeed. I knew I'd survive,' he later told his brother's wife and her son. 'I eked out a lonely living in the middle of New York as if I was up in the wilds of Montenegro.' The boy stared, riveted, while he spoke about the dog skin he had made shoes from. The boy had never seen his own father, but he imagined he must have looked like this uncle with the short, grizzled moustache who now came into their kitchen in shoes of strong-smelling leather (maybe even dog-leather?), hugged his mother and him, slipped some money for sweets into his pocket like uncles do, and in the evening told them tales of his adventures. What an uncle, what a man!

He made it good in America but died of a broken heart, my grandmother told my father, who later told me: 'He never married and therefore died unhappy. "Everything I've done and all the roads I've travelled have been in vain because I'm dying without a son," he said before he died.' My mother, while she was alive, maintained he would have lived longer if he'd stayed in America: 'But he came back, saw your father and fretted for the son he'd never had – that's what killed him in the end.'

He slaved away all his life, only to die in misery. But he left all his worldly goods to his sister-in-law. That saved her from the penury she faced after her husband's death and would have had to raise her child in. 'All my young years I ate the fruits of my uncle's labour; I fed on his sweat and suffering,' my father used to say.

The man from Crmnica laboured, suffered and died. That's the whole story about each and every one of us: the complete biography of the human race. He was buried fifty years ago, and what's left of him is going up in flames tonight.

Now it's all over, I thought as I watched the flames rising into the night sky. The hill was burning for the third time in ten years. The fire would be my father's final defeat. He no longer had the strength to raise the property from the ashes again. After my mother died, the enforced loneliness he was ill-prepared for exacerbated his depression. He hardly ever left the house anymore. He would just sit in the darkened living room all day. I asked myself what he was thinking about, but in fact I didn't really care. I just hoped he *was* thinking and that at least his thoughts might manage to break through the tall, smooth walls of depression which surrounded him.

That night the hill was on fire, but he didn't go out in front of the house even to watch the flames which were swallowing up all his labours. From the balcony of my house I watched his terrace, without hope that he would appear or maybe even step through the door he had decided to die behind. His wife had died, and mine had left me. Two men, each in his own house, whom not even a fire blazing a hundred yards away could unite; not even to watch the spectacle of it devouring their property.

The burning hill sounded like the crackle of an old record. Or the hiss of a cassette. Something you could get rid of by pressing the Dolby button. But now the flames spread out of control down the slopes of the hill. I turned on the local radio and learnt that the first houses had been evacuated. Behind the first houses, of course, were more houses. And then mine. I was horrified by the thought that the whole neighbourhood had again pooled its efforts and was trying its hardest to stop the fire. Actually they were obstructing the fire brigade in doing its job. I could just imagine the neighbours gossiping about me. 'He's the only one who's not here,' I could hear them whisper to each other. 'It's their property that's burning and he's not here. Why do we have to put out their fire?' they asked themselves, ignoring the fact that they were out there protecting their own houses, not my olive grove. They were only fighting the fire in my olive grove because they feared it could encroach on their houses. 'My olive grove' wasn't mine anyway.

They said on the radio that the government had sold all its Canadair aircraft to Croatia because it had assessed that the country didn't need a fleet of water bombers. That was in the springtime. The coastal area had been set alight in the first days of June and was still burning – from Lastva above Tivat to Budva, Petrovac, Možura and all the way to Lake Skadar. Now Ulcinj was ablaze too: the flames had spread from my great-uncle's hill to the first houses in the suburb of Liman. The walls of the Old Town were also at risk, the radio reported.

Since the government had sold the aeroplanes, the fire was being fought with helicopters. They were hauling up water in what looked like sacks and dropping it on the fire. The instant the water fell on the ground, smoke and steam obscured its elemental beauty. Everything vanished momentarily in grey, but the flames only needed another minute or two to re-establish their reign over my father's property.

I soon tired of the scene. Three helicopters were now in operation, and it was plain to see that they would defeat the fire in what would be one more triumph of technology. Once technology and nature were pitted against each other in this way I felt there was nothing left for me. And yet I simply couldn't make up my mind as to which was more monstrous: nature itself or the methods people employ in order to dominate it. Before turning and going back into the room, I glanced over to my father's house. The lights were off, but I knew he wasn't asleep.

It was at that point that I heard the bleating of goats. The neighbour must have been herding a flock along the road towards the house. 'Eh, mate!' I heard him call, and that sound made the blood freeze in my veins. I wasn't prepared for a conversation with him. I wasn't in the state of mind to thank him for saving my father's goats from the fire, or to invite him in for a drink and have a good talk like good neighbours and real men are supposed to.

But he was already standing at the gate, which I always kept locked, and waving to me. Great: now there was no escape. I put on my boxers and went down to open up for him.

'What a tragedy, eh mate?' he droned. Fortunately he didn't expect me to answer. As he drove the goats in through the gate he continued: 'Everything your father did has burnt down. I only just managed to save these ones here. I got them out when the barn caught fire. There was no saving it. Such a great shame, ain't it mate? But that's life for you – people slave away, and sometimes you wonder what for. You slog and sweat, and then everything goes up in smoke in a flash. *It was destroyed by the flames*, they say. But it wasn't the flames – it was God.'

With this kind of attitude, he was bound to be considered a wise man by those who knew him.

Finally all the goats were in the courtyard, and I realised I was already sick of the situation. The goats themselves immediately set about what they do best: surviving. These creatures, who had only just eluded death, now grazed indifferently and stank to high heaven. The billy goats were the most accomplished in that; they stank even worse than my neighbour, who doggedly came up behind me every time I tried to move away from him to get a breath of fresh air.

'You know, old son –,' he schmoozed, determined to get some reward for his good deed, 'I always tell people there's no better *rakija* than yours.'

'Let's go upstairs,' I said, too weak to fight against the kind of incivility where people invite themselves into others' houses.

But I hadn't set one foot on the stairs when I was compelled to turn around abruptly, feeling as if someone was watching me. And sure enough, my paranoia was justified once again: the black he-goat was looking at me intently. His yellow eyes were staring at me in the dark. Their slit-shaped pupils looked like cracks in the earth, ready to swallow me up. He threateningly flared his nostrils, from where a gleaming trail of saliva trickled. His sharp little teeth chewed the grass I'd just walked on, and he kept his eyes on me. I was sure we were thinking about the same thing: he about how to eat me, and me about my flesh disappearing into his mouth, his teeth sinking into my body and tearing off piece after piece.

'You all right, mate?' I heard the man say behind me. I turned back and saw my neighbour, whom I'd completely forgotten. For the first time in my life I was glad to see him. For the first time I found comfort in another human being, despite his gap-toothed smile and half-witted gaze set beneath a low brow and red lop-ears. *Away, away from the animals!* I thought as I rushed up the stairs. My neighbour ran after me in surprise.

'Whoa, easy does it, mate. You look a bit pale,' I heard him say.

I led him into the house and cast one more glance at the he-goat. He was still standing in the same place and staring at me. It was as if he wanted to make it clear to me that I'd opened the gate of my house for him, that he'd entered and that he'd never leave. He'd stand there and wait for me until the end, whenever my end would be.

'I don't have any *rakija*. Do you drink whisky?'

'I drink everything,' he said.

I poured myself a full glass and just two fingers for him because I wanted him to leave as soon as possible. We sat in the armchairs in the living room, opposite each other. I put the bottle down on the table between us, hoping it would obstruct my view of him, but it was in vain: the table was too low and the bottle too small.

Through the balcony door, I could see the tips of the flames. They must have been frazzling what was left of the hill. Yet I found comfort in the flames. They were the perfect excuse for me not to look at the fellow in front of me. He'd think I was fretting because of the fire or that I felt sorry for my father. He tried to start a conversation but soon gave up and decided to leave me to my sorrow.

'I'll pour myself, mate, don't you mind. You just go ahead and think,' he reassured me.

After that we sat in silence. When he'd quaffed all my whisky and my neck was stiff from looking out through the balcony door, he left. As he was going, he said: 'You're a good man.' I nodded, refusing to look at him. When he closed the door behind him, I burst into tears.

That's how *she* cried, too, as if she was imploring someone. And that someone was *me*, I sometimes thought, and yet it was as if she was beseeching someone who wouldn't hear. The only purpose of crying is self-pity, which brings us the greatest satisfaction – a wet orgasm after emotional masturbation. We pity ourselves because there's no one else who would. Self-pity is held in great stead. Only someone who cries and weeps convulsively over themselves can hope to gain the sympathy of others. But it only lasts an instant. Everyone turns back to themselves in a flash because people are only capable of ongoing agony in relation to themselves. And who can blame them: being alive is an unquestionably tragic fact which can induce nothing but tears.

When she finally stopped sobbing, she left me. All at once she wiped away her tears, and instead of a tearful glance she sent me one full of hate.

'You've destroyed me. I curse every day of our life together,' she snarled.

I saw clearly where this was heading. Two or three sentences more and she'd say I'd made her want to die, I thought. But she didn't.

'Life with you was hell,' she said instead, 'a hell I'm now leaving. I'm going to start life again. On second thought, I should be grateful to you because you've aroused the desire for life in me again: a life after you. Now I know there's a life after death.' She laughed hysterically. 'Life *after you*. Thank you for everything,' she shouted as she threw her things into her suitcase.

She left before I could say anything in return. I simply stood in the hall, staring at the door she'd slammed behind her, left alone in the house which until just a moment ago had been our home. What did I expect? That the door would open again, that she would come in, laugh her golden laugh and once more grace this damned house with her smile; with the smile which made me fall in love with her in the first place; the smile I married? It was only this morning that she left me, yet I can no longer remember the reason why. What happened between us? What was it that became so unbearable? I thought about her but couldn't come up with a single reason why she found me so abhorrent, nor of how I'd become estranged from her, incapable of living close together. I knew now that I loved her. I thought about her smile and loved it like the very first day I met her, and it seemed as if nothing untoward had happened at all, nothing had changed. I realised that her leaving had brought everything full circle: she had gone and everything returned to nothing.

I remembered watching her singing in the kitchen in the immaculate light which came in through the open window, like the illumination in baroque paintings. She stood there like an angel with wings outspread, too tender for this world. It seemed only a moment before her mangled, fragile form would float heavenward and her wings would fall into the mire in which I reside. But then she started singing, and the terrible dissonance destroyed the picture.

'Darling, you look like an angel but sing like a toad,' I told her.

As a matter of fact, everyone becomes unbearable once we get to know them a little better. That's why the most beautiful women are those on painters' canvases, where they're limited to their appearance. Beautiful they are, and that's all we need to know about them. Because any other detail about their biographies, habits and thoughts would repulse us and turn delight into disgust. I can just imagine how the girl with the pearl earring must have stunk. Europe at that time didn't have bathrooms, so it's hard to think of European women of that era as anything other than carriers of the plague bacillus. This woman, as we know, was a maidservant. Before she sat for the painter determined to immortalise her beauty, in other words the lie about her, she must already have cooked the main meal, scrubbed the floors and done all the shopping. She's sure to have worked up a sweat at least three times, and being in the same room as her must have been awful. But there's not a man alive who doesn't desire to kiss her when he sees her on a museum wall.

Art always lies, as a matter of fact. It seduces us with its lies like a killer seduces a girl standing in the rain in front of the school and waiting for her mother, who's running late because her lover needed several minutes longer to reach orgasm that day. It takes us by the hand just as that girl is, blinded by lies, and leads us away from the truth, away from life. Art creates the impression that things have meaning and always happen for a reason, but the truth is different, of course: we never find out why, nor do we perceive the meaning of what happens to us. Things are neither beautiful nor justifiable. They simply stink like the sweaty body of Jesus did up on the cross, or the masses who tried to stone him and the disciples who bewailed him; they stink like the saints and sinners, the convicted and the executioners, da Vinci's *Mona Lisa* and Vermeer's *Girl with a Pearl Earring*, and especially van Gogh's shoes, which Heidegger, amid the stench of beer and sausages, claimed to be those of a peasant. We, the living, stink too; we wash in vain because filth, not cleanliness, is our natural state. We clean ourselves but always get dirty again. And we stink hideously: from the day we're born until our dying day, and even after we're dead. We stink *in both life and death*.

Only now that she's gone can she be beautiful again, and only now am I able to love her again. Because now I'm forgetting all I had learnt about her, and can allow only her beauty to remain. Her smiling face. I will cherish that image just as precious paintings are stored in high-security museums.

Apropos women ... I heaved myself out of the armchair and sat at the computer again. I connected to the internet at the first attempt and typed '*free cumshot pics*' into the search engine. It came up with 40 million porno sites, and I chose one at random. I saved several women's faces to my desktop. Splattered with sperm, they stared up adoringly at the studs who'd just ejaculated on them as if they were pagan fertility gods. Cumshots are my favourite segment of pornography: the wanton spilling of seed, the defiant and futile squandering of fatherhood.

Ready to masturbate, I thought! After all, masturbation is the ultimate consequence of the Cartesian concept of the *subject*. I gazed at the image on the screen: a siliconed Korean knelt in front of a circumcised black. Talk about multicultural. Political correctness is only tolerable in pornography, I thought – this is its true place. Because what is political correctness if not a pornography of correctness?

But it wasn't to be; this happens to me all the time. My masturbation has become excessively intellectual and too discursive for it to be possible. For months I've been unable to feel sexual arousal and instead resort to fulfilling a need to deconstruct porno images, can you believe it? My own hunger for the grotesque will destroy me, I yelled, pacing round and round. It was clear that my need to discover the grotesque in every detail would be the end of me: I look at everything with contempt because I see discord and misery in it all. Yet the only alternative to repulsion is compassion, which is equally lethal. In the end I'll die, and when they've buried me everyone will hold me in contempt. There will be no one to mourn for me.

'It's unbearable how my brain works!' I roared.

Going out onto the balcony, I gripped the railing with both hands.

'I can't take this repulsion anymore,' I cried, 'no one would be able to. But what can I do when I keep seeing all those things, when the wretchedness and filth drive me to disgust and pity, and when they crucify me like Christ. I'm like Christ on the cross, who instead of love for the mob who stoned him feels only disgust. And the stinker who cuffed Christ while he was carrying the cross: what if Jesus saw in him only a wretch who'd found out the day before that his wife was cheating him, and who hit *him* today because he didn't slap *her* yesterday? What if that's how it was? What if Christ simply loathed him? What if he laughed at those grotesque creatures and then breathed his last, adrift in the ocean of sorrow which washed over him, sorrow because of all the misery on Earth. What if that's how it was? Everything would go down the plughole and there would be nothing but agony, like everything really has gone down the plughole and my life is nothing but agony. Death is the only fact which one can build optimism on – only death can finally bring hope.'

I stood on the balcony, howling out this tirade, and then stopped myself when I suddenly remembered my father. The terrible thought that I might wake him forced me into silence. I glanced over to his house, but he hadn't turned on the light or come out onto the terrace. He hadn't heard me, after all. I had avoided the reproachful question,

'What are you doing, for goodness' sake?' which I always found the most shameful and frustrating. Once again there was no sign of my father. I tried to recall when I'd last seen him, but I couldn't quite remember: I now wondered if he left the house at all anymore.

If *I* don't wake him, the dogs butchering each other down on the road will, I thought. A huge black tyke was tearing away at an unfortunate hunting dog. And a whole pack of dirty mutts and mongrels had come bolting up behind; canine freaks combining all the worst features of their forebears. The black tyke seized the slender hunting dog by the neck, immediately drawing blood and maddening the black leader's entourage – that incestuous, degenerate pack. The long-bodied dog died in agony as dozens of jaws rent at it, pulled at its limbs and tore it apart on the sticky, hot asphalt. That will wake my father, I thought, and everything will end in a row, like every other conversation we've had since my mother died: without her standing between us as both gateand bridge. Without her, our relationship was finally reduced to its very essence of mutual antipathy. My father had grated on my nerves even when I was a child, when I would be annoyed by everything he said or did. The trauma I carry with me from my earliest years is my father. I must have had a hundred nervous breakdowns in my childhood, and each of them because of him. Every time my father thought of giving me a goodnight kiss, of coming into my room, stroking my hair and saying something to me which *he* thought was affectionate – *he* who never learnt anything about children, who never learnt to live with his child, who never really accepted the fact that he had a child ... Every time he stroked my hair and kissed me on the neck after his 'affectionate' and fortunately brief monologue ...

He even kissed me that evening after Milan had fallen from the gnarled, enchanted, 500-year-old maple. They said it was me who had talked him into climbing it. I don't remember that, and I don't know why Milan climbed the tree that particular day, like I know he had many times before. Perhaps he climbed it to needlessly prove to me once again that he was the elder brother, and thus braver and stronger. It turned out that a man was hoeing around the olive trees on the property next door: he heard our argument and me telling Milan that I hated him and demanding that he climb the tree all the way to the top. Milan refused because it had rained and the bark was wet, and then the man heard me saying I would climb it instead. Soon there came a scream and the sickening sound of a bone breaking.

The body of his seven-year-old son was at the city mortuary in Bar that time my father leaned over my bed, covering me with the bridge of his body, and said, 'Don't cry, we love you.' I listened to his steps receding, heard my mother's sobs and the door of their room close. It closed once and for all for me. From that moment on, it was no longer the long hall and the two doors which separated us. Between us lay dead Milan, the blood trickling from his small, fractured skull and being borne away by the water from the old Turkish drinking fountain. From that moment on, we were separated by my guilt. My father never said that to me. He didn't have to: it was enough for him just to look at me, or even worse, to kiss me. Every evening I awaited my punishment, but it never came. Instead there was the *goodnight kiss*. Only today do I realise how cruelly I was punished – that kiss was the punishment. I was 'forgiven', and it had been 'decided' that Milan's death would never be mentioned in front of me. I was left to take care of my punishment myself. They could just as well have said: We won't mention it but we know it was your fault, just as you know it was your fault.

Every time my father kissed me I cried hysterically, spat into my palm and tried to rub clean the place on my skin he'd kissed; the spot he'd blemished with his lips, which in the very act of forgiveness spoke: *It was your fault.* That kiss was an imprint on my skin, a mark branded into me every evening. Those who forgive us are our harshest judges. I clenched the bedcover with my teeth, pummelled the mattress with my feet and cried into the pillow. For hours and hours. In the end I'd drift off to sleep in the oblivion which came with the exhaustion of my young body. Fatigue finally brought salutary bluntness to my mind and senses. First my father and every thought of him would disappear; then the door which had unsuccessfully tried to protect me from his coming; and after that there would no longer be the room or the bed. Nothing any more, and no one.

The lights in his house didn't go on. I feared he might come out onto the terrace and that I would soon hear the creak of his gate and his fast steps as he stormed towards my house, ready to give me yet another telling-off.

My mother cursed the day she bore me. She was in hospital in Podgorica, melting away before my eyes as uterine cancer ate her up from the inside; she literally dematerialised as the emptiness of her womb spread like the expanding universe, and she disappeared into that void like light is devoured by a black hole. And as she lay there dwindling away, she told me that although she was dying it was with the greatest happiness because she wouldn't have to see me or my father anymore. After being *condemned to an existence with us*, now at the end she'd at least be able to *unexist without us*. Those were her words. What surprised me most about them was that my mother had never had the slightest inclination towards philosophy. I'd never have thought that her last words would be an attempt to philosophically review her life just as it was about to be snuffed out. That amazed me, although my amazement was actually out of place. With sufficient suffering, everyone is capable of relatively accurate philosophical perception, at least as regards their own suffering. It's a fact that suffering makes people wiser, just as happiness stupefies them. And after the amount of suffering my father and I inflicted on my mother, one could actually have expected something even more philosophically profound and weighty. Yet the end result was certainly an achievement: you can't get much deeper than the insight into the solace of death – than dying in joy.

My mother only gave up on us at the very end. Right up to her last breath she tried to reconcile my father and me, to find a way for the two of us to love each other. She gave us her all. She gave herself up for our hatred, and we consumed her. We ate her up from the inside, from the womb which he, the father, had penetrated, and I, the son, had fled. But flee as I did, my father still entered me. I fled from the womb straight into a life where my father terrorised us not only from without but also from within.

A father manages this feat because, over time, we recognise him *in ourselves*. We realise to our horror that what we fear most – the father – is already deep inside us. We spend our whole life fleeing from the father figure but never really manage to escape, not even when he's dead. In the end we die, hoping that death will grant us release from him.

The agony of my mother's life was even greater because she ran towards death while fleeing from both husband and son; from the torture that both of us inflicted on her. But I've decided not to end up like her. I've expelled him from my life. I've driven him into his house and left him to books and Bach. I've left him to his depression. That was the only way for me to survive: *to be by myself, without him.*

Yet my mother never seemed to tire in the peace negotiations she brokered, shuttling back and forth between my father and me in what she termed an attempt to kindle love between father and son. Truces were made, only to be broken the very next day, for the most part unintentionally. The antipathy was simply too strong for her sacrifice to be like a restraining dam, and too broad for her to bridge it. I only have the two of you, she would say, and I'd give my life to see you happy and getting along together. Only at the very end, when they had her put in a hospital bed and it became clear she'd never leave it alive, did she realise that her lifelong sacrifice had been futile. At that point, she felt thwarted and cheated, and was filled with the desire for revenge. And since my father wasn't available, she took it out on me. She called me close, conspiratorially, with her gaze riveted to the door lest someone barge into the room and foil her little plan. When I put my head against her chest to try to hear what she was whispering, she demanded that I kill her.

'Put me out of my misery, don't let me suffer like this any longer,' she murmured. 'All my life I was against euthanasia, but now I realise how stupid I was. It's my only choice now. You're my son, you have to do this for your mother.'

Her words were urgent, and she seized my head in her hands.

'Be a man. I've never asked anything of you before, but this is different. Be a man at least this once and have pity on your own mother.'

I tried to explain to her rationally and, to my mind, almost affectionately, as if speaking to a retarded child, that I couldn't do anything of the kind.

'You know I've never accepted *such* responsibility. I never have and never will,' I told her. 'You've had your whole life to kill yourself and put yourself out of your misery. You've had cancer for two years now, knowing that you're going to die in terrible pain. But instead of taking care of things yourself, you've waited until the pain is unbearable.' I was yelling at her now. 'You just sat and waited, and now you heap it all on me. Suddenly I'm the one who has to decide about life and death – me, someone who avoids obligation at all costs, refuses to influence people's lives and has just one ambition: to go unnoticed. Now I'm supposed to destroy my life because you didn't dare to put an end to yours. You didn't have the courage to end your life of misery, and instead you've decided to make mine even more miserable,' I screamed.

I stopped talking when I saw the tears in her eyes. She sobbed loudly. Her crying stabbed into my brain like long, hot nails.

I realised that I'd managed to offend her again just before her death, just when she was most vulnerable, when actually I pitied her. I'd offended her and riddled her with venomous words, when my intention was to say something affectionate and comforting.

But like a mortally wounded beast, she decided to bite once more. She cursed the day she bore me. Naturally, this could in no way upset me, because I also curse the day she bore me. I told her that, too, considering sincerity a virtue and holding that an upstanding person wouldn't lie to their mother in the hour of her death.

'Get out and at least leave me to die in peace,' she shrieked through her tears. That brought in the doctors, who as usual were hovering about the hospital corridors all day, ready to swoop down like vultures when they hear the cries of the dying.

All at once the room was aflutter with those white-coated scavengers, along with nurses stinking of nicotine. My mother asked them to throw me out of the room. This was just what they'd been waiting for; I'd obviously been getting on their nerves to such an extent that they despised me. So I sat out in the corridor until evening and whiled away the time by watching the goings-on in that brothel. People die in its rooms, pervaded by despair and fear, while its corridors are awash with lust and greed; with doctors lining their pockets and nurses supplementing their marital sex life. It was unbearable to see all the loathsome things which go on there, the common bribes and adulteries so familiar to anyone who has ever waited in a hospital corridor. I expected my mother to make the last sacrifice for me and save me from those insufferable scenes; to die as quickly as possible and spare me the obligation of waiting for word of her death in that disgusting corridor. My mother didn't betray me this time either: she died before evening. I tried to enter the room to give her a farewell kiss on the forehead, but the doctor said that before her death she'd expressly forbidden me from coming anywhere near her. I wasn't to touch her at all, he told me with a malicious grin.

She said that despite the fact that I was the only one who'd been with her as she lay dying. My father didn't visit her once in the whole time she was ill. He just sat riveted by depression to the armchair. He didn't even get up from the chair the day I buried Mother, leaving just myself and the two cemetery workers standing beside the grave. I didn't inform anyone about Mother's death. I didn't have an obituary notice printed, and of course I didn't permit the outrageous perversion of announcing her death in the newspaper. I had her buried in the town of Bar, where we knew no one. That way I could be sure that nobody would come to the funeral and spoil things.

I paid the workers well. They misunderstood the gesture and considered it their duty to pretend to be deeply touched by her death. When we'd buried her I couldn't make them leave the grave. They just stood there, crossing themselves ceaselessly in compensation for the lack of mourners. 'The poor woman. To die so alone and for no one to come to the burial,' one lamented. 'May the dark earth rest lightly on her after such martyrdom,' the other said. I desperately wanted to be alone but they refused to go. Instead, they came up with new and ever more pathetic folkloric creations. This introduced an element of the ridiculous, which was superfluous because funerals are ridiculous as they are, in common with all situations where people feel obliged to be serious and dignified. I was reminded once again that the nicest thing we can say about a person is that one day they will die and cease to bother us. In the end I had to pay the workers double before they finally agreed to leave.

At a cemetery, surrounded by the dead, we're at the source of cognisance. At a cemetery we learn at first glance all we need to know about life – that we're going to die. I sat down on the dry stone wall by my mother's grave and lit a cigarette.

The wind blew several snowflakes into my face. I looked around and saw that I was alone at the cemetery, which extended out to all four corners of the world. Row upon row of stone crosses marched to the horizon, where threatening black clouds were mustering. War is the father of all things, I thought: an army of the dead against a heavenly army. Thunder rumbled through the valley. Both the cemetery and I witnessed those sound effects of nature in impassive silence. Wherever I looked, I saw graves mounted with crosses, upright and dignified, marking lives spent in humiliation and submission.

All around me, as far as the eye could see, stretched the future.

II

I realised I would have to leave the house as soon as possible. It was still out of the question for me to enter the bedroom, so I left it locked. But since the wardrobe containing my clothes was in there, that restricted my choice of attire for the night. I decided that anything would do and opted for the white linen suit hanging in the hall. True, I knew it would make me look like a pimp, but I considered that persona quite appropriate for a writer. Because what do writers do if not pimp out their life to lustful readers? They always write about themselves whether they want to or not, just as they're always occupied with themselves, whatever they do. To be a writer therefore means to pimp oneself, which is a perfect, self-sufficient form of prostitution, integrating both the pimp and the whore – both the marketing and the finished product.

So there I was, dressed up in the white suit and walking along the road past my father's house. I thought I could hear Bach playing inside but I wasn't sure because an easterly breeze was shaking the tops of the olive trees. Their murmur merged with the ever-present din of the cicadas, making the summer evening a wall of sound. Then I was down on the road, in the shine of the street light, which was working for a change. And finally I found myself in the car, and the engine of my SUV rumbled as I flipped through the CDs in the glovebox, searching for Sonic Youth and their *Song for Karen*.

Uncle's hill was still burning and the fire brigade was busy. They had parked their ridiculous red truck in the middle of the road, forcing me to squeeze between it and the illegally parked patrol car the police had arrived in. They'd come to ensure order in our suburb during the fire, but as usual they caused even greater chaos. My neighbours were there too, of course, with their emaciated cows, their scrawny, mangy dogs, and their children, who were the most undernourished and grubby of all. On top of that, these offspring were thick-headed, full of juvenile gazes which exuded a blend of primitivism and prurience – that most dangerous of all pernicious combinations of human characteristics. The adults, cows, dogs and this dubious brood were all milling around on the road, all of them equally incoherent in expressing their fear of the fire which seemed to blaze more brightly the more the fire brigade endeavoured to put it out. They all held their heads in desperation, mooed, thrashed their tails, wailed and barked. Every living thing becomes unbearably sordid the moment it fears for its life. And, as a rule, those who count for least are most afraid. There's no pitiful human being who won't make a drama out of their death if they find out they're incurably ill. Everyone around them will immediately be informed of their misfortune and will even be expected to show sympathy. In keeping with the old *friend-in-need-is-a-friend-indeed* truism, I saw that my neighbours' relatives were starting to arrive too; people whose only thought was how fortunate they were that their own house wasn't on fire. The relatives shook their heads in fake concern and consoled the wretches who were preoccupied with their bad luck and the forest igniting right next to their house.

There I was, hurriedly departing that Golgotha of human dignity. *Tunic, Song for Karen* – an awesome piece of white noise about death – blared from the car as I drove down into town. And there I was, thinking how diligent the pyromaniacs had been that night: the rubbish containers were ablaze all along the street. Like torches on the wall of a cave they illuminated the main thoroughfare leading down to the centre of unbridled touristic repulsiveness.

But I didn't get far. There was a commotion like a mass-meeting in front of the mosque which forced me to park the car and continue on foot. I literally had to struggle through the crowd. So many people could only have gathered because of a fatality, I thought. Maybe the muezzin had fallen from the minaret. Perhaps he had been taken out by a man with a rifle who, after a gruelling and stressful day, was just trying to get to sleep when the bearded guy started bawling his *Allahu akbar*. Or maybe he'd woken someone who'd just fallen asleep, an irascible man who was already at wits' end without that holy droning – a walking time bomb who could explode at any moment. Yes, that's probably what happened; the muezzin called a bullet instead of the believers. The transcendental can be irritating, I mused, especially when it comes unwanted. But that supposition proved to be wrong: no one had killed the muezzin. Instead, it turned out that a son had killed his father, after doing in his mother and brother too.

What incredible things you hear if you only mix with the crowd! Impelled by curiosity, I joined the mob in front of the mosque. People whispered about a crime they said was terrible and 'unprecedented', while I thought that an unprecedented crime would truly be something new. It would be hard to add an unwritten chapter to the comprehensive history of crime. Surely everything has been written about already, and all that happens from then on is just the perpetual repetition of the same code of crime.

'A father killing his son is sort of imaginable, but this?' people repeated in their astonishment. Those good folk of Ulcinj were ill-informed: patricide is a reinforcing bar in the foundations of this world. Sometimes it is symbolic, but sometimes people – particularly those of modest intellect – resort to literal patricide. 'Can you believe it? Such a peaceful family, who'd have thought!' People's comments reminded me of the crime reports in our daily papers, every single one of which ended with the sentence: 'The neighbours are shocked by the crime. The murderer and the victims were a harmonious family, to all appearances, and there had been nothing to herald this tragedy.' If asked, people are always stunned when a crime occurs, even one as commonplace as patricide, which every adult has committed in their infantile mind, while those who haven't yet broken free of the deadly embrace of the father commit it later. There's no family in this world which cannot be the scene of the most terrible murder. As long as they live, parents destroy their children, and their children pay them back for it and don't relinquish their thirst for vengeance until they've sent their parents to the grave. Every family home can turn into a slaughterhouse. A tiny catalyst of just a single word is often all it takes for the history of abuse and hatred, hidden under a semblance of harmony and love like in an old-fashioned memento chest, to end in bloodshed.

And yet, although a variation on a well-known theme – an evergreen crime, so to speak – this murder was interesting in its own right. The murdered father had been *a lovely man*, people said: a retiring, pious man who minded his own business. 'He never did anyone any harm, and look what happened to him,' a voice called from the crowd. The others agreed, while I was hoping that the fellow would soon finish his tribute to the deceased and move on to the gory details. After all, that's why we find murders interesting.

The son was an absolute no-gooder, they said. It had been clear from an early age that he'd be a reprobate. But his father, that *lovely man*, was eternally forgiving. 'Don't underestimate the power of forgiveness,' he told his friends, who believed in the power of punishment. To my mind, his downfall was caused by him preferring forgiveness to corporal punishment. The boy stole. Whatever he could swipe from the neighbour's garden and whatever he could stick into his pockets at the market, he took it. And then there was grandma's jewellery, grandfather's antique pistol and his cousin's bike. He even stole when he knew he'd be found out and punished. They say his mother died of shame. They caught him pickpocketing the mourners at her funeral. Over time, the neighbourhood began to blame him for every single burglary. Not that they were far wrong: their suspicions were justified most of the time. But occasionally they'd accuse him of things he hadn't done, just enough for him to become acquainted with injustice and to realise that no one has a monopoly on it – you constantly inflict injustice on others, and they constantly inflict it on you.

There would be a furious banging on the gate of their house, interrupting the father's afternoon rest. Roused from sleep, he would go out in his striped pyjamas and wearing a hairnet which he refused to go to bed without, even if he was dead sick. The irate 'visitor' would proceed to shower him with a tirade of abuse. 'Do please calm down, Mr Karić, we'll sort it all out,' the father repeated. As he led the 'guest' into the house, he'd glance up at the first-floor window and see his son peering down into the courtyard through the curtains. When their eyes met, the father would smile, letting his son know that he forgave him and would take the blame for everything himself. The boy would run into the hall, and time and time again he heard his father enduring insults and excusing his son's escapades, which had long since grown into full-blown scandals. The yob and the rake in him came out ever stronger. When he turned twenty, old Karić the neighbour yelled at his father in the kitchen just like he had ten years earlier when the boy had broken the apple tree he'd climbed to steal the fruit. Now the boy had got Karić's daughter pregnant.

His father had sorted things out in the past, and he knew he'd sort them out now, too. After showing Karić out, the father went up to his son's room and gave him a homily which was supposed to be soul-stirring. He spoke about the power of love and forgiveness and appealed to the debt of responsibility we have towards others. After this sermon, which was futile and thus tragic, he kissed his son on both cheeks and went to the mosque, bent with sorrow as if he bore it on his back. His son must have thought it would be the same story that day when old Karić dashed to their house and demanded that he marry his daughter.

All this I gleaned from the flurry of anecdotes about the son who killed his father, which partly stemmed from memory and were partly dreamed up by people as they went to read the green obituary notice on the wall of the mosque. The son had promised his father that he'd marry the girl, people said, but that was another lie: one day before the wedding he'd fled to America. His father reached him in New York, where he was working in a restaurant run by a compatriot, and told him he had to come home because the girl was pregnant and would soon be giving birth. She hadn't had an abortion because he couldn't countenance such a sin. The girl kept the child because the father had promised Karić his son would return and marry her. But his son hung up and fled to the other end of America, even farther away from the past. He even made it as far as Los Angeles, only to receive word there that the girl had given birth to a son and, after leaving hospital, had drowned herself and the baby in Bojana River. In order to avenge the disgrace brought upon his family, old Karić went down to the quay that night and killed his would-be son-in-law's brother – a boy of just ten. And as the father held the bloodstained body of his youngest son in his arms, Karić came up and spat on him.

'If you'd've killed that rotter when you should've, this good'un would still be alive,' Karić said, and with tears in his eyes he fell to his knees before the dead boy. He wept convulsively, kissed the boy's hand and repeated the sad refrain over and over like a scratched record: *Forgive me, forgive me, forgive me…*

'This is all because of you. It's all your fault,' Karić flung at the father as he was being handcuffed and bundled into a police car.

At that moment I realised all the things I miss, all the fascinating stories I don't get to hear because I refuse to mix with people on principle. People said the son had already been taken to Montenegro's largest jail in Spuž. The inspector who questioned him now sits in his office for hours, drinking, and doesn't speak a word to anyone, they say. But word had already leaked out to willing listeners in the pub next to the police station about what the son said at his questioning, and now the whole town knows the story: *I killed him because he forgave me.*

When he heard that his brother had been killed because of his sin, the son decided to go home for the punishment he felt he had long since deserved. 'I loved my brother more than myself,' people claimed he said. 'As much as I've hated myself all my life, I truly loved my brother,' he allegedly uttered, not caring about the obvious contradictoriness of the statement. In any case, the son returned and stood in front of his father. 'Kill me now at last,' he said. But his father embraced him and burst into tears. 'My son, now you're all I have left. Promise me, swear to me by the grave of your brother, that you'll never leave me again,' his father beseeched him.

The police counted twelve stab wounds on the father's body when they responded to the son's call and the words *I've killed my father*. He waited for them in the hall, still holding the bloodstained kitchen knife in his hand. When he was questioned he admitted everything. 'I have just one condition,' he said. 'I want the death penalty.'

He told them that he'd only come back to Ulcinj to be punished. He returned because he believed his father would kill him for all the evil he'd caused. Taking his own life would have been an option if he'd had the courage, but he admitted he had always been a coward. So he came for the punishment he desperately wanted. Instead, he received forgiveness and couldn't stand it anymore. That's why he killed his father – because he hoped the law would be merciless and someone would finally kill him in return. He admitted everything but demanded the death penalty. 'All my life I've just wanted punishment,' he said. 'I committed every new crime in retaliation for not being punished for the previous one. My father forgave me for everything and that made my life hell,' the son cried before the bewildered police officers. 'You don't know how hard it is to live without punishment, how terrible the world is when there's nothing but forgiveness on the horizon.' After all I'd heard, I found I had the deepest sympathy for him.

Reflecting on how our parents constantly grind us down and destroy us whatever they do, *through their very existence*, just as we grind them down and destroy them through our very existence, I went into one of Ulcinj's myriad cafés and ordered a double whisky at the bar. But I didn't get to drink it in peace because Dirty Djuro came up to me and offered me sex with one of his daughters: 'Just 15 euros for a blow job, just 25 for the real thing.'

Interpersonal relations are a nightmare from which there's no waking up, I thought to myself.

Djuro came to town as a refugee back when the war in Croatia began. He claimed he could repair various appliances and even offered to do it on the cheap. People are miserly and therefore they chose to believe him. It took a few years for them to realise that Djuro never repaired anything for anyone. He'd arrive at a house like an ill omen, called by a householder determined to save money. If Djuro was supposed to fix the fridge, he would remove the motor, and then also offer to 'repair' perfectly functional water heaters, irons and vacuum cleaners. He took a piece out of every appliance and promised to come back the next day with new parts, insert them and reassemble everything he'd dismantled. After he left a house, nothing in it worked anymore. And he did all this damage for just half the price of what tradesmen charged for repairing a single fridge.

As a consequence, not one day went past when he didn't get a beating. Around town, he'd run into the miserly numskulls whose houses he'd devastated and whose appliances remained unfixed because in the meantime he'd sold the parts he removed. The fellow would beat the living daylights out of Djuro, and no sooner had he got to his feet and brushed the dust off, he'd fall to the ground again, bloodied by the blows of one of the local repairmen furious at having their prices undercut and their customers taken away. In the end there was no more work for Djuro, but by then his daughters had grown up and he realised he could earn money on their budding, increasingly curvaceous bodies.

They called him Dirty because his clothes were always slimy like the cassocks of Orthodox priests. And because he pimped his daughters. But whatever people thought of him, they had to admit he was endowed with entrepreneurial spirit. He started business with two of his daughters. The elder, sixteen-year-old Tanja, he advertised as a *buxom blonde who swallows*. The younger, Zorana, who had her first john on her fourteenth birthday, was sold as a *tight, small-breasted brunette*. Later, his third daughter, Mirjana, came of working age and ran as a *sweet anal fantasy*.

Djuro stuck to his low-price policy in prostitution too. He drove a rusted red Moskvitch with *Dirty Djuro & Daughters: Sex for Every Pocket* painted on the side. Half an hour later we drove up to his flat in this rattletrap, which looked like something out of a bad film. The old pervert had detected straight away that I was easy prey. 'Talk about horny,' he told me. 'Two more whiskys and you'd even do me! Luckily there are beauties like my daughters.'

They lived in a cellar converted into a two-room flat. A narrow corridor led from there to the business premises – a three-room brothel. The door was opened for us by Djuro's wife, a gap-toothed old lady with breasts worn out from feeding the horde of children who gambolled about the flat like a litter of puppies. Her face spoke of a great weariness and the desire for an early death. I was wondering what was left for a mother of three, four or five children, when suddenly two more appeared, making a total of seven. When someone multiplies life to such an extent, even if they don't understand it, they at least feel its worthlessness. Children are like money: the more of it you print, the more of them you bear, the less they're worth.

This hyperinflation of children hampered our forward progress through Djuro's flat. As soon as the children saw me, they ran towards me. The burliest of them, and thus the most dangerous, grabbed me by my trousers with chocolate-smeared hands. Another knelt in front of me and cried, announcing a demand I didn't understand and which obviously had nothing to do with me anyway. A third, the smallest one, bit into my shoe.

'Don't worry, he's just teething,' Djuro told me. 'Follow me, I'll take you to Tanja.'

I carefully shook off the ankle-biter, not wanting to break his milk teeth, and headed after Djuro.

'Look, I've made sure that each has her own room,' he said. He wanted me to know that he was a devoted father. They were young women now and needed to have intimacy. Besides, he added, there was no need to economise on space because he'd made a good deal with the tenants. In return for being able to use the whole cellar, the family offered them sex for free.

'They're all old men and don't want it more than once a month,' he confided in me. 'And imagine: there are some who want my wife. You can give them beauties like my daughters, but the old farts want my wife – that old walrus!' he sniggered.

We went into Tanja's room. She was lying on the bed in black underwear. I noticed that her knickers were frayed at the edges. She pursed her fleshy, shoddily made-up lips in an effort to look sensual. The bra holding her enormous breasts was smeared with sperm. I handed Djuro the money and pushed him out of the room.

The Olcinium Trilogy

'I've had my eye on you for a while,' Tanja said. 'But I didn't make any advances because I thought: a cool cat like him can have any woman he wants, so why would he pay for me?'

'Very flattering of you,' I mumbled and tried to have a look around the room. But she hadn't finished.

'You'd be surprised if you knew how many well-to-do, handsome men come to see me.'

'Believe me, I'm not surprised,' I told her.

'But it's clever ones like you who turn me on the most,' she purred, looking me in the eyes.

We find a bent for the intellectual in the most unexpected of places, I thought. Everyone is driven by the eternal *Why*: the physicist in a Zürich laboratory, the art historian in the Vatican Library and the whore in Ulcinj. They're all equally far from, and thus equally close to, an answer: it's just as appropriate and legitimate to seek answers in atoms, books or smelly provincial phalluses. Therefore, everyone has equal right to intellectual snobbery – or rather no right – and everyone pondering the questions of existence is equally laughable.

I was blessed by an interruption in the conversation because Tanja now devoted herself to her ritual of cleansing. Leaning over the washstand, she soaped up the coves of her armpits and then the fjord between her legs. She hummed a cheerful melody; I think it was *Put on something folky, let's do the pokey-pokey*. Finally, I had time to study her room.

On the camp bed, leaning against the metal bars, was a teddy bear. It faced a pink pillow in the shape of a heart. Beneath the bed I saw an open book; something by Virginia Woolf. Probably *A Room of One's Own*. Tanja tried to satisfy as broad a target group as possible, I said to myself. The camp bed was for the sadists, the teddy bear and the pink pillow were to please the paedophiles, and the book was for intellectuals like me but could also come in handy for slapping the masochists. Djuro's family left nothing to coincidence – it was a well-organised, carefully thought-out, proper little family business.

That's what I thought until I saw the photo on the wall above Tanja's bed. It was of her and her father, embracing and smiling. They were standing on the terrace above *Mala Plaža* beach with the open sea behind them on a fine spring day: the air was clean and radiant, and the world was steeped in a blue we otherwise see only in toilet-cleaner ads. Djuro hugged his daughter around the neck, laughing and kissing her hair. One of her arms hung around his waist. She was looking up at her father, and he was leaning down towards her. Her eyes were full of adoration and love in just the way that young women in the paintings of the Old Masters look up into the sky, searching for God, or at least the saints. She really must love her father, I thought. Ten minutes beforehand she'd had sex with a man who her father pimped her to. And it wasn't hard to imagine that he'd take her off for another fat toad of a man to lie on, straight after the photo was taken. Her father had made a whore of her and ruined any chance of her ever being anything else, at least in a small town like this where everyone knows everything and nothing is ever forgotten. She was forever doomed to be a cheap whore, thanks to her father. For as long as she lived she would put out to old men and pimply teenagers because that was the only future she had: ever-worse customers and ever-lower prices. And then death in contempt and loneliness, if she didn't get AIDS first or some maniac cut her throat or suffocated her with a pillow. All that because of her father. Yet despite all that, she looked up at him with a love which couldn't be faked.

I left the room in a hurry. Traversing the kitchen in the greatest urgency, I was waylaid by Djuro.

'Let me introduce you: this is my mysterious son Petar. "Why mysterious?" you may ask yourself,' he blathered, although I was only asking myself how to flee that cellar as quickly as possible.

I breathed with difficulty because I suddenly became aware of the claustrophobic quality of the space around me, and that feeling merged with a growing rage inside me.

'He's mysterious because no one knows who his father is,' Dirty Djuro guffawed. 'Look at him: a donkey of sixteen, a handsome lad, but he doesn't look like his father – his *alleged* father, I should say,' Djuro snarled and spat.

Then he grabbed the lad by the ears.

'As to who his father is, you'll have to ask my wife. I only know he's not mine. Either my wife is a whore or he was sent by God to test me, like Father Bogdan said. I don't believe in God, but I fear Him. So I say to myself: in case this is some kind of test, I'd better tolerate the little guy till he grows up. One more mouth to feed? I won't even notice. But just look at him,' he shouted and grabbed the lad by the genitals. 'Talk about well hung, eh? Anyway, I've done my part of the deal with God: if this is His child, then I've been good to him like a real father.'

I heard the tail-end of Djuro's theological dilemma as I fled from the cellar where that big happy family lived in harmony and love. I hurried to make it back to my car because I couldn't spend a second longer amid the river of flesh pouring towards the promenade and the cafés. These were anthills emitting *turbofolk* music and the beastly odour of humans ready to copulate. And so I desperately strove against the current of the Styx, which was dragging me back into that seething human crowd. I felt I was sinking in a human multitude like a person going under. Drowning in humanity – what a terrible way to go!

Somehow I made it to the pavement and leaned, panting, against a pole to catch my breath, finally out of harm's way. 'Hey mate!' I heard and flinched. 'My old friend!' the voice went on, and now a heavy hand was laid on my shoulder. I stared at those fingers with skin as rough as the bark of a centennial tree and as thick and knotted as Montenegrin mountain sausages. Each of those fingers seemed strong enough to squash the life out of me, but I wasn't afraid of them at all, nor was I afraid of the wielder of such powerful and at the same time absurd fingers. Everything is equally absurd, even that which kills us. We realise this as soon as we overcome our fear of what threatens to destroy us. I laughed, gazing at the grime under the giant fingernails. I was amused by the thought that anyone could kill me, even a man who doesn't use nail clippers – someone so primitive that he doesn't even clean under his nails.

'It's you, mate!' yelled the giant, who was now standing in front of me. I measured him from head to foot. What I saw was a six-foot-something, 300-pound hulk, his shaggy hair encrusted with cement – *so he's a building worker*, I thought, and with bloodshot eyes in a yellow face – *so he's an alcoholic with a destroyed liver*. His cheap, tattered jeans and worn-out army boots, in which he seemed to step-dance in front of me, only confirmed the sad sketch I'd made out at first glance.

The colossus evidently knew me. As if that wasn't compromising enough for me already, he expected me to recognise him. 'It's me, Uroš!' he shouted, making all the passers-by turn and look at us, like we were game-show contestants and they were the crowd, allowed to be malicious spectators of my humiliation.

Uroš was an unlucky wretch I went to school with until Year 8. After years of daily abuse, the gang of kids set on him by arch-bully Žarko Primorac broke both his arms. Uroš's dim-witted parents were determined for their son to have the education they didn't, but this event finally made them decide to take him out of school, and by all indications he didn't re-enrol. Uroš was my best, or, if you like, my only school friend. The day they broke his arms I was standing in the corner of the schoolyard like I did every day. I munched away at my hamburger and watched the ever-bloodthirsty onlookers form a circle around Primorac's bully boys and Uroš, whom they spat on and kicked every day. I never said a word in his defence, and obviously I never ran up to offer help. I'd just eat my lunch and wait until the mob split up, after having had its fill of inflicting torment and humiliation. Uroš would wipe the blood from his face and come over to sit next to me. He never blamed me or expected me to do anything for him.

Now he did. He expected, even insisted, that we go and sit in a nearby café and have a drink. When people grow up they lose the few good traits they had as kids, I thought. That's why we're always disappointed when we meet long-lost childhood friends. Friendship is ultimately only possible in childhood because the concept of it demands a naivety which only childhood can ensure. Only children and idiots can have *friends*. That's a word that goes together with an exuberant *ta-da-da-da!* Who else, other than children and idiots (i.e. the larger part of humanity) could believe there exist people so noble and good that we could believe them, confide our innermost thoughts and feelings in them and expect their help when things take a turn for the worse, which in all honesty things always do. If someone manages to cultivate what they consider *a lifelong friendship*, that merely means the friendship hasn't been properly put to the test. There's no friendship which won't crumble beneath the weight of a friend's bad character or the weight of evil, which all people are condemned to carry in their core due to the very nature of being human.

'So how are you doing, my old friend?' Uroš yelled.

Seeing as he'd interrupted me in contemplation, he deserved for me to be ruthless, so I replied, 'Sorry, but I was just thinking about something. Be quiet for ten minutes, remember what you wanted to say and tell me later.' And good old Uroš really did fall silent. He guzzled his beer and grinned, evidently managing to convince himself that he was glad to see me. When people resolve to be good-hearted you can do what you want with them – it's simply impossible to offend them. And that's fair enough. To be good-hearted means to transcend oneself and to rise above one's own nature, therefore so-called 'good people' use their 'goodness' to create an unforgettable pleasure for themselves, one of the most profound a person can feel. They enjoy their own goodness to such an extent that the rest of us have no obligations towards them whatsoever. In fact, the worse we behave towards them, the greater is their goodness towards us, and thus the pleasure they're rewarded with is also greater.

'Well then, Uroš, how's life treating you?' I said when I'd finally resolved to speak to him.

'Pretty well,' he replied. 'Can't complain.'

In the first few years after his parents had taken him out of school he refused to leave the farm and go into town, he told me.

'You know, I was really offended by what Primorac and his guys did to me,' he said almost apologetically, as if he was telling me amazing things I'd find hard to believe. 'I felt kind of humiliated. Things were fine on the farm. But in town I might run into one of my old *school friends.*' Those were his words, school friends. 'I forgave them, but I never wanted to see them again. That's why I avoided town.'

Then the war broke out. His father told him to enlist in the army to go and fight in Bosnia.

'And that's what I did,' he said, and I believed him.

That's just like him, I thought – he never used to ask any questions.

'I killed a few people in the war. Later it gave me sleepless nights, but over time you get used to things,' he explained, and went on to present his pitiable philosophy of life. 'I always forgive myself. Whatever you do, you always accept yourself again afterwards, isn't that right? Each of us does terrible things which we're mortally ashamed of, but we keep on living. That's why I wasn't angry at the guys who bashed me up back at school – I knew all the bad things I'd done, and if I forgive myself it's only fair that I forgive them. To think badly of others you have to think well of yourself, and I can't do that. I know myself pretty well and I know I'm no better than others.'

He killed during the war, but he stayed in the background whenever he was ordered to burn houses and rape women, he told me.

'I hid then, I must admit, but I'm no coward. When there was shooting, I fired like the others. But I couldn't do anything to the women. I felt sorry for them and simply couldn't do it with them. Others did, but not me. Maybe it was because I myself was maltreated as a boy. Could that have been it?' he asked me.

He returned home. The next winter his parents married him off, and he and his wife came to live in town.

'In Ulcinj we had it better than in the country. Now that I had a wife I was sort of proud and didn't care what others thought of me,' he said.

Sometimes he'd run into those who'd abused him. Some of them looked at him with a derisive smile, others with shame. One of those he met was Žarko Primorac.

'He came up to me, and God was he friendly! He invited me for a few drinks. After we'd had two or three he started apologising,' Uroš told me. 'We were at the bar for a long time that evening. And he cried, man did he cry! In the end I took him home to my place, and all the way he held my hand. He gripped it like a vice, as if he was hanging over an abyss and my hand was the last thing for him to cling to. And he didn't let go of it until I promised we'd see each other again.

'When my son was born, Primorac became the godfather. He was always considerate of my Miloš. He never forgot a single birthday, Easter or Christmas, and would always come with presents,' Uroš said. 'To tell the truth, I'd never have been able to buy him things like that, so let his godfather, I thought. If I, his father, work on a building site from dawn till dusk just to make ends meet, let him have toys from Primorac if that's the only way he can have them. The boy's got it hard enough because of my poverty, and it's not his fault.

'Then I had a chance to go and work in Nigeria for six months,' he said, as if it had been a lucky break. 'I slaved my guts out like here, but at least the money was better. When I came back I took a taxi home. The whole boot was crammed full of presents – both for her and for Miloš. *Now I'm going to give them something nice for a change,* I thought. *All the presents from Primorac have made my son like him more than he likes his own father.*

'Nena, the old landlady, was waiting in the courtyard. She burst into tears when she saw me,' Uroš said. 'I asked her what was wrong and where my family was, but she didn't answer. She just cried and said *My good Uroš* over and over again. *Where's my wife?* I asked her. I wanted to go into the house, but Nena stood in front of me and wouldn't let me in. *You no longer have a family or a home, my good Uroš,* she told me.

'So, old mate, my wife had left me. And who with? With Primorac the godfather, of course, and she took our son with her. They didn't even wait a week after I'd gone, Nena told me. They got up early one morning, packed their things before dawn so the neighbours wouldn't see, hopped in the van and were gone. They didn't call anyone, so no one knows where they went. I looked for them for a while but then gave up. I drank my Nigerian pay – it had only brought me bad luck anyway. *And may it be the death of you,* I said to myself. I didn't leave the bar until I'd drunk away the very last dollar. There's no way, mate – if you live all your life with nothing, you'll end up with nothing. And if I had anything but straw in my head, I would've known that money isn't for me. I had everything except for money. Then I went after money and lost everything,' he said.

He didn't blame anyone except himself, he added, and he forgave both his wife and Primorac. He only missed his son. But he hoped that Miloš would come and look for him one day. He hoped he'd remember his old dad when he grew up and, wherever he was now, that he'd return to Ulcinj to see him, if only for a day. Yet Uroš still knew that nothing mattered and it was *all the same* – a phrase which had become the refrain of his life.

'You know, I've thought a lot about everything. I've had the time,' he said laughing. 'I mean, what else are you going to do when you're left all alone? I thought a lot, and in the end I realised *it's all the same*. And if I hadn't run into Žarko Primorac in the street that day, and if he hadn't shouted me drinks, and if we'd drunk by the glass and not by the bottle, and if I hadn't felt sorry for him when he cried, and if I hadn't promised we'd see each other again, and if I hadn't taken him home to my place, where he met my wife – it still would've been *all the same*, because everything would've been up shit creek anyway.

'Even if Žarko Primorac had had one ounce of decency in him, which he didn't, and if he'd remembered that he'd already done me ill enough for the rest of my life – after all, they carried me out of school with broken arms, and because of him I never went back – and if he'd remembered that that sentenced me to mix cement and cast concrete for the rest of my life, and if he'd realised that it was he who destroyed any chance of me ever being more than a day labourer, which he didn't, and if that had made him think *I'll never do him harm again*, which it didn't, and if everything had turned out differently, it would still be *all the same*.

'The Devil would've found a way of fleecing me, I realised in the end, because I've never had any luck, and never will,' he said. 'Whatever I do, it'll be *all the same* – I'll croak it alone, and the last thing that'll pass through my head will be: *Die properly now, and may all the misfortune die with you!*

'Miloš can come and see me, and maybe his biggest wish when he grows up will be to see his father. But what will he see? A shabby, dirty drunkard with a scraggly beard who sleeps in derelict workers' huts, washes once a month, eats every second day and is dying of a bleeding liver because he's had his fill of every kind of poison in this life: from what you drink in the bar because you want to and what you down every day because you have to – because others say you must. What should Miloš do? If he comes and sees me like this, I'll die of shame that my son has seen how wretched I am. And if he doesn't come, I'll die of shame that not even my own son cares about me. Whatever's in store, it's *all the same* to me. Just like it's *all the same* to him, too. If he comes, he'll be haunted by shame until his dying day because of what his father was like. If he doesn't come, regret will catch up with him: he'll remember the day that his father died and he didn't go to see him, and he'll feel ashamed because of it. Whatever he does, he'll be dogged by misfortune, just like everything I ever did was plagued by misfortune. And so you see, my friend, that's why nothing matters to me.'

I thought for a moment that I should pay for our drinks because I'm rich, after all, and he's poor. But I let him pay because it was *all the same*, just like he said. We should never prevent people from putting their money where their mouth is. Although he had to turn his pockets inside out to find enough money to pay with, he was in good spirits when he left.

'I'm glad to have met you again,' he said, and was gone before I could answer.

Actually, I'd really wanted to tell him an edifying and comforting story, something about the Austrian writer Thomas Bernhard. It always soothes me to think of Bernhard because we cannot but feel comfort when we hear of others' misfortune being greater than our own. If I'd managed to tell Uroš about Bernhard, he would have gone to sleep happy that night. Because I would have told him that the story teaches us an important thing: that human misfortune is always the same and equally possible everywhere. A starving farmer in the paddy fields of Asia and a depressive writer languidly chewing *Sachertorte* and sipping *Julius Meinl* coffee in a Viennese café have equal reason to be unhappy. We have equally good reason to be unhappy, he and I, because human misfortune doesn't derive from a social system or a geographical location, but from existence itself. Simply *to be somewhere* is reason enough to be unhappy. Actually, it's enough just *to be*. I'd tell him that others have also been *cast into life*, just like we have, and condemned to an existence we didn't want, just like us. It was like that both for him, who had to walk to school from his village in worn-out shoes, and for me, who was driven to school by his father every morning in the Mercedes bought with his uncle's money. Both for him, who went hungry all through school, and for me, who knew that but never offered to buy him a stupid school lunch. Both for him and for Žarko Primorac, who paid the ever-hungry and venal proletarian children with doughnuts and pastries so they'd abuse Uroš in the schoolyard, and do it during the break so that his humiliation was public and visible to all, and thus all the more terrible for him. Both for him and Žarko Primorac, and for me, who never ran up to offer help. And for the suckers who'd bolt down the food Primorac bought them, wipe their mouths on their sleeves and get down to the job. They bashed Uroš mercilessly although they had nothing against him. But they beat him diligently to make sure their boss was satisfied and would buy them delicacies the next day, too. If Primorac hadn't found Uroš particularly repugnant and if it hadn't been for his sadistic urge to abuse and humiliate him, they'd never have eaten chocolate-filled doughnuts in their impoverished early years. Uroš did suffer, but they got the doughnuts they'd craved for every day of their hungry childhoods. Yep, that's probably what they think of when people say *every cloud has a silver lining*. He and I do, too, to the same degree. If he'd just let me tell him that, he'd have been able to realise how comforting it is.

But Uroš undoubtedly saw I was unhappy. He had to see it because the first thing people think when they meet me is: *God, how unhappy that man is*. That's why he said 'I'm glad to have met you again'.

He probably said the same thing to Primorac when he went boozing with him, I thought, because it was clear that Primorac was unhappy too. How great is the joy of those who envied us our apparent childhood *happiness* when they meet us as adults and see that life has made us just as unhappy as them. Life levels us all in misfortune and despair, and every advantage we once had turns against us. But it drives those deprived of all chances, like Uroš, beyond rage and bitterness, and they end up in shame. Instead of being resentful towards others and towards life itself, he awaits the end in shame. Ultimately, Uroš, who was abused by Primorac, could find consolation solely in the fact that life maltreated Primorac too. Each of us is both an executioner and a victim – everyone abuses everyone else. The sadist will come to feel like a martyr sooner or later, and a martyr who lives long enough will also commit contemptible acts which will ensure lasting notoriety. There was nothing else for tormented Primorac to do but to enjoy the feeling of once having been the one who abused: he remembered that when he encountered Uroš. That's why he was so glad to have met him again. That meeting of executioner and victim was to their mutual satisfaction, which is a real rarity in the rich and complex history of executioner and victim, so fraught with negative emotions.

I thought about Uroš as I cruised through town in my car. The rough road took me up to the TV transmitter on Pinješ Hill. I stopped the car and sat there, sipping my whisky and looking at the lights of the town. I located the CD I'd burned for moments of particular desperation. It had two tracks on it – *John Walker's Blues* by Steve Earle and *Leif Erikson* by Interpol – and I played them over and over until I'd emptied the bottle.

That's why I dipped into humanity again: to buy more blasted whisky. That was the only reason for socialising that night. I bought two flasks of Glenfiddich, sat in front of the supermarket and downed several fiery gulps. The golden fluid would flow and I'd find the strength to move back to the car, I thought.

But it seemed that not even such a simple plan could be achieved. However little we expect of life, it gives us even less. Disappointment is inevitable, and not even the complete absence of hope can free us of it. I only wanted to drink whisky and then scoot off home. Instead, I was forced into a conversation with Samir the Wahabi.

I could see him striding towards me like a harbinger of doom. He came straight at me, and the people he bumped into on the way were flung back as if they'd hit a brick wall. If there could be an Islamic comic superhero, some kind of Arabian Hulk, it would look like him, I remember thinking. Even while he was still some way off, I saw he was yelling at me and waving his index finger threateningly.

Samir was usually harmless. You would find him standing around town with his thick black beard and funny white crocheted cap. He was a bogeyman for infidels on his gnarled legs, whose lankiness was further emphasised by the baggy, three-quarter pants he wore. Ranting and raving, he warned the people of Ulcinj about sin and doom. He was therefore considered a local loony, one of many.

Samir had once been a promising young talent, a brilliant pianist, whose rendition of Bach's *Goldberg Variations* brought him to the cusp of fame. He was invited to study piano at the Mozarteum University in Salzburg, which he accepted, and the people of Ulcinj saw him as a 'local boy made good' who had a great future ahead of him, and they predicted he would become one of the world's leading pianists. But just two years later he returned. Some said he'd been raped: that a group of students had abused him on the piano and then whipped him with conductor's batons as he staggered, bleeding from the anus, all the way from the recital hall back to the dorm. Others spoke of an Austrian girl he'd been due to marry. They loved each other and were happy, until one evening she was found hanging from an oak tree in front of the Mozarteum. According to that story, she wrote in a farewell letter that she'd chosen to die because her parents wouldn't allow her to marry him, and she wouldn't marry any other. Apparently, the letter was sewed to her belly with red thread and stated *I'm leaving, my love, and taking our unborn child with me*, but the abundance of details made that version seem less convincing.

Whatever really happened, Samir sought consolation in the mosque. The fingers which had once flown over the piano keys now turned the pages of the Koran. What Austria hadn't given him he now received from Saudi Arabia. People could scoff at Samir while he stood at the traffic lights berating and Koran-bashing them, and they also felt pity for him. But I envied him, because the only truly happy person is the zealot prepared to put everything on the line for what they believe. Of course, what we believe reveals itself as a lie in the end, and what we were prepared to give everything for turns out not to have been worth a thing, not even something as trifling as our life. But that disappointment comes later. Before it grips us, before reason sets in and the tide demolishes the sandcastle we've placed all our hopes in, the moments of happiness we live are the only ones we will have. I never had that hope, and that's why I envied Samir. One moment of blind faith in anything, even in the most utter nonsense, brings a person more happiness than all the reason and knowledge in the world; for reason and knowledge do nothing but destroy any possibility of happiness and reveal everything we've tried to link our life to as worthless. That's why we float like balloons, bloated to bursting point with reason, just waiting for the moment when one tiny extra bit of knowledge will blow us to smithereens – when our body, as fragile as the membrane of a balloon, explodes from the despair which fills us.

When he stood in front of me and sent me what must have been his best reproachful look, I finally understood what he was saying to me.

'You'd better put away that bottle!' he commanded. 'Don't bring more evil upon yourself. I can see there's more than enough of it in you already. Don't you know it's forbidden to consume alcohol?'

'Of course, but not for me – I'm not a Muslim,' I said.

'I know *very well* who you are,' Samir replied. (Why not come out and say he knows *everything* about me? I thought.) 'I know that your great-grandfather was an Orthodox priest, and that's why I'm appealing to you – because the Bible also forbids alcohol.'

I tried to explain to him that I'm a non-Christian to the same extent that I'm a non-Muslim, as well as telling him that all I knew about my great-grandfather was that he was an idiot who plunged his family into misery with his religion. Nothing that Samir had to say from now until eternity was of any interest to me, so I asked him politely to go away and leave me in peace. He replied that he saw evil in me, that even among the throng in town that night he could see evil radiating from me.

Then all at once he changed his tone. He calmed down, pulled up one of the Coca-Cola crates and sat next to me.

'I'm whispering because they're everywhere around us. I can see them following you like they follow me,' he said.

We sat on crates there in front of the supermarket: one of us drunk on alcohol and the other with religion, but both with a vision of evil and ruin around him. Samir told me he believed we were both being pursued by spirits. He claimed they were called djinns.

He spoke eloquently and what he said was not uninteresting, but it certainly was threatening. As we know, the only things we take seriously are those which threaten us.

'Allah, blessed be His name, said: *We made the djinns of scorching fire*. According to some it was the fire of lightning, others say it was the fire of the sun,' Samir explained.

Then he demanded that I reject the image of the world I have.

'There is no one single reality. Reality is tiered and consists of three worlds: material, psychic and spiritual,' he declared mechanically. 'The djinns live between this world, where you and I are now, and the world of pure spirit – they're denizens of the psychic world,' he said, tapping his finger against his forehead.

'The djinns have no permanent shape and can therefore take any form. They have a soul and therefore, like man, are responsible to Allah. Some of the djinns are on the right path and are Muslims. Others are forces of evil in the struggle against Allah. They lurk in the shadows waiting for us and are constantly assailing us,' he told me, visibly agitated. 'They attack me when I'm praying, just like they attack you when you're drinking. But I defend myself again and again, while you give in to them.

'Sometimes you can hear them at night and it sounds like they're romping around your bed. Sometimes they look like ghosts, other times like dogs. Beware of the black dogs in particular! The Prophet said: *The black dog is a Devil! Were dogs not a species of creature, I should command that they all be killed. But I am afraid to kill a whole species. Even so: kill all black dogs because they are djinns.* Those were the words of the Prophet,' Samir claimed.

I learnt from him that evening that being unclean, both physically and spiritually, opened the door to the djinns. When I masturbated I flung the door wide open to evil, he warned me, and I realised that it would be hard for me to ever close it again! According to Samir, masturbation was a call to evil to take us over. When it did, there was only one way to expel it: by turning to what is holy. He explained that the djinns flee from the holy, just as they flee from light and water.

'What is dark must be made light, and what is impure must be cleansed.' With that he abruptly got up and, without looking back, vanished among the crowd of people who were unaware of the danger awaiting them and lived their lives open for evil.

My good Samir, I thought as I lurched off towards the car: everyone is evil and everyone is a liar. As long as you search for evil around you, you're blind to the evil within, and everything is inside you.

That's how my father used to speak to me. He'd sit in his armchair on the terrace for hours, as if petrified, and read Saint Augustine's *Confessions*. If he hadn't moved his hand from time to time, just to turn the page, you really would have thought he'd turned to stone. He sought refuge in that immobility, erecting barricades against everything around him, and whenever he said anything it felt like a stony monument was addressing me. He only spoke words of warning and censure because his self-seclusion and hermit-like asceticism evidently gave him the strength to judge me. This was only possible because he'd never been strong enough to pass judgement on himself – he'd always been weak and indecisive. In the end, he fled beneath the skirts of Saint Augustine, read him, and assumed the pose of a statue of him. Surely he can't have thought that would be sufficient for his salvation;

surely he can't have seen a salutary *transcendental* and a *vertical* in it, to use his words.

'You can't run and hide – all your holy-roller stuff is in vain because none of it is real,' I yelled at him. 'There's only torment, for which you're too weak. Some flee from it into death and decay, and some into religion, which also ultimately leads to death and decay. There's only the torment, from which you all flee; and there's me, determined to endure every little bit of the agony I've been granted for as long as I exist,' I shouted.

He pointed a trembling finger at me and muttered his Augustine: *You are one of those who live their life ever destroying and never creating; all that is good comes from God, and all evil from human freedom to choose.*

That was our last quarrel. I left him on the terrace with Bach playing on the gramophone and Augustine in his hands, all alone in that empty house which he filled with the transcendental after my mother died. We told each other all we had to say and then I left him for good. Since then, we've known nothing about each other, just as we knew nothing of each other before. We've felt nothing but antipathy for each other and yet we regretted that things had to be this way – regretted that we never really had a chance for love to grow between us.

The fastest and least unpleasant way back to the car led through the abandoned underground car park. From there I knew I'd be able to squeeze my way through the row of ramshackle houses to the park, and then walk up the alleyways to Pinješ Hill, where I'd parked the car. The risk of running into someone I didn't want to meet, if we abstract from the fact that I never want to meet anyone, was minimal. This shortcut to the car led round the back of the multitude thronging in their own sweat and stench on the promenade in search of summer amusements. It led through the dark beyond the reach of the street lights, under which tens of thousands of people bobbed and collided in their mindless trajectories like a disarrayed army of ants trundling the same streets as they did every evening, every summer.

Near the deserted Socialist-era supermarket, there was a car park from which a broad staircase led underground. The Communist leaders, recruited from the impoverished proletariat and simple-minded peasantry, made up for their modest origins by hatching megalomaniac plans for the future. They saw everything they built as a cenotaph to them – that which future generations would remember them by, because they believed in the idiotic idea that human life doesn't end at death but endures through people's deeds.

Once I read in the local paper that the car park with its three levels covered every bit of 100,000 square feet. This was not including the nuclear shelter, whose dimensions are unknown since the information is still treated as a military secret. The building would make a perfect vault or crypt, and I assume it would be possible to transfer the remains of all the Yugoslav Communist leaders there. In the process, the coffins of their immediate family members could also be brought to the shelter so that they could be together in death, too. The Yugoslav Marxists lived according to the maxim that the family is the basic building block of society, so it seemed appropriate that the same social organisation should be upheld in the afterlife, too.

But this gargantuan child was useless as a car park. When the weary tradesmen had completed the final construction tasks and the pig-faced municipal president cut the ribbon to declare the place open, no car could drive into it accompanied by the town sirens' festive blare. The underground car park was ready but lacked a short stretch of access road. The newspapers of the time justified a car park which no cars could enter as being 'part of the anticipated dynamic development of the town'. The car park was just the first step: the next five-year plan would see 'construction of the road into and out of the car park, as well as a range of associated infrastructural facilities to enhance the attractiveness of the Ulcinj area as a tourist destination'. The municipal president delivered his vision of the future road in a speech to a meeting of the town's youth. The gist of his argument went like this: if today's generations went and built *everything*, meaning the car park *and* the access road, they'd run the risk of pampering generations to come.

Just as their fathers had done a hard job by fighting for and winning the country's freedom, they too had done a hard job by building the car park. Every new generation had it easier: half a century ago we had nothing; now we had our freedom and the car park; the access road was the only thing missing. These were his main points, and it revealed a glimpse of the future concept of development. The car park was evidently conceived as a story without end – an everlasting building site which every generation would contribute to until the end of the world.

In the meantime, however, the car park was a hole in the centre of town, where the local population disposed of their rubbish on a daily basis. And as I was going down the stairs into this notorious rubbish dump, I almost tripped over rusty television sets and fridges several times, along with piles of good old jumbo rubbish bags which the more environmentally conscious citizens dispose their refuse in. The light bulbs which had not yet been smashed by local hooligans flickered in an effort to illuminate this mausoleum to the belief in progress.

The abandoned car park provided the inspiration for many local urban legends. It began with the story about a band of drug addicts who gathered *under the town*. Then a dead girl was found in the car park. She'd been raped, some said. Others claimed the killer had cut off both her hands before she died. The police ultimately reported that the girl had died from tumbling down the stairs, and that she'd tumbled down the stairs because she wanted to, and that she'd wanted to because she was the victim of a paedophile, incestuous father, which caused her to commit suicide and saw her father end up in jail. But before it irrefutably became a 'family tragedy', the case ran the gauntlet of neighbourhood gossip, with every teller of the story inserting some figment of their darkest desires and frustrations. They said the girl had been anally gang-raped. Or that she'd been forced to have oral sex, again with several men. Or that she was found with her eyes gouged out, which meant that suspicions were directed towards the Satanists. Or that her kidneys had been plucked out, which saw the blame being levelled at the human-organ traffickers who'd passed themselves off as an old married couple from Italy and managed to

The Olcinium Trilogy

deceive their victims with the image of friendly, senile tourists travelling the impoverished European fringe to bring humanitarian aid to the local population. The dead girl was a blank slate, and the town testified to its own repulsiveness. Let people give free rein to their fantasies and hell will open up before you. A smelly sulphurous torrent of their thoughts will gush forth, full of slimy desires spawned from their souls like monstrously deformed infants; full of suppressed fears dredged up from that cemetery of bones and putrid corpses inside.

There were a few more fantasy murders as well as several real suicides down in the car park, which became a chasm into which the people of Ulcinj stuck everything they didn't dare to say or even think, like in the fable about the emperor who had goat's ears but banned anyone from saying so. But no hole is deep enough to accommodate all the evil of humanity. If someone managed to wring all the black out of just one human soul, like the ink from a squid, the whole world would disappear in murk. Only demented minds could split atoms and search with microscopes for the perfect weapon; just peer into one human being and you'll find all that's required to obliterate life on Earth.

When I was down in the car park I felt comfortable for the first time that evening. I'd always known there's no place people can find happiness except underground. Up above me humanity raged, producing a clamour which penetrated even the thick reinforced concrete of the construction. The footsteps above my head sounded like tiny nails being hammered into the coffin I'd voluntarily entered. Alas, even below ground I wasn't alone: one unpleasant surprise follows another – that's the story of my life.

I sat on a heap of abandoned books at the nethermost point of the car park, in front of the giant steel doors of the nuclear shelter, and browsed through some of them. There was quite a collection of religious trash: *One Hundred Ways to Attain Salvation, Interpreting God's Signs* and *Self-Awareness*. I lit a cigarette and looked attentively at the piles of rubbish around me. The harsh landscape of garbage is comforting, devoid as it is of promise, and thus of hope and subsequent disappointment. Everything around me was spent, disposed of and utterly forgotten, as if it had never existed. I sympathised with every one of the discarded domestic appliances, kitchen cabinets and light fixtures. Each of us awaits the same fate which befell them. People will use us and then forget us just like they used and forgot those objects. Intermittently, people are useful to us for some reason and so we bond with them. But the very next day, they bother us and we wish for nothing more than for them to vanish from our lives. Every day we discard people like we discard rubbish. We discard and will be discarded, that's the simple truth. We're cast into a world which constantly discards us. In the end we're left alone with ourselves to wander the waste dump of our lives. All around us are discarded friends, lovers, and people good for one day; those we avoided and those we got rid of.

For a moment, I thought I saw the silhouette of a person between two old fridges. I told myself not to be ridiculous, that no one had come here for years. The locals think the place is cursed, and tourists only come down for a pee or, in moments of great sexual urgency, to have an unfulfilling quickie. But they never come down this far. Whatever brings them here, they perform it at the base of the stairs, from where they still have a comforting glimpse of the world above them.

Despite the convincing argument I consoled myself with, the silhouette emerged from the darkness again. In front of me now stood a dark-skinned boy. He looked at me with a measured gaze, his eyes full of suspicion. Then he held out his hand to me, which I naturally took as an extremely hostile gesture.

The impertinence of beggars knows no bounds. They're people who demand compassion from us again and again, despite them having none for others. They act as if there was no other misfortune in the universe apart from theirs. When a person dear to you dies and you drive the streets of the town in despair, waiting for the sedatives you've swallowed to take effect, you stop at the traffic lights and a beggar woman with a child pinned like a brooch to her flaccid breast will come up and ask you for money. What does she care for your suffering? She's got enough of her own and is determined to get something in exchange for it. Even in the midst of the worst tragedy that could befall you, beggars will still stubbornly assail you, demanding that you pay them for *their* tragedy. And if a person, in their greatest despair, decided to end their life by jumping off a high-rise building, I'm sure the beggars would reach their hands out through the staircase windows and demand alms from the plummeting figure.

As if that wasn't enough, beggars also unscrupulously exploit their physical deficiencies. Once at the traffic lights near the railway station in Podgorica, a Gypsy stuck his withered leg in through the open window of my car. I hadn't noticed him as he came up, dragging himself along on his crutches. With the cool calmness of a hit man, he thrust his leg in through the window and kicked me in the face; his foot stank abominably. I hastily opened the door, knocking him back and into the adjacent lane, right in front of a truck which had stopped at the red light. With a bit of luck I was able to push the bastard beneath the moving vehicle. He got up on his crutches again with amazing speed and came at me again, cursing. Fortunately, I had a can of Coca-Cola in the car, the perfect projectile, which I landed right between his evil little eyes. This time he hit the asphalt properly. In my rear-view mirror I saw the blood trickle from his forehead onto the asphalt. Later, when the police questioned me, they asked why I fled the 'scene of the accident', as they called it. I told them that the formulation 'scene of the accident' was quite inappropriate to my mind because the event had really made my day.

'You fled because you didn't have the courage to face up to what you did,' the officer shouted.

I explained to him that I only drove away because the traffic lights had turned green and the impatient drivers behind me were blowing their horns, unwilling to let me revel in what I'd done and savour the sight of that miscreant bowled over backwards.

Now here I was, faced with another such situation; the boy with the outstretched hand edged towards me, step by cautious step. Uh-oh, I thought, one misfortune never comes alone: behind him several more beggars brazenly stepped forth from what I had considered the dark of non-existence. I counted them: there was one man, two women, and five children of indeterminable sex. Now that a whole family of beggars had appeared, I realised I'd better get out of there quickly. One of the women had a lump on her back the size of a mirror ball in your average disco, while the other's face was wrapped in bandages embellished with bloodstains. Both of them were also lacking vital limbs; at least an arm and a leg each, I estimated at first glance. But their anatomic minimalism didn't mean the effacement of all beauty, and I discerned something well-proportioned about their figures, a kind of pragmatic symmetry. One of the women lacked a left arm and a right leg, while the other lacked a right arm and a left leg, so the diagonal presence and diagonal absence of limbs intersected on their bodies. This symmetry, which my aesthetically trained eye immediately perceived, allowed them to move about with the aid of just a single crutch. With it propped under their one arm, and hopping on their one leg, they could flit around with reasonable dexterity. If the absence of limbs had been vertical – if they'd lacked an arm and a leg on the same side of the body, say – getting about would have been much more difficult for them. That would have lessened my problem because I wouldn't have needed to fear they could accost me or – horror of horrors – even touch me.

Now as they came closer, I saw that the father of the family wasn't intact either. He had no arms from the elbows down. He also lacked ears and a nose, which was only fair in a way, because what would he do without hands if he wanted to pick his nose or dig in his ear with a little finger? And was that a limp he had? His legs looked as if they'd been beaten into the shape of an X. Again, two diagonals, I noted. The children, as so often happens, combined the features of their father and mothers. They all looked the same: dark-skinned and dirty, with pale, gummed-up eyes. It would have been impossible to distinguish them if it had not been for their bodily imperfections.

Should I Stay or Should I Go, I thought, as this family of invalids shuffled towards me, accompanied by whooping and the rhythmical clacking of crutches. But I didn't take to my heels because just at that moment the writer in me awoke, after having lain dormant for years.

Literature thrives on human misfortune, and the beggars in front of me were a prime example of the agony of existence. It occurred to me that if I couldn't squeeze a good story out of them, I'd never be able to write. Having now found a way to exploit them, I decided to spend a little longer in their company. Yet at the same time, I realised that they also had an idea or two about how to exploit me. Perhaps they'd decided to club me to death with their crutches and then eat me. A fatso like me would be food for them for a whole month, I worried. My body would never be found, if I was searched for at all. No one saw me enter the car park, and no one would ever think of looking for me here; my mind played out a paranoid scenario.

Fortunately, I found a way of giving them the slip. I scaled the fire-escape stairs up to the ventilation duct of the nuclear shelter. It was clear to me that those invalids would never be able to make it up here, and sure enough, the head of the family scrutinised the stairs, almost to the point of sniffing them like a dog. As I'd assumed, he concluded I was beyond their reach. He turned to the family and spread his arms – or what he had left of them – in a gesture of helplessness.

They all gathered beneath me and called out in one voice for alms, obviously without thinking for a second how pointless their demand was. I watched them from my vantage point like populist leaders behold the crowd from the balconies where they hold their speeches. The small children reached out their trembling little hands towards me. Only then did I notice that every hand had only three fingers. The Serbian three-finger salute, I thought to myself!

So I yelled down to them like Slobodan Milošević at one of his rallies in the nineties, 'I love you too!'

'We're hungry, give us alms!' called one of the one-armed women. 'Please … May God grant you health,' said the other.

That cheered me up no end; a person afflicted by leprosy had just wished me good health!

'See, you're laughing,' said the head of the household, determined to seize on my good mood. 'Give us food and we'll make you laugh all night long.'

Ha, these weren't beggars but entertainers! The five grubby children had perhaps taken *The Jackson 5* as models. Since that was a respectable way of providing for oneself, I promised to throw them a few crumbs. I took a good swig from my bottle.

'If you want to eat, tell me about yourselves,' I proposed. And that they did.

They were originally from Kosovo. They'd had a hard time all their lives, the father emphasised, as if that didn't go without saying for every human being. 'Me and my two ladies went from town to town,' he explained. 'Then the children came along, three little angels,' he sighed wistfully.

'With swarthy faces,' I added with compassion.

He claimed that they'd worked hard but never earned enough for a house of their own. Therefore, they slept in caves. In a cavern near Prizren they came across a colony of lepers. They tried to flee, but the lepers blocked the exit with their bodies, a barrier more effective than electrified barbed wire. They let him go, but his wives and children were held hostage. Every day he had to bring the lepers food, he said. That went on for months. Then they were liberated by NATO, which was bombing Serbia at the time; it seems a pilot missed his target and his rocket hit the cave. They fled through the flames as the cave collapsed behind them.

A period of prosperity followed for the polygamous family. Infected with leprosy but as yet unaware of it, they roamed from village to village after the residents had fled to Albania to escape the Serbian army.

'The soldiers left us alone,' the paterfamilias said. 'We told them we're Balkan Egyptians,[1] and they had nothing against us. Nor we against them. And when they came in trucks and took away everything of value in the villages, there was still enough for us.'

But when the Serbian army withdrew and the Kosovar villagers returned to their ransacked homes, difficult times were in store for

---

[1] Albanian-speaking Romanies (Gypsies) who believe that their ancestors migrated from the Indian Subcontinent to Europe via Egypt.

the family. Everyone beat them up and they were blamed for all ills, the head of the household complained. When irate villagers raped his wives and broke his legs with a pickaxe, they realised they'd better run for it. They ended up here in Ulcinj, and regretted it a hundred times. No one gave them a lousy dinar here, he bellyached. It's as if the people here had no feelings. But the worst was yet to come …

'We have no education,' they told me. 'So how were we to know that we'd come down with leprosy too? We caught if from those miserable lepers in the cave.'

'When my missus came up with a lump on her back, I got worried and took her to see a doctor. And he called the police,' the head of the family said. 'Men with gas masks came, armed with hoses, and evacuated the dispensary. We and the doctor were quarantined. He was let out the next day when they established he wasn't infected, but we were held there for a few days more. And then one evening we were brought here to the abandoned car park. If we ever came out or so much as poked our noses out of the car park, we'd be killed, the police warned us. But I no longer had a nose then – it had fallen off all by itself.' He laughed heartily at the police's stupidity.

From then on, the years were filled with misery. Two more children were born, and they lost the odd arm and leg. But all in all they led a peaceful life, he said. The police's threat had been quite unnecessary. 'We're not going anywhere,' he emphasised.

'If anyone tries to drive us out of the car park, we'll fight for our right to stay,' the whole family chipped in.

The car park had become the home they'd been searching for all their lives. They claimed to have everything down there: food, a roof over their heads, and peace and quiet.

'In the world outside we get beaten up and abused, and we'd be strangers wherever we went. But down here we're masters of our own home,' the head of the family explained. 'Outside my children would be despised, but here they grow up surrounded by love. Outside they'd grow up seeing others beat and humiliate me, while here in the car park I can gain their respect. That's important because I'm their father.

We stay because we're happy here,' he said, unaware that he'd just convincingly refuted Tolstoy, who claimed that all happy families are happy in the same way.

I have a vision, I wanted to tell them. I am a piper with a funny Tyrolean cap, which Thomas Bernhard would find laughable, and am dressed in green knickerbockers with suspenders like Heidegger used to wear. I march along blowing my pipe. And just as the rats faithfully followed the Pied Piper of Hamelin, whom German towns hired to rid them of the bright-eyed rodents, so the abandoned, homeless and sick shall follow me. I play my pipe, and the leprous beggars totter after me up the stairs, and we leave the car park into the summer night full of neon and lust. The music from my magic pipe needles its way through the blaring bands on the café terraces and makes it through to every old lady about to be poisoned by her relatives so they can share out the inheritance; to every child who will be suffocated by its mother in a shanty on the outskirts and thrown into a stream clogged with plastic bags and old umbrellas; to every AIDS-infected young woman who trembles in her room, dreading the moment when people will find out; to every raped boy; to every alcoholic dying of liver cirrhosis down in the cellar, banished and abandoned by his ex-wife and children upstairs; to everyone on the verge of suicide, standing on a rickety chair with a noose around their neck – my music is like a waking hand which reaches out to all the tuberculosed, the blind and deaf, the paraplegics and lepers. They are my army! Arrayed in a column behind me, they limp, lurch, stagger, crawl, drag their withered legs, and roll along in their wheelchairs. They follow my footsteps, just like the rats followed the Pied Piper. This is my grisly army beneath banners of blood-drenched bandages. Like avengers, we enter city after city and leave our mark in parliaments, malls, schools and hospitals. With every step we take we spread disease and disaster. We sneeze, pee, bleed, and leave bacilli on everything we touch. Wherever we go, we remake everything in our likeness, and all that is living falls before the contagion. Now they are all my soldiers. Faithfully they form a mighty column, and I think:

O children of the dark generations, silvery do shine the evil flowers of blood on our brows, and the cold moon in our broken eyes, o my blighted brethren!

This is my grisly army, and there are ever more and more of us: all the beggars of Delhi, all the homeless of Brooklyn, all those who have grown up beneath Cairo and all the hungry of Kinshasa. Longer and ever longer is the column behind me, and the choir of a billion diseased voices, in unison, roars the cheerful refrain played by the pipe: *Death to Everyone is Gonna Come*. Here we are now on the sea shore, and here I am walking on water. *Death to Everyone ...* I play and mark time as I watch the cliffs over which my army, my grisly army, plunges into the sea and vanishes in the blue depths. I play faster and faster, now it is already *tempo furioso*: without a tear, without a scream, without regret and remorse, all that is mine falls to its death.

III

'Master?' I was roused from reflection by the father leper's rasping voice. 'Give us food now, we've done our part of the bargain.'

What can I give them when I've got nothing but whisky, I asked myself rhetorically. I took another swig and threw him the bottle.

'Don't overdo it with the fire water,' I was even bold enough to warn them.

As they were trying to bend over and pick up my Glenfiddich, I used the distraction to zip down the safety stairs. Just when I thought I'd gracefully backed out of things, albeit without saying goodbye, the greedy kid grabbed me by the trousers. I shot him a reproving look. He tried to hold me back with all the three fingers of one hand, while demanding alms with the open hand of the other. So I gave him a gentle kick in the stomach with the tip of my shoe, in a fatherly sort of way. I hardly touched him, but the little monster raised such a racket that his father and mothers, after examining him and establishing he was all right, headed off after me seeking revenge. 'Liar, bastard, scum!' I heard them fume as I ran for the exit.

It was three in the morning when I found myself in the world outside again. The mob of tourists was gradually dispersing.

I drove slowly. The roots of ruin can be seen in every stone by the roadside if you care to look, if you only try to learn, I thought. The road I was driving along was the one the Montenegrin army climbed when it came to take Ulcinj from the Turks. Up in the clearing, where you can look out into the blue emptiness all the way across the Adriatic to Otranto on the one side, and down onto the plain of Štoj and the salt pans on the other, they clashed with a small Turkish unit. After that they advanced down through the streets of Ulcinj to the walls of the Old Town. But their attack was repulsed, and they let out their rage by burning down part of the town. It would later be rebuilt, and today the suburb is called *Nova Mahala* or New Quarter – talk about a euphemism! The wooden houses and hundreds of little bridges burned through until dawn, illuminating the path into the future for the people of Ulcinj.

When he finally captured Ulcinj, King Nicholas had a church built beneath the walls of the Old Town. They say that parts of the Cyclopean ramparts, thousands of years old, were used to build the church. Pieces of the damaged walls which had plunged down into the sea from the besiegers' cannonade during the siege were masoned into the church. Later, a new settlement was raised around the church. For that they levelled the Muslim cemetery where the people of Ulcinj had buried their dead for centuries; they knocked down the gravestones, threw them into the sea, stamped and trampled the ground, and built their houses there as if it was virgin land.

Where is there any chance of human happiness in all this, I wondered. Amid the death, destruction and dispossession which had been present from the very beginning and would last until the end. It seemed impossible to find happiness, and I gave myself up to the satisfaction of moralising for a few moments, before stopping the car and parking in front of the wall surrounding the Orthodox church.

That was the closest I was going to get. The shortest route to the Old Town led through the courtyard of the church, but I never thought of going that way. If Catholicism enraged me and Judaism bored me, if I pitied Islam and disdained Protestantism, Orthodoxy filled me with sheer disgust. That's why, instead of going through the church's courtyard, I went the long way round, past overflowing garbage containers which the municipal services hadn't emptied for days. If I have to choose between the reek of rubbish and the stench of incense, I always choose the first. Rather dirty streets than seedy cassocks, I said to myself. If I'm stupid and desperate enough to seek salvation and place my hope in it, I'll search for it on the asphalt, certainly not before the altar. I choose the world the way it is rather than swallow the lies for the weak.

With these thoughts in my mind, I arrived at the gates of the Old Town. I could hear steps coming towards me along the dark street, and a man ran past me carrying what looked like a dog or a child in his arms. I caught a glimpse of his face and saw that his eyes were full of tears, while his contorted lips revealed the despair he felt. Behind him, like penguins bereft of any trace of amiability, there waddled several headscarved women in pantaloons. Not one of them was taller than five foot or weighed less than 160 pounds. They looked like pygmy sumo wrestlers. John Waters would have paid a fortune to have them in one of his films. These kerchiefed penguins shrieked unbearably. It was clear they were bemoaning something, but aren't we always doing that, and mostly bemoaning ourselves? Like grotesque performers, they tap-danced in their tiny wooden-soled slippers over the cobble-stones worn smooth with time. Although they'd never realise it, time would render trivial every pain they'd ever felt and would make both them and whatever they were lamenting that night pass without a trace, like the wind blows through the desert.

I was heading for Terra Promessa, where I was a regular and could sit on the terrace and drink for hours. It was a nice bar with a perfect view of the sea where they played Johnny Cash and Merle Haggard: *some of the best that conservative America has produced*, the waiter once commented. He had a strange ideological profile I never quite understood.

'I travelled a lot when I was young. I was even at Woodstock,' he told me once. 'I was a liberal. But then I thought a lot and read a lot, and there you are – today I'm a conservative.'

That was unusual because people are normally conservative because they *don't* think or read.

'You do understand, of course, that any ideological definition is completely pointless,' I said to him. 'Accepting any idea simply means that we haven't yet thought about it enough, because everything becomes absolutely unacceptable as soon as we think twice about it. Do you realise how paltry your dispute with the leftists is?' I asked him. 'In trying to improve the world, you make life even harder for everyone. You enact laws and rules which make our already

The Olcinium Trilogy

wretched existence even more miserable, and then you even fight wars, although that isn't so bad – fortunately people die in war, so those lucky beggars are at least put out of their misery. You do understand, of course, that you're all going to snuff it in the end. And what's more, it will be in despair. There won't be a single idea, song or slogan behind which you'll be able to hide from the fact that you're dying, that you don't know why you've lived or why you're dying, that you've never known what is good and what is evil, and that you've always only ever done evil, especially when you most firmly believed you were doing good. But that really doesn't matter because not only will the border between good and evil blur for you in the hour of your death, but you won't even be sure if good and evil exist at all, and you'll feel at your death that good and evil are just ideological constructs which were necessary to help you scrape through,' I told him.

He didn't answer, but he realised it was better to avoid conversing with me. Since then we've developed a wonderful relationship: he brings me my drink in silence, and I drink in silence. He exists solely as the one who serves, and I solely as the one who pays him for it. A whisky or two in the 'promised land', and then I'd drive home to bed, I thought.

But a foreboding that the future wasn't going to be so nice grew on me as I walked along the narrow lanes. The people I met on the way were shocked and emotional. Women were leaning on the windowsills and crying, while men stood in front of the houses and smoked in silence. I tried to make out what they were whispering about. I heard just one word of Albanian, a language I've never learnt although I've been immersed in it all my life. They repeated that one word, and it followed me like a hissing snake all the way to Terra Promessa. It slid after me down the dark alleys overgrown with ivy like a giant serpent bearing misfortune on its back. *Pus*, they said over and over again.

The bar was empty, and there was no music. I took that as final confirmation of my presentiment that some misfortune had struck. Misfortunes happen all the time – what else is there anyway? – but people only notice it on occasion. Usually they take all their life to realise that everything was misfortune, from their birth onwards. Admittedly, a certain subtlety is required to see a reason for sadness in the birth of a child. Therefore, people only show sorrow when misfortune takes a vulgar manifestation, like when an aeroplane crashes or miners are trapped underground. Then they turn off all music, which for them is a form of entertainment, despite the greatest value of music being that it is so lovely to mourn to.

The waiters stood at the bar, spreading their arms and shaking their heads in a demonstration of helplessness and disbelief. I cleared my throat several times in the hope of attracting their attention. They only came after I'd resorted to more radical methods: taking a crystal dish for ice from the next table and throwing it on the floor at their feet, where it smashed to smithereens and made it *crystal clear* to them that I was demanding my drink.

My conservative waiter explained to me the strange events I had witnessed that night. *Pus* is the Albanian word for well. A child had fallen into a well and died. But, strangely, the boy hadn't drowned. He fried to death.

In his sleep, the boy's father had heard someone lifting the lid of the well, one of many which residents of the Old Town still have in their courtyards like mementoes of a bygone age. Some thirsty tourist again, he thought, and turned his head to the other side of the pillow. Then he distinctly heard someone fall in, and squeals like those of a slaughtered animal came from that hole in the ground and woke up the whole neighbourhood. When they saw their son's footprints in front of the well, his mother fainted. His father took a long rake and managed to haul up the little charred body; the unfortunate boy was burnt beyond recognition. One bystander suggested lowering a bucket to see what could have burned the boy so quickly. It was brought up full of molten lava, caught fire and fell back into the well.

'But there's no volcano here, or at least there wasn't until now, so how's this possible?' the waiter marvelled. 'What's more, lava has also been found farther up the coast, at Možura, and it looks like lava was the cause of the fire there. There was also lava at *Velika Plaža* beach, and the underbrush is still burning from it. I bet they'll find lava in Bratica, too. The fire brigade can't get at it there. The road to Bar is cut off and the whole town surrounded by flames. What if a hidden volcano beneath Ulcinj explodes tonight?' the waiter asked. 'What will happen to us then?'

I paid up and hurriedly fled the scene because his story contained an apocalyptic tone I found particularly unnerving. But we flee in vain. Misfortune comes in bunches, like poisonous flowers or bombs dropped to destroy the last sanctuary of our solitude and calm. I escaped the waiter only to run into Dirty Djuro again, for the second time that night. I'd made it to the gate of the Old Town when he intercepted me like a jet fighter invisible to my radar.

'My friend, let me take you to *Servantes*. My daughters are doing a dance number there,' he said.

Servantes, as I was to learn, was a newly opened cabaret-bar on the Slave Market in the Old Town. Here I always used to come across panting, sweaty tourists photographing the slave cages, which gape shamefully empty today although the world is full of people who ought to be locked up. I've always appreciated that place as one of the few surviving pieces of evidence that the town I live in belongs to Western civilisation. The Ulcinj corsairs were once the scourge of the coastal towns all the way north to Istria. The Ottoman Empire sank their fleet in Valdanos Bay in the mid eighteenth century after the corsair leaders refused obedience to the Sultan. In any case, the corsairs abducted people throughout the Mediterranean and sold them here at their Slave Market. The documents bearing witness to this lead us to believe that Ulcinj's Slave Market was famous far and wide. The slaves who changed hands here were taken all the way to Constantinople in the east and Vienna in the west. Historical sources which don't seem particularly reliable allege that the man who later wrote *Don Quixote* was also brought here, sun-parched and fettered, and sold. Inspired by the knowledge that the inhabitants of Ulcinj had enslaved Miguel Cervantes, which was undoubtedly their greatest contribution to world culture, I imagined today's Slave Market as the perfect venue for an artistic event; a place where writers would read from their oeuvre and then be auctioned off to the literature lover who bid the highest. After paying an adequate fee to the publisher, readers would be allowed to take a wet whip and flog a writer they particularly hated. Or loved. Ladies who dreamed of having children who'd become artists could be impregnated by gifted authors. Such a concept would create the opportunity for countless debates about the social role of writers, freedom of artistic expression and the commodification of literature.

But other art forms were in demand in *Servantes*, I thought to myself as Djuro led me into the smoky premises illuminated by green and red neon lights. His daughters were doing a striptease on an improvised stage in the centre.

Located behind the Romanesque church, which had been converted first into a mosque and then into a museum, a dilapidated stone house had been made into a brothel and named after the famous writer. The people of Ulcinj gave him no peace even in death. Djuro had announced that the programme would be spectacular. But his daughters had problems with the choreography, to put it kindly. Their movements were devoid of the slightest trace of elegance, and they tried to tie them into something which could only be called 'erotic dance' with a lethal dose of sarcasm.

Through the thicket of *oohs* and *ahs* accompanying this performance I heard a deep male voice addressing the barman: 'A double pepper vodka for me, and a double of your best whisky for my friend here.' I looked for the owner of that impressive voice: he was an elderly, grey-haired man in a fine jute suit with a neatly trimmed beard, a topi above a high forehead, and keen eyes.

We exchanged several polite sentences. That was the least I could do for a man who'd bought me a drink. He was, as people like to say, a man of the world: an old-school gentleman with good manners and an education which can only be provided by classical lyceums and top-notch European universities. Only when you finally meet someone with good manners do you realise why they're so important – they allow you to communicate with others without getting too close to them. Good manners can help you to keep at a hygienic distance from people, which is impossible to maintain when evil fate forces us into contact with primitives who constantly desire to become intimate with us and are offended when they learn that we don't want any proximity.

'Is this your first time in Ulcinj?' I asked him.

'Not exactly', he replied. 'It would be truer to say I've been here all along.'

'That amazes me,' I said. 'This is a small town where everyone knows everyone else, and I don't remember having met you before.'

'You know, what I really meant is that I feel at home everywhere, metaphorically speaking,' the stranger remarked.

'Truly cosmopolitan spirits are rare today,' I said, and drained my glass. 'People have everything within arm's reach, the world is at their feet and all knowledge at their fingertips, but the world is still ruled by ignorance and prejudice.'

'You're quite right,' the old man agreed. 'It's the same with me: nothing vexes me more than prejudice. You just can't explain things to some people because prejudice makes them blind and deaf. I have always most highly prized openness for new ideas and a freedom of mind. Those who have that are my people,' he averred, rapping his knuckles on the bar.

After a brief pause he continued, 'My dear Sir, although we've only just met I feel I've known you all my life – you're a man of style, that's clear as soon as anyone sees you.'

'The same could be said of you,' I returned the compliment.

'Yes, yes,' he muttered, 'I guess people have accused me of many things, but no one has challenged my style. Therefore, I say to you, because you'll understand me: this little orgy behind us here will come to a bad end,' he said with confidence and conviction. 'That's the problem with people – their lack of style. Their inability to transcend their limitations. And so every attempt to rise above oneself ends in obscenity; the more ambitious the attempt, the greater the obscenity.'

There was nothing to add to his words. It's rare to encounter a kindred soul. Sophisticated people are condemned to solitude. Therefore, when we meet a like-minded person, we should make sure to enjoy their company. Determined to chat a little longer with the old man, I ordered another round of drinks.

Then Samir the Wahabi strode into the premises. *Servantes* really brought out his messianic syndrome. He cursed the naked girls and the men who were watching them.

'Go home to your wives,' he yelled. 'God will punish you all and scorch you with His wrath.'

That was all Samir managed to say before someone hit him and he fell to the floor. Diligent feet kicked him and a barrage of fists found their mark. He was carried out of the café, covered in blood, and thrown into the nearby bushes.

'If you ask me, he came to grief because he moralised,' I said to the old man. 'He came at a bad time and said the wrong things. It's as simple as that. To go into a brothel and lecture a pack of sex-hungry men about God and punishment is bound to end badly.'

'Why do they do that, I ask you?' the old man growled and banged his fist on the bar. 'Why do they confound the already hopeless tangle of their lives with things like morality, philosophy and religion? Why don't they ever choose the simpler way when it's so obvious? And why the remorse when they do choose a path? All this and the whole world is just a conspiracy of fools, my dear fellow. It's all been devised to make life miserable for us people with spirit. Couldn't some good Gypsy ensemble have played here tonight instead? Couldn't people have sat here in peace and drank some of the quality local wines? I beg your pardon, a man of taste will refuse wine – whisky then. Couldn't they have served a single malt from the Scottish Highlands? Couldn't they have all been contented tonight? But no! This is just an example of how easy it is for everything to fall apart. And where has this got us to, I ask you? Instead of whisky, blood flows – not that I have anything against it. But where there's blood, there's wine. That short trajectory from blood to wine contains all the lies of this world, all that makes people's lives miserable. Turn blood into wine and you've turned the world into a hell where they drown people in cauldrons of seething guilt and roast them on the pyre of illusions – a hell for those condemned to eternally repeat one and the same question: why?

'I feel we've got to know one another pretty well. Instead of music, we have the tears of a martyr – a fool, to be frank, who suffered due to his own arrogance. That's how things go, *my son*,' he said. Seizing my hand in his torrid fist, he intoned: 'There are still so many things I have to say to you, *my son*.'

'Old fool!' I thought. He started off well, in fact he did brilliantly, but now he's gone and called me *son*. If we continue the conversation it will turn out that I remind him of a son he lost long ago, some sad story about losing a beloved child will pop up like a zombie, and everything will end up in pathos, cheap advice and tears. I'll have to put him in his place, I thought. That will offend the old man, but I have no choice.

'Our conversation is over. Good night to you,' I said and headed for the door.

'You know, of course, that it won't be as easy as that. Let me assure you that you don't really want to leave me, *my son*,' he replied, maliciously accentuating those last two words. 'Let me tell you a few interesting things about you. Is it not true that your wife left you, not one day ago? I have your attention now, don't I? The wife you loved has left you. They say: *love*, but what does that mean other than *to suffer when you lose it*? You loved her, and you lost her. So it seems. But *on second thought*, as you like to say, you'll realise that you didn't lose her, nor could you have, because you never owned her. She was never *yours*. You don't *have* other people, just as they don't *have* you. You live separate lives. Sometimes people are useful to you, like when you take what you need from a toolbox. Other times they're an obstacle to be avoided, and sometimes removed. Ultimately, you're left to your own devices in an extremely hostile environment, where everything that exists is there to make your life difficult and ultimately destroy you.

'*I know all that*, you'll say. Yes, you did, and yet you got married although you knew better,' the old man said. 'I can just see the two of you: it's quite plain that you take devotion for love and don't discern the difference between tolerance and love. You say to yourself: I love her, but actually you only just put up with her. You think: I put up with her because I love her, and love means denial. That explains everything, you think. But why then do you get up every morning before dawn, open the bedroom door a crack to check she's sleeping, and sit down at the computer? Why then do you search for pornography on the internet and spend those early-morning hours, those precious moments of solitude, masturbating? Then regret befalls you, or is it that you're worried she'll discover your dirty little habit? You take your hands off *Richard*, so to speak, and shun the computer, but you still can't sleep. There's no sleep for you since she's lain in your bed. You wake every morning at the same time. Three minutes past three, it says on the clock, whose red numbers blink on the shelf above your head. You're woken by strange noises. You hold your breath to try and hear them better, you listen hard, but you can't tell where the noises are coming from. Sometimes you think you hear footsteps outside the window. Or is that the rustling of sheets from the kitchen – you imagine they're white and hover over the table, borne on a wind which opens the window and rushes into the room. At other times you're sure that someone, or *something*, is up in the roof; that it scratches its nails on the plaster and gnaws at the rafters; and that that someone or *something* will keep maltreating you until you lose your mind. You get up and search the house, trying not to wake her. She mustn't find out, you think: *that* would be too much for her. You search the house but find nothing.

'*I love her*, you think now as you sit in the car, staring at the gate of the clinic and waiting for her to come out, purged of your child. But when she lowered her head onto your lap, as helpless as a broken, golden doe; when she lay on your legs, blinked with tears in her eyes and fearfully said *I'm pregnant*; when you, at those words, pushed her aside and brutally shouted *What?*; when she doubled up in the armchair, buried her face in her hands and cried; when you told her you could put up with her but not a child, and she had to get rid of it straight away; when you told her a child would eat away your existence like a brood of rats and would kill you, you finished what she'd begun; when you told her you weren't capable of devoting a single shred of attention to the child and that you already had a child – her – and she must therefore choose between you and the child; when all of that was in the air you actually wondered: *Do I love you?*

'And before she could even think things over you threw her into the car and drove her to the clinic. She'd leaned her head against your shoulder and nestled up to you, but you didn't say a word. You refused so much as to look at her. Was her transgression so huge that not even a love like yours could brook it? Was her pregnancy too great a transgression to forgive? You harshly threw her off you, onto the seat beside you; then you threw her into the car like a sackful of rubbish; soon you cast her out in front of the clinic as if it was a rubbish container. She emerged from there an hour later, bent and black, a shadow of the person you *loved*.

'When she came to her senses in the morning and realised what she'd done, and above all what you'd done to her, she left you. "Everything I thought I had to sacrifice the child for is gone. Everything I discarded the child for so I could keep you no longer exists. So everything that was a reason to stay with you is now a reason to leave you. My love for you is *aborted*," she said.

'That's why I ask you: why are you leaving me and where are you going? Haven't you decided to tread the so-called path of virtue?' the old man asked. 'But where does it lead? And even if you lived the life of a righteous man and arrived at the wisdom they preach, what would await you in the hour of your death? What would you think of when your soul, that most precious of all things, was separating from the body? I'll tell you: you'd feel only fear of what lies ahead. Only fear and remorse, as long as your wisdom and righteousness were guiding you. At the peak of their wisdom and hour of their death, people repent every moment they've lived, except those where they suffered the most. You can arrive at that wisdom, and it will only reward you with more suffering. I knew a man who said: *When I'm desperate, I'm strong.* Is that a wise man or a saint, as some may call him, or is he simply crazy?

'Finally, I appeal to your humanity,' he said. 'Stay here with me. In the name of compassion. Have pity on the poor old man now, since you didn't pity your mother. You may have let your mother die in excruciating pain, you may have left her, but don't leave this old man. You may have been deaf to her words when she begged you to kill her, but don't be blind and deaf to me,' he pleaded.

Tired, angry and nauseated, as if I couldn't live a moment longer, I closed my eyes.

I woke beneath the walls of the Old Town. I must have stumbled on the way home and fallen asleep there.

I looked around me. It was first light. The sun was slowly rising, but its terrible heat wouldn't unfold until later. The streets were empty and there was no one to offend my retina. I'd always imagined the empty town as a perfect backdrop for my life. At dawn, the colossal crime machine is still warming up. The mighty engine doesn't start with a rumble and a whistle until everyone has done their morning toilet, had their first coffee, kissed their daughters in their beds, said goodbye to their families and gone down to the street, that conveyor belt for the production of abominations. At dawn the world seems least defiled – only then is it tolerable. All the sordidness of the day has still to happen. I remembered the old hi-fi my father used to play his classical-music cassettes on when I was a child. Sometimes I'd press the *PAUSE* button, and he'd come in from the kitchen and start the tape again. Now is that moment between me and my father, I thought – the moment after I'd pressed *PAUSE* on the matrix of the world and before the tape started turning again. I inhaled deeply and closed my eyes, determined to imbibe some of the morning's silver-blue silence.

Suddenly I knew that the morning had died and everything had started again. The machine was set in motion: I heard the rushing sound of cars in the street and passers-by calling out to one another. As if a dam had burst, thousands of people plunged down towards the town from the surrounding hills and it vanished beneath a flood of human bodies. Cheap flip-flops fluttered like the wings of bats. Bony feet with toes and nails now covered the asphalt, the façades were wrapped in human skin, and gouged-out eyes blinked in place of traffic lights and public lighting. People literally trampled one another. They'll all pour into the sea, I thought. Only the roofs of houses could still be seen above the torrent of *humanity* spewing through the town.

I ran for the pavement, determined to flee before the masses swept me away. But when I tried to look at my face in a nearby shop window, all I could see was the river of nameless people behind me.

Suddenly I heard the voice of a boy or a girl, I know not which, coming from the neighbouring house, chanting over and over again, 'Pick it up, read it. Pick it up, read it.' Immediately I ceased weeping and began most earnestly to think whether it was usual for children in some kind of game to sing such a song, but I could not remember ever having heard the like.

I looked into the vortex of sunburnt and peeling human bodies behind me and thought of that voice and its ethereal song. Then it became clear to me: I've finally gone under in the sea of *them*, I thought. Finally, I can see no more difference between myself and *them*. I was drowning, but it wasn't the feeling of horror I'd always expected it to be. Instead, I felt relief. I had to reach the point where I could no longer see myself; I had to disappear for myself so I could finally feel relief.

We see so much sadness around us every day. We see it, and yet we don't recognise it, I thought. To loathe people means not to understand anything, and even worse: to not understand them properly. Loathing is nothing but superficiality at its worst – when superficiality is fortified by conceitedness. We loathe people because we think we see them the way they are. We're proud of our loathing and work on it assiduously, cultivating it like a rare plant.

But all that is a lie. We hate people because we don't understand anything, and that lack of understanding is all the more profound because we think we do understand. We find everything around us grotesque, but actually it's only we who are grotesque – we, the seekers of the grotesque. That's how we see things before we understand. And when we do, we realise that everything is just endlessly sad, including us and everyone else. There's nothing more to understand. There's just that sea of sadness which you cannot sail and cannot walk on; there's no room for miracles here. Just that sea of sadness, in which we drown. We thrash about with our arms and legs, sometimes managing to lift our head above the surface in our panic, and sometimes we even think we're going to come through. But how wrong we are. In the end we drown, like all others before us have and all others after us will, I said to myself. We drown, the sadness swallows us up and closes over us as if we'd never existed, and only when we stop struggling and end our ridiculous attempts at resistance do we find relief. We need to go the whole path from repulsion to pity, from rejection to acceptance. We have to drown to finally find relief.

The man who brought me my father's goats was unhappy. If you saw him, you'd say: what an idiot. And yet how much wisdom was needed to come up to me – someone like me – and say *You're a good man*. How much wisdom, or whatever it was, doesn't matter in the end; he was able to comprehend another's despair, and nothing else counted. He saw how unhappy I was. Only a fool could fail to see how unhappy Uroš was. Or the family of lepers in the car park. How unhappy Djuro's daughters were, and Djuro himself, I thought. And then I desired to tell them that. I felt a need to tell them that I hadn't seen it before but that I saw it now. I got into the car and sped off to find them.

I had to see the lepers urgently. I ran down the stairs into the underground car park and started calling them right from the top. 'Hey, lepers!' I shouted. I rushed along the dark terraces of the car park and then went down as far as the nuclear shelter, hoping to find them where I'd left them. But I found no trace of them. They've probably fled into some dark nook and are now looking at me in fear, determined to stay hidden, I thought. 'I come as a friend,' I yelled, trying to get them to come out. I wanted to offer them money and medicine for their ailments. *And with medicine in hand he descended among the lepers*, I laughed in desperation.

Back to the car, then straight to Djuro's flat. I dashed to the cellar door and hammered at it. There was no reply, not even from Djuro's wife who I imagined had to be home. I put my ear to the door and listened for the crying of Djuro's brats. Instead I heard the old woman from the floor above cursing and threatening to call the police if I didn't go away immediately. It wouldn't have worked anyway, I reflected as I was leaving. I'd have gone up to Tanja, handed her the money and said: *This is all for you, I only ask that you leave your father – that you go away and try to save your life, and thus save and justify mine.* But after all that she would just have told me that she couldn't. She'd never leave because she loved her father.

I hadn't set foot in my father's house or spoken a word with him since my mother's death. In fact, I couldn't remember when I'd last seen him. How long had it been since I'd last looked from my terrace, like the balcony of a theatre, and seen my father sitting in his armchair out the front of his house? He used to sit there for hours and would stay there when night fell, motionless, staring at Uncle's hill, with Saint Augustine's *Confessions* on his lap.

That morning I felt the urge to see him. There were so many things I had to say to him and so much we had to discuss. I knew that sooner or later we'd have to do it, so why not straight away? I knocked resolutely on his door, ready to face the scathing indifference he'd receive me with. And when he didn't answer, I thought he must be sleeping, because it was still early. So I went round the back of the house to the summer kitchen, where my mother used to make dinner for the guests who dropped in less and less over time. My father, and then all of us, withdrew into ourselves, until there was no one to visit us any more. The key hung on a hook in the stone wall above the sink as it always had.

I entered the dark hall. All the blinds were closed and light only made it in through the holes in the roof, which my father probably hadn't felt like mending. I tried to turn on the light, but there was no electricity. It was easy to imagine that my father didn't care about that – he probably didn't even open up when the debt collectors rang and didn't want to go into town to pay the light bill even after they'd finally disconnected him.

I opened the door of the main bedroom just a crack. The sheets and blankets on my parents' double bed were smooth and tucked in neatly. It was clear that no one had lain in that bed since my mother last straightened up the house, that morning when she was taken to the hospital in Podgorica to die. My father must be sleeping in my room, I thought. But my room was locked. I called him and banged on that door I grew up behind, but there was no reply.

I looked for him in the bathroom, too. Water was dripping from the tap above the bath. I tried to turn it off, but it was no use: the rusty thing would keep on dripping until someone replaced it. I heard a swarm of flies buzzing above the toilet bowl, which stank terribly. The bath was covered in brown, slimy layers of filth.

The house looked as if no one had lived in it for years. It was the chef-d'oeuvre of my father's ascetic concept, a way of life he adopted in his old age which involved renouncing anything that demanded the slightest effort.

It was clear that no one had cleaned the house since my mother died. Tapestries of spiderwebs stretched from one end of the living room to the other. Half a loaf of bread lay on the kitchen table, mouldy green and as hard as stone. Beside it stood a half-drunk bottle of wine, now vinegar, and everything lay under two fingers of dust, like a shroud. On my father's desk, draped with a sheet on which the damp had traced dark spots, stood the ancient *His Master's Voice* gramophone. Solid mahogany with a huge brass horn. It was a present I gave him, a valuable acquisition from my Year 12 excursion to Florence. When I returned, I had triumphantly presented him with several Bach records and the gramophone.

'It was made in 1933, and its first owner was a German industrialist who committed suicide a few years later,' I told him, repeating what I'd been told in the antique shop. 'His name is engraved in gold on the back, *Leopold Kleist*, but that's not why I bought it. You see, Leopold

Kleist married a girl who was a direct descendant of Bach's – his great-great-granddaughter, so to speak. This was her gramophone and she listened to the music of her ancestor on it,' I said.

That was a lie, and the whole story was a device of the cunning Italian trader. But my father believed it because he needed to believe. He just looked at me with his eternally sad eyes. He didn't hug me or say thank you. He didn't have to: I knew how much the present meant to him.

Only then did I notice that all the bookshelves in my father's study were bare. Where had all those books gone? I gazed in puzzlement at the emptiness of the library he'd assembled throughout his life. All four walls of the room had once been covered with books, almost like wallpaper. 'Here we're protected from the world by an armour of knowledge,' my father used to say. Now the shelves were bare save for dead flies and rat droppings. All that was left were seven solidly bound red volumes on one of the lower shelves. I remembered the angelic voice singing, *Pick it up, read it. Pick it up, read it.* I lowered the tomes onto the desk with a thump, and through the cloud of dust that rose I saw that I'd just discovered my father's diaries.

Before I opened the blinds and light flooded into the house; before a Bach record crackled on the gramophone; before I went out onto the terrace and sat in my father's wicker armchair; before I glanced at Uncle's scorched hill, above which smoke was still rising; before I heard the bleating of goats in the courtyard; before I managed to calm down and before I thought everything now seemed quite acceptable – before all of that I took my father's diaries off the shelf, laid them on the desk and opened them, and with a start I became aware of the word which the man had pondered all this time; the word which had been wholly on his mind and hounded him. With a tremendous sense of fear which nearly destroyed me, I read what my father had written trance-like, in a shaky hand like a cardiogram, every day of the last years of his life; like a grisly army with its banners, a single word stretched in a column from line to line, from page to page, from one volume to the next, and from the first to the last – just one word: son.

SOUNDTRACK FOR *THE SON*

1. MONO – *Moonlight*
2. JESSE SYKES AND THE SWEET HEREAFTER – *Reckless Burning*
3. GRAVENHURST – *Animals*
4. NOIR DÉSIR – *Le vent nous portera*
5. SIGUR RÓS – *8*
6. SONIC YOUTH – *Tunic (Song For Karen)*
7. INTERPOL – *Leif Erikson*
8. STEVE EARLE – *John Walker's Blues*
9. BONNIE PRINCE BILLY – *Death To Everyone*
10. THE WORKHOUSE – *Peacon*
11. J.S. BACH – *Suite No. 3: Air*
12. AMANDINE – *For All The Marbles*
13. BAND OF HORSES – *St. Augustine*

Quotations:

GEORG TRAKL on p. 10: *Georg Trakl: Poems and Prose. A Bilingual Edition*, Northwestern University Press 2005, trans. Alexander Stillmark

THOMAS BERNHARD on p. 10: *Gathering Evidence: A Memoir* by Thomas Bernhard, Vintage 2003, trans. David McLintock

ST AUGUSTINE's *Confessions* on p. 83 (trans. Albert C. Outler): www.ccel.org/ccel/augustine/confessions.xi.html. Retrieved 18 June 2013

The
Coming

Chapter One   93
which tells of a gruesome crime, anger, snow and the corruptness of human nature

Chapter Two   105
in which the snow continues to fall, we meet good Hedwig and old Marcus, and stroll with Emmanuel from Schikanedergasse to Naschmarkt

Chapter Three   115
which describes human resourcefulness and falling cows, while a butcher tells us his tale of cold and loss

Chapter Four   127
which tells of books and a conversation in Saint Anna's Hospital, presents the multiple murder from a different angle, and shows us Fra Dolcino fleeing the wrath of the Church and finding refuge in the Franciscan monastery on Bojana River

Chapter Five   139
which tells of trust, a lie under pressure, proud pregnant women and an old liaison, and the demands of the murder victim's brother for revenge in this world or the next

Chapter Six   150
in which Emmanuel tells of the false messiah Sabbatai Zevi, a secret society of his resolute followers, the burial of The Book of the Coming and the day of its resurrection

Chapter Seven   158
in which we briefly enter a public house, venture into a dark marsh and hear of self-pity and grace as Lazar tells his story; we meet singing nuns, and a company of drunken friends confess their sins

Chapter Eight   175
in which we learn of an unhappy love affair and the deaths of loved ones, Hedwig reveals to Emmanuel her last and greatest secret, we hear of the cruel death of countless animals and are overwhelmed with powerless remorse

Chapter Nine   184
which tells of an ugly awakening, the devastating power of sincerity, the End which has not come, and the heralding of a long-awaited advent

Chapter One

The smell of blood reached us even before we entered the house, yet there were no signs of a break-in at the front door. Clearly the murderer had rung the bell and a member of the household had opened up for him. I turned around to Janko:

'Perhaps it was someone they knew.'

'Psssht!' he hissed, probably afraid the murderer was still in the house.

I looked back. Curious neighbours were already clustering around our patrol car behind the row of cypresses which skirted the Vukotićs' property. Some kids were roaring down the road in a souped-up yellow Fiat with music blaring and almost lost control at the bend. They spotted the crowd, slowed down, and drove back.

'Turn that off,' someone yelled at them, 'there's been a murder here!'

I forced the door with my shoulder and took a step into the house, gripping my pistol as tightly as I could, with both hands. It felt cold, as if I'd just picked it up out of the snow. Janko came in behind me and lit the way with his flashlight. We heard a movement in the dark, or at least we thought we did, but it was hard to tell. We were on edge. Terrified, to tell the truth. It was my first murder, after all. Sure, I'd seen a lot of corpses before, but I don't think any sane person can get used to death.

When we heard the noise, or thought we did, Janko flashed his light into the kitchen. I stepped forward, ready to shoot. Then my legs caught on something and I fell. My cheek was warm and wet. 'Fuck this,' I called, 'turn on the light.'

I was lying in Senka Vukotić's blood. I found some paper towels in the kitchen and wiped my face and hands, while Janko photographed Senka.

'I think I moved her,' I told him.

There was a large wound on her head. It turned out that the murderer had dealt the first blow with an axe. Evidently that didn't kill her outright, so he knelt down and cut her throat. We didn't find the knife, but the axe is at the lab in Podgorica for analysis.

The trail of blood led to the internal staircase. The lab later reported that the murderer had been wearing size seven gumboots with worn-out soles. As soon as he set foot on the stairs, Pavle must have fired at him: two shots, we found the buckshot in the wall. It's incredible that he didn't hit him. We combed the house several times but couldn't find any trace of the murderer's blood. That's what fear does to you – Pavle was firing from above, from the top of the stairs, at a distance of no more than five yards. But before he could reload the shotgun the murderer was upon him. From what we've been able to reconstruct, it seems the first blow struck Pavle in the right shoulder. As the murderer swung the axe again to deal the mortal blow, Pavle dashed off into the bathroom and tried to hide.

But what happened next makes us certain that the murderer knew the family and had been to the house before: instead of going after Pavle he went into the children's room. He knew they had children – that's the point – and he knew where to find them. He grabbed Sonja in the bed by the window. She was seven, Jesus Christ… One blow was enough for a small child like that.

Meanwhile, Pavle realised he'd left the children at the tender mercies of the murderer. He ran into their room and found the intruder on the floor – the killer had needed to set down the axe to grab Helena, who'd hidden under her bed. That was The Second Chance Pavle had that night. He didn't get a third. Although he now had the axe, which put him at a clear advantage, the murderer overpowered him and cut his throat, like he did with Senka down in the hall.

Helena tried to run away but she didn't get far. We found her body in the living room, on the couch in front of the television, which was still on. Judging by the bloodstains, the murderer sat down next to her. Our psychologists are trying to unravel what that could possibly mean. One thing's for sure – he switched on Animal Planet.

Then he left. No one saw him, no one heard him, and he left no fingerprints or DNA. There won't be any further investigations because, as I'm sure you know, homeless people laid waste to the house and ultimately set it on fire.

Quite a story, don't you think? I reckon you've got something for your two hundred euros! Inspector Jovanović exclaimed.

'You can say that again!' I said, patting him on the shoulder. I ordered a beer for him, paid, and went outside. But I didn't get very far. Each day I went back to the pub, sat behind the same sticky bar and listened to the same story like a bloody refrain I couldn't get out of my head.

* * *

I remembered all that again as I sat in a long line of cars that evening and stared at the fire-blackened ruins of the library covered with snow. It was like a white sheet spread over a dead body: although it conceals the body underneath, everyone knows there's been a crime.

I was beginning to realise that I'd need at least an hour to get out of that traffic jam. It was cold that night, and the snow had turned to ice because there was no one to clear it off the roads. A driver had probably failed to brake on time and crashed into the car in front, and even on an evening like that they managed to get into a fight about it. The police were already on their way to restore order. I could see the blue rotating lights through the snow which was now falling ever more thickly. Luckily, I'd filled up before the Ulcinj petrol station closed and all the staff were sent home. I heard that when the petrol station ran dry, they rang the head office in Kotor to ask for another tankload. They called all morning, and finally around noon they got through to someone. The fellow told them everything was over – no one needed anything now, least of all petrol. 'I mean, what are people going to do with it? It's not like they can escape,' he said, his voice thick with depression. He complained that his wife had kicked him out of the house. She'd told him to get lost – she at least wanted to die without having him around. And with nowhere else to go, he simply went back to the office. There wasn't another living soul at the Hellenic Petroleum depot. When the workers at the petrol station finally realised that the end of the world also meant they'd lose their jobs, they divided up the money in the till. The gas cylinders they'd sold to customers in happier times were now heaved into the boots of their cars, and plastic bags full of sweets, cigarettes and bottles of whisky were crammed into the back seats. They didn't bother to lock the door when they left. Now they're probably guzzling down Chivas Regal and their children are gorging themselves sick on sweets to make sure nothing will be left. Like they say, it's a shame to waste things.

The fuel gauge under the speedometer told me I had enough petrol for all I needed to do that evening. The motor rumbled reliably. I turned up the heating and put in a new CD. Odawas sang 'Alleluia' while several men with long black beards marched past in formation. They were rushing to the mosque because it was time for prayer. The lights on the minarets blinked like a lighthouse. But it's too late now, I brooded, we're still going to hit the rocks. You can crawl under the red altars, run into the minarets – slender rockets ready to take you away to a different world, but it will be as promised: tonight, no one will be able to hide.

That night warranted an update of all our dictionaries, if only there had been time, so as to add the definitive new meaning of '*dead*line': everything anyone in the world still planned to do had to be done that night. Working under pressure? I was used to it, even though I initially imagined that being a private detective in a town as small and peaceful as Ulcinj would be safe and easy. Cheated husbands, suspicious wives – who could need my services apart from unhappy people in unhappy marriages? That's what I thought, at least.

* * *

When I first rented an office in the centre of town I furnished it minimally but tastefully, by anyone's standards. Posters of classic old movies went up on the walls: *The Maltese Falcon* with Humphrey Bogart, *Chinatown* with Jack Nicholson ... The posters were to discreetly prompt clients to compare me with the best. A little pretentious, I admit, but it proved effective. A massive oaken desk dominated the room. Period furniture was installed to give clients the impression they were engaging a company with traditional standards – and people still believe in tradition, although tradition always betrays them if they don't betray it first. The desk sported a black Mercedes typewriter: a real antique and pure extravagance. I wanted everyone who came in to know that we didn't allow any newfangled gadgets like computers in the firm. I wanted clients to know that our methods were time-tested. A detective needs to seem timeless. I wanted people to think: wow, this is a hard-boiled, old-school detective who can be a real tough guy where necessary; a Sam Spade type of character who's seen a lot and knows the mean streets but isn't afraid to jump back into the thick of things if circumstances require.

As soon as I opened my agency, though, it seems all of Ulcinj decided to start killing, robbing, abducting and raping. And there was plenty of adultery too: it must be close to a dozen marriages I've torn apart. I'll always remember those jobs most fondly, given the rest of my blood-soaked career. I follow the adulterers to their hotel, make myself comfortable in my car, and knock back a swig or two of whisky – just enough to give them time to undress and get down to business. A few photographs as evidence, and the matter is settled. My own experience in such matters is rather scant, I should say, or at least not as extensive as I'd have liked it to be, but one thing's for certain – women cope with adultery much better. A woman sees her partner's adultery as a betrayal: she's angry and offended. But a man who's just found out his wife is cheating on him sees it as a humiliation and irrefutable proof that he's not man enough. When a woman finds out she's been cheated on, her femininity is abruptly heightened. It's as if she has a 'femininity switch' which her husband inadvertently activates by having an affair. But a cheated man crumples like a used condom. Little in this world is as fragile as masculinity – I've learned that lesson well.

Another thing which quickly became clear to me: whether I'm solving *serious crimes* like murder or *crimes of the heart* (as one romantically inclined and, to my delight, promiscuous lady client once described adultery), the most important thing is to understand *what the client wants.* The ones who hire me to find out if their partner is cheating on them thirst for evidence that their suspicions are justified. If a wife is cheating on her husband, she's a bitch; if she isn't cheating on him, he's a swine for suspecting her. Faced with the choice between a negative image of her and a negative image of himself, he always chooses the former. Each of us obviously has unlimited potential for swinishness. Whether and in what form that potential comes out is just a minor technical detail. So I always make a point of presenting extensive evidence of adultery – a photomontage works wonders, irrespective of whether the said adultery actually took place. If it didn't, it still could have, so in a way I'm communicating a deeper truth. And after all, the client comes first. If the client is satisfied, my own satisfaction is assured.

Things are more complicated with murder. To generalise a little, I'd say there are two kinds of murder-investigation clients: those who want to know *who* committed the murder, and those who want to know *why*. With the latter it's easy: you have a chat with them. When they drop in to inquire how the investigation's going, you invite them down to a local bar … people loosen up after a drink. Sooner or later they'll give you a hint as to their suspicions, and then the case is as good as cracked. From then on you just confirm the story they themselves have come up with. Tell them you're close to solving the case, but make them wait a little longer. For some reason people consider what they call *arriving at the truth* to be a thankless job. *The truth is a hard road*, several clients have said.

But those who want to know *who* the murderer was are hard to please. They usually want to take revenge, so you can't just point a finger at the first passer-by. It usually ends up that after trying to resolve the case for a while, I give up, cancel the contract and just ask them to cover my expenses.

The way people think is to a detective's advantage. Tell them any old story and they'll exclaim: *I knew it!* Whatever tale you tell, even if it's got as many holes as Swiss cheese, people will say: *Yes, it's logical!* There's evidence for everything – all you need is a story to back it up. By way of illustration, let's take the World Cup football final. A penalty shoot-out will decide who gets to be world champion. The last shot is taken by the best player on the planet. Whether he scores or misses, people will say: I knew it! Because it's *logical* that the best player will score when it's hardest, just as it's *logical* that the best player will miss in a decisive moment because, as we know, fate is often unkind.

My point is that a detective's work isn't so much about finding out the truth as inventing a story which people will accept as the truth. It's not about discovering the truth but about discovering what truth is for those people. Truth always appears as a fiction and takes the form of a story. I am a storyteller.

* * *

Still stuck in the un-moving traffic, I looked back on my detective career and remembered when the first of the e-mails arrived which caused my *grand illusion* to collapse … Funnily enough, around that time I found myself in a similar situation to now: caught in a long line of cars after leaving Inspector Jovanović with his beer and his inability to accept that the massacre he'd described for me did actually happen. Fortunately, this inability didn't prevent him from selling me the information. The massacre at the Vukotićs' would always be an 'incident' for him – something which happened despite the fact that things like that don't happen. Or always happen to someone else. I believe we're able to overlook the horror of our own lives, and we owe our strength to that blindness. Lies are all that liberate us: one drop of the truth would be enough to destroy what remains of our life.

I remember it was feeling every bit of 40 degrees centigrade that day, and the wind had turned into a dry sirocco from North Africa. The fishermen, who sleep with radios close to their ears, had hauled their boats up onto the sand the night before. Ulcinj doesn't have a marina, so an accurate weather forecast and quick legs are all that saves their boats from the waves determined to smash them on the rocks. Radio Dubrovnik got it right again yesterday: the sea did rise after midnight.

It was as if someone had created a vacuum over the town. Everything under the sky was gasping for breath. I searched for a whiff of fresh air in the park across from the pub. Then I went up to the bar: a whisky with two ice cubes. All in vain: wherever I went I breathed in the heat. It was as if the world had turned into an oven which was open right in front of my face and I was leaning into it. But isn't it like that with every change: we decide on it not *because* of things, but *despite* them?

All the local schizophrenics were out on the streets that day – drinking Coca-Cola, ranting, smoking as they walked, and often changing pace and direction as if they didn't know where they were going, making them indistinguishable from tourists. The town was full of people whose diagnosis was unknown but whose condition obviously required immediate hospitalisation.

A little later I found myself driving through a horde of tourists: moving like a herd of animals heading to a watering hole. That's how they go down the steep Ulcinj streets to the beach, knocking over and trampling everything in their path. They walk right down the middle of the road because it's wider than the sidewalk, so they can move faster, and speed is important because it allows them to occupy a spot on the beach closer to the water. They don't move to the side when a car comes – experience has taught them that the driver won't run them over. They don't react to the honk of horns and don't comprehend verbal abuse.

I saw on television that farmers in America have jeeps with rubber grill guards. The driver just drives straight ahead and anything in the way gets pushed aside. The vehicle doesn't injure the animals but directs the movement of the herd. Give a little gas, and then it's just straight ahead. *Go West*, eh? But America is far, far away. For someone who's decided to go to the pine forest today and get nicely drunk amid the pinecones and the scent of resin, the mistral and the shade, the problem is not just the pedestrians, not just the tourists – his *fellow citizens* are enough of a calamity. The ones with cars are the worst: they have driver's licences, names, surnames and even biographies. They have everything except regard for other human beings.

People can rein in their desires. They really expect little of life. Simple things count – like getting in the car and driving to where there's lots of whisky and ice. But however little we desire, we end up getting even less. I sat and waited in a line of cars hundreds of metres long. People were hot and edgy. They sounded their horns, some cursed and swore, others were calm because the priests had taught them to accept fate (another word for chaos). After one or two minutes which seemed like one or two hours, the line gradually got moving again like a giant snake. I know from experience that when there's a traffic jam in Ulcinj it's always because of some brain-dead neanderthal stopping and talking with another driver, or because he's parked in the middle of the road so he can go into a betting shop. We passed the culprit of that day's stoppage: a square-headed young guy with a look of vacant stupidity who had stopped in front of the bakery and blocked the lane leading down to *Mala Plaža* beach. He ordered a pizza from his car and waited for it to be made and brought to him. Then he didn't have the right change, so he waited – meaning *we* waited, for the assistant to go and fetch change for a twenty-euro note. All this was done without any hurry, with the greatest philosophical composure, paying no heed to the other people and cars, to the heat and the horns blaring … like a cow in serene Zen meditation – for only cows on the road manifest quite the same indifference toward the surrounding world, a tranquillity and resolve to do the first thing which comes into their heads: usually to dump a load of dung right where they're standing.

A person's degree of primitivism in an urban setting can be gauged by his indifference toward other people and their needs, by the firmness of his conviction that he's alone in the world and has a right to do whatever he wants here and now, regardless of the misfortune it may cause other people. His place is in *nature*. There he learned that to exist means to mistreat. He's unburdened by the illusions of *Homo urbanus* – for him nature is not a delicate equilibrium, a sensitive and complex organism; nature has only mistreated him and his tribe throughout history, harassing them with droughts, storms, floods, and frosts; they've fled from nature and have brought nothing but nature with them because they *are* nature. A person's degree of primitivism in an urban setting can be gauged, I maintain, by the disturbance he represents for other people. A primitive person is unable to exist in quiet discretion: he always creates noise, unsightliness, and stench. He does everything he can to be noticed – he constantly *emits* his existence. His being is a blow to the senses and an insult to the intelligence. He mistreats us with his very existence. When he celebrates, a considerate, tasteful person unfortunate enough to live next door to him is bound to suffer. What a primitive person enjoys inflicts pain on the civilised.

I read in the paper about an Austrian in Vienna who shot his Bosnian neighbour. It turned out that the Bosnian had driven the Austrian out of his mind for years with the loud Balkan folk music which he listened to in his apartment every afternoon. The Austrian complained to the police several times, and they intervened in accordance with the law, but that didn't prevent the Bosnian from continuing to mistreat the Austrian. When he realised that all legal possibilities of protecting his calm and privacy had been exhausted, the Austrian shot the Bosnian in the head and calmly turned himself in to the police.

That story stuck in my mind because it tells us that the law can't protect us from the primitive, who is nothing but a walking disaster. However brutal the law is, it can't compare with the brutality of nature. When law is about revenge, as in the case of capital punishment, it's closest to nature – and thus furthest from the law.

That's why it's so unbearable here: primitivism is not some random excess but the very *essence* of local culture, which therefore isn't a culture. If you're not primitive here you're a foreign body and you'll be made to feel it every day. With a lot of effort, luck and money you can construct a fortress and preserve your own order of things inside it – for a while. You can erect high walls, dig moats and build draw-bridges to shut off your world *for a while*. But they'll find a way in: like in Poe's 'Masque of the Red Death', their *nature* will get through and wipe your little world off the face of the earth.

Here people dump garbage by the roadside and turn the landscape into a landfill. Their sheep and goats, which they need in order to survive in their suburbs, wander the asphalt and graze the parks, or what's left of them. Their children imitate the cherubs in fancy fountains and pee in flowerbeds in front of the passers-by. They shit on the beaches and in neglected recreation centres. Music is the form of art they like most because it doesn't demand interpretation or reflection. Like the salt strewn on a vanquished ancient city they sow the world with noise – repulsive music lasting late into the night is what they need in order to enjoy themselves. Walls and billboards are plastered with pictures of their big-titted women with frightening faces and grimaces which we can only assume are meant to suggest lust but which actually attest to nothing but stupidity and vacuousness. The males of the species thrust their ever-erect organs into that void, and from that nothingness *their* children are born to ensure the continuation of *their* world, nation, family and culture – of *their* kind.

There are times like that day, stuck amid all those people, every one of them a nerve-grating nuisance, when anger grips me so tightly that no insult I could ever think of and no salvo of sarcasm I could fire at their civilians – their women and children – could bring relief. Those are times when anger grips me so tightly that I can't move, as if the black monolith from *2001* was weighing down on my chest, times when anger is all that exists – when I'm anger itself. Then I think: death. What comes next has to be death. If there's anything after and beyond anger, it can only be that. Those were my thoughts that day as I nestled into my car seat, gripped the steering wheel – and waited.

It's fascinating that something as dependable as death becomes so utterly unreliable if we dare to count on it for release, because as a rule it arrives too late. The only mitigating circumstance is that, because it takes its time in coming, we're never truly disappointed. They say that *Homo sapiens* are animals endowed with reason. I'd say that, despite this reason, they're animals punished with optimism. Because as soon as the pistol is removed from their forehead, the boot lifted from their neck and the blade pulled from their belly, they think: things will get better. But before they can even cross themselves and pronounce *faith, hope and love* a few times, they'll be cast face-down in the mud again, and then death won't seem so terrible and unfair.

Nope, not this time either – everything's as it was before, I said to myself, and noticed that the people around me were starting to get out of their cars. They raised their eyes to the sky, called out to one another, seized their heads in their hands, and spread out their arms in wonder. Then the first flake fell on the windscreen. I opened the window and peered out: as serene and dignified as a Hollywood White Christmas, snow fell on Ulcinj that June day.

Chapter Two

in which the snow continues to fall, we meet good
Hedwig and old Marcus, and stroll with Emmanuel
from Schikanedergasse to Naschmarkt

from: emmanuel@gmail.com
to: thebigsleep@yahoo.com

Even here, in this room where I'm confined – *for my own good*, they never fail
to say – the first snow brings serenity and joy. And even though the narrow
slice of landscape I see through the window is now my whole world, that
world is sublime in its beauty once it's covered in white. The west wind casts
snow on the gnarled branches of the plum tree, the browning grass of the
hill and the bristling willows. There are other days when the lake is a leaden
grey and impossible to distinguish from the sky, which is eternally grey here
in the Alps. The surface of the water sometimes shakes as if someone were
walking on it, unseen and unheard. The water ripples and the little waves
move towards me. They won't shake the willow branches dipping into the
lake and don't have the strength to reach the shore. If it weren't for me
patiently awaiting them every winter as I stare out through the window,
probably no one would notice their so portent existence.

Those waves which won't foam, let alone carry away or smash anything,
are a sign: they herald the first snow. The wind which raised them will soon
strengthen and bring driving snow to the lake. A flurry of snowflakes will
descend on the landscape and white will re-establish its order. But not before
several large, watery stars have stuck to my window. By evening, ice will have
covered the glass: I'll press my face up against it and feel the cold on my forehead. Outside everything is at rest, and inside everyone has fallen asleep. That
is my time: I can melt the ice with my breath right through until morning. Every
few seconds I breathe life into a shape – and a being on the window-pane
starts to move. Now it's a bird, next time it's a wolf. And however often the cold
comes for them and the ice reclaims them, I bring them back with my breath.

My world lacks breadth, perhaps. It lacks people, above all, because apart from the village children in summer who go scooting down the grassy hillside on sheets of cardboard and plunge head first into the lake with a scream – hardly anyone calls by. But there's no lack of order. My world is as ordered as a Chekhov play. If I mention a plum tree, children will come and pick its fruit in the autumn. If I look at the willows, some youngster is bound to jump from them into the water by the end of the summer to demonstrate his manliness, which in my world and all others is always done in primitive and superfluous ways. And then there's the lake! It, too, is a nail which someone will hang their coat on by the end of the play. Its waters are calm and buoyant, it accepts visitors… and sometimes keeps the particularly careless and weak. As I say, there's no lack of order in my world. Nor any lack of excitement: there are quite enough changes for my liking.

Not to mention memories. When you're confined, you learn to live backwards. Tomorrow will be the same as today. The only future you have is your memory. The only uncertainty which awaits you is what you'll remember tomorrow. You go back and tell yourself stories in which you're the main hero. Most of those stories never happened, but who cares – they could have happened, and that's all that counts. Your past contains innumerable possibilities for lives different to the one you live. So: go back, young man!

I go back to the hall of our Vienna apartment in 5 Schikanedergasse. I'm seven years old. From my hiding place behind the shoe cabinet I can see that my nanny has fallen asleep in the armchair beneath Lucien Freud's painting. The picture had belonged to our neighbour who committed suicide after the bank took away all his property, but not before *papa* bought the picture from him 'for a fair and reasonable price', as he and my mother emphasised every time Freud was the topic of conversation in our drawing-room. Fair and reasonable wasn't good enough for the bank, which confiscated and flogged off all the neighbour's possessions, turning the heir of a tailor's shop which had *clothed the Viennese for over three centuries* into a homeless pauper who had no choice but to drown himself in the Danube, a way in which people in a similar quandary had ended their lives for more than three centuries.

So Hedwig, my nanny, was sleeping beneath the picture painted by the grandson of the great dream interpreter. My parents had gone to visit Aunt Esther, who'd been dying for at least as long as I'd been alive. When they took me to see her the first time, she was lying like a big white polar bear on a wide, heavy bed, the same one I found her on when we'd visited the last time, at New Year. When they introduced me to Aunt Esther, she said: 'The boy is most irritatingly blue-eyed – I can't help it, but those misty blue eyes have something distinctly Prussian about them.'

Three paces and I was at the front door, which I closed behind me noise-lessly. A descent down the wide, marble staircase awaited me. The stairs were made so that they not tire a person out. *Papa* always made a point of emphasising what he called 'the humaneness of Vienna's stairs'. I don't think we ever went up to our apartment together without him remarking that these stairs could teach you all you needed to know about Viennese architecture. Although it mirrored the narcissism of tradition and the power of the former empire, it above all reflected the idea that 'buildings, even the most palatial ones, are to serve people' – I think those were his words. To his mind, Viennese stairs had to be made so that walking up them was no more strenuous than a Sunday stroll on Stephansplatz. Vienna's opera houses were the only buildings on the planet fit to host operas: everything else was a barbaric blasphemy which ought to be banned by law. The proportion of the height of the ceiling to the length of the windows in Viennese cafés was simply perfect, and visitors got the impression they were drinking their *kleiner Brauner* in the very centre of the world. Overpriced Parisian cafés were claustrophobic and kind of obscure, *papa* claimed. The cafés in Rome, on the other hand, seemed frivolous: when you were drinking your espresso there you felt the visitors and waiters were about to tear off their civilian clothes or uniforms and show themselves in costumes, revealing their true nature as characters from a commedia dell'arte. In a nutshell: *papa* loved Vienna, and a life outside that city was unimaginable for him.

The stairs which were made so that even the oldest residents of Vienna, at least those who were still mobile, could mount them with a minimum of effort, were also made so that I could imitate the hops of a kangaroo – the animal which fascinated me most at the time – and go bounding down them two steps at a time without danger of falling and getting hurt, although I doubt that was the intention of the constructors. When I'd jumped the last few steps, it was just four more hops to the main door of the house. One more after that and I'd finally be out on the snow-covered pavement, staring at the bright sign on the other side of the street: *Carlton Opera Hotel*.

I was a sickly child. If my chronic bronchitis improved for just a second, I'd be bed-ridden with sinus pain. There was probably no day I didn't have a cough, a sore throat or an annoying cold. To top it all off, there were the allergies. I wasn't allowed to eat strawberries: just a morsel of the red fruit sufficed to cause an attack of asphyxiation. We also discovered under dramatic circumstances that I was allergic to penicillin. I was two at the time. After I'd been given an injection of penicillin an intensive red appeared, starting at the point of the injection. Then my temperature shot up, and it took them days to get it to come down again. Just when *maman et papa* had given up hope for me, my fever subsided, and the doctors wrote CAVE PENICILLIN in thick red letters on my medical record card.

What I want to say is that I wasn't allowed to play most children's games. Running out into the snow in only a jumper – without my fur coat, cap and gloves – was a blatant violation of the unwritten but no less rigid rules. It was always the same: I'd use my parents' absence for my street adventures. I'd always return home before they did. Poor Hedwig would be waiting for me in tears after having woken up, called for me, looked in all the hiding places in the apartment, and burst into inconsolable sobs. It meant nothing to her that I came back running every time: she seemed not to perceive the pattern behind such simple repetition. She'd always be worried out of her mind as if I'd run away for the very first time. She waited for me on the landing at the apartment door, beside herself with anxiety. Instead of scolding me when I returned, she'd lift me up a little, embrace me and repeat: 'Oh Master Emmanuel, thank goodness you've come back to me.' That woman is up with the angels now, I'm sure. 'Don't worry, I won't say a word to *monsieur et madame*,' she'd tell me. She demanded only one thing of me – precisely the one thing I couldn't promise her, however sincerely I regretted the misdemeanours I'd committed each time: *that I never, never do it again*, she repeated in the tone

The Olcinium Trilogy

of voice I imagined Heidi's grandfather used to tell her important lessons. And sure enough, she never gave me away. But *I* would go up to *maman et papa* while they were still taking their coats off and admit everything. 'This child is beyond our help,' my mother would sigh and start to cry. 'May God protect you because I obviously can't,' she sobbed and withdrew into her room, complaining of a headache.

Papa would tell Hedwig to give me a warm wash and put me to bed. Later he'd sit on the edge of my bed until I fell asleep and tell me in a low voice, like a lullaby, how much my mother had suffered because of me. It wasn't good to return her kindness like this, he whispered. I felt warmth washing over me, my limbs became as light as wings and I sank into sleep, with his gentle, patient voice a distant echo in my ears: *She's made so many sacrifices for you. She'd do anything for you…*

Whenever I was outside, opposite the Carlton Opera Hotel, an irresistible adventure would begin. There was a story connected with that hotel which probably all nannies in the neighbourhood told to give the children a fright. I heard it from Hedwig: *A horrible man hung himself in the hotel. He'd done terrible things during the war many years before you were born. The army he commanded was defeated. But, being cunning, he dyed his hair black, grew a beard and moustache to conceal his identity, donned glasses, changed his name – and disappeared. Forever, people thought. Until one day a woman happened to go and see a doctor who practiced in an apartment on the top floor of the Carlton Opera Hotel. She realised it was the same evil man whose hospital she'd been detained at during the war. She called the police and demanded they immediately arrest the doctor, whom she blamed for the death of her husband and thousands of other innocent people. The horrible man probably knew what was in store for him when he saw the police car pull up in front of the hotel. The police called on him and demanded he give himself up. In the end they broke into his surgery and found him hanging from a light fixture, dressed in the uniform he'd worn during the war. Boys like you mustn't go there because the ghost of the doctor still haunts the halls of the hotel. They say that if he finds children who go there despite the warning, he lures them into the lift with sweets. The lift is like a cage: its doors clang shut and he takes them straight down to hell.* That's what Hedwig used to tell me.

I entered the hotel and saw the terrible lift. Just a few steps lay between me and that shaft to hell. To the left was the reception desk, which was always staffed by several pretty and friendly young women. They knew me by now and called out: 'It's you, Emmanuel! How is the little Master today?' I'd cautiously go up to the desk, raise my hand in greeting and lay it on the marble top. That was part of my rescue strategy: if the doctor appeared in front of me, I counted on the young receptionists whisking me behind the desk. I'd stand there for a while looking at the lift: it was an imposing contraption with thick, black bars and glass which definitely fitted the part. When one of the guests got in, the bars closed behind them and the lift would head upwards with a creak of chains. But when I heard the lift coming down, I'd think it was the evil doctor coming for me. Fear would get the better of my curiosity and I'd turn tail and bolt from the hotel.

I'd run until my cough made me stop. But I didn't go back home. No way, my adventure had only just begun! I'd turn into the first street on the right and stand in front of the windows of old Marcus's shop. There were bottles of liquor with colourful labels – I liked the green ones best, which looked as if they had nothing but smoke in them. More interesting still, Marcus's window displayed a whole range of chocolate bars from exotic parts of the world. *Brazil*, it said, *five, five*, and then a funny sign. *Ecuador, six, five*, and the funny sign again, and *South Africa, Kenya*, and again numbers with signs I didn't understand... There outside that luxury food shop, which after Marcus's death was turned into a kebab outlet, I learned that everything I don't know or don't have can be substituted by things I imagine and believe in. There was no chocolate taster for whom those delicacies were more real than for me. Experts could try a little cube of chocolate with their eyes closed and unerringly identify its origin and the class of the cocoa, but what was that compared to the stories I could tell about those chocolates? I trembled with excitement at the yellow, green and orange wrappers with little maps of the countries from which these chocolates arrived in my world: on packhorses through the jungle, on rafts through foaming rapids, in seaplanes through clouds and storms, on ocean-going ships past icebergs and waves as tall as the Staatsoper... The wrappers also showed palm trees, whose fronds the natives used to make huts to shelter from the tropical rain; I saw lions, black women with long necks carrying wicker baskets on their heads, and to top it all off there were stern warriors with spears and blowguns which fired poisoned darts deadlier than the fangs of a cobra; I convinced myself that every thought and word was true.

I'd stand there in front of the shop window until Marcus, who was forever sitting behind the counter reading, looked up through his glasses with lenses as thick as the jars in Hedwig's pantry. Then he'd come hobbling up to the door and pull me inside. 'You've come out without your woollens again –,' he'd reproach me, 'you'll be in bed with fever again for a whole month!' And before I could say a word in my defence he'd slip a hot cup of tea into my hand.

His shop always smelt of cinnamon and tobacco. Gentle music was playing which I'd recognise years later as Bach, whom my friend prized above all other composers. Business was going from bad to worse, so Marcus smoked most of the luxury cigars himself when their use-by date expired. He'd blow out the smoke of a thick cigar and say to me, imitating black-and-white-film icons: *When you take poison, you have to do it with style*, a lesson even Socrates read to humanity. Alas, in vain.

Marcus wasn't a man of many words. If I tried to ask him something, he'd reach me one of the books he kept under the counter and say with a crafty smile: *Here, read this*, only to return to his cigar, book and silence. When I'd drunk my tea, and I made sure not to hurry, he'd see me out and send me on my way: 'And now straight home!'

Later, when I was at high school, Hedwig told me that Marcus had sold the shop and used the money to pay for a place in a retirement home in Aspern, on the outskirts of Vienna. Since he had neither children nor any close relatives to look after him, he thought it was the best way of providing for a peaceful retirement. Before leaving our area for good, he met Hedwig on her way back from shopping and asked after me, although I hadn't dropped into his shop for years. He told Hedwig that he'd lived in Aspern throughout the Soviet occupation. After the Russians shot his father in 1946, he grew up with his grandfather there. *The old man's reign of terror was no better than the Russians'*, he told Hedwig, who then told me. Marcus also mentioned that his father lay in a shallow grave in Aspern, as well as his grandfather, who had maltreated him as long as he'd had a breath left in his body; there were other gruesome memories, too, which he hadn't been able to lay to rest and put behind him. Since that's how things were, he felt it was only right that he also be buried in Aspern when his time came. And with that he politely said goodbye and headed off down the street, leaving a trail of smoke; I can just picture him with his cigar, like an old steamboat proudly chuffing away on its last voyage, to the salvagers.

I didn't go to visit him. Not out of laziness or because I didn't care about him. On the contrary: because he was so important to me. Marcus had known he mustn't give me any of the chocolates from his shop window, however often I came, because that would ruin everything: our little game, all my reveries about faraway countries which began at his shop window, and our whole delicate and sincere friendship. And I knew I mustn't go and see Marcus in the nursing home: he wouldn't be behind the counter, on the throne of his empire, but enfeebled in a bed or wheelchair. No, it was best this way: kind old Marcus would forever stay in his shop, pretending to be strict and sending me home at the end of my visit.

I ran through the ankle-deep snow. Then I turned round, and when I saw through the veil of snowflakes that Marcus was no longer watching to check that I'd turned into Schikanedergasse as he'd told me, I kept going straight on towards the Naschmarkt market.

They said on this morning's news that snow fell in Ulcinj in the middle of summer, and now people will probably ask themselves why. Why, indeed, does snow fall? In the childhood stories I'm telling you it falls to bring peace and joy. I don't think my story is different to that of most other people: childhood is a widespread phenomenon. And childhood's most pleasant moments are often concentrated in blissful, snow-covered winter days.

James Joyce, for example, has snow fall so as to set the final scene of one of the most touching stories in the history of literature, which, although not as long as the history of snow, is similar to snow in that it reveals the foot-prints of those who've trodden this world. The ending of 'The Dead', where Gabriel Conroy realises that his wife will spend the rest of her days at his side but that the greatest event of her life was in the past, when a young man died because of his love for her, and Gabriel comprehends that everything he can give her in life is worthless compared to what the dead Michael Furey has already done for her… Oh, perhaps I take it all too personally. I have a soft spot for sad love stories.

Now you know why the snow falls for me. The world shines differently beneath the snow – that light falls from the sky, covering us, all we can see, and everything our senses perceive. However many times we've seen snow, the spectacle is always as fascinating as the first time. You can consider snow to be just congealed water, of course, but being rational is only good up to a point, beyond which reason destroys all joy in life. Things like snow have to stay unexplained, and therefore pure, so we can enjoy them. To stand beneath the sky as it sprinkles us with snow and reflect on the atmospheric processes which formed it is not irrational but is certainly a sorry state deserving of sympathy. For such a person, snow is just a nuisance – one of many which await them before death, the greatest unpleasantry lurking at the end.

I remember *one snowfall* better than all the others. It was during the war years, though I don't remember exactly because they've all merged into a continuum of nausea and I can't distinguish them any more. I didn't experience those years then and there, but I did spend them with you as I sifted through newspapers and books, remembering every cutting and every Web link to do with the time and place where you were living. Human nature is hopelessly corrupt and this corruption is to be found in every system which people establish. So it is with the market, so it is with the Church, so it is here, too, where I'm confined *for my own good*. It's fortunate that there's corruption, I must add, because how else would I manage to get a computer into my room if no one was bribable, and how else would I get hold of the books I need so as to be with you as often as I can?

Yes, snow was falling that winter. There was a power failure. It lasted for days, so I walked with you every night through empty Ulcinj. The ice cracked beneath our feet as we talked about all that needed to be done, about how wise and careful we needed to be to survive one more year. That's how a person cracks too, you told me: they stand firm and look as if they're going to outlast eternity. But then just a little brush with misfortune, one hardship on top of that, and one more which treads on them and they shatter like shop windows on city squares under bombardment.

The north wind blew away the clouds over Ulcinj and the cold descended on the landscape to preserve it, like the canvasses of the Old Masters are conserved. The radiance of the stars reflected on the snow-covered ground. Now, when the sub-stations had burnt out and the power lines were down, when people lit their houses with candles and there were no street lights, the town shone brighter than ever before. Radiant it was, like cities beyond the memory of the living, from times which no one now remembers. We know these things only from books printed on paper *as white as snow*, paper which awaits the moment when *snow falls on the margins* and it shall finally be revealed to us *why* snow falls: so that we see the word impressed on paper more clearly and also read the word – the text from which everything began.

Chapter Three

which describes human resourcefulness and falling cows,
while a butcher tells us his tale of cold and loss

The line of cars was finally starting to move. I drove past the market and the suburb of Nova Mahala before heading down the narrow streets towards the Port. The thousands of people who'd been packed together like sardines on the beach that June day were now fleeing in panic. Every few seconds, one of them would bash into the side of the car. A few moments earlier they'd been putting on sun lotion to get a better tan, and now they left greasy pawprints on the windscreen when they tumbled over the bonnet. I stopped and looked down at the beach. I saw a family encamped under an umbrella: a man, a woman and three small children. Tourists from Kosovo have the custom of taking woollen blankets to the beach. The older members of their thirty-head immediate families lie on them all day, smoking and drinking *çaj rusit*, their heavily stewed black tea, which they sip out of small glass cups like a designer hybrid between a schnapps glass and a Turkish coffee cup. Now the blankets and the hot tea will come in handy. How could I not have noticed before: they have a panoply of beach/ mountain gear good for both summer and winter outings. This pile of things in their PVC bag means they're equipped for all climatic conditions, from –50 to +50 degrees. The family under the umbrella sat huddled in the blankets and stared towards the left-hand end of the beach. In the wind-shadow of the headland where Hotel Jadran used to stand, a group of beachgoers were splashing around and playing volleyball in the shallows. They can only have been Russians.

I stepped on the gas a bit and drove round to Hotel Galeb, which was demolished a decade ago. The town council promised to build a new, luxury hotel complex in its place, but today there are only eerie ruins with no function except perhaps a sentimental one: to remind the small Jewish community, which has settled not far from here and bought houses from the old-timers, of all its demolished temples and houses in their original homeland over the sea.

I continued on and came to the monument to the fallen fighters of the Second World War. This memorial, located just above *Mala Plaža*, the cove and the Old Town, hovers with outstretched wings like an oversized dove of peace and victim of radiation. Although a white dove, it doesn't seem peace-loving: it strikes me as an animal trained to carry bombs instead of letters, as if the sculptor's chisel caught the very moment when it was preparing for indiscriminate bombing. The monument has been decaying for decades, but the town councillors don't dare to have it demolished and sell the site to one of the local tycoons. If they did, they know they'd be shot by one of the former Partisans, who might need a walking stick to get around but still have a sharp eye and a steady hand.

I needed all of half an hour to get through the throng and make it home from the monument – a drive of one or two minutes under *normal* circumstances, without people running about in the snow in their swimming trunks and flinging themselves in front of the car. But the last and biggest obstacle of the day was still ahead of me.

At the last bend before my modest home, a cow was lying on the road. I got out of the car, lit a cigarette and went up to my neighbour who was standing beside the animal and scratching his head. I asked what had happened and he replied with a candid, if somewhat rambling description of the events which had led up to one third of his assets lying here on the carriageway. Of all that he wanted to explain, the only important thing was made clear to me by his pointing finger: the concrete wall on the right-hand side of the road. I knew all the rest. A good four metres high, the wall was built to prevent rockslides from hitting the road. As far as I know, there are only two species on the planet capable of climbing near-vertical slopes: the Himalayan chamois and its predator, the snow leopard. Now the neighbour's cow had tried to graze on that near-vertical hill. It was driven by hunger because people in our region keep hundreds of cows which they don't feed. Every morning they let them out of their sheds, and herds of the stressed animals – the nightmare of every respectable Indian – roam the town until dark, feeding on the sparse grass in the parks and scavenging among the garbage which farmers leave at the market when they close their stalls. The cows are thus forced to climb over stone verges, like goats, and to use the roads, like people. The eternally hungry bovines have already browsed off all the fig bushes, grape vines and gardens in the neighbourhood. The only grass within several kilometres grows up on the hill above the retaining wall. Where many cows do not venture, one will boldly go. And that cow fell. The poor animal tried to land on its legs but the bones broke from the impact and were jutting out of open fractures on its legs. A bloody trail led from the place of the fall to where it now lay at the end of its tether, with no more strength to move.

In the meantime the neighbour's family went in action. They hopped around the cow like Lilliputians around Gulliver. His mother carted up a wheelbarrow, his youngest daughter brought a set of rusty knives and the eldest arrived with an axe in tow. Finally his son appeared, brandishing a chainsaw and full of enthusiasm about the impending massacre. When you live alongside other people you get used to all sorts of things, but slaughtering an animal in the middle of a main road still seemed a bit extreme even by our standards.

'What else can I do?' the neighbour whined in his defence. 'She's too heavy to move, and I can't just leave her here for the dogs. We'll have to cut her up, take the pieces back in the wheelbarrow and put them in the freezer, there's no other way. The butcher will be here any minute. I called him because this cow was my favourite – I can't kill her myself. I'm afraid, and my hand will tremble,' he said.

'I know this is a difficult time for you, but I won't stay. Don't take it amiss. I haven't had a proper drink yet today,' I apologised.

I glanced in the rear-view mirror as I was driving away and saw the lumbering figure of Salvatore, the butcher, arriving with his slow gait at the place of execution.

When I finally made it home, I hastily knocked back the double Cardhu I'd decided to treat myself to. I threw myself into the armchair and turned on the television. Snow in Ulcinj in summer hadn't made the headlines because it was hindered by other, even greater wonders of nature. CNN reported a rain of frogs which had blighted Japan. The reporter was standing under a fly tent next to some Japanese who were calmly eating sushi. He tried to interview them, but they didn't share his fascination with the event. *I hope the frogs stop falling soon – my lunch break ends in ten minutes,* one of them muttered between two mouthfuls. It sure is hard to fascinate the Japanese, I thought. Even if Godzilla emerged from the ocean dressed in a white shirt, black miniskirt and little white socks like a schoolgirl, with its eyes bound with pink lace knickers, Nipponese passers-by would hardly bat an eyelid.

The news then took me to America, where people still appreciate a good miracle. A devastating earthquake had hit Los Angeles. Footage from a helicopter showed a bridge broken in half. Desperate people were clinging to a twisted steel framework and paramedics were trying to pull them up. Just as it looked as if the valiant rescuers would succeed, the ground shook again. A red pick-up rolled backwards, hitting another car. And, seconds later, dozens of vehicles came crashing down on the paramedics and their desperate rescuees like an avalanche of metal.

'Los Angeles is in flames and people are trying to flee the city in panic,' the anchorman said.

A new report followed with another human drama. A residential building was ablaze and firefighters were trying in vain to climb up to a group of occupants who'd sought refuge on the roof. Rescuers on the ground held a safety net and called out to the desperate people to jump. They threw themselves off, one after another, and were caught down below by evidently well-trained Californian firefighters. But an old lady refused to jump. Although the CNN cameraman was filming from his shoulder while running through the crowd of onlookers, I could make out in the unsteady footage that the lady was holding a tiny dog in her arms. In the end she finally jumped, but fear had a hand in things – she came down hard on the lawn, a good five yards from the safety net. The camera zoomed in on her crushed body. A Scottish terrier slipped from her arms, which would never move again. One of the firefighters triumphantly held aloft the little dog, like a shaggy trophy. 'It's alive!' he shouted. The bystanders clapped, and the camera closed in on the bewildered animal licking its paw.

Fox News showed images from New York. Manhattan woke up to find itself under water: experts couldn't yet explain why, but the sea level had risen dramatically. Whereas the CNN reporters focused on the despair which the abrupt and violent acts of nature had driven people to, the right-wingers on Fox News emphasised the optimism of their born-again viewers. The preacher in a megachurch in Texas announced euphorically: 'We told them and they didn't believe us, but now the End has finally come, rejoice, o Christians!' and behind him a gospel choir of fat black ladies blared *Jesus is coming, hallelujah!* In a student dorm in Iowa, two boys from respectable Wasp families sang *It's the end of the world as we know it and I feel fine* accompanied on acoustic guitar by a stoned, raven-haired Tanita Tikaram lookalike.

MTV reacted promptly and to the point: Strummer roared *London is drowning and I live by the river*, while an autocue at the bottom of the screen advertised the upcoming *MTV Apocalypse Awards*.

A stuffy Euronews correspondent reported from a mountain peak in Switzerland on avalanches which had buried villages in the valleys. I also learned from him that Holland had been struck by a tsunami. The information coming in spoke of hundreds of thousands of dead. Their correspondent in Russia reported about a doomsday sect, breakaways from the Orthodox Church, who saw the dreadful cruelty of nature as a sign of the Second Coming of Christ. Emaciated-looking Ivans and Natashas with colourful headscarves, who were obviously doing their best to look like matryoshka dolls, were hurrying to hide underground. Their reading of the Bible seemed to be that only those who buried themselves alive would survive the end of the world. Be it because of the rush or out of laziness, these God-fearing folk didn't dig their own holes but hid in one which turned out to have been excavated by Gazprom as part of a new gas pipeline. When the believers refused to leave the company's land, the Russian president sent in the army, who mowed them down and threw them into another pit which wasn't Gazprom's. The reporter openly voiced his revulsion at this inhumane act of the Russian authorities, but it seemed to me that the believers had achieved a significant symbolic and practical victory. They were under the ground, so they'd got what they wanted.

I turned off the television because there was a knock at the door. It was Salvatore.

'Please forgive me for coming unannounced like this, I know you don't like visitors,' he said and extended me his right hand; in his left he was holding a butcher's knife. 'Your neighbours are waiting for me down at the cow. I told them I needed some knives from your place and would be straight back. I know we've never had much to do with each other – we've hardly ever spoken. But I hope you'll understand: I just need a little of your time.'

Salvatore had the stature of a serial killer from a horror film but the manners of an academic. I invited him in because I have a soft spot for politeness, which is a rare virtue in this mountainous and uncultured country. I noticed out of the corner of my eye that I'd left the gate to the property open in the rush to get to my drink. One careless moment and people invade your world, I thought: and not just anyone, but people in bloodstained butcher's aprons!

'Life is harsh,' Salvatore said when I'd poured him a drink and sat him down on the couch. He'd never been shown mercy, nor did he expect any. Whoever counted on mercy came to a bad end – he'd seen it many times. Today he sat and drank with me. There was no respite. Whatever happened, life always had to go on. One month earlier he'd suffered a great tragedy, one which would've destroyed most other people. But even as a boy he'd learned to live with loss: to mourn for a moment, and then soldier on. The dead can bury the dead, right? And before long he was back at work. If people don't have work they delve around in their past until life caves in on them. But he wasn't one to philosophise, he said.

He wanted to tell me about his tragedy. He arrived at the shopping centre in Bar at six o'clock each morning. The parking lot was empty.

For years he'd been the first to arrive at work, although he had to drive there. He got out and leaned against the car, lit a cigarette and looked up at the bluish slopes of the Rumija mountain range. After years of looking, one glance sufficed to tell him what time of year it was.

He liked to watch the slopes burning in the summer light. The midsummer glare is merciless. It's different in September, when the days are shorter and morning comes later. Then the light is velvet, as if everything is shrouded in haze. In September the world looks like the old pictures which they write about from time to time in the paper. The people in those pictures are usually naked and have a sleepy look. He thought he looked like that too when he examined his face in the rear-view mirror of the red Zastava, he told me.

Salvatore's eyes were bloodshot and dull. He watched films until late at night and also drank, but only a little more than moderation, he emphasised. A man had to have an outlet sometimes. His wife and children were asleep when he returned from work; he didn't disturb them. He wasn't one of those men who got drunk and maltreated their family, he said. He sat in front of the television and thought about things. Different things. He had a few beers. It'd been like this for fifteen years since he'd been working at the shopping centre. At first he only worked one shift. But then their second son came along, the eldest started school and life became ever more expensive. He began working weekends, but that didn't bring in enough extra income. Then he agreed with his boss that he work two shifts: from seven in the morning till ten in the evening, seven days a week. His children lived like all the others: modestly but without want. He knew his life wasn't like that of other people, but that was the price he had to pay so his children could have a normal life. That's just the way things were. His father, too, had slaved away from dawn till dusk to raise him. People struggle and then die. That's just the way things are, he said.

He never rang when he came home. He made sure the door and the lock were well greased so they wouldn't squeak when he opened them, sneaked into the hall and locked them again. He turned the television down low so only he could hear it. When he went to the fridge or to the bathroom, too, he was careful not to wake the family. Over the years he learned to go without being heard. He even managed to get into bed without waking his wife. When he went to work in the morning, they were still sleeping. He opened the door of the children's room a little and looked at his sons. Dragan was already thirteen and resembled him. Mirko was still small. Children at that age look like their mother.

'When I drive to Bar, I imagine their alarm clocks ringing,' Salvatore said. He pictured Dragan, half-awake, stumbling towards the bathroom. After him Mirko came running, complaining that he needed to go urgently. Mirna, his wife, was already in the kitchen frying eggs. She'd contracted chronic arthritis as a young woman and every movement caused her pain. But she had a normal life with a husband and children. Like every other woman.

'When we got married I told her: "As long as I'm alive I'll make sure you can enjoy a normal life. You'll be able to live like all other women,"' he said. He imagined them eating, going to the fridge and taking out the jam and milk he'd bought the night before on the way back from work. Breakfast was over; now the boys got dressed and ready to leave for school. Before they left the house, Mirna gave them a euro each. 'This is from your Dad,' she'd say, and they'd run off cheerfully down the street. 'I see all that while I'm driving,' he said.

He'd smoke a second cigarette. In the distance he heard a Lada and knew it was the cleaning lady being brought to work by her husband. Like every morning, they'd say a polite hello and she'd unlock the front entrance. Then he'd go to the cold room and she to the cleaning storeroom, and they wouldn't meet again until the next morning.

As he prepared the meat for the day he heard the other shopping-centre staff arriving, through the cold-room door: Mirjana from the fruit and vegetable section, who was now engaged and spent the days making plans for her marriage; Zoran from the purchasing department, whose wife had been diagnosed with cancer and who wandered from doctor to doctor, getting deeper and deeper into debt, searching in vain for a cure; Branka from the health and cosmetics section, who had problems with her alcoholic father; and Aida from the bakery, who had a mute child.

He also heard the voices of the regular customers. For example, there was a lady who they knew by her first name, Stela, whose son had moved to Canada. He married a black woman there. Stela objected, but he didn't listen. Even as a child he'd been obstinate, she said. She begged him not to get hitched to that woman. Now he was punishing his mother by not getting in touch for years. Every morning Stela would buy her two croissants and then rush home: 'I have to get back – just imagine if he rings while I'm out!' she fretted day in, day out.

Although Salvatore spent most of the day in the cold room, he knew everything about those people. It was as if he listened to a radio programme about their lives all day. They chatted, argued, bitched and rejoiced about things, and he listened to it all just as if he was out there with them. At first it'd been hard to get used to the chill and isolation of the cold room, but over time he realised that it didn't matter. When he heard how hard other people's lives were and how they struggled, he was ashamed that he'd complained about his life so much.

Every morning, first thing, he sharpened the knives. He took his time and did it meticulously. 'You can see yourself in my knives like a mirror,' he said. He couldn't stand blunt knives. The blade had to pass through the meat without resistance. The cut had to be straight and clean. He was horrified when people mangled meat instead of cutting it. Some almost seemed to hate the meat they cut. It was as if they let out all their frustration on the pieces of veal and pork they got their hands on. One look at the cuts a butcher made would tell him what sort of person he was. An angry, resentful person was easiest to recognise. Butchers like that always made more cuts than necessary. They cut and realised it was wrong. Then, in their rage, they cut wrongly again. They ended up rending the meat like a wild animal. He'd seen butchers like that: if their wife had offended them or their children didn't respect them, they stabbed the meat and tore at it. There were ones who bellowed as they cleaved the meat. Some made a real mess in the butcher's shop: they dragged the pieces of meat across the floor, stamping on them and kicking them. But not him: he left all his problems at the cold-room door. When he finished work, he left everything spic and span. It was as clean as a hospital, he said.

Until noon, when he had his first break, he made sausages with a lot of garlic; then he prepared burgers and three sorts of meat patties. Next he marinated meat in oil, salt, pepper and *herbes de Provence* – but not paprika because it would dominate the taste. He filleted pork, cut beef for soup-making, and set aside prime-quality filets and rump steak. It was like that in the summertime: however much you prepared, the café owners bought it all.

He would take a bottle of beer out of the fridge and sit down on the bench behind the butcher's shop in the shade. He smoked two cigarettes and watched the cows and sheep tottering about the meadow, torpid from the heat. Mirjana would come and sit next to him. She would bum a cigarette like she did every day.

'What are you up to?' she asked one day.

'Watching the animals. I could watch them for hours. I grew up with animals: we had cows, sheep and goats at home,' he told her.

'I don't like animals – they scare me,' she said. 'When my husband and I have kids and they're a few years old, maybe I'll get them a dog. I've read that dogs are good for kids. Children who grow up with dogs become better people because a dog has the traits of a good person. The dog brings them up to be good, in a way. A dog is OK, but I'd never let a cat into the house. I'll invite you to my wedding. Will you come – you and your family?' she asked. Then she threw away the butt and returned to work without waiting for a reply.

He glanced at his watch: twenty past twelve. He had time for one more cigarette. He stared at the cows which were now lying in the meadow. They didn't move or give any signs of life. He was musing on how they looked almost like rocks, when he was roused from his reflections by a voice calling his name. Turning, he saw two police officers standing beside him. Come with us, was all they said.

When they were driving in the police car he tried to find out where they were taking him, and why. The men in uniform said they were under orders not to tell him any details. The car pulled up in front of the mortuary. 'Even then I didn't know, even then I didn't think,' he said. Only when he'd set foot inside the mortuary did he notice that he still had his apron on. He'd been working all morning and the apron was blood-smeared, as was the cap which he kept on all day in the cold room. *They'll think I'm a psychopath*, he thought. He was relieved when he saw the mortuary was empty and no one could be intimidated by his appearance. At the end of the corridor he saw Mirna. She ran towards him, all in tears, and threw herself into his arms. 'Dragan's dead,' she howled, 'someone's killed our son,' she screamed and dug her fingernails into her cheeks. The blood mixed with her tears and she smeared it over her eyes and hair in her anguish.

Then the doctor appeared. He also had a bloodstained white apron and a cap. The only difference between them was the gloves the doctor wore, Salvatore said. The doctor instructed the police officers. One took Mirna to the toilet so she could wash and calm down, the other accompanied Salvatore and the doctor to the autopsy room. On a metal table in the middle, illuminated by a neon lamp, lay his son.

'Twenty-nine stab wounds, probably made with a knife, and three slash wounds: two short ones on the chest and a long one which tore his stomach,' the doctor explained.

'It was a blunt blade – an ordinary kitchen knife like you can buy at any market,' Salvatore told him.

'How do you know?' the doctor asked.

'You can see I'm a butcher,' Salvatore said.

He asked the doctor and the policeman to leave him alone with his son.

Through the door of the autopsy room he heard Mirna crying and the voice of the policeman trying to console her.

'I know how you must feel: I also lost a child. But you have to calm down. If I'm not mistaken, you have another boy? You have to settle down and keep going for his sake,' he said. Their voices receded – they'd probably gone outside for some fresh air.

He sat down on the bench in the corner and looked around the room. It was clean and everything was in its place. The sharp implements were neatly arranged on a long table. The panes of glass in the door were immaculate, without the fingermarks which are always a tell-tale sign of negligence. The floor tiles had been polished. The only stain on them was a little puddle of blood from his son's right arm, which hung down from the autopsy table.

Salvatore got up, raised the boy's arm and laid it alongside his body, parallel to the arm on the other side. 'That was how Dragan slept: stretched out and flat on his back,' he said. He pulled up the white sheet to cover his son's body. On the shelves he found some paper towels. He wiped the blood from the floor and shone the tiles with a moistened towel. Then he sat down on the bench in the corner again.

It was cold in the room. He could see the steam of his breath. 'For a moment I thought I was back in the cold room and everything was alright. As if it was still morning and the whole day lay ahead,' he said.

Chapter Four

which tells of books and a conversation in Saint Anna's Hospital, presents the multiple murder from a different angle, and shows us Fra Dolcino fleeing the wrath of the Church and finding refuge in the Franciscan monastery on Bojana River

from: emmanuel@gmail.com
to: thebigsleep@yahoo.com

It was the article about the library fire which finally opened my eyes. The papers and Web portals were full of headlines about the killing of the Vukotić family, which is why I didn't notice it earlier. I find it unforgiveable that such a tragedy is reduced to a spectacle to be served with morning coffee. All the pain and fear of the murder victims, and all the sorrow and despair of those who survived them, is transformed into a product to increase newspaper circulation – a topic of conversation to while away the time and be utterly forgotten as soon as the front pages scream in bold about a new murder. Every day we do and say unforgiveable things, without our hand or voice trembling. We defend our right to the unforgiveable with the utmost decisiveness. Doubt and trepidation only come when fear takes over and when our lives, which we once claimed a sovereign right to and defended at whatever cost, have slipped completely from our control.

That terse report in the 'Community' column told me that the Ulcinj Library was set on fire the very same evening that the killers broke into the Vukotićs' house. As I'm sure you know, the library fire was started a few hours before the murder. Although the fire station is just twenty metres behind the library and right next to the police station, the report in the paper suggests the firefighters arrived late. They didn't set about extinguishing the fire until the damage had become irreversible and the flames had engulfed the roof of the building. By then, the book which the fire was meant to destroy lay in cinders.

The chaos in the centre of town facilitated the work of the Vukotićs' killers. I can see them now, driving towards the house along a little-used track in the dark, without headlights. They kept off the busy road to avoid detection. Although they had done an efficient job with the library, these well-organised and devoted zealots remained cautious and used the narrow dirt road leading up to the property from the back. There were no houses there, whose lights might give away those coming with evil intent – only scrub and forest between there and Cape Djerana. And forest is a good keeper of secrets.

Four men in black balaclavas opened the narrow, ground-level window and crawled through it into the cellar. The ease with which they moved and their noiseless steps showed they were adept at crime. They didn't want to wake the residents before the task was done. They quickly found the safe hidden beneath the floorboards under a thick, sumptuous carpet which, even in the dark of the house, they could be sure was Persian. One of the intruders knew the combination for opening the safe. It clicked open and he withdrew a thick book with a hard, leather binding. As he leafs through it, I can see it was written by hand in a language unknown to me. The writing seems scattered, and the pages are yellowing and battered at the edges. It was as if the paper didn't absorb the ink – the letters and words are just lying on the pages, ready to flutter up and away at need.

The burglars made certain that this was the book they were looking for. But their work wasn't yet done. One of them lifted up a vase from the kitchen table and smashed it on the floor with all his might. As intended, the noise roused the residents. The woman of the household came first, running down the stairs and shouting *Who's there?!* While one of the burglars inflicted fatal wounds on her, the others ran up to the first floor, where they overpowered her husband and mercilessly killed the children. They then left the house through the front door, which they intentionally left ajar. This was meant to mislead investigators: if you hadn't witnessed the crime you'd think the woman opened the front door and let the killers into the house.

I spoke about this with Doctor Schulz today. He was particularly interested in the part of the story about the burning of books.

'Why did they burn down the library?' he wanted to know, and above all: 'Which book burned in the library? And which was stolen from the Vukotićs'?'

Dr Schulz often reminds me of my childhood: people like him are becoming steadily rarer. It's as if they belong to a different time and disappear with it. He sits patiently in his armchair beneath the large portrait of Lacan and listens to me with the greatest attentiveness. Sometimes he takes notes of what I say. These are obviously of no real significance because all our conversations are tape-recorded, he just jots them down to add a dash of pop-psychological flavour. But he plays his role flawlessly, with no intention of adding to the interpretation – without innovations, which would destroy everything. *Rereading* is the vogue term: people produce *rereadings of rereadings* and in doing so only conceal their inability to read the text in full. Dr Schulz reminds me of Bruno Ganz and his playing of Thomas Bernhard: if you go to the Burgtheater to see *The Ignoramus and the Madman*, be it the première, the second showing, or the second season, you'll see the same actor playing the same role in the same way. Even the vanilla-scented tobacco Dr Schulz smokes in his pipe is always the same.

'I wonder what could be written in the book you're talking about?' he said. The question was rhetorical, of course, but it served well as an introduction to what was to come.

'So you're studying the case of a burned book – I must admit I also find this a fascinating topic,' he began his most instructive and interesting discourse. 'My fascination goes back to an event during my studies. Its elusive implications have accompanied me up until this day. You are… how should I put it… our conversation here was portended that day, so many years ago.

'The event I'm taking about occurred in 1977. I came here to St Anna's towards the end of that year to attend a seminar given by Lacan. Even back then I found its title threatening: *The Time of Conclusions*. One morning we gathered in the amphitheatre; we were all young and full of faith in ourselves and our mission. We listened with bated breath as he, brilliant as ever, outlined the seminar he was going to hold. "Now I'd like to hear your questions," he said after his introduction.

'You may not have noticed, and maybe it's imperceptible today, but my greatest failing is vanity,' Dr Schulz told me. 'When we're young, our vanity is simply ludicrous, but no less dangerous. If you'd known me back then, you could have been sure that I'd be the one to ask the first question. And not any old question: it had to be one which told the teacher that this pupil had mastered his lessons. It was intended as a kind of declaration of loyalty: this pupil wanted to tell the teacher that he'd remain true to his teachings although he knew their weak points.

'"What is your greatest desire: to bequeath your work to the world?" I asked him.

'*You haven't understood anything. On the contrary, before I die I want to completely destroy my work*, Lacan stated, and he meant it. This wasn't a threat or a vow, and even less a confession, but a cold conclusion. Back then we didn't believe our teacher would destroy every hope that we could help humanity and destroy our last illusion about the practical value of the discipline we'd devoted ourselves to.

'Why did our teacher want to destroy his work? Attempting to understand this led me on to the question: Why does an author destroy his book? Did you know that Kafka wanted to have almost his entire work destroyed? He entrusted the task to two friends. One, a woman, complied with his wish, while the other, a man, betrayed his friend's trust. It's the latter, Max Brod, who we have to thank for having Kafka's writing today.

'Destroying a book is the culmination of the drama of fatherhood,' Dr Schulz said, getting up from his armchair beneath the portrait of Lacan. 'And of the drama of *sonship*, if you like,' he added. He looked out the window and continued speaking, which created the strange impression of him talking to me and ignoring me at the same time. 'A son who burns a book is staging a revolution against the Father and his Law conveyed in that book. But a Father who burns his work deprives the son of his name and his Law. A burned book is the spot where the bond between father and son is severed.

'In *Totem and Taboo*, Freud goes back to the primal horde, only to find the tyranny of the father there too. The primal father imposes tight restrictions on his sons and punishes them harshly for any disobedience. The sons desire freedom and therefore band together to kill and eat their despotic father. Here we have the first of many revolutions, which will all run according to the same Oedipal scenario. But, as usual, remorse comes instead of freedom and leads the sons to resurrect their father's ban. All this is accompanied by the posthumous veneration of the father. Here, of course, we note the root of religion,' Dr Schulz said.

'Oh, if only it were so simple that a murder, even the murder of the father, could resolve things… The catch is that neither the actual death of the father nor the proclamation 'God is dead' really brings liberation. The Law remains when the Father is gone. Since freedom can't be attained by patricide, one tries to achieve it by destroying the Law – the book which civilisation and culture are based on. To burn a book means to kill one's father, as poignantly described by Gérard Haddad, whom I met back at the seminar. But even if the father is killed twice, he still returns.' Then Dr Schulz suddenly turned towards me: 'As far as I can tell from the brief description you've given, those book-burners of yours must belong to a millenarian movement. The history of those movements is the history of book-burning and contempt for the Law.'

After those words, Dr Schulz paced the room in circles several times and then stopped at the bookshelf. He took out a book and laid it on the table, then sat back in his armchair. I memorised the title: *The Pursuit of the Millennium* by Norman Cohn. When he was sure I'd registered it, he added: 'But, like I say, I was more interested in the figure of the father who deprives the son of himself – the father who feels revulsion towards fatherhood.'

That same evening I asked my corrupt fallen angels, the paramedics, to get Cohn's book for me. I had it the very next day, hidden under my bed. The book would turn out to be irrefutable proof of the 'butterfly effect': a work written by a British academic, which an unconventional Central European psychiatrist discreetly showed his Vienna patient in a solitary clinic in the Alps, would lead to the solving of a murder mystery in a town on the Adriatic.

Everything is interrelated, I say to myself, repeating that worn out phrase. The signs are a sure guide, but it's so damn hard to read them correctly and even just recognise them… Given the preoccupation or even obsession with health which I grew up in, I ask myself today if I couldn't and shouldn't have recognised the sign that everything would end in illness? You see, if *maman et papa* were dedicated to something, it was so-called physical health. They therefore perceived my asthenia as a punishment of God, while my corpulence, which they fought against in vain, must have seemed a heavy blow of Providence indeed. Every morning *papa* washed himself in ice-cold water. That superfluous and painful ritual had been part of family tradition ever since his grandfather, an officer in the Austro-Hungarian army, had served in Sarajevo. He washed that way for the first time and realised that the absence of civilisation, which in his case began and ended with the absence of warm water, certainly toughened a man. Mother's morning toilet, on the other hand, lasted longer than it took to create some twentieth-century artworks. Jackson Pollock could have finished a painting in the time it took *maman* to do 'all that was necessary for a lady to be ready to leave the house', as she put it. This would be followed by a slow breakfast – cereal, yoghurt, fruit – and a schedule of morning gymnastics designed to keep her eternally healthy and young. My priorities were different: chocolate cake, for example. It and everything else I truly desired only became attainable in my parents' absence.

Hedwig had a good heart and, equally important for this anecdote, a good appetite. No sooner would *maman et papa* leave the house and I sadly blink my little eyes, than Hedwig would whiz down to the neighbourhood baker's to get some pastries, which we proceeded to devour in the pantry. We chose that secluded spot for our secret little ritual as if to highlight the gravity of our transgression. And that just whetted our appetite.

Hedwig was with me for days on end. She'd practically only leave the house when she went out on errands or was called to the school which her daughter, Marushka, attended.

The time I had to spend alone was particularly hard for me. I'd stand by the window, with black thoughts populating my little head. Everything that entered my mind spoke of the End and of irretrievable loss. Schikanedergasse would suddenly turn into a street being swallowed up by a swamp: I saw a flood of water coming and pushing in through the doors of the houses. Reeds started to grow among the parked cars and bent in a black wind bearing fallen leaves. Huge brown leaves rotted while still in the air and fell to the ground like dust. It was as if the whole world had turned into a grave, with the undertaker shovelling earth into it. We'll be buried alive I thought as my heart slowed its beat, we'll perish beneath the water and dust with nothing to show that we ever existed.

The Olcinium Trilogy

I was obsessed at that time by an article I read in the paper about a rifle which had passed from hand to hand and circulated through the Balkans for almost a century. It so happened that every owner of the rifle was shot and killed – but not before he himself had killed someone with the accursed gun. Belgrade historians made a list of the various owners of the rifle and also those killed by it. They then fed all the available genealogical data into the computer. It turned out there was a certain order to all the killing which had at first looked so random and indiscriminate. For example, a grandson of the rifle's first owner was killed by his grandfather's weapon. The great-grandson of his killer shot a man from Herzegovina with the same rifle. The dead man's son later took possession of it and, without knowing that he was using the rifle which had killed his father, shot a certain Perović from Nikšić, who was a descendant of the rifle's first victim. When the Belgrade historians joining the dots on the rifle's huge, ramified family tree designating those who killed with it and those who were killed by it, they ended up with an outline of a butterfly with spread wings.

I concluded back then that everything I do, and everything I think, can have terrible consequences for people I don't even know. A sequence of events unfolds, unforeseeable for me but entirely logical in itself, which can forever change the lives of people, even those who'll come after me. For the first time, I clearly formulated the idea which has possessed me up until today: if I could comprehend the pattern by which the actions of people in one place and time impact on the lives of people in another, I'd be able to understand how the world works. I'd be in possession of the matrix which governs the unfolding of history. Then I'd be able to make sure that none of my actions caused sorrow or pain to others.

After that, *maman et papa* would enter my mind. I'd see their car racing along a winding forest road at night. The car's headlights would illuminate the huge trees which stood by the roadside like grim sentinels lining the travellers' way to a secret and sinister destination. Another time I'd see them crossing an intersection, with a busload of schoolchildren inexorably speeding towards them from the side. Or I'd see their car breaking through the crash barrier and plunging over a cliff into the sea, which beat and foamed against sharp rocks far below. The ending was always the same and had them dying in the crushed body of the car.

Those visions were so real, so convincing, that I'd instantly be overcome by a fear that they really were dead. No one could dispel my fear, not even Hedwig when she returned to the apartment. She'd come running up to me: 'Master Emmanuel, it was all just a dream!' she'd say. I'd spend the rest of the day glued to the window in fear and trembling incessantly. I'd stare down the street and wait for the only thing which could bring relief: my parents' return. But fear wasn't the worst. Along with it there came a paralysing guilt. The feeling that I was to blame for their death was all-powerful and pervasive, and inseparable from the fear. I think you could say that I feared my thoughts and acts had evoked their death. An unbearable weight pressed down on my young shoulders like a boulder determined to crush me: not their death itself but the thought that they'd only died because of me.

By the time they finally returned I'd be a trembling heap on the floor. They'd reprimand Hedwig, who each time, rightfully, perceived that as the worst injustice and withdrew downcast into the kitchen. I'd be taken to my room and put to bed, as usually happened when they didn't know what to do with me. Through the bedroom door I'd hear my mother crying. The realisation that she was miserable because of me dealt yet another blow to my tormented body.

Later, when the voices in the apartment died down and the streetlights were on outside, Hedwig would slink into my room, sit at my feet and read me stories from her hidden book. 'As we agreed, no one is to hear a word about this,' she'd whisper and put her fat finger to her lips. That was another of our rituals: she'd take the book from her apron, wink to me – her accomplice – mutter 'Now, where did we stop last time?' and start reading me the latest adventures of the Son of God, who asked *Father, father, why have you forsaken me?* as he suffered to save us all, me included.

Dr Schulz knows the things I've told you about myself. He knows a lot. But there's one thing he doesn't know, the most important thing, and I'm going to tell it only to you because it's the key for you to unlock the secret of the Vukotić murders: there's a *third book* – one which its author called *The Book of the Coming*. It is the reason for all this happening.

For you to understand, we have to go far back into the past.

I first found out about the author while reading Marcel Schwob's *Imaginary Lives*. And as these things usually go, I discovered that book coincidentally and indirectly via Borges, who turned out to have read Schwob before he was even twenty and went on to virtually become his pupil.

One of the twenty-two literary portraits Schwob wrote is the story of the heretic Dolcino. The historical Fra Dolcino was born around 1250, we can assume. We have to be more careful when trying to determine his place of birth: most researchers consider that he *might* have been born in Novara. Schwob's Fra Dolcino pursued his sacred studies at the church of Orto San Michele, 'where his mother raised him so he'd be able to touch the beautiful wax figurines with his little hands'. The boy grew up with the Franciscans, and the friar who instructed him claimed he was accepted into the order by Saint Francis himself. I see myself standing beside the sweet boy as he learns to speak with the birds, which aren't afraid of him and often come to land on his shoulders. The boy snaps out of his daydreaming and remembers he has to go to the monastery, where Schwob says he 'sang in a sonorous voice with the brethren'. Barefoot, he rushes like a whirlwind through the crowded lanes and markets.

The boy lived from begging and found great enjoyment in mendicant ways. Schwob describes how, one summer day, the townsfolk were cruel to the boy and his brethren. Hungry and thirsty, they took refuge from the heat with their empty baskets in an unfamiliar courtyard. Here the boy experienced a miracle – the first of many great miracles which years later would lead him to believe he was *the chosen one*. A curtain of grapevine formed before his eyes, and leopards and other wild animals from faraway lands frolicked behind it. Young women and men in bright raiment played violas and lutes. When the boy lowered his gaze to his basket, it was full of fragrant loaves of bread, reminiscent of the time Jesus fed the five thousand with five loaves and two fish.

Fra Dolcino's biographers note that Dolcino was falsely accused of theft – in Vercelli, by all accounts. Although innocent, he was tortured. Humiliated by his mistreatment, he fled to the city of Trento, where he came across a sect whose name sounded so pure: the Apostolics. Later, in 1300, he was to don the white robe and become leader of the Apostolic movement.

Now Dolcino was indoctrinated with the esoteric teachings of Gioacchino da Fiore. Thomas Aquinas refuted Da Fiore's ideas in *Summa Theologica*. Nevertheless, Dante placed Da Fiore in Heaven. In his *Inferno*, Dante also mentions Fra Dolcino, whom Mohammed warned to prepare well for the conflict with the Novarese.

Under the influence of Da Fiore's teachings, Dolcino would turn the *Apostolics* into a brotherhood known as the Dolcinians. Night after night, Dolcino listened to the stories of the older brethren about Da Fiore's wisdom and kindness, and also about the history of the world, which Da Fiore divided into three ages. There by the campfire high up in the mountains, in the empty lands where neither merchants' caravans nor soldiers pass and the Apostolics were safe, a lamb appeared to Dolcino in a dream. It came down the hill towards him with a flight of tiny red birds hovering above it.

Dolcino wakened his followers at dawn and told them the revelation which had come in his dream: there had been the age of the Old Testament, he said, when people were created to settle the land; there had been the age of our Lord Jesus Christ and his apostles with their modesty and poverty; then there had been the age of decay and disaster caused by the Church and its greed. 'But an age will come, the age I am bringing –,' he proclaimed, his eyes streaming tears and his voice trembling like a sparrow in the January frost, 'an age of modesty and poverty, when the sword of worldly power and might will no longer hang over our heads. The lamb said to me: *You are my word and my promise, I am coming with you to stay forever.'*

Now Dolcino and his band of revolutionaries wandered the Novara area. They were joined by the poor and the ignorant, inebriated not so much by the promise of a better world to come as by the prospects of plunder. The Dolcinians, who after their teacher's 'sermon on the mount' no longer doubted they were the beloved of God, gave themselves over to forbidden bodily pleasures. Churches burned late into the night in the lands they passed through, as did the houses of any who refused to renounce the authority of the Pope and were promptly slain. Dolcino absolved the marauders, rapists and killers of their sins. The Dolcinians knelt before him, ragged and filthy, with the dried blood of yesterday's victims under their nails. 'To the pure all things are pure, but to the corrupt and unbelieving nothing is pure,' Dolcino recited the words of Paul the Apostle. And no sooner had his followers crossed themselves than they were ready for new misdeeds.

A certain Father Tomaso hung from an oak in front of one of the many churches the Dolcinians committed to the flames. When he'd seen the rabble carting away the pewter, candlesticks and fabrics from his church, he turned to Dolcino and thundered: 'You call for a return to Christ, but you're blind to his works and deaf to his words! Does not our Lord say: *For many shall come in my name, saying, I am Christ; and shall deceive many... And many false prophets shall rise, and shall deceive many... Then if any man shall say unto you, Lo, here is Christ, or there; believe it not. For there shall arise false Christs, and false prophets, and shall show great signs and wonders; insomuch that, if it were possible, they shall deceive the very elect.* Are those not his words?'

Challenged to a theological duel, Dolcino decided to withdraw without loss. Instead of parrying the presumptuous priest with a sagacious response, which his followers keenly awaited, Dolcino just muttered: 'Kill him.'

The Church soon set about hunting down Dolcino with all the means and forces at its disposal. The *Statutum Ligae contra Haereticos* was passed in Scopello on 24 August 1305. This amounted to Fra Dolcino's death sentence: from that day on, his end drew rapidly nearer like a stone falling into a well.

The most interesting period in Dolcino's scarcely documented life, from the point of view of your and my story, is the time between 1300 and 1303. Fleeing the wrath of the Church, he spent these years 'somewhere in eastern Dalmatia', the sources say. But we can assume that Dolcino didn't feel safe even there, at the 'edge of the world'. I can see him now at a marketplace in the hinterland of Split and running into one of the Franciscan friars who he'd begged with as a boy. The meeting was cordial and their friendship deep. Torn between loyalty to the Church and loyalty to his old friend, the friar chose the latter. He was journeying to the Franciscan mission in Ulcinj, which had been extended into a monastery in 1288 by the kindness of Helen of Anjou. Since he was continuing on his way at dawn, he suggested to Dolcino: 'Why not come along? Your secret will be safe with me.' And Dolcino thought: Ulcinj is *terra incognita* indeed – they'll never find me in that land of dragons!

The fugitive Dolcino and his friend travelled south through Dalmatia. Several weeks later they arrived on the banks of Bojana River in the town which would be marked on Venetian etchings over a century later as *Dolcigno in Dalmatia*.

Dolcino spent his days by the river. He carved pipes from the reeds that grew there, and with their music he charmed the fish of the water and birds of the air. But Dolcino had a mission, and he couldn't build the Kingdom of God on earth while hiding in Ulcinj. The night before departing back to his home region, where he would once again head the Dolcinians by Lake Garda, he had another dream. He saw that he'd die at the stake. But that wouldn't be his end: he dreamed that he'd be resurrected. He entrusted this dream and the date of his resurrection to only one person – his good and faithful friend, the Franciscan friar. He took down Dolcino's words and locked the manuscript into a chest, which he secretly immured deep in the walls of the monastery.

One peaceful evening by Lake Garda, Dolcino met Margaret of Trento, who before dawn would become his lover. He'd lead his followers all the way to Mount Rubello, there to dig in and await the final battle. One year later, the army of the Church would come against them with all its might. A thousand of his followers would be killed, while Dolcino and Margaret would be captured and burned at the stake. Schwob writes that Dolcino 'asked just one favour of their executioners: that in the hour of their suffering they be allowed to keep on their white robes like the apostles on the lampshade in the church of Orto San Michele', where his mother had taught him faith. But he begged in vain – he was forced to watch his lover burn to death. Before his own turn came, he was castrated, blinded, and had his nose, ears and fingers cut off.

As his head blazed like a torch, Dolcino remembered the day as a boy when he was driven by hunger, thirst, heat and the absence of human clemency – and saw leopards and heard the song of happy people. Before he breathed his last, he had a vision of himself descending from the mountain bringing baskets of *pane dolce* to the people of the valley: a gift to the poor from his master, the Saviour.

Chapter Five

which tells of trust, a lie under pressure, proud pregnant women
and an old liaison, and the demands of the murder victim's
brother for revenge in this world or the next

Salvatore finished his story. He sat there with his elbow on his knee
and fist on his chin, staring into the emptiness before him. He stayed
like that in silence for a while, like Rodin's *Thinker* who'd just reached
the end of all thoughts. I thought I saw tears in his eyes. But Salvatore was a tough guy. He jumped to his feet, downed his – or rather
my – whisky, and said in a very businesslike manner: 'So that's agreed,
then?'

Like everyone who approaches me, Salvatore didn't trust the police.
And quite justifiably so, because even if the police found the killer, his
tracks could be covered again for the right price. If the police failed to
protect the felon in any way, there was always the court: the criminal
could rely on its corruptibility even if the case he'd paid to cover up
was taken all the way to the Supreme Court.

Salvatore therefore wanted me to find the killer.

'You're a wreck of a man: you don't *need* anything any more, you
don't *want* anything any more, not even money. I can trust you,' he
told me. I took that as a compliment.

'I'll think about it,' I said.

'You'll do it, I know,' he smiled and shook my hand.

Salvatore's story didn't surprise me because he'd been dogged by
misfortune all his life. His first and greatest misfortune was to be born
in this country. As with the majority of things which cause us lifelong
suffering, he had his parents to thank. We're all victims of our parents'
inability to resist the reproductive urge. We've all been at the receiving
end of the fascism of nature, whose casualty count far surpasses that
of any criminal regime or system we've seen – and every single one
of them has been criminal. Instead of pictures of Hitler and Stalin,

textbooks which teach schoolchildren about the greatest enemies of humankind should show a picture of a forest in spring.

His parents went one step further in crime against their son: they decided to raise him in this country. Salvatore's father, Simone, had been stationed in Ulcinj when fascist Italy fell. Enchanted by the natural beauty of the town, and even more by the beauty of its women – one of whom would later become his wife, this cheerful and ever primped-up stereotype Italian decided to stay on. They say he left an olfactory trail of hair grease and aftershave behind him so that when you went downtown you'd always know where he'd been that morning. He came to Ulcinj as an occupier and ended up as the object of town jokesters and the jealousy of many a husband.

Simone lived in Ulcinj more or less peacefully. What occasional bother he had was mainly of his own making – at least up until the Trieste Crisis. Then anti-Italian demonstrations were organised throughout the country. Party leaders came from Podgorica to ensure that the 'spontaneous expression of popular rage' in Ulcinj went off according to plan. One of them heard there was an Italian living in town. The people of Ulcinj said in Simone's defence that he was good-natured – a harmless clown, whose only flaw was being a Casanova. But the Comrades from Podgorica were unyielding: Simone was Italian, therefore he was suspicious and had to be punished.

And punished he was: he had to march at the head of the demonstrations and carry the biggest *Trieste is ours* placard – him, of all people!

* * *

I laughed at that anecdote again as I parked in front of the house. The muezzin's call came up from town once more. I didn't have much time – this night was going to be short. I planned to read the peculiar mails again and try to find some clue in them. While reading, I'd help myself to some whisky: there's nothing wrong with a man enjoying his work.

One day you open a mail and, whoom, you find out you're a father. All your life you've refused every possibility of fatherhood – the very thought is repellent. You're doing just fine, you think. You don't have time for anything more and everyone else can just jump in the lake. Your liver is a write-off and every next bottle could kill you, if your heart doesn't get you first. They've prescribed heart tablets but you don't take them properly. You fervently hope the doctor was right when you asked: *How much longer have I got?* and he replied: *With a lifestyle like that – a few years at best.*

You'll go for sure, but not in peace (not that you deserved it, but you hoped for it all the same). And then the twist: you get a mail and suddenly you're a father. You of all people, who was overcome by despair and anger because of neighbourhood children toddling around all summer's day on the terraces of their parents' houses too close to yours, waddling about and tirelessly repeating their *ga-ga-ga*, which sufficed to evoke applause and ovations – at least from their parents – who always channelled all their interpretative potential into trying to tell who their unsightly child took after. You of all people, who was struck and horrified by the uniquely proud gait of expectant mothers, who with every step seemed to want to say: *Look, I've fulfilled my function, I've justified my existence, I'm a mother.* As if she'd written *Anna Karenina* rather than getting pregnant! As if she was going to deliver the ultimate explanation of human misfortune rather than just reproduce, as nature has done for thousands of years and will do after her, too. You of all people, who felt nausea around men who, with the help of the whole feeble-minded community, convinced themselves that their lives were meaningful when they became fathers; these were men who got married when they didn't know what to do with themselves, and when they didn't know what to do with the marriage – they had children, and later they didn't know what to do with the children; in the end they died, but only after they'd become religious and turned for help to the world's oldest breakdown assistance service: the Church. You of all people, who maintained that the most intelligent, sophisticated and sensitive people doubted, re-examined and repented: they bequeathed us art and philosophy, but not progeny. It was the others who multiplied. Creatives died in loneliness, while the others produced herds of offspring. Humankind was thus the product of the careful selection of the worst. Yes, you of all people, who said and believed these things.

When I first saw the woman who I'd eventually conceive Emmanuel with, fatherhood was the last thing on my mind. She strode into my office briskly and proudly, with an air of ceremony. Just like Dragan Vukotić came strolling in some twenty-five years later. Unlike her, he immediately offered me money: he threw an envelope full of large banknotes onto the table and delivered me a speech he'd obviously painstakingly prepared. He told me he had the means – money wasn't an issue – but he expected me not only to find out who his brother's killer was but also to catch him before the police did. I was to bring the killer to him, and he'd mete out justice himself. There was no doubt in my mind that he meant what he said. And from what I knew about this unpleasant new client, it wouldn't be the first time. One of his building sites would be the tomb for his brother's killer: he'd throw their body into the foundations and cover it with concrete, or he'd brick them into the attic of one of his buildings. He was a tireless developer, as if he hadn't already raised dozens of building and earned tens of millions of euros. *Why do people who have fifty million to their name work hard to earn another?* I remember thinking as I slipped the bulging envelope into the pocket of my jacket.

She didn't offer money, but she offered what I desired much more – herself. And she did so in a stylish, discreet way by telling me she *had a lot to offer*. The next morning she woke up in my bed. As soon as she opened her eyes, she woke me too. 'Don't tell me you've forgotten: you have a lot of work today,' she said, and turfed me out of my own house.

I went into town, had two or three drinks at the Port and then got down to business. The case seemed simple: one of those leading to an explanation which ultimately no one is satisfied with. The explanation of the death of loved ones is usually quite banal, and for some reason people find that hard to accept. I've never had any problem with banality. For me it's always meant convenience.

Her father had disappeared and it was my job to find him. He had been in love with this town and had spent his summer holidays here for thirty years, she told me. In fact, he lived in Ulcinj for more than half the year: he arrived as early as April, when the shad fishing season begins, and went straight from the plane to Bojana River, where his fishing crew was waiting. He didn't leave until December, after the mullet season. At first she thought he might have drowned because he'd been known to go out in heavy sea with a sirocco blowing: she imagined he'd tried to return to the river but the swell capsized him in the estuary. But his boat was moored by his cabin and all the fishing gear was there. She checked his bank account: he'd withdrawn a certain amount before he disappeared, but nothing significant.

I went out on Bojana River by boat and had a talk with fishermen who'd known him. What they had to tell me was of no help: *A peaceable sort of guy, great to have as a neighbour. We were so surprised when he disappeared, who'd have thought – but there you go, these things happen.* So I puttered down to his cabin. I'd forgotten to bring the key, so I forced the door.

Inside it was like a pharmacy: spick and span and orderly. Jars stood in file like German fusiliers at inspection. The bed was made and tucked in, barracks-style. His clothes were all on coat-hangers in the wardrobe and he'd tied sprigs of lavender to them to keep away the moths. That was a first warning sign for me – I don't trust orderly people. You can only expect the worst of someone who worries about things so diligently. I decided to search the cabin.

When I found photographs of a boy in the sleeping bag under the bed, I realised where this was heading. The boy was only ten, with black hair and a face full of birthmarks. The photos showed him naked on a sandy beach – they'd obviously forced him to pose. One of the photos had a phone number on the back: it began with the calling code for Albania.

If the old pervert had gone to Albania, there was only one person who could have taken him there: Johnny. After a few years in Germany, Johnny had come back with a hoary, moneyed Teutoness and a powerboat which was the fastest on the coast at the time. The old woman died soon afterwards and left all her money to him; Johnny soon drank and whored it away, and now all he had left from the whole German episode was the powerboat – still fast enough to smuggle goods and people to Albania.

I found him sleeping at the dock, thoroughly drunk, with his head on the table. After I'd poured a bucket of water over him and slapped him around a bit, he was ready to cooperate.

'I've chucked a case of beer and a bottle of Scotch into your boat so you know I value your labour,' I told him.

'Gimme me a cigarette and tell me what you want,' he said.

'The German who disappeared two weeks ago: what do you know?'

'Five hundred deutschmarks and I know everything.'

We met at three hundred. And it was worth every cent of it. You don't hear a story like that every day, even when you're in my line of work. As I'd assumed, Johnny had taken the paedophile to Albania. Pimps were waiting there and took them to a house by the beach, where boys were kept confined.

'You know me, I've seen lot – thank God I've got a strong stomach – but *that* made even me feel sick,' Johnny said. 'I left him there and went back to the boat. Not five minutes had passed and I'd just opened a warm beer, when there was a commotion in front of the house. Then shots rang out. A lot of shots, several magazines full, I'm pretty sure it was a Yugoslav service pistol. *Stuff the old man,* I thought, and started up the powerboat to move away from the coast a bit. Through my binoculars I saw a man with an Albanian skullcap coming out of the house, carrying a boy in his arms. Two women ran out of the undergrowth towards them. I turned the steering wheel and stepped on the gas. Fortunately the old man had paid me in advance.

I stayed there with Johnny until evening. We didn't talk. What was there to say? We just drank beer after beer and watched the river flowing by. I didn't feel like going home, where she was waiting for me, impatient to hear news of her father who she seemed to truly love.

She was a wonderful girl and didn't deserve to find out. As soon as I heard Johnny's story I decided I'd lie to her. And I did. For a month I told her: 'I'm onto something,' then 'I'm making good progress,' and finally, 'I think I'm really close now.' She became more and more vulnerable and would burst into tears ten times a day without visible reason. The whole thing had become an ordeal for her. I had to put an end to it and was just waiting for the right moment.

One morning I woke up and thought how happy I was with her. I kissed her hair and leaned over to whisper a few affectionate words. The time had come – I broke the news to her at breakfast that her father was dead. I told her that he'd been fishing near the far arm of the Bojana River delta. He must have strayed into Albanian waters. Border guards came and hailed out to him in Albanian. He answered in German … They shot him. He was buried there, in Albania – the grave could be anywhere.

'I knew it,' she repeated through her tears.

'I'm sorry,' I said. 'Now you'll have to find a way to continue your life. I presume you'll be going soon: you must have a lot of commitments waiting at home.'

She looked at me as if I'd stabbed her in the back. When I returned from work that evening she was gone. She didn't leave a farewell letter, only an envelope with money and the message: *For the extra costs.*

As it turned out, she also left me a son, who'd send me mails a quarter of a century later. Now I stood at the computer printing those texts, although I knew his fantasies wouldn't help me in the investigation. Before I left the house, I checked I had everything: key, mails, revolver and bottle. I'd left my phone in the car and could hear it ringing. It was Dragan Vukotić. He wanted to know if I had any news for him.

'Not yet, but soon,' I said.

'And when might *soon* be, seeing as we won't be around tomorrow?' he snarled.

'Listen, I'm onto a hot trail and following it like a bloodhound,' I told him. 'I think it's just a matter of hours until I nail him down.'

'I hope you do, for your sake – I'll have my revenge, in this world or the next.'

The fellow's name was Lazar – I learned that from the Vukotićs' neighbours. It was incomprehensible to me how a police force, even one as ignorant and apathetic as ours, could overlook such an important detail. They probably gave up on their work, which they were never terribly motivated about anyway, and laid down their batons and pistols to sit and wait like so many others. But not me: I, with my Protestant work ethic, have always felt lonely amidst Balkan irresponsibility and laziness.

So his name was Lazar and he worked for the Vukotićs as a caretaker. The neighbours weren't able to tell me when the Vukotićs first employed him, nor where he originally came from. And they didn't know, of course, where he'd gone after killing the family which had accepted him. 'The Vukotićs led a secluded life: we didn't feel welcome there, and so we never dropped in,' they told me.

As soon as I found out about Lazar, every piece of the puzzle fell into place. The Vukotićs had opened up for him because they knew him. He robbed them because he knew the house: as caretaker he had access to every corner of every room. He'd probably discovered they had a safe while repairing the floorboards in the living room. It was presumably then that he conceived the crime he ultimately committed. Only one thing had me fazed: the safe which my son speaks about in his mails. Inspector Jovanović didn't mention a safe when I bribed him to tell me everything he knew about the case. So now I phoned him. He answered, drunk and despairing.

'Listen, mate, I think you forgot to tell me one important detail about the Vukotić murders,' I reproached him. 'Was there a safe at the house and had it been broken into?'

'Yes,' he mumbled and replaced the receiver.

Good, I said to myself: I have a suspect who had a motive. Now I just have to find the scumbag. The way things are going, I'll still manage to get tanked up tonight.

The snow seemed to be falling more thickly now. A right bloody blizzard! Even with the high beam on, I could hardly see two metres in front of me.

Lines of refugees struggled past by the roadside. When the snow first came in June, people still hoped it was a *practical joke of nature*. But then the sea rose and carried away the joke. When day dawned, the foundations of the hotels and planned skyscrapers on *Velika Plaža* beach, hyped up to be a copy of the bluish, futuristic towers of Abu Dhabi, were under water. A few days later the sea swamped a village of weekenders up behind the beach. Ugly, illegally built houses sank in the swirling waters as the sea took over the responsibility of the building inspectorate. Whoever fled when the first waves were lapping their houses was able to take a few belongings with them. The optimists copped it bad, as usual: they'd thought the worst-case scenario was far-fetched, so they eventually had to be evacuated by helicopter from the rooves of their houses. People struggled to the town in makeshift rafts and boats and kissed the ground when they landed, as if they'd discovered a new continent. But the water kept surging further inland until it also flooded the suburbs. Camps were organised in hilly parts of town for the people who'd *been forced to leave their homes*, as all reports in all languages said in the same pathos-ridden tone. These folk now plodded the town like zombies in search of food. The shops had long been closed because supplying a town surrounded by water was impracticable, so the impertinent starvelings forced their way into houses and tried to steal food. Contrary to all international conventions on the rights of refugees, the residents shot them and threw their bodies out onto the road so cars would run over them and hungry dogs tear them up.

They announced on the radio that there'd been another fifty-centimetre rise in the sea level *globally* – they used precisely that word. In Ulcinj itself, the water reached all the way up to the town council building. They took the opportunity to remind listeners that the Bojana River sometimes used to overflow its banks in winter months before the dam on the Drin River was built, with the flood-water coming all the way up to where the post-earthquake council building was built. The studio guest was an environmentalist, an idiot who claimed this was yet more proof of the theory that all of nature was in equilibrium.

'The water has returned to where it once was, you see, because water has a memory, just like the planet remembers,' he said with thrill in his voice.

'But what's happening now, in your view?' the compère wanted to know. 'Where is this wave of cold coming from? And these floods?'

'I don't know,' the ecologist admitted, 'but I appeal to listeners not to be taken in by stories about a catastrophe, because one thing is certain: there is a rational explanation.'

Of course, just like there's an irrational one. As usual, all we lack is an explanation which might explain things.

'And now to recap on today's main news,' the anchorman recited: *People all around the planet are awaiting the end of the world tonight.*

Then the international news editor took the microphone. Among the mass of trivia he read, a story from Izmir caught my attention. A man with a deranged son had decided to clean up an overgrown and neglected olive grove. It had once belonged to a prominent dervish who taught that the olive tree brings people closer to God.

Although he was getting on in years, the man worked day after day in the olive grove. It was close to the sea but far from the road. The only way up to the dervish's host of olive trees was along steep, narrow paths, over dry stone walls and through thick scrub. But the man didn't mind. The more effort he invested in the task he'd set himself, the sooner God would heed his prayers and heal his son, or so he thought.

When the young man asked if he could go with him and help with cleaning up the olive grove, his father concluded that God had heard his prayers and taken pity on him. Ever since childhood, the young man had lived in the confines of his room, alone with his attacks of madness and the medication which didn't help. His father naturally interpreted the wish to join him in this good work as a first sign of his son's recovery.

They set off together for the olive grove one morning. That evening, the son returned home alone.

The police inquest revealed that he had killed his father and thrown his body into the sea.

When they asked him why he did it, he said God had ordered him to.

Chapter Six

in which Emmanuel tells of the false messiah Sabbatai Zevi,
a secret society of his resolute followers, the burial of
The Book of the Coming and the day of its resurrection

from: emmanuel@gmail.com
to: thebigsleep@yahoo.com

As I've mentioned, Fra Dolcino left a manuscript in the Franciscan monastery on the banks of Bojana River announcing he would be resurrected. It was hidden in the walls of the friary. Several years later, when it became clear that all further resistance to the furious Novarese besieging Mount Rubello was futile and only defeat and death lay ahead, he entrusted his secret to a handful of his closest pupils.

Over three centuries later, in the garden of the imperial palace in Istanbul, the Sultan asked: *Where do you wish to be exiled?* Sabbatai Zevi replied: *To Ulcinj.* He had Dolcino's secret in mind.

What we read today as the biography of Sabbatai Zevi *may* correspond to the historical truth about him. On the other hand, it may be that most of the things we know about him, starting with the year of his birth and through to the year of his death, are only what he *wanted* us to know. Sabbatai Zevi was a first-rate manipulator, a Wildesque figure before Wilde, with his life as his *chef-d'oeuvre*. His antics, sometimes incomprehensible and ludicrously inconsistent but always spectacular, were part of a grandiose project intended to convince the Jews that he was the Messiah. There's not the slightest doubt that he believed it himself.

The year of Zevi's birth is given as 1626. Was that really so, or did Zevi dictate that year to his biographers so that the very date of his birth would seem to confirm his messianic status? After all, there's a Jewish belief that the Messiah will appear on the anniversary of the destruction of the Temple. Zevi's playing with dates of greatest significance to Jews doesn't end there: the self-proclaimed Messiah was born in Smyrna, now Izmir, on 9 August.

That was a Sabbath. He died in Ulcinj on 30 September 1676. That was Yom Kippur.

Zevi died ten years after the failure of his key prophecy – the one according to which he was the King who would return the Jewish people to Israel. Zevi had presaged that this would occur in 1666. He certainly reckoned with the interesting associations awoken by the three sixes. In fact, his whole biography is in three sixes: the year of his birth, his unfulfilled prophecy and his death all end in a six.

The books say that Zevi stood out even as a child. He didn't easily get on with the other boys studying to be rabbis. He had periods of deep melancholy alternating with phases of wild euphoria. (Dr Schulz would definitely have recognised the symptoms of bipolar disorder.) At the time, many considered them a sign that the young Zevi was *the chosen one*. At the age of twenty-five, Zevi proclaimed: 'I am the Messiah and will return my people to Israel,' and he immediately declared the abolition of God's Law. He called on the followers gathered around him to eat non-kosher food. He put on a lunatic performance and publically wedded the Torah. In a later phase of his messianic madness, he tore up and trampled on the Torah, and then desecrated leather tefilins containing the holy verses. This man, whom two women had left because he'd shown no interest in them, now became sexually insatiable. He demanded of his followers that they bring him their maiden daughters to create a harem. What was more, he claimed he could have intercourse with virgins and they would remain pure.

Zevi's theologians wrote: 'As long as taboos regarding incest prevail on Earth it will be impossible to carry out union *from above*. The mystic annulment of the ban on incest will allow man to *become like his Creator and learn the secrets of the Tree of Life*.'

While Zevi enjoyed the pleasures of promiscuity, the Sultan was worried. On 6 February 1666, he ordered that Zevi be arrested. The Jewish prophet had become a danger to his throne. Jews from all over Europe poured into the Empire to follow the Messiah. Others were preparing to sell all their belongings and follow him to Israel. Many Christians, even learned ones, attentively and optimistically awaited confirmation that Zevi held the truth. Henry Oldenburg wrote to Spinoza: 'All the world here is talking of the return of the Israelites to their own country. Should the news be confirmed, it may bring about a revolution in all things.'

Instead of leading to revolution, Zevi was led in chains before the Sultan. He was given the choice: Islam or death. If he didn't wish to adopt Islam, the Sultan was prepared to let him demonstrate his power: a master archer would loose an arrow at his breast, and if he was indeed the Messiah it certainly wouldn't be difficult for him to perform a miracle and stop the arrow. Zevi didn't hesitate for an instant: he removed his Jewish cap and donned a Turkish turban. The Messiah had changed faith at the last moment.

Aziz Mehmed Efendi, as Zevi was called after his conversion to Islam, didn't relinquish Judaism completely or sincerely, and certainly not voluntarily and free of coercion. He continued to perform Jewish rites and even to preach in synagogues. The fact that he'd become a Muslim didn't prevent him from continuing to claim he was the Jewish Messiah. The Sultan, who'd hoped Zevi's conversion would make Jews flock to Islam, watched this messianic carnival with increasing consternation.

In the end, he decided to banish Zevi. It seems this is just what Zevi had been hoping for. He tried to persuade the Sultan that Ulcinj was an ideal town for exile – at the outer edge of the Empire, at the end of all roads. He'd be quite far away and out of sight there, in the fortress above the sea.

Ulcinj was populated at this time by pirates: both local buccaneers and Barbary corsairs. It was the most recalcitrant town in the whole of the Ottoman Empire. The people of Ulcinj feared neither God nor master. Being so wild and reckless, they'd sabre Zevi if he dared to bother them with his follies, the Sultan thought. 'Let it be Ulcinj then,' he pronounced.

The Ulcinj pirates were a plague on shipping and even raided the Venetian possessions in the Adriatic. In the years to come, the Sublime Porte's conflict with these outlaws would escalate into an undeclared but no less savage war. The Pasha of Skadar was ordered to attack and set fire to a dozen of the Ulcinj pirates' vessels. When the Sultan sent a missive to Ulcinj the following year demanding that further ships be burned, the pirates killed the messenger and threw his body from the town's walls.

The Venetian authorities, for their own part, were itching to take action but realised that Ulcinj lay in Turkish territory. They didn't want to risk war with the Empire. Instead, they sought to resolve the problem by diplomatic means. One Venetian dispatch even appealed to the Sultan's vanity: 'All the inhabitants of Dalmatia and Albania are astonished that you allow the pirates of Ulcinj to so audaciously flout your authority.'

The ship carrying Zevi and twenty-nine families of his followers approached Ulcinj. A black cloud was circling above the town and the travellers watched it in trepidation. As they disembarked on the beach below the fortress, the birds were on the sand, waiting with beady eyes. They seemed to be sizing up the newcomers, whose hands trembled and knees knocked: 'As if we'd arrived in Hell!' one of the women wailed. More and more of the feathered creatures poured forth, cawing, from caverns beneath the fortress, which would ultimately collapse in the earthquake of 1979, and rose up above Zevi and his following like a black flood to sow fear in even the bravest hearts. Imagine the sky above us in black turmoil as we ascend the stone stairs towards the fortress gate. Anxiety and despair are in the eyes of Zevi's followers, but in Zevi's I see only joy, for the circling murder of crows which blocks out the sun has shown him *the sign*.

Fra Dolcino's followers had been unable to keep the secret he'd entrusted to them. Drunken mouths let it slip out and inquisitive ears were listening. As stories have a way of finding those who want to hear them, the story about Fra Dolcino and his hidden manuscript made it all the way to Smyrna. Zevi listened with disdain to those who spoke of Dolcino being a madman, illusionist and trickster. He knew Dolcino had hidden his book because he intended to return. But there could only be one Messiah. Therefore Zevi was determined to destroy the book of the 'false prophet'.

Zevi spent his days in Ulcinj in writing and prayer. He carved the Star of David into the wall of his tower and there he spoke with God, whom he'd never renounced. Zevi left Ulcinj only twice: once he went to Bojana River to try and find Dolcino's book in the ruins of the Franciscan monastery; the other time he travelled to the Archdiocese in Bar to try and find some trace of the book or at least rekindle his hope that the search would bear fruit.

Zevi would have gone to the very ends of the earth to find Dolcino's book: his thoughts probed the distance in search of it. But the whole time it seems to have been right under his very nose.

Twenty years after Zevi's death, the Morean War was raging. A Venetian fleet assembled in the sea off Ulcinj. It was 10 August 1696. Historical documents state: 'The aim of the attack was to take the town and destroy the pirate nest because all attempts by the Venetians to wipe out the pirates in battles at sea had been unsuccessful.'

The blatant lies of history! As he was deploying his ships before Ulcinj, *General Providur* Daniel Dolfino IV thought back to the day his uncle told him Fra Dolcino's secret. His uncle had spoken slowly, and he, still a boy, had stared widemouthed and absorbed every word. The air around them had burned on that serene, summer day, just like today, when he and his army were finally so close to the book he'd sworn to retake for Christendom.

The *General Providur* believed he'd find the book hidden in the wall of the church which the infidel had turned into a mosque. When the monastery by Bojana River had been destroyed, one of the Franciscan friars, who knew Dolcino's secret, had taken the book and hidden it in the church in Ulcinj's Old Town. But Ulcinj fell to the Mohammedans. *Today people captured on pirate raids are sold as slaves in the church square,* Daniel Dolfino thought with disgust. *And there, overlooking the square, is the tower where the Jewish prophet who became a Mohammedan lived until his death. Pah, work of the infidel!* With God's aid, order would soon be returned to that part of the world: shipping in the Adriatic would be free of the infidel threat, Ulcinj would be Christian again, and he would finally get hold of the book which had fired his imagination for so many years – the book he believed to contain the answers to so many questions humanity could only ask with fear.

It's noon, and a mistral from the sea fills the sails of the Venetian ships. Standing beside the general, I can see the deadly determination in his eyes. *Fire!* he commands his troops.

The siege of Ulcinj lasted almost one month. In the end, the Venetian troops re-boarded their ships and returned to the Bay of Kotor. They'd managed to take the town of Ulcinj and well nigh raze it to the ground; they'd also blocked off the aqueduct. But the pirate stronghold had not fallen.

Rain beat against the windows of the Venetian headquarters in Perast. In the library, *General Providur* Daniel Dolfino wrote his report to his superiors: 'We were unable to take Ulcinj, but if the main goal was to punish the audacity and arrogance of the pirates, we have at least taught them a lesson.' History books would describe his campaign as a partial success. But he alone knew how immense and utter his defeat was. All the honour and glory of this world would be worthless to him after that. Until the end of his earthly days he'd dream of the former church – now a mosque – up in the unassailable Ulcinj fortress; he'd dream of opening the book whose words would take him by the hand and lead him to where only the elect may go.

Back in his Smyrna days, Zevi arrived at the idea that all books and human knowledge are not only superfluous but a diabolical burden on humanity's shoulders. He was completely obsessed by this idea during his ten-year stay in Ulcinj. Knowledge, he told his followers, prevents us from hearing the clear message of God. We may thus assume that Zevi was familiar with the teachings of Thomas Müntzer. 'Bibel, Bubel, Babel – Bible-babble and Babylon: all that clutter has to be discarded so we can turn directly to God,' Müntzer wrote. 'The scholars think it's sufficient to read the Word of God in books and spit it out raw, like a stork spits out frogs for its young in the nest.'

Müntzer was Luther's student: a brilliant intellectual who burned with hatred towards everything that in the slightest way resembled intellect. Not inappropriately, they dubbed him the *Apostle of the Ignorant*. In his reckoning with books, Müntzer elevated the illiterate masses to author-ised expositors of Scripture. The weakening of the authority of the Catholic Church also weakened its Truth, which at that time was the backbone of the world. Now, in place of that backbone, doomsday movements embedded implants fashioned in smithies and sheds, forests and caves. Their peg-leg-ged Truth was crooked, crippled and lame. The common people took the matter into their own hands and Europe was ravaged by myriad groups guided by grotesquely distorted ideas. The people intervened in the corpus of the Christian idea, carrying out their operations with butcher-like preci-sion. After this surgery by the 'popular experts', Christian Europe resembled Frankenstein. All across Europe, cities blazed, outlaw communities replaced liturgy with sexual perversions, cannibalism took over from Communion in places, and the ground was soaked with blood. Under the rule of mille-narians, one contemporary wrote, 'the world is awash in a torrent of blood which will rise as high as a horse's head'.

Unlike Müntzer, who rejected all books, Zevi recommended the world one title – the one he himself authored and titled *The Book of the Coming*. But it will only be read when he arises and brings the Truth. For the interim, he left a fake book in this world of lies: *The Glory of the Return*, which he wrote by candlelight during the long nights in his tower, before the Star of David. Zevi considered that this book, which explains his teachings and the future of his people, contains just about as much truth as the world can bear. He bequeathed a difficult task to his followers, who would pass his words from mouth to mouth through many generations up until today: they must destroy his fake book, as well as that of the false messiah Fra Dolcino, before he can return and bring with him the real Holy Book. His followers had to find and burn those two books, otherwise his coming would be prevented and his people would continue to roam the world without peace and without a home.

Zevi left Ulcinj in the same way he arrived – spectacularly. Back when he disembarked on the beach below the fortress, black birds had risen up to meet him. On his last day he was strolling through the town in the company of two followers. They came across a group of people gathered around a fig tree, crying. A woman held in her arms a lifeless boy who'd fallen out of the tree. Then Zevi said: 'O Lord, send back this child and take me instead!' The boy opened his eyes and started to cry, while Zevi fell down dead on the cobbles. As the people lifted up his body and bore it away in wonder and gratitude, a murder of crows circled above them.

Now you know it all. The Ulcinj Library was burned down because Dolcino's book lay hidden there among all the worthless titles. Daniel Dolfino IV had been right – Dolcino's book really was hidden in the wall of the former church, now a mosque, in the Old Town. Workers renovating the church after the cataclysmic earthquake of 1979 found it, after which it was kept at the Ulcinj Library. The staff there didn't know its value and consigned it to a depot for old books no one wanted.

About a hundred of Zevi's followers had gone with him to Ulcinj. Although they'd all formally adopted Islam, in their hearts they'd never renounced Judaism. After Zevi's death, they scattered to all parts of the world: some returned to Smyrna, while others went as far away as Australia. They in turn died, but their descendants learned to preserve the secret of their faith about what lay buried in the hill cemetery above Ulcinj. Where did the devotees come from to carry out their assignment and await the coming of the Messiah? Who'll ever know – perhaps from Turkey, where they're called Dönmeh, or from California, where Yakov Leib HaKohain of Galata in Istanbul went to gather the faithful and prepare them for Zevi's return.

When Zevi had felt his end drawing near, he crept out of the fortress and climbed up to the cemetery with a group of his disciples. There his *Book of the Coming* was buried in a tomb, following ancient rites. The Messiah would thus have his Holy Book nearby when he arose at his burial place in Ulcinj.

Zevi's fake book, *The Glory of the Return*, was stolen from the house of the Vukotićs, who'd bought it at auction in London. Zevi's followers are fiendishly cunning: they burned down an entire library to cover up their burning of one book. And in order to conceal their theft of the other, they killed an entire family and left misleading clues.

From the Vukotićs', they went straight to the old Jewish cemetery where *The Book of the Coming* lay waiting in deep, sylvan oblivion. There, on the grave of Zevi's true book, they performed a ritual according to rules laid down by the Messiah himself and burned his fake script.

The first book had been destroyed in the library fire. The second was burned at the cemetery. The third was now dug out of its tomb: the Messiah could come again.

Chapter Seven

*in which we briefly enter a public house, venture into a dark marsh
and hear of self-pity and grace as Lazar tells his story; we meet
singing nuns, and a company of drunken friends confess their sins*

What drove Lazar to kill the Vukotićs that evening? Or rather: what
stopped him from killing them *before* that?

If I hadn't lived through the war here, I wouldn't know. But I
saw what happens when the safety net of social relations fails and
social masks are dropped – when *the truth about us* gets out. I saw
the collapse of the world in which we'd played our little roles as
good people and friendly neighbours. Like when a dam bursts, the
water floods through, and the peaceful valley of the world we knew
is suddenly swamped by the deluge of our desires. All the dead of the
wars of the 1990s are a bodycount of the fantasies and deepest desires
of our neighbours and fellow human beings.

A man lives with his neighbours in 'peace and harmony' for
decades. Ask anyone in the local area about him and they'll tell you
he's a peaceful, friendly guy. Isn't the crime news in the papers always
the same? Don't people always describe their neighbour in the same
way, and then – out of the blue – he commits a terrible, bloodthirsty
crime? He conforms to social conventions for years and years. But then
comes a day when he follows his own desires: he goes into the house
of people he's lived alongside in peace and love for decades and kills
them all. Who is the man living next door? Who is the criminal from
our wars? An *ordinary man*, a good neighbour of forty years standing,
who under the sway of ideology, religion or whatever, blows a fuse and
commits the crime? No: he's a killer who wished to see his neighbours
dead for forty years and one day finally did what he'd *always wanted*.

It's the same with *sincere* friends. My good friend is drunk: he
comes up to me and insults me; he tells me he despises me – no, he
hates me, a hatred I deserve for things I've done, some of them in the

distant, common past, which he enumerates and describes with what feels like the inhuman precision of a surveillance device. When I see him again the next day, he stands before me with his head bowed and apologises. 'Please forgive me, I was drunk,' he says.

What is my friend actually apologising for? Not for what he thinks and feels, but for having *said* what he thinks. He apologises for truth having punctured the condom of interpersonal consideration under the influence of alcohol. His apology is a request for me to reject the obvious: yes, that is what he really thinks about me. Hypocrisy is at the very heart of so-called good interpersonal relations. It's the very core of our everyday forgiveness. Usually we forgive what is done to us and manage to ignore the fundamental question of *why* it was done to us. Even if we forgive from the position of a good Christian, we do so in the full knowledge that there's a final arbiter, our God, who considers the claim for clemency once again. What's more, we forgive in full awareness that we have to forgive for our own sins to be forgiven. So that the outcome of the trial in which we are being judged be favourable, we have to relinquish our authority in the trial where we are the judge and transfer the matter to the 'Supreme Court'. We forgive, fully aware of the existence of the Heavenly Bank of Sin, in which every transgression counts. Our interests in the Bank of Sin render us fundamentally incapable of forgiving: a person can only truly forgive if their grace is disinterested. Ours never is, therefore it isn't grace.

* * *

One of the Vukotićs' neighbours told me he'd seen Lazar drunk several times at the Lonely Hearts bar, where I didn't go because it was frequented by the local working class. An essential precondition for joining the struggle for the rights of the working class is that you not know the working class. After all, ignorance is the precondition for every struggle: as soon as we get to know something well, we can no longer imagine fighting for it.

The local proletarians met at the Lonely Hearts to dream of better days and drink away their wages. Despite the flood and snowstorm, the place was packed that night. The owner of the Lonely Hearts was nicknamed Pasha. No one remembered his real name any more. He was a petty crook from Bosnia who came to Ulcinj like so many others to escape the war. The natives of Ulcinj are wise: they know that current adversities will be replaced by the adversities to come. One occupier will replace another – one despot will be deposed by the next. This makes them paragons of patience, in no hurry to replace their current misfortune with the next in the sequence of misfortunes. In fact, if the misfortune lasts long enough you become so used to it that you can't imagine your life without it. The natives of Ulcinj know how to get on with people like Pasha: they let them live next door and just don't allow their bars, quarrels and shams to affect their lives.

Pasha owed me a favour, like many other people in town. His problem was that he treated people like idiots. That's not a bad basis for success in life, in principle, as long as you're not an idiot yourself. Pasha was.

Things were bound to blow up in his face sooner or later. I made sure he survived the blast. Therefore, when I entered the Lonely Hearts, I expected that I'd just need to do a bit of the mandatory, folksy *not-on-your-life-mate* haggling, and that Pasha would then tell me where to find Lazar.

In 1999, long lines of Kosovar refugees poured into Ulcinj, fleeing from the Serbian troops or NATO's bombs. Many of these displaced people dreamed of making it to Europe. Pasha offered to help them achieve that dream.

Serious criminals sailed from Montenegrin harbours for Italy in boats full of refugees. Some of the vessels made it to the other side of the Adriatic, others sank and took with them many a dream of good wages, second-hand Mercedeses and savings for building garishly painted villas near Prizren and Priština with decorative plaster lions on the balconies.

Of all the human traffickers, Pasha was the cheapest. This was partly because he operated with the lowest overheads and partly because people paid him to take them to Italy – but he didn't take them there. Pasha would load his clients into a truck and cart them through Montenegro all night: from Ulcinj to Kolašin, from Kolašin to Nikšić, from Nikšić to Risan, then round the Bay of Kotor, via Budva, and back to Ulcinj. The others all used boats, but he stuck to good old terra firma, Pasha boasted. At dawn he'd unload the people on the sandy beach of Bojana Island near Ulcinj, at the southernmost tip of Montenegro. The refugees looked around in confusion because they couldn't see a single structure or anything that might have confirmed to them that they were really in Italy. 'Just keep walking a bit, and when you meet someone, wish them *Buon giorno*!' Pasha instructed them, before hopping back into the truck and speeding off.

The refugees would roam along the beach with suitcases in hand until they came across a local watchman who, to their astonishment, would reply to their *Buon giorno* with obscenities in Albanian.

Pasha's plan had only one flaw: it overlooked what would happen next. The refugees would realise he'd ripped them off and would then have no other goal in life than to kill him. I'm a well-informed man: as soon as I heard they were after Pasha I sent him to a friend's place in Bar, where he hid until the furious refugees had returned to Kosovo.

While I waited for Pasha to familiarise some new female staff with the house rules, I realised that the Lonely Hearts had extended its range: along with the terrible drink, guests could now pay for hideously ugly prostitutes. One of them, a wench with part blonde, part black hair and a few missing teeth, offered me the services of one of the *beautiful girls*, she emphasised.

'No thanks, I've already got a full collection of STDs,' I said.

'Then at least buy me a drink,' she insisted. She was obviously thirsty, and a gentleman always helps a damsel in distress.

'Aren't you the local Sherlock Holmes?' she asked as she was quaffing her brandy.

'More like Philip Marlowe,' I corrected her. 'Holmes keeps women at an arm's length, whereas Marlowe takes them under his wing, only to destroy them later.'

'I love Holmes films,' she avowed, determined to continue our cultured conversation. 'What I like most is when he shows how clever he is: you know, when he just looks at someone, and the next instant he can tell you everything about them after having seen just a few details, which only he has noticed. Can you do that too?' she wondered.

'I could give it a try,' I said. 'Since you don't stink of sweat like the other whores in this joint, I infer you weren't working today. Therefore I assume Pasha has set you aside for himself because only his mistresses are entitled to days off. I see you've swabbed two inches of powder on your face and also note that you've washed your hair. That means you want to appeal to Pasha and be attractive for him. That, in turn, means that you hope to stay his mistress. Who knows, with a bit of luck he might even marry you. After all, doesn't every man ultimately want to settle down with a good woman by his side? But that's not going to happen: even if we live to see tomorrow, the day will bring a girl younger than you. Then Pasha will give you the boot. You're afraid of that, and it's on your mind. Warm?'

'You have no idea,' she snorted and demonstratively relieved me of her company. I wouldn't want to sound pretentious, but I'm pretty sure I managed to drive her to tears.

Half an hour later I was in the boat, passing what remained of the petrol station. Pasha had done me a favour: I now knew that Lazar lived in one of the stilt houses on Saltern Canal and had done so ever since coming to Ulcinj.

The canal had once been navigable. When King Nicholas of Montenegro captured Ulcinj, he named the canal Port Milena in honour of his wife. Princely sailboats would moor there. The establishment of the nearby salt works turned the canal into a giant fish pond because the salt it released into the water attracted the fish. Dozens of stilt houses sprang up on the canal; local fisherfolk would lower nets into the water, and when they raised them again they were full of catch. Later the canal devolved into a cesspool because the houses which grew up all around discharged their sewage straight into it. Soon there were no more fish in the canal. The people left too. Punting on the canal had once been a favourite pastime of the Montenegrin royal family. Now going to the canal meant venturing deep into a marsh.

My trusty boat cut the calm water, which was topped with floating pieces of furniture from submerged houses. Two crows were riding on the carcass of a cow and blithely pecking at its entrails. Drowned people drifted past, too, their bodies grotesquely rounded like blow-up dolls. I pulled my scarf over my face and tried not to inhale the stench. Whenever the boat bumped into them I'd use the oar to push aside those bodies – their hearts now home to beetles and worms, not love – and then continued on my way. Just like a slice of bread always falls butter-side down, drowned people always float with their face in the water, it occurred to me.

I paddled along the former boulevard leading to *Velika Plaža*. The roof of a truck protruded from the water in the parking lot in front of the shopping centre. There had been no power in the region for weeks. The metal lamp-posts swayed in the wind. The billboards still announced summer fun: a buxom singer performed on a terrace by the sea, a tanned brunette advertised sun cream promising protection from skin cancer, and there was a new line of fruit ice cream which *took care of your children's teeth*. I passed abandoned auto repair shops and bakeries. Restaurant terraces where cheerful tourists had bobbed and skipped to folk dances from home were now swimming pools for ducks.

Large snowflakes descended silently from the dark sky. It was frigid in the marsh, the kind of damp cold which really gets into your bones. People kept saying this was the cold of the End, but I remember well the cold of the beginning, from my childhood. On the coldest of winter days, when the salt works' canals turned to ice, I'd go there to hunt ducks. I'd creep through the snow-covered dunes and, small as I was, hide in the reeds around the edges of the frozen ponds. I tied rags or strips of hessian around my boots. That allowed me to run on the ice and gave me a decisive advantage – it made the hunt possible in the first place. A duck on the ice is slow. It has trouble taking off because it needs a run-up, which is difficult on the ice, and its clumsy legs let it down. A duck on the ice is like Ollie in the Laurel and Hardy films: fat and ungainly. It falls over a few times before getting the forward motion needed to take off, and that gave me the chance to reach it and kill it with my stick. I remember the duck would sometimes get airborne, and then I'd hit it with my stick like a baseball player slams the ball.

A lamp was on in one of the stilt houses – like a lighthouse showing me the way, I thought. I turned off the motor, trying to sneak up on Lazar unnoticed.

I found father and son there in the small, cluttered space, huddled up to an old woodstove. The old man was sitting in an ancient armchair with springs sticking out, one of those communist replicas of 1950's American design, which were once used to furnish hotels on the coast.

He sat there calmly, like A. Lincoln in his Washington memorial.

'He's blind and deaf – he has been for twenty years,' Lazar said in a low voice.

But the old man was nodding to a rhythm only he could hear.

'I know who you are, and I know why you've come,' Lazar whispered. I've been expecting you. The police or someone else. As soon as I killed them I knew I'd be punished. I'm not afraid of punishment. Look where I live and how I live. Punish me – it'll be my salvation.'

I sat down on a stool close to the stove to warm my frozen toes. I pulled the bottle out of my coat pocket and took a good swig.

'Why did you do it?' I demanded.

'The real truth, Sir, is that I don't know. Back then I thought I knew: I was furious and felt I had to kill them all that instant. But when I look back at what I did, and I have time to look back at my actions – what else is there to do here? – I realise I didn't have a reason. At least none which people would understand.'

'Still, if we tried, you'd be surprised what I can understand,' I encouraged him.

He explained that he'd come to Ulcinj from Vojvodina in northern Serbia, where he'd lived with his family and his father.

'It feels like he's always been old,' he said, pointing at his father. 'Look at him: can you believe he was once young?!'

Back home, in the plains of Central Europe, Lazar had been a repair man: people would call him, and he'd go and get their things running again.

'It was an honest job, but honest jobs don't earn much money. I got used to poverty, and I always knew I'd die poor. But my family wanted more, so I became the scapegoat for their *miserable lives*, as they called them. Have you ever felt the contempt of your own children?' he asked. 'Do you know what it's like when your children say to your face that you're *a loser, a coward, a weakling, a sucker*? That your father is *an old vampire who refuses to die and make us happy*? For days on end, even on Sundays, I'd be rushing from house to house, eternally tired and dirty, but that wasn't good enough for them. No sirree, they always wanted more. My father and I became unwelcome in our own home – the house I'd built with my own hands.

'That's why we left. I'd heard there was a lot of building going on in Montenegro on the coast and that tradesmen were in demand, so we moved here. And it worked out: I got a job at a building site. We were doing well, me and the old man. Until I took a fall from the scaffolding. Now I'm lame in one leg and drag it behind me like a club-foot. There are lots of strapping young men looking for work, so who needs an old limper?

'Just when I thought I couldn't earn a crust here any more – just when it looked like the two of us would have to hit the road again, the Vukotićs gave me a job. Madam Vukotić opened the gate and immediately took pity on me. She asked me inside, gave me a good meal, and I started work there the very next day. She was a kind woman, Senka – soft-hearted, and that went to her head. It's not good to pity people. Don't mind me saying so, but you look like someone who understands that. It's not good even to pity oneself. I'm inclined to self-pity, you see, and that's really made my life hell. It's a great evil: I've killed people, but I still feel sorry for myself.

'We moved into this stilt house here. How should I put it – it's not exactly five-star luxury, but at least it's rent-free. My pay at the Vukotićs' was substantial. We lacked nothing, and we two old boys could have gone on like that for years. But I kept thinking about my wife and children and the house, as much as I tried not to; every night my thoughts flew back to Vojvodina and I'd cry the whole night through when I thought what grief and injustice had befallen me. It was driving me nuts, and I started drinking and gambling at the Lonely Hearts … You know how it is: when you gamble drunk you lose, and then you need another drink.

'My pay at the Vukotićs' was good, like I said. But I needed more, and the Vukotićs had enough. I thought I could take from them without them noticing. A little for them was a lot for me.

'So I stole from them. Nothing big, you know: a tenner or twenty from the purse Senka used to leave on the kitchen table when she came back from shopping and went up to her room to get changed. A vase or two, or a piece of jewellery.

'One day when I was painting the tool shed Senka brought me out a cold glass of lemonade. And then she said nonchalantly, like just in passing: "I'd ask you not to steal from us any more." She didn't wait for an answer but simply turned and went back into the house.

'That night I thought I'd die of shame. There was no one for me to confide in, so I sat here with my deaf father almost through till dawn, even though he was mostly sleeping in his armchair like he's drowsing now, and wrung out my heart. I'd become a good-for-nothing in the eyes of the people who'd been so good to me, people whose kindness meant we still had work and a roof over our heads and weren't forced to wander the world in misery as a cripple and a geriatric.

'I tried to apologise to Senka and promised it wouldn't happen again. She told me with a compassion which hurt, as if I was a lowly creature crawling the earth, that no explanation was needed and that she knew very well what extremes people can be driven to by poverty. She said she didn't hold anything against me and that, as far as she was concerned, nothing had happened: "We've taken you in and decided to help you – we'll give you another chance."

'But not one month had passed, and I took to stealing again. The Lonely Hearts may be the cheapest bar in town but it was still too expensive for me. This time Senka invited me into the house, served me some chocolate cake, and then raked me over the coals in front of the whole family: although they'd already forgiven me once, I kept on stealing from them. They were disappointed, she said, but they realised I had it hard and knew I'd have nowhere to go if they gave up on me, so they wouldn't send me away. But I should be aware that it was *truly deplorable* how low I'd fallen – those were the words she used.

'Instead of vexation and regret, this time I felt anger. When they saw me out into the garden and Senka gave me instructions for mowing the lawn, I was brimming with hatred towards her. Yes, they'd helped me when I was in a tight spot. But did that give them the right to humiliate me, what's more in front of the children: I often told stories to them about the olden days and they seemed truly happy listening to them. What would the children think of me now? *My transgression is one thing. Please punish me, Madam Vukotić, I seethed inside as I turned on the lawnmower, but don't put me down in front of the children. Perhaps you think I'm so wretched that I don't even deserve punishment. Is that what you want to say, that even punishment is too good for me? Don't those who are punished, even those who are punished most harshly (especially them!) warrant a modicum of respect? Don't those who are punished at least regain their dignity in the end? Isn't it a terrible crime to rob the punished of their human dignity, bigger by all means than the one I committed in stealing? Did you employ me to work for you, Madam Vukotić, or for you to practice your kindliness on me? When I trudge off home in the evenings, do you stand in front of the mirror and admire your own virtue?'* Lazar foamed with rage, squirming in his chair.

'I kept on working as best I could. I pruned the orchard, hoed the garden, repaired the water heaters and pipes, but I was determined not to put up with any more humiliation. For days on end I quietly practiced a speech to give to Senka, one she'd *have to* listen to. Oh yes: no one would interrupt Lazar mid-sentence any more. *You have my gratitude but that doesn't mean you can look down on me. I work for you, but I'm not a lesser human being,* I was going to tell her.

'One day I was in the tool shed making a new handle for the axe, when she popped in to look for an improvised watering can. "Madam Vukotić –," I spoke in as decisive a voice as I could muster. "Not now, Lazar!" she snuffed, rummaging on the shelf. Fed up with everything and white-hot with anger, I stormed up to her and grabbed her by the arm. She wheeled around abruptly: I felt her sweet breath on my face, and the tips of her large breasts brushed me.

'She hadn't expected this. For the first time since we'd known each other it wasn't pity she felt. I could see fear in her eyes. *What now? What's he going to do to me?* she was thinking.

'For a few seconds I stood before her, proud, enjoying that superiority. Then she pushed me aside, moved away, and declared in that same condescending, matronly tone, which drives me mad even now when I think about it, that her husband wouldn't find out what had just happened. I should be ashamed of myself. She hadn't expected this from me, but she'd forgive me one more time. As she left, she added: "You don't need to worry about your job. You're a walking disaster – you don't need punishment when you've got yourself."

'I left their property, determined never to go back again. I sat and drank at the Lonely Hearts until evening, muttering to myself: *Lazar may be poor, but he still has pride. He'll make sure no lady looks down on him again.*

'Drunk, humiliated and livid with rage, I went back up the hill to their property. I had the key to the gate, so I entered the grounds without being seen. I took my tools from the shed: knife, spade and axe. I put my work gloves on. When I look back at that night, I don't think I intended to kill anyone. I just wanted respect. But why then did I put the gloves on, you may ask? I have no answer to that, at least none people would understand. I rang the doorbell, determined to speak my mind to Senka, say thank-you for her kindness and leave with my head held high.

'I had to ring three times before she came down and opened the door. As soon as she saw me, the browbeating began: I'd really gone too far now. Did I know what time it was? I couldn't wake them this late, and I was drunk as well. She told me to go home and sleep it off, and they'd decide what to do with me the next day. I tried to speak, but she went on and on, bombarding me with words which came down on my head like a hammer.

'I shut my eyes and swung the axe,' he said.

'But the children and her husband: why them?' I asked.

'They were woken by the noise. If only I'd killed her with the first blow … But she staggered and knocked over the vase before falling to the floor. It smashed damn loudly, like a gunshot. That's what woke them. It's all because of the vase that they're now dead.

'Pavle was at the stairs and saw me kill her. He went for the shotgun. I had no choice. I had to go all the way and get rid of them all,' he said calmly. 'I'm pedantic – when I start a job I always finish it. Then I removed all the traces, or so I thought. I threw the knife into the marsh. Only then, drunk with alcohol and blood, did I realise that I'd forgotten the axe. Since then I've been living in anticipation of the police coming to get me.

'It was hardest with Helena. I'd got on with her the best, and I'll miss her the most. I took her to the couch and switched on the television for her. She liked watching programmes about animals. I sat down beside her and, to tell you the truth, I started to cry,' Lazar said.

I lit a cigarette and knocked back a good swig from my bottle. I looked at the old man. He muttered in his sleep and his dry lips moved quickly. It looked like he was praying.

'Are you going to take me to the police station now?' Lazar asked.

'She was right,' I said.

'Who?'

'That woman, Senka – she was right: we don't need punishment when we've got ourselves.'

On the way out I turned to look at them once more: the killer and his old father by the stove. 'How much money did you take from the safe?' I asked.

'What safe?' Lazar replied, startled, as if shaken from deep thought. 'The Vukotićs were prudent: they kept their money in the bank. If there was a safe in the house, I didn't know about it.'

I got back into the boat and left the marsh as quickly as I could. Like people say, trouble never comes alone. As if the cold and the snow blowing in my face weren't enough to make me miserable, I'd run out of whisky. I disembarked at the town council building's parking lot, broke into the first café and deposited a bottle of Jameson in my coat pocket. I stood in the dark, leaning against the bar, calmly watching Christmas turn the streets white. Many people had turned off the lights in their houses. They stood at the windows waiting, or knelt by their beds and prayed for mercy. Maybe they lay with the blankets over their heads and talked about the past. I went round behind the bar, poured myself a drink and switched on the radio. A witty DJ put on the Sex Pistols and Johnny Rotten screamed *No Future*. I looked at my face in the mirror and sent myself a sincere, warm smile. *Fucking hell, those were good times*, I sighed.

Then my phone rang and shattered my moment of nostalgia like a harbinger of doom. Dragan Vukotić still wanted to avenge his dead brother. What should I tell him – that I had Lazar, and he was longing to be punished? That I had an excellent story with just one unresolved detail: a safe, whose existence I couldn't vouch for because the house had burned down? No thanks, I thought, and hurled the phone out into the snow. I went outside. A howling came from the maternity hospital: a dog had been shut inside and now stood in the dark amongst the empty cradles yowling for someone, anyone, to come.

A group of nuns stood at the traffic lights and called on the occasional passers-by to embrace Christianity. 'Accept Jesus now, the End is nigh!' they shouted. It was like when market stallholders yell, *It's all gotta go!* The group had a well-defined division of labour: some did the hard sell for salvation while the others sang. Their song brought a lot of things home to me, like that they'd actually had no choice but to join the monastery. They certainly wouldn't have made it as a rock band, I told them.

'You mean you don't believe *even today*?!' I was asked by the most inquisitive – or maybe the stupidest.

'No,' I said, 'but you know how it is: I will as soon as I get cancer.'

Our parting feelings for each other couldn't exactly have been called love. Each of them spat after me three times and then hurriedly crossed themselves. Dealing with an old-fashioned gentleman like me is one thing, I thought, but what are they going to do about these fellows who are at least as fervent as them? Six bearded men strode angrily towards them, gesticulating aggressively and going ballistic with umbrage.

As they passed me, heading for the nuns, one of them pointed to the Jameson I was carrying: 'That's *haram* – you'll burn in hell!' he promised.

'Cheers,' I seconded.

If any pub is open tonight, it'll be Johnny's, I reckoned. I got into the car. It started up straight away. Then the shape of a man emerged from the snow, approaching with mighty strides. It was Salvatore.

'Get in,' I told him.

'How are you tonight?' he asked politely.

'Same as ever. When you look at it, it's a day like any other, don't you think?'

'I was up at your place. When I didn't find you, I told myself to go for a walk through town, thinking that perhaps I'd meet you. And there you go: I run smack bang into you. It's a small world. Anyway, you know why I'm looking for you. I thought that by now you could perhaps tell me who killed my son, and why. My wife is waiting for me at home – it's she who sent me to look for you. She said: "Go and ask him so at least we can wait in peace for whatever this night will bring."'

There was nothing for it, I had to improvise. Salvatore listened in silence as I explained what I'd learned: his son had been killed by a madman – an escapee from a mental hospital in Kotor:

'The doctors and nurses left the hospital and a horde of lunatics is now free to roam the country. I pursued the killer for days. Tonight I finally caught up with him in the marsh. It was either him or me. I couldn't get him to give himself up, so I had to shoot. He was swallowed up by the dark water. Now he's lying there somewhere in the mud.'

Salvatore buried his head in his hands and sobbed. 'I knew it,' he said after wiping away his tears. 'What sane person would do that to a child?'

'You can go home,' I told him. 'It's over. It's all over now. I've done what there was to be done. Go back and tell your wife that everything's in its place again.'

He shook my hand firmly and looked at me with tearful eyes full of gratitude. I watched him in the rear-view mirror running off through the blizzard to take the good news home.

I arrived at Johnny's just in time to witness a collective confession. My regular drinking mates were preoccupied with the looming Apocalypse, which they now took for granted. Alcohol was flowing in hectolitres and Johnny was handing out bottle after bottle from behind the bar without a break, obviously determined to have the pub drunk dry by the end of the evening. As they used to say in Partisan films: *Not one grain of wheat should be left for the invaders!* In this final hour, the drunken gang felt the need to let out its deepest secrets and worst sins. They demanded that Father Frano hear their confessions.

'I can't, guys: most of you aren't Catholic, let alone christened,' he said in his defence. This pragmatic country priest had come from Dalmatia thirty years ago and had had to learn quickly how to get on with the wily local flock which gathered in his church on Sundays. He knew that God had no need to listen to the garbage these drunkards would confess. 'We'll do it like this –,' he proposed, 'you'll confide in one another because the most important thing is to be frank with your neighbour and with yourself. God is satisfied with that.'

It really must be high time if even Catholic confessions have become like AA meetings, I thought.

Božo was the first to open up his heart. There was silence while he spoke, apart from the sound of clinking glasses. He made a dramatic pause after every act of adultery he admitted, and Father Frano gave him an indulgent look to embolden him to continue. When Božo finished, his listeners were mildly disappointed: infidelity, drunkenness and domestic violence – all in all, Božo had lived an ordinary, mainstream life.

Frowns crept over the men's faces when Zoran began to tell his sins: 'I'm a poof. Johnny will probably tell you himself when it's his turn, but he's one too: we've had something going for fifteen years. The wife and the kids don't suspect anything, neither mine nor his. I can see in your eyes that you condemn me. I knew it'd be like this, and that's why I never told you. Now you're probably asking yourselves: *How many times did the bugger look at my backside?* I know you are, there's no need to be ashamed. The answer is: not once. I want you to know that you've always just been friends to me. Before you reject me, ask yourselves if I've ever betrayed you … Now that you know the truth, I just want to ask you one thing: please don't turn your back on me.'

An ambiguous request, to say the least! I'd always found him pretty unbearable: his macho pose, easy rider and cowboy boots – what a put-on! I could imagine him wearing red lace knickers under his leathers.

Then it got even worse: Fahro admitted that he'd been sleeping with Božo's wife for years. Even Father Frano seemed bewildered – he was obviously losing control of this little nightly collective confession. It was as if someone had opened Pandora's box and now people, one after another, were saying things which in different circumstances would cause friendships to be broken off and blood to flow.

When Johnny recounted having been raped by three young men at high school in Bar, Father Frano began to cry. Is there anything more unbearable than the moment when people *open up their heart*, as the expression goes? I'd rather watch open-heart surgery than be around at times like this when the toxic waste of human lives leaks out.

In tears, Father Frano described the day he stopped believing in God: 'Nothing spectacular happened that day, I just woke up in the morning and realised that I knew *nothing* about all the people I had advised on how to lead their lives. I didn't understand the souls I had to give pastoral care to, nor did I respect them. I was just the guy that peddled God,' he blubbered.

'That morning I opened my eyes and my whole dismal life flashed before me, right up to its unavoidably wretched end. But I didn't have the strength to throw off the cassock and put an end to the lies. Above all, I didn't have the courage to appear so naked before my family. My vocation as a priest was a great source of pride for them, and leaving the priesthood would definitely be the ultimate disgrace. I thought: if I tell the truth I'll hurt many, and if I keep lying I'll only destroy myself,' Frano said.

Fuck this life! Is this ordeal ever going to end? I screamed to myself. I downed shot after shot of whisky, getting absolutely plastered in the hope of falling unconscious from inebriation and escaping this hell of cheap sincerity – that bastard born of despair from an illicit liaison with fear.

Out of the corner of my eye, I saw Gogi kneel in front of Frano and lower his head into the priest's lap.

'I killed a man,' he said, and an icy draught flowed through the room. 'I've killed a man,' he repeated and stood up, tears running down his face. 'I've killed more than once,' he shouted, drawing a revolver from his pocket and pointing it at his temple.

I couldn't stay a second longer. I felt sick from all the whisky I'd drunk and all the repulsive things I'd heard.

'Stupid, bloody fools!' I yelled and stormed out into the blizzard. *Now everything's fallen apart, I've just lost all my friends.* As I was striding swiftly towards the car, I heard the shot. That was the seal on our doom.

Chapter Eight

in which we learn of an unhappy love affair and the deaths of loved ones, Hedwig reveals to Emmanuel her last and greatest secret, we hear of the cruel death of countless animals and are overwhelmed with powerless remorse

from: emmanuel@gmail.com
to: thebigsleep@yahoo.com

Dr Schulz was particularly intrigued by my father being a detective. 'How interesting, how very interesting,' he muttered into his beard as he paced in circles, gnawing on his pipe and puffing at his vanilla-scented tobacco.

'You see, the desire for an Apocalypse is a sure sign of the inability to cope with anxiety – the inevitable angst of waiting for the endgame which we hope will provide an outcome and an explanation. Not to mention the anxiety of waiting for an answer to the question: is there an outcome and an explanation at all? This anxiety grows as we get closer to an answer and as it becomes ever clearer that there is actually no answer. When we desire an Apocalypse, we're instinctively reaching for the remote control so we can fast-forward through our own life history to the end, like we might do with a gripping detective film. It's like we can no longer resist the urge to find out who committed the crime,' Dr Schulz said.

'God the Father, who brings the Apocalypse, does the same as the sleuth at the end of a well-crafted detective story. At the end, God assembles all those involved in the crime – and what is history but a crime story with humanity as its cast? He gathers everyone together, be they now living or dead, and explains the role of each character in turn: he discloses their hidden motives and intentions, exonerates the innocent, brandmarks the guilty, reveals the truth and clarifies the meaning of every seemingly senseless move by each of the actors. When a good sleuth and God are finished, no further interpretation is possible, there's only applause,' Dr Schulz exclaimed and clapped his hands loudly because he'd noticed that my thoughts had wandered off.

When he was in a good mood or I'd done or said something to arouse his intellectual curiosity, which must have been simply irrepressible in his younger days, Dr Schulz would launch into a long monologue. Of all the days I've spent in this asylum – where I'm confined *for my own good*, they never forget to say – I best remember those when Dr Schulz held one of his inspired discourses.

'Do you want to hear about the funny side of the end of the world?' he asked me once, and, in his usual way, continued without waiting for my reply. I swallowed his words avidly as he spoke about the apocalyptic prophecy pronounced by the Montanists in the second century AD. The sect was founded in 156 AD by Montanus, a prophet who seems to have had the ability to speak in unintelligible languages. This phenomenon has virtually become part of pop culture today: we know it under the name 'speaking in tongues' and it's an everyday practice in Pentecostal churches. It's also common in mental institutions, where we call it schizophrenia. In any case, Jesus had scarcely gone, but Montanus believed he'd soon come again. The prophet wrongly predicted the date of Christ's return, but his cult lived on for several centuries.

'Elipando, Bishop of Toledo, described the uproar which took hold of the city's inhabitants on 6 April 793. He wrote that a monk by the name of Beatus, a manic street preacher, called the people together on the main square and told them the end of the world was coming that same evening. The city was panic-stricken. Later, when the people realised that the End hadn't occurred, they were enraged and went on a spree of plundering.

'Who better than the Pope to answer the question *When's the next time round?*' Dr Schulz laughed loudly. 'Pope Innocent III was unequivocal: the Second Coming would occur in 1284, that being 666 years after the advent of Islam. Jesus didn't come, despite the Pope's authority. Since the Pope was infallible, by inference Christ himself must have been wrong.

'Botticelli couldn't resist Apocalypse forecasting either. On a painting completed in 1500, he added a caption in Greek saying that the great cataclysm was coming in three and a half years: "Satan will be chained and cast down, as in this picture."

'Martin Luther believed the End would come by 1600. Tommaso Campanella was even more precise: the Earth would collide with the sun in 1603,' Dr Schulz said.

'Isaac Newton devoted a large part of his life and thought, which was not only mathematical but also theological, to the attempt to find what he considered the Bible code. And ultimately he succeeded, as he himself asserted. In 2003, the media were all abuzz about hitherto unpublished writings by Newton which state that the end of the world will come in 2060.

'The *London Stories about the End*, if I may call them that, are especially cheerful and bring out the British sense of humour,' Dr Schulz explained and refilled his pipe. 'In June 1523, a handful of London astrologers calculated that the end of the world would be on 1 February of the following year. It would begin with a flood in London. The water would then cover the entire world. Tens of thousands of people left their homes, fleeing before the predicted deluge. When the day of the prophecy came, not a drop of rain fell in London.

'The prophet William Bell said there would be a devastating earthquake on 5 April 1761 which would destroy the world. Previously he'd predicted a quake for 8 February. "So it didn't occur, but don't worry – it'll be on 8 March," he assured his listeners. Oops, wrong again. People left their homes and took to the hills yet again on 5 April, and when there was still no earthquake, an angry mob threw Bell into the London madhouse, Bethlem.

'In his *Book of Prophecies*, Christopher Columbus wrote that the world was created in 5343 BC and would last for 7,000 years. The End would therefore come in 1658. He got it wrong, but what can you expect of a man who was searching for India and discovered America?' Dr Schulz gibed.

He wasn't always in such a good mood. There were days, oh there certainly were, when he was gloomy and almost inscrutable. The warm laughter which had resounded in his study the day before would unexpectedly switch to a cold keenness, a presence almost like a scalpel, and I felt he could dissect me with his thoughts if he wanted.

And again, there were moments when he seemed to truly sympathise with me, when a story I told him in confidence shook him more than I thought a person in his position was allowed to be shaken. Sometimes I felt he sympathised with me so completely and sincerely that *I* suddenly had the desire to help *him*, as paradoxical as it may sound. Gentle and pensive, he'd listen to me without interrupting with a single gesture as I told him about my love for Marushka.

I was in love with Marushka even before I met her. One day Hedwig dropped her wallet and it fell under the sink. When I stooped down to get it, I saw her picture on the floor. She was my age, pallid of face and ethereally beautiful. I knew from what Hedwig had told me that she was of fragile health and that her chronic bronchitis had developed into asthma at an early age.

I often imagined her coughing blood and holding up a snow white embroidered handkerchief in her slender fingers. There was something compellingly romantic for me in that scene of beauty separated from death by a single strand of maiden's hair. I'd always be there to keep her from falling. I'd bring up a chair and offer her a glass of water. She'd then raise her angelic blue eyes to me and, not letting go of my hand, say: *thank you*. The love between us couldn't last for long. Her illness would tear her away from me, I imagined, and for that very reason I was convinced that she was the love of my life: the only love I'd have would be unhappy, but I'd fling myself into that tragedy like the Spartans charged the Persian hordes.

We met at the Amarcord brassiere, where I used to go in my late teenager days to watch the tumult of Naschmarkt. This marketplace had exercised a magnetic pull on me even as a child. It was strictly off-limits for me, needless to say. Yet how many times had I toured Naschmarkt wide-eyed, absorbing every nuance of the fruit and vegetables on display, every wrinkle on the faces of the dark-skinned porters and the fat saleswomen with their stentorian laughs and wide, aproned bellies which looked like they were hiding kangaroos. Amidst all those sounds, colours and not always pleasant smells, I felt a heady excitement such as only comes over us on the greatest of adventures – asail on the most distant oceans, braving the most perilous battlefields and scaling the highest mountain peaks. My heart beat like a tin drum whenever one of the saleswomen leaned towards me and spoke to me in her poor German. What a treasury of stories Naschmarkt was for me! Green olives and white cheeses, smoked salmon and pickled legs of pork, dried figs from the Adriatic islands and dried tomatoes from Turkey, early cherries from Italy and late oranges from Egypt: every market stall had the power, like an invisible lock, to sluice me into a dangerous new world far away from Schikanedergasse. But you mustn't think I really wanted to travel to all those places: my journeys were so spectacular because of my confinement, and my confinement was so agreeable because of my journeys. Any change would only have disturbed that delicate equilibrium and would only have been for the worse.

As I mentioned, the Amarcord was directly opposite Naschmarkt. Here I'd drink Julius Meinl coffee, smoke and gaze out at that unofficial Vienna theatre of life, where I staged and played some of the most exciting episodes of my childhood. When Marushka got a job as a waitress at the Amarcord because Hedwig's wages working for us weren't enough to cover her education, I began dropping by every day. They served Guinness on tap and crispy roast duck in spicy orange sauce; everyone there knew me, from the cooks to the regular guests – failed artists who hung around all day in the alcoves, waylaying visitors careless enough to sit down at neighbouring tables and abusing them with tales of their 'new art projects'.

When Marushka and I left the Amarcord together for the first time and I accompanied her to St Stephen's Cathedral where she lit a candle on the anniversary of her grandmother's death; and when we sat in the Bräunerhof afterwards drinking tea; and when I took her to the bus stop; and when she gave me a kiss on the cheek before running to the bus – we knew our relationship was inconceivable for everyone else. And precisely for that reason it was the only conceivable one for me.

We were as discreet as only those can be who know that to be noticed means danger. The slightest carelessness on our part could have brought a torrent of adversities, because *maman et papa* weren't the only obstacle to our love: Hedwig would oppose it just as forcefully, if not more so. But I'd been good at keeping secrets since childhood – was I not Hedwig's pupil, after all?

And then, within less than a year, Marushka and I were left alone in the world. First of all my mother died. They searched all the way from Vienna to Thailand to find a cure for her illness, but in vain. She passed away in a Swiss clinic in 'the miraculous hands' of a quack who 'healed those whom the medical profession has written off', as the pamphlets claimed which kept turning up in our home for months after the funeral. Knowing my mother, I have no doubt that she believed until the very end that she'd come through it. She could never accept the idea that she'd die; even the possibility of ageing and of her beauty waning was unthinkable for her: off the edge of all mental maps, deep within the dark territory no thought would penetrate, because those who enter there must abandon all hope. Her mother was like that too – the grandmother whom I never met. Apparently she had the habit of saying: *If I should ever die*… My mother, keeping with her convictions, didn't write a will. *Papa* followed her example, which cost me a fortune in lawyers' fees over years of litigation with his relatives, who descended like a flock of vultures on his estate. Fortunately it was quite large. *Papa* was a weak but good man. And a good father, too – except that he wasn't my actual father.

Before long, Hedwig also died. After *papa* was buried, I insisted that she not leave – she was to stay and live with me in the apartment. At one stage I was determined that Marushka should move in too, but she energetically rejected the idea and forced me to repeat after her, for the umpteenth time: *My mother must never find out*. Hedwig did actually stay, but today I know it would've been better if she hadn't. She hovered about the apartment like a ghost. I'd find her polishing a piece of furniture endlessly, as if in a trance, and raining down tears on it. Poor *madame*, poor *monsieur*, she'd say all of a sudden at dinner and burst into tears. Everything in the apartment reminded her of them. Schikanedergasse became Hedwig's Calvary: the memories caused her great sorrow, and everything which still existed turned into a monument to the ephemeral. There was so much death all around: the neighbourhood changed, people died or moved away, and she no longer even knew the saleswomen at the local baker's. Everything that had been hers, except for Marushka and I, was now in the world of the dead. She didn't show it in any way, although it must have caused her pain, but *I know she knew* that we were no longer hers either. Then one day she joined the shadows she'd been living with in her last few months. She'd been with them in the other world for days on end, and it was only her body which periodically came back to us. So when she died she didn't go away: she just didn't come back.

Her death didn't bind me and Marushka together. After they'd all been buried, you might have thought that nothing more could stand in the way of our happiness. Indeed, there was nothing – apart from my illness, which took on new and ever more frightening forms with every passing day. It worsened after my mother's death, only to culminate in my breakdown on the day of Hedwig's funeral. This turned out to be just the first in a series of breakdowns which ultimately led me to this hospital, here in the Alps.

They came on fast: first I'd have an attack of vertigo, then a terrible pain in my head, and next I'd black out. I'd wake up in a bed at the casualty ward where they'd rushed me from the library, the park or the street where I'd collapsed with inhuman cries, they told me. I'd seen a rapid flux of sights, places and epochs tied together into a story whose connecting thread I was unable to apprehend, and that seems to have literally driven me mad. Sequences of historical events alternated with the sequences of stories of those who saw history from the side, askance – its victims. From the beaches of Normandy to Petrograd, from medieval abbeys to the glass-and-steel towers of multinational corporations, a story unfolded in my mind, imperceptibly fast and incomprehensibly complex, but one grand story; and whenever I felt I was finally so close, just one proverbial step away from decoding what at first looked like a chaos of random threads of information, I'd stumble and seize up, drowning in merciful nothingness, with my body sinking in behind.

As if that wasn't enough, the pangs of remorse became more frequent and abrupt. To defend myself from those feelings of guilt would have aroused an even stronger sense of remorse in me because I considered my condition rightful punishment, and evading that punishment seemed unforgiveable. It all climaxed one day when I ordered my favourite roast duck at the Amarcord… and then realised I couldn't live a second longer in a world kept in motion only by death. I was inundated with images of hundreds of millions of feathered animals lying on conveyer belts and having their heads sliced off by razor-sharp precision machines. Their cries – through which I clearly discerned the triumphant, self-contented tones of a Black Mass – stabbed into my mind like steely knives. Billions of chicken's legs jerking in their death throes grated at my brain. Cows' heads were severed from their bodies and blood gushed from the necks, bespattering the faces of rubber-suited figures that dragged the carcasses down endless slaughterhouse corridors. Pigs grazed on vast pastures by the sea, only to throw themselves off the cliff one after another, as if at some invisible sign. Lambs were separated from their mothers, whose skulls were then crushed with sledgehammers, and the little animals were herded from their pens to a tract fenced in with barbed wire. There they were gassed to death and mountains of their bodies shifted by bulldozer to restaurants and cafés for our consumption. The thought about how much death was needed to maintain just one human life, my life, made me bolt from the restaurant like a wayward maniac. They didn't find me until evening – wandering aimlessly through the marshes of Lobau.

Marushka will never forgive me for the choice I made. I know she searched for me in all the hospitals in Austria, but I'd covered my tracks. I'd reached the end; she has to keep going. But she can only keep going if she forgets me and forsakes me. I know what she'd wish: to care for me and give me more and more of her unconditional, almost maternal love, the worse my condition became. That would cure me, she believed. She'd lay her life at the altar of my illness. But I can't bear a single sacrifice more for my sake. Instead, I decided to erase myself from her life and liberate her from me. I divided my inheritance into two trusts: one which I manage and use to pay for my luxurious confinement here with a view of the willows and the lake, and a second, which she'll manage when her children are born. That's the closest I'll ever get to fatherhood. I realised that during the first of our fruitless attempts at physical love. Each and every one of them ended in my complete incapacitation, such that we ultimately gave up. I'll never be capable of giving life – but at least I can give money and all that money can buy.

When my mother died, Hedwig handed me a slim book bound in red leather, which she announced as *my mother's diary*. And, in a way which had become habitual, she added in a conspirative-cum-demanding tone: 'This has to stay between us.' My mother turned out to have kept this diary in the period between the separation from you – forgive me for being so direct – and her marriage to the man who would play the role of my father through until the end as well as could be expected under the circumstances.

The Olcinium Trilogy

The diary told me nothing about my mother I didn't already know. They never concealed from me that *papa* wasn't my father – a fact underscored multiple times in the diary. But it did reveal the greatest secret: the name of my real father. First you withheld it from me, then my mother; I doubt that *papa* was involved in the decision, although he's sure to have gone along with it in his good-natured way, as with everything else my mother insisted on. Now, thanks to Hedwig, it's become my most precious possession. You may take the mails you're receiving from me as interest on the value you've renounced but which I, nevertheless, will duly reimburse.

PS
We'll see each other soon. At last, I'm coming. Dr Schulz has approved my visit to you: he considers it could be of the greatest significance for my recovery.

Chapter Nine

which tells of an ugly awakening, the devastating power
of sincerity, the End which has not come, and
the heralding of a long-awaited advent

I woke up in the cold amid a vile stench. I'd vomited in my sleep and made an absolute mess in the car. Before I'd gone to sleep I'd started the motor and turned on the heating, determined not to go home. The fuel ran out during the night and the motor died. Fortunately, some whisky shimmered yellow at the bottom of the bottle.

The snow kept falling. The streets were still empty. Everything just went on: the story about the End concluded like so many others. My head was heavy and still ringing with last night's confessions. Never again would the penitents be able to stand in front of each other. They wouldn't be honest with one another or themselves. Even if they went out drinking together again, nothing would ever be the same. Everything they'd once buried had now risen up out of the deepest dark, the densest forest and the thickest ice to plague them. How many love affairs, friendships and families were destroyed in one moment of nightly candour … How many secrets of the dead were released into the world to rob the living of their peace … How many husbands and wives are sitting at opposite ends of the cold kitchen table this morning and staring into their steaming cups of coffee because they no longer have the strength to look each other in the eyes … How many sons and daughters are staying in their rooms this morning because they don't dare to face up to their parents … How empty the confessionals in the churches are this morning after the whole planet turned into one big confessional last night … yet in the churches, the truth was spoken in such a way that it remained secret: the priest heard it under oath that he'd keep it confidential, and this prevented it from becoming public and destructive.

The non-occurrence of the catastrophe was a catastrophe which ultimately made the world impossible to live in. The Apocalypse had been a kind of solution, after all. The truth was an incident people had waited for: a comet colliding with the earth, a wave inundating the land, a bomb destroying a tower ... One drop of the truth and this world became impossible.

The truth is that I 'fathered' him and then deserted him, albeit unwittingly. He ended up in a mental hospital. And even while confined there, he sought my help in vain. He didn't receive a single word from me, nothing but the address to which he could send letters of confession. He won't receive absolution for the sins he committed and the confessions he made to the one, whose sin he is.

People are born as sin, a product of sin, and their whole life is a struggle against sinfulness. Sin is unavoidable and undeniable, and the only means of correction people have is death. Yet they consider that if they produce more life they'll help fill the gaping hole in front of them – a hole they don't know what to do about except to learn to ignore it, if they can't manage to plug it in some way. That's why people have children in an ultimate egoistic act, as if it was going to fulfil their life. They cast their children into new emptinesses in an attempt to cover up their own. Then they're overcome by worry, which they think will redeem them. And so the tragedy goes on without end, and generations are sacrificed in vain because their birth was a blunder which rectified nothing. So many generations, so much reproduction – and not the slightest change. Only the same human drama which has been played from the first day on, a play which remains the same old tragicomedy however much set and technology is put on stage, however many actors and supernumeraries are involved.

The power to give life is far more destructive and sinister than the power to take away life. Every living creature has that power, however dirty, ugly and stupid it may be. Every father is a father because he was unable to withstand that power. His child will foot the bill for that paternal potency until the end of its days.

In the end, to top it all off, you're stricken with remorse. I have nothing to say to my son other than: I'm sorry. But everyone is always sorry. He's sorry too. Instead of feeling anger because of *what they did to us*, we end up feeling guilty for *what we've done* because we unfailingly feel that our inherent nature is even more corrupt than the circumstances we were born in.

He sent a letter, and with the letter came the snow. His breath has found a way into all the fortresses I had built around me and crept in beneath all my locked doors. He has followed me like a bloodhound down all the paths I've fled. What else can I do now but end my flight: to turn around and meet him face to face, like facing a mirror? What can I do now but look down the road and wait, even today, *especially today*, when all flights have been cancelled and the trains and buses are stranded in snowdrifts?

And an anger rose up inside me like a storm surge, like a black ocean pounding down on my chest. I opened the side window, shook out all the heart pills and threw the jar into the snow. Taking a big swig of whisky, I pressed myself back into the seat and my numb hands gripped the steering wheel. I breathed with difficulty. The pain became unbearable – my chest felt like it'd burst open any second and *a stranger* would spring out into the world. I shut my eyes: now I just needed to wait. There was a rushing sound that seemed to be coming from afar, coming ever closer. I wasn't sure if it was the bus Emmanuel was coming with, the final storm which would flatten everything along with the tidal wave which would immerse us all, or my blood seething. Come, I thought. Yes, come.

SOUNDTRACK FOR *THE COMING*

TILLY AND THE WALL – *Nights of the Living Dead*
R.E.M. – *It's the End of the World as We Know It*
THE CLASH – *London Calling*
BAT FOR LASHES – *The Big Sleep*
SEX PISTOLS – *God Save the Queen*
NICK CAVE – *Jesus of the Moon*
CUT CITY – *Just Pornography*
THE SMITHS – *Meat is Murder*
THE STONE ROSES – *Made of Stone*
THE JESUS AND MARY CHAIN – *Darklands*
BEGUSHKIN – *Bitter Night Choir*
ODAWAS – *Alleluia*
THE TWILIGHT SAD – *Three Seconds of Dead Air*
BELLE & SEBASTIAN – *O Come, O Come Emmanuel*

Till Kingdom Come

Prologue: Water

I think I remember how it all began.

The winter was unusually mild that year. But it dragged on, as can happen by the Mediterranean, until it swallowed the spring like an Aesculapian snake eats an egg. The rain poured down day after day, for months. Soon it was half a year. The sardine season was almost over, but people still only went out if they had to, and only in their raincoats. The fishermen gathered every morning in their little cafés by the shore, where everything stinks of fish and seaweed, ready to drink their espresso and head out before dawn as usual. As if the old reality would come back if they held on to their little rituals for long enough. They sat in silence, scrying their coffee sludge, like the last survivors of an exterminated tribe which still doesn't understand why its world has disappeared. They listened in vain to the weather forecast, as bleak as a pagan mass. There was no good news: the rain wouldn't stop, the sea wouldn't drop, and they wouldn't be heading out. The men whose families depended on the catch despaired and drank glass after glass of grappa. In March, only the most persistent went after shad and then vainly stood in the rain trying to sell their fish to non-existent customers. The prawn season, the most profitable of the year, was delayed at first, and then it became clear that it wouldn't take place at all. Even if they had managed to head out, risking their necks in the waves which broke with a roar in the shallow water of the bay, it would have been a pointless effort. The sea was icy cold – just 12 degrees – although May was drawing on. Prawns only come with the warmer currents. They herald the beach tourists, but they wouldn't be coming either, it seemed. The nature people knew, whose unwritten laws they thought they could rely on, had betrayed them. The things they considered certain failed to occur. What no one in their families had any memory of, and therefore couldn't tell them about, had now happened. The most dogged of the fishermen kept setting their alarm clocks so they could get up at night and tip the water out of their boats, which would fill again even before they made it back to their beds. The others let their vessels sink. When all this finally passed, they would pull them up onto the shore and their skilful hands would clean, repair and refloat them.

Once, out of curiosity, I went down to the marina at three in the morning. I wrapped myself in my raincoat, opened the parasol I had taken from a burglarised storeroom at the beach and sat down on a bench. I opened a bottle of Vat 69 and watched the boats lying at the bottom of the bay for hours. That's what the Ulcinj pirates' fleet must have looked like after it was sunk by the Sultan's navy at the entrance to nearby Valdanos Bay. I thought that same, vacuous thought again and again, vainly trying to think of some other words, until I finished the whisky and threw the empty bottle into the sea. Only then was I able to free myself of the thought of the corsairs' sunken ships. Whoever finds my bottle will get the message: I wanted to say that I have nothing to say. I trudged home, took the basins of rainwater off the bed and slept through until the next evening. It seemed to me, when I finally opened my eyes, that the rain was beating down as if it intended to flatten everything beneath it.

If you wanted to go outside, gumboots were the only suitable footwear. But they were no good now either because the water was getting faster and deeper. In the end, wherever you went, you arrived wet up to the waist. The foundations of the houses absorbed the damp, and before the eyes of the tenants it climbed the walls towards the ceiling. Everything we touched was water. We slept on wet sheets under cold, clammy covers. The floorboards were swollen to bursting-point. Parquet flooring buckled like the ground after mighty tectonic shifts, such as shook the Earth in pre-human eons. The contours of the floor changed from day to day. Windows, even those with heavy shutters, were no help against the rain. It came with a wild westerly one moment and with a sirocco the next, constantly changed the angle at which it fell, attacking now frontally, now from the side, until it had crept through every invisible opening in the walls and woodwork. In their rooms, people made barriers of towels and babies' nappies beneath the windows. When they were sodden, they would be wrung out in the bathroom and quickly returned to the improvised dykes.

Roofs let through water like a poorly controlled national border. Like in a bizarre game of chess, families pulled pots and pans across the floor: Casserole to f3, frying pan to d2. The whole town suffered from sleep deprivation. Everyone finally understood the terrible power of Chinese water torture: the beast dripped all night and drove everyone out of their wits. Some tried to protect themselves from the sound of the drops which fell louder than bombs by stuffing cotton wool in their ears. When even that didn't help, they would turn on their televisions, radios and computers, trying to make noise to block out the monstrous aquatic symphony. Those who had small children would find brief salvation in the children's crying. No one attempted to calm them. They screamed with hunger, fever or colic, but their parents made no attempt to feed them or lull them to sleep. Mothers later recounted guiltily that they had hoped and prayed the crying would go on forever. In the end, the children did tire and fall asleep, and the parents would again be at the mercy of the sound which tormented them. That winter, children learned that crying is useless because no one will help us. And parents learned the lesson that everyone who tries to find salvation in procreation realises sooner or later: that the children will betray us, just as we betray them.

Ultimately, everyone gave up the struggle. Those who would never have lain in bed and gazed at the ceiling now sat and smoked all night, staring vacantly and watching the containers on the floor fill ever quicker, until they decided it was time to stop emptying them.

The winter firewood was already used up, and going out to gather new wood in such a gale made no sense. The stove would only smoke, producing no heat, and there were no prospects of it drying the rooms, let alone the walls, where the rising damp was puckering the plaster.

The alleyways ran like rivers. We would long ago have been inundated if the town was not built on a hill. The stormwater drainage became clogged before the New Year. The Central Canal gave way in the middle of April.

Now what we called the Central Canal is an interesting thing: it had not actually been dug for the passage of water. The people of Ulcinj originally made that tunnel because of a different enemy; one of flesh and blood. It led from the old fortress by the shore to half a kilometre inland, all the way to today's promenade, where you find one boutique after another with second-rate Italian wares and jewellers peddling trinkets from Turkey.

At first, the tunnel served for the rapid evacuation of the residents of Kalaja, the fortified Old Town of Ulcinj, who, it should be said, were pirates. They had the custom of plundering Venetian cities, and it seems they particularly liked attacking Perast, a small, wealthy town in the Bay of Kotor, which was practically defenceless because its menfolk were valued mariners in the fleet of La Serenissima and thus were constantly *sul viaggio*. Therefore, from time to time the Doge would send the fleet to Ulcinj to take revenge. The Ulcinj pirates evidently considered a good plan of withdrawal no less valuable than a wise plan of attack: the secret tunnel they dug allowed them to flee from the superior Venetian forces. We can just imagine the bewildered Venetian soldiers wandering through the eerily empty Kalaja, where they were met only by starving dogs and seagulls. There was no trace of the corsairs because they had already reached the swamp in the town's hinterland. They made their way through the water lilies and reeds in small, fast rowboats, rushing to *Velika Plaža* beach, where their ships lay hidden. From there, they would embark and launch a counter-attack. With a bit of luck, they would be able to approach the Venetian fleet from behind, while the infidels were still in the fortress, busy with plundering and getting drunk. If the Venetians had already left, never mind: the pirates were still alive, and what had been burnt and stolen they would plunder back again, inshallah. Today we'd say: the main thing is that merchandise changes hand and capital circulates.

The Olcinium Trilogy

People I knew told me that the tunnel was wide enough for a VW Golf to pass through. I never tested the claim: probably because of the disdain I feel for empirical proof.

In any other town, a pirates' escape tunnel would be a tourist attraction. The fact that it was left to become a drain should not be ascribed to a conscious plan of the local authorities, but to their negligence – a unique blend of idleness, impudence and fanaticism – which is interpreted here as consistent non-interference in God's will and His competencies. When Communism collapsed, the local population rediscovered God and started flocking to the mosques, and it became common to complain about dysfunctional municipal services at the local council and for staff to reply that the heap of rubbish which lay stinking in front of your house was there because God wanted it to be:

'If He wanted us to remove the dead horse from your parking slot, we would already have done it,' an official told me once.

'If who wanted you to?' I asked nervously.

'Out, get out!' he shouted.

As I hurried away down the corridor, fearing that I had involuntarily experienced proof once again that dialogue is the most overrated thing in the world, I heard the fellow banging the drawers of his desk and repeating to himself: '*If who?* Whaddaya mean *If who?*?'

Searching for a path, the water found the tunnel. It was as simple as that. And then it worked its way out of the tunnel: it breached the fifty-metre tall Cyclopean walls of the Old Town and, true to Kant's definition of the sublime – as beauty we experience as fearful – surged into the sea in a mighty torrent.

It may have been a state of emergency, but there was no lack of alcohol in the shops and the black-market cigarette trade still flourished. In Suljo's crummy shop, where everything was twice as expensive as elsewhere, I was the only buyer anyway. When some local informed me that Suljo's stocks of Rubin white wine, brandy and Johnny Walker were, if not inexhaustible, then at least sufficient for me to drink for another year of floods, all cause for concern disappeared from my mind. I kept buying my cigarettes via the Tadić delivery system: you call them at any hour of the day or night, and the Tadićs bring you a carton of cigarettes within half an hour. The combined IQ of all the Tadićs put together did not exceed 200, but they had certainly organised a proper little family business: the father sold cigarettes at the market, while his sons darted about town on rattletrap Vespas, delivering them to bars and houses.

'For every four cartons you got a free Coca-Cola,' the youngest Tadić told me one evening around midnight as he slugged a litre bottle into my hand.

'Listen,' I said to him, 'I see you got the idea of the free Cola from pizza delivery services, but if you think about it you'll realise how absurd it is. Cola may go with pizza, but with cigarettes you need alcohol or coffee.'

He looked at me bluntly through the streams of sweat running down his face. He was computing inside.

'We can't give away liquor. That wouldn't pay off,' he told me after a pause for computation which seemed as long as the Peloponnesian, Hundred Years', Guatemalan, and all the Punic wars put together.

'Alright, but how about a hundred grams of coffee?'

'Yeah, that would work,' he beamed.

'There you go! Do it like that from now on. But I'll keep the Cola all the same – it goes with whisky.'

* * *

Now that I was provisioned with everything an honourable man could need, I gladly accepted Maria's invitation to go to Bojana River for the May-Day holidays. That was typical of her and part of her charm which I found so irresistible: she thought it was perfectly natural and normal to leave a flood-stricken town and go to where there is even more water, just for a change of scene.

She, Goran and Radovan woke me before dawn, bursting into the house like a SWAT unit. Even before I could open my eyes, Maria was rummaging loudly in the kitchen trying to find a vessel to make coffee in, while the other two attacked what was left of last night's Vecchia.

'Come on, get this into you,' Radovan passed me a glass of alcohol. 'You know what they say: you have to fight fire with fire.'

Then Maria arrived with coffee in a Teflon frying pan.

'You don't have any detergent, and this was the only thing which was clean.'

Goran found glasses beneath the armchair and the bed, and Maria ladled the coffee into them.

'The three-day rule applies here,' he said.

'Which is?' I asked.

'The same as the three-second rule: what's been on the floor for less than three seconds or longer than three days isn't dirty and you can eat and drink out of it,' was his reply.

Radovan came from some godforsaken place in the Krajina borderlands. He claimed he was a close relative of a well-known Bosnian Serb folk singer. Having a nationalist bard like that in the family opened many doors for him here. That's the kind of time it was. Montenegrin ethno-fascism was comparable with the German variety in terms of its intensity. Its relative lack of coherence and effectiveness at killing can be put down to Montenegrins' legendary laziness and incompetence in organisation.

Radovan brought his wife, children and mother with him. His daughters were spectacularly ugly – prime specimens of negative natural selection – but they were not nearly as shocking as his wife. Even the budget of an average Hollywood movie would not have been enough to rectify her appearance. Such disfigurement is a rarity, even in the history of literature. At first she reminded me of one of Tolkien's orcs, but later I realised what ought to have been obvious all along: that God created the woman not in his own likeness, but in that of Dorian Gray.

Radovan claimed to be a talented cook and even to have *hands of gold*. There was no one who believed it and gave him a job, so he just used his hands for lifting bottles of beer, and he was able to fit more amber fluid in his small body than the laws of physics allowed, I can vouch for that. He was a first-rate liar and intelligent enough to know that you can always rely on people's greed. He found business partners in cafés and bars, where he would booze with them until the small hours. Then, when they were drunk enough, he would ply them with the bizarrest of 'business plans' and ardently describe 'investment opportunities' until they took the bait and turned their pockets inside out for him. The way Radovan conducted his business did not differ substantially from the functionings of global financial capitalism, which is a euphemism for the Ponzi scheme. The *Radovan scheme* differed from the Ponzi scheme only in so far as Radovan never paid a single instalment to anyone – not one cent of profit. Since I was interested in psychoanalysis, I understood that Radovan could be said to be part of real-existing financial capitalism. He never paid any dividends as an enticement for further investment, which would mean greater losses in the long-run, and there was no false hope in making gains – as soon as you gave money to Radovan, you knew you'd get fuck all back. You could even say that his dealings were closer to the Truth than those of large financial institutions are, and thus closer to Virtue. But there were few who appreciated that, and every now and again he would be beaten up by one of those to whom he had caused grief. But what can you do – everywhere and at all times, people are passionately intolerant of the Truth.

Goran also gave him money several times. Not out of greed, which he had been cured of, but out of a compassion and kindness which probably only still exist in Russian novels. How many times did I tell him, *Don't do it, you know he won't give it back, you know you're throwing your money out the window.* But Goran would just shrug his shoulders, smile and say, *He needs it more than I do.*

Goran was my best and perhaps my only true friend. He lived with his father, a tyrant who first drove Goran's mother out of his kingdom and into her grave, and then pushed his sister into voluntary exile at the age of seventeen. Fleeing head over heels from her father, she married the first good-looking, sweet-talking man she met. He would turn out to be the same as her father; but before she realised her mistake, she already had two children, and there was no escape for her any more. Hiding her misery from her husband, she would meet with Goran; she lamented to him, cried and said she'd kill herself, then always went back home because she had to feed the children.

Goran worked as a waiter during the day, and at night he went out to sea to try and catch fish to sell so he could put some money his sister's way. Now and then he would rebalance his and his sister's budget by selling the odd matchbox full of grass he'd got from Albania. Goran dealt with the best of intentions, like everything else he did. He spent his free time with me. I couldn't help him – I was never able to help anybody. We drank, told each other intimate things, and then parted, taking all our own misfortunes away with us again. I would watch him from the terrace as he headed away down the path with a light step. He had a proud, dignified bearing which suited him like height suits a cypress.

The morning they came to pick me up, he was particularly cheerful. He put on a brilliant parody of a broad Montenegrin drawl, full of all those lofty and pretentious ways of saying stupid things, which Montenegrins are masters of. He made two or three toasts, each more verbose and vacuous than the one before. Then Maria got up and ordered us to get going.

Radovan's light blue Trabant was waiting for us in the parking slot. He apologised as he tried to unlock the door of the old wreck – his BMW was at the garage.

Even today you can still find discussions on the Web about which was the worst car of all time: the Yugo 45 or the Trabant. But whoever trashes the Trabant has obviously never been in one. Put it this way: if you like to compare a good car with a ship, a Trabant is a rubber dinghy in a force-ten gale. After all, a Trabant can be repaired the same way as people repair boats. The body of the car is made of plastic, and in seaside towns you could see specimens of Trabants among the sails and oars in the maintenance area of the marina, raised up on blocks in a row of yachts and smaller craft. There's just one good thing about the Trabant, and it certainly came out that day in flooded Ulcinj: it doesn't sink.

We set off on the watery voyage to Maria's villa. Maria came from a family of weak fathers and masterly mothers – one where the *men* were married off. It was a mystery as to what had driven her great-grandmother to take her seven-year-old daughter by the hand and leave Trieste, where she had an enormous estate and social standing to match, and end up in Ulcinj, where people gossiped about and feared her. But once here, she bought a property on top of Pinješ Hill, where your gaze goes out across the Adriatic towards Otranto. She had a mansion built there, whose beauty could compare with any *villetta* by Lake Como, and which made everything ever built in Montenegro, including King Nicholas's ostensibly luxurious palace, look like a dump.

That woman would go for afternoon walks by the sea clad in the finest dresses, striding the town and creating a public scandal because the women of Ulcinj rarely went out at that time, and only if accompanied by a man and covered from head to foot.

Maria's grandmother enjoyed a home education: they engaged a governess from Rome, and her piano teacher – only the best would do – came all the way from Moscow.

The self-willed young woman ignored her mother's advice that she stay single, without children. She married a Montenegrin officer from Cetinje, who fled from her when he was sober and beat her when drunk. He died in a Russian prostitute's bed in a quayside brothel by choking on his own vomit while Maria's mother was still in nappies.

Maria's mother, Elletra, followed the family tradition of choosing a wimp for a husband. He did not die young like her father, and immediately after Maria was born Elletra banished him to the outhouse in the pine forest at the far end of the property. Happy there in his pigsty, he tippled and screwed around with the servants. When Elletra could no longer tolerate a bordello in her own backyard, she paid him out and he left for central Serbia to open a café. As Elletra expressly demanded, and in keeping with the contract they both signed, he never tried to contact Maria. Elletra later turned the outhouse into a larder with a collection of alcohol that the best of hotels would be proud of.

And it was to that store that Radovan now ran off, returning with a whole cardboard box of cognac. Elletra's cook came waddling after him. He moved like a penguin because he was lugging two crates of Nikšić beer. Since he was short, the crates scuffed over the asphalt and screeched like Cobain's teeth as he, already poised for suicide, played an MTV Unplugged concert on speedball which made him pogo up and down like a wild thing. If I ever come down with delirium tremens … Or rather, *when* I come down with delirium tremens, I won't see white rabbits but a line of penguins with cook's caps on their heads riding down the slopes of Mount Lovćen towards Kotor on empty beer crates and plopping into the sea one after another like ice cubes into whisky, I thought.

'This car is wonderful,' Radovan said. 'Its only weakness is that the boot is so small.'

He zipped back to the larder and this time brought a box of Chardonnay, which he dropped onto Maria's lap, as she had the honour of sitting in the front.

'Just a tick longer, have a smoke and then we'll be off,' he said, vanishing into the garden. He came back with a children's inflatable swimming pool, which he made the cook blow up. The fellow sweated from the exertion and I could imagine that he hardly restrained himself from butchering us and stashing the pieces in his freezer. Radovan then roped the swimming pool to the back of the Trabant and put another crate of beer and a few bottles of wine in it, taking care not to overload the vessel and cause it to sink.

As we were leaving, I thought I saw the silhouette of Maria's mother up in the attic window.

A Trabant pulling along a children's swimming pool loaded with alcohol didn't grab the attention of the people of Ulcinj who, as happens with the poor in spirit who live in expectation of famine, cholera and family deaths, had lost all sense of humour and love of the bizarre – the only things of lasting worth among all that has gladdened, frightened or troubled us in our time on this earth.

Ulcinj was deserted and we passed through the town without any great hindrance. The real fun began when we came to the area behind the *Velika Plaža* beach. From there to Bojana River we had fifteen or so kilometres' drive across the Štoj Plain. In Ulcinj, the water ruled like an autocrat, but in comparison with the reign of terror it unleashed in Štoj it was an enlightened dictatorship, perhaps a bit like the way Tito ruled Yugoslavia. In Štoj, the water was Pol Pot. Bojana River had burst its banks, and Lake Šas had also overflowed. A tide of shit rose from the septic tanks which the residents of Štoj had emptied their bowels into for decades. Dead cows and sheep floated around us. It was hard to avoid them because the water came half way up the windscreen. Our raft of alcohol bumped into bloated carcasses several times, but otherwise Radovan drove a perfect slalom.

'If you were in Noah's situation, what sorts of alcohol would you take with you on the raft?' Maria asked us, holding a perfumed hanky over her nose.

We agreed that it wouldn't be necessary to take a sample of every species of drink because not all of them deserved to exist. The world would be a better place without some drinks, and that is not the end of similarities between alcohol and humankind.

Maria would have liked to turn Noah's raft into a floating wine cellar.

'Guys, for ideological reasons I wouldn't save a single Californian wine,' she said. 'Some of them are good, some are perhaps even excellent, but Californian wines are anti-wines. Where there is no tradition, there ought not to be any wine either. Do you also get the feeling that they're instant wines concocted like Nescafe? The only thing more scandalous than Californian wines is Californian cognac – because cognac is a perfume among drinks, the essence of tradition.'

The rich are fundamentally conservative, and Maria was no exception. However decadent they are, however many transgressions their life is full of, however ardently they promote liberal values, or the manners of their class, and however much compassion they may have for people of colour, the disabled and the LGBT community, the rich want one thing above all: for everything to stay as it is – for them to stay rich, that is.

Goran enthusiastically accepted her thesis. He considered there should only be a place for a very few types of cognac in the new world.

When Radovan announced he would load the raft with good old-fashioned rakia, and add the occasional crate of beer, it became clear that our apocalyptic fantasy was a confirmation of Béla Hamvas's theory that there are wine-, vodka- and beer-drinking peoples.

As far as I'm concerned, there has only ever been one drink – Scotch whisky, single malt. There was no need for any other kinds of alcohol – neither in this world nor in any other. When I later succeeded in life, as they say, and finally had the money for single malt, I didn't drink anything else. A raft loaded with select oak barrels of single malt didn't need to be seen as the seed of a better, future world – it already was the best of all possible worlds.

Entertained by imagining utopias – the path to which is always paved with corpses, or at least carcasses – we arrived at the Bojana River in good spirits. The water had not carried away Goran's hut, although it had been a close call. The small wooden structure, sheathed in tarred and rusty corrugated iron, built to the highest standards of the slums of this world, had proved exceptionally sturdy. There are times when the glass towers fall and all of modernity founders with its information systems and social structures, when gravity overcomes everything which people's pride has put in its way, and then only holes and hovels survive the universal destruction.

The Bojana River wasn't always the cloaca it is today. Fishermen once used to net schools of grey mullet here, and at night they would sit together with local wine and home-grown tobacco telling tales of the good old days and big catches. But the little river had the misfortune of being discovered by rich Muscovites, who brought along their lovers – badly bungled crosses between the male ideal of female beauty and the female need to please the male eye. These Frankensteinish brides came with their Luis Vuitton handbags and their shrieking chihuahuas in tow. Later, prostitutes from Novi

Pazar opened their all-inclusive spa centres. Then hordes of Montenegrin tycoons descended on the river like tribes of barbarians set on razing Rome to the ground, and this perfect landscape lay in their path, perfectly vulnerable. The moguls' excess of money and lack of taste spawned architectural monsters by the waterside, and in a truly just society they would be publicly executed in the town square and their brains sent to advanced research centres for close examination in the hope that future experts would be able to prevent aesthetic crimes – the most terrible of all.

Radovan sped back to Ulcinj to kill one more wretch's last trace of trust in humanity. The three of us, in a silence disturbed only by the clink of glasses, gazed into the river, which was carrying away the remains of a world lost in the flood. For hours we watched the millions of destructive raindrops compress into the stream of the river. At night, only a few lanterns upstream impaired the perfect darkness we gladly consigned ourselves to.

When Radovan came to collect us three days later, I asked Goran and Maria to wait for me in the car as I prepared to take my leave. I stood on the terrace and let the sorrow flood through my whole being, a sadness which numbed my limbs and then took away my thoughts. I floated in the weightlessness of that potent melancholy, sensing beyond any doubt that something majestic had ended, a grandeur I would remember till my dying day. I knew it was over and that I wouldn't be able to talk about it because, however much detail and eloquence I described it with, the essence would slip away – it was essential to me alone and could not subsequently be interpreted and shared with another person, not even with the future me. I knew that no future intimate bond would be complete enough for that feeling to be shared because, however many words I used, no one would find what I was talking about more significant than some second-hand anecdote.

Our return to Ulcinj ended in catastrophe. Radovan insisted that we drop in for a drink in Štoj on the way. There another guy from the Krajina borderlands ran a pub called *The Second Chance*. As soon as we set foot in that hole it became clear to us that the name was not without significance – here you had a pretty good chance of picking up AIDS, or syphilis at the very least. Prostitutes roosted in artificial-leather booths lit by imitation candles; the girls were from Moldova, as it turned out. Radovan was a welcome guest here. You could even say a stakeholder. He and his fellow countryman went off for a conspiratorial conversation in 'the office', they told us. The three of us dragged ourselves to the bar. The waitress threw a few bottles of Nikšić beer at us – lukewarm, the way bricklayers drink it.

By the time Radovan came back from his 'meeting' and buttoned up his flies, I was starting to slur my words. He insisted we have another drink, claiming he had reason to celebrate. One drink turned into five, or ten, it makes no difference. They carried me out of *The Second Chance* and heaved me into the Trabant.

They woke me when we arrived at a petrol station because our East German wreck finally gave up the ghost. We even tried to jump-start it for a hundred metres or so – in vain, of course. I stumbled several times and fell face down in the slough. Since I was wet and barely able to walk, Maria took me home. I don't know many people who would haul a drunken pig three kilometres through a flooded town in the diluvial rain, fully aware that he would never thank her for it.

Somewhere on the way, I realised from what she told me later, I tried to kiss her. I wasn't pushy, just wet and icky with vomit – my worst possible manifestation. It takes a special feeling for melodrama and tragedy for a man to declare the love he has been harbouring for years to his victim, the unlucky *object* of his love, at the worst possible moment.

She turned me down, though I don't doubt she did it with a ladylike tenderness which would make anyone she turned down love her even more hopelessly. I then gave a romantic speech, whose details she spared me, but clearly it was in keeping with the genre, and thus unbearable. When cynics 'open up their heart', as the phrase goes, they ought to be shot on the spot like rabid dogs. It becomes clear at that moment that the best in the man – his razor-sharp humour, his cold, refined, analytical mind, the dignified distance he maintains towards everything, including his own life – is actually just a mask. His confession and tears wash away that mask and you have an intellectual wretch before you who has pretended to be an aristocrat of the mind; instead of a rare being whose reason has overcome instinct, you have a rotten hulk kneeling in front of you for whom you feel nothing but disgust.

That's what I told her later, too: 'You should have killed me.'

'Would you be able to kill me?' she asked with a laugh.

'I'm afraid I don't know any more,' I said, but it didn't sound half as good as it would have one day earlier.

She was getting sick of pulling me along against the current, so she called the servants. She took me to a garden, where we sat under an orange tree and waited for the little kitchen hand to come in the pick-up. Then they threw me in, drove me home, took off my wet things and left me on the bed, unconscious.

I woke up in Sarajevo, a city I had never been to. I had a clear memory of the previous night. We had been drinking at the Piccadilly, a bar behind the cathedral. The father of one of the boys in the group, who owned the place, had the waiter bring us a bottle of whisky as soon as we arrived and got settled in the booths. By ten, we were all drunk – it doesn't take much with teenagers. I wanted to clear my head and decided to go for a walk and get a trolleybus at the Skenderija sports centre. Snow was falling silently through the universe. Each plume of steam from my mouth revealed perfect snowflakes, and whoever saw them would have recognised the structure the world was created from, based on the principle of endless iteration. I walked past the Markale market hall, the Eternal Flame, and went down Tito Street to the Sarajka department store, where I turned left and stopped outside a bar. I remembered with the precision of the clearest, crispest photograph, although I had never been inside, that I once went in there with a friend the time he bought a matchbox full of hash from the barista before a school excursion to Venice; we smoked it in Cividale del Friuli, another city I had never been to. Recollecting the details of an excursion someone else was on, not me, I arrived at the banks of River Miljacka. It seethed and swirled, flowing as fast as that piddling river could, I recalled.

The trolleybus had broken down at the Olympic Village. I was still drunk and needed to keep walking in the cold air, so I decided not to wait for a bus. I set off for the suburb of Dobrinja, taking a route I had never gone before. The avenue was deserted and I headed down it, ploughing through snow which seemed immaculate. When I unlocked the door of the flat, I heard water flowing in the bathroom. Then I trod on something. I lifted it up from the floor, and in the gleam of light from the upper, glazed section of the bathroom door I saw it was an empty jar of zolpidem sleeping tablets.

I knew the layout of the flat intuitively and, without turning on the light, I undressed, went into one of the bedrooms and crashed. I didn't care whose bed it was. I remembered all this when I woke up. I jumped out of bed and went to have a shower because I was supposed to meet a young guy called Amar, whom I didn't know, in the old bazaar that morning. I found a winter coat in the wardrobe and put on my sturdiest boots. I went outside, donned cap and gloves, and was heading for the tram turntable in a Sarajevo suburb when I saw a reflection in a drop of rain on a pine needle, and only then did I realise I was standing on the terrace of my house by the sea; it was night, the fourth of May, and the water was draining away from Ulcinj; the sky had opened up, the lights of the town shimmered beneath the stars which had finally come out, and I didn't know what was happening to me.

TIME

1

These spatio-temporal lapses continued in the years which followed and became ever more frequent and prominent. To begin with, they occurred just after I had woken up: lying in bed in my grandmother's house in Ulcinj, I would open my eyes in Brussels, Paris or London and recall the circumstances which had led me there. I would return five minutes or half an hour later; it was totally unpredictable. Later the lapses became even more common, I'd say almost regular. They could happen at any time: while I was going for a walk, eating a meal or, worst of all, in the middle of a conversation. I would simply fall silent and be somewhere else. The person sitting next to me would call my name, but it didn't work. Most of them simply got up and left. The well-intentioned and devoted ones would call an ambulance. After a few abortive calls, which ended with me coming round in front of the astonished medics and having to apologise, make them a coffee and beg them to be discreet ('My condition is certainly strange, and this is a small town – you know how it is when people find out about things'), the ambulance dispatchers learned to ignore the calls. 'Just leave him,' they'd say to the good Samaritan. 'Get on with your business and don't worry about him. He wanders a bit, and then he comes back as if nothing had happened.'

I was unable to perceive any pattern in those lapses or determine what triggered them. At first I thought it might be alcohol. But abstinence didn't help: on the contrary, it made things worse. My condition could be described as an absolute lack of interest in the present, let alone the future. My mind was constantly going into rewind because everything I cared about was in the past.

2

I don't believe those stories about pristine beginnings. True, time spoils everything. And yes, everything gets worse over time. But what is prone to spoil is not necessarily good in the beginning. Everything is bad, even at its inception.

Nor do I believe the stories about the wisdoms pronounced by children in their alleged innocence. I'm sure there are children cleverer than I was, and perhaps there have been three-year-olds who walked the earth and had something vital to say. But as a small child I only ever blabbered nonsense. We derive that habit from our childhood, ultimately, and it remains with us even in our so-called mature years and through to our death. There is little consolation when you realise that, until the end, you will write and say things it would have been be wiser not to. And it is small comfort that occasional people manage to utter a few last words before they die which are not necessarily wise but at least not stupid.

When I was a boy, a year seemed as long as eternity to me. Once my grandmother planted an olive seedling in front of the house. I pranced around the fragile sapling for a while and then decided to be pragmatic and ask when we would be able to pick the first olives.

'In ten years' time,' she said. She could just as well have said 'never' – it would have meant the same to me. But from then on I imagined a year like an olive tree. The tree grew as the year passed: quietly and slowly, visible only to the persistent and patient eye.

For me today, the years don't *pass*: they fall like trees – not olive trees but the massive trunks of the northern forests. One minute they're standing tall beneath the sky, the next they're beneath the boots of the lumberjack. Nothing remains of their might except the tremble of the moist earth when those giants come crashing down.

Yes, today the years fall like chainsawed trees. And the warning voice which shouts, 'Timber!' is in vain: they always fall on me. They fall, and it hurts. Maybe the logic is: the more we get battered, the better we can measure time.

Why not throw away our watches and purge all digital devices of the numbers signifying the passage of time? Clocks only ever measure the time of material things: an abstract entity we measure life with, although it is a sterilised and preserved entity which passes life by. *People's time* is entirely different: it doesn't flow uniformly, no two minutes or hours are the same, and its only real measure is the desolation it leaves in its wake.

History is an uninterrupted series of catastrophes – shipwrecks, avalanches, take your pick – where nothing is less important than whether my poor self is going to be dragged under or buried alive. Only arrogant fools expect satisfaction from history; the ordinary, little person is always on the losing end in every brush with history.

And yet that house of ruins, that past built of catastrophes, is all we have.

Maria and I shared a love of Walter Benjamin. Both she and I placed him before all other philosophers, even before the majority of poets, but not above Trakl and Celan. How many bleak winter nights we spent in drunken discussions about his *Arcades* and the Angel of History ... We both had a passion for knowledge, which is so rare in our time. Living in a provincial backwater surrounded by people who consider selfishness and greed an expression of faultless utilitarianism only intensified that passion. If you've never lived in the backwoods, you don't know to what extent your enjoyment of knowledge sets you apart from others ... How complete is the solitude of bibliophiles and thinkers, and how strongly such people bind together and become totally dependent on each other when they meet, against all probability, near the scaffolds of the soul that are our small towns.

I'm sure I still know all of Benjamin's historic-philosophical theses off by heart today, just as Maria did. In the second thesis he says:

'One of the most remarkable characteristics of human nature, writes Lotze, alongside so much selfishness in specific instances, is the freedom from envy,

which the present displays toward the future. Reflection shows us that our image of happiness is thoroughly coloured by the time to which the course of our own existence has assigned us. The kind of happiness which could arouse envy in us exists only in the air we have breathed, among people we could have talked to and women who could have given themselves to us (...)'

3

As if it wasn't bizarre enough that I experienced the memories of other people, whose identity I woke up in, what I considered *my own* memory lost all narrative continuity over time. Not only did I not know what I had in common with the people I remembered, but I didn't even know what I had in common with the *me* I could remember.

My time seemed to shrink and then to scatter in all directions, forwards and backwards, up and down, into yesterday and tomorrow, exploding into thousands of droplets – fragments I tried again and again to unite, in vain. It was like a ball of wool which rolls down the hill into a stream and ends up all tangled in the waterweed, or like a piece of Czech porcelain from grandmother's chest of drawers which falls to the terracotta floor. It demanded an exceptional effort to re-sort the findings about my own existence and assemble an even slightly convincing narrative about myself. Social contacts were becoming ever harder for me. I was terrified of questions and prop-phrases like 'remember the time we ... ' or 'you know how ... ' because I had no answers to them. Actually I did, but they weren't socially acceptable. A short, honest 'no' was out of the question. No, I don't remember. No, I don't know you. No, I really don't know who you are. Lots of little 'noes', which each individually and all together meant one thing: no, I don't know who I am.

In turn, the solitude I had always found consolation in now ceased being a matter of choice and became a necessity. If I wanted to stay outside of institutions I could be put into for my own good by people I knew nothing about, but who claimed to be well-intentioned and even friends, I had to reduce my contacts with the outside world. In that way I created the time I needed to tell me about myself.

I built myself of water. I tried to give the water shape and hold it back, at least for long enough to glance at myself briefly in the mirror. All that I touched and all that I owned ran between my fingers, trickled away from me, met weirs and then changed course and shape, flowing, falling, gushing away and sinking into the ground, only to well up again, elusive and completely unable to retain any shape.

It was no easy task, but I managed to put my life in order so that I could function in spite of my 'condition', which was constantly worsening. There is only one recipe for happiness, and that is to desire as little as possible. A simple life, even if spent in privation, is the closest you'll get to happiness. When you accept that you have little, most of the problems which have dogged you will vanish – because those problems were fuelled by all the futile efforts to gain more. It's a simple matter: to have a lot takes a lot. Everything I had gained cost me dearly. It wasn't worth it.

4

I only went out at night, when I could stroll through the deserted town to my heart's content. No one was out in the streets after one in the morning except the schizophrenics hurriedly walking in the squeaky flip-flops they wore summer and winter alike, looking straight ahead. They were my brothers. Their families kept them under lock and key during the day because people in small towns try to hide what is considered shameful. They would let them out at night to get their fill of fresh air and wear themselves out on their sometimes long and always frenzied walks. Before dawn, they would be rounded up, like animals which have strayed from the flock, and returned to their rooms, where they would sleep all day on sedatives.

Drugged-up kids would squeeze into unmanageable cars and race to discos in the suburbs. They didn't notice me. Young couples had fast sex in the woods and on the beaches. They had enough problems of their own even without me turning up – difficulties and embarrassments which , when the night's amorous experiences were recounted the next day, would morph into anatomically impracticable acrobatics and fireworks of passion. Teenage sex is proof that Karl Kraus was right when he maintained that intercourse is a poor substitute for masturbation. Out of consideration for the ordeal they were going through, I always gave the young people a wide berth and tried not to disturb them.

But most of all I liked the dawns. In nature, I have to admit, there is no kitsch. That is also the nicest thing which can be said about nature. It is people's perspective which fouls everything up. When dawn comes like the writing on the wall and the day which arrives in its wake is unwelcome, like all it can possibly bring, there can be no kitsch even in the scene of a person standing at the shore and watching the morning rear up, slowly and terrifying like Godzilla – that gleaming monster one should flee before, to find a refuge and try to survive until the following night. Yes, the dawns were beautiful.

Beauty is difficult.

5

I wrote for the newspapers and that's how I made ends meet. For a while, I used the money my grandmother had left to me, but I soon learned to save, and what I earned from six articles would last until the end of the month.

I wrote quickly and with ease, and what I wrote had an audience. They were commentary pieces at first, fiery and provocative. People liked to read them, especially those who didn't agree with me – and there were quite a lot of them. If you tell people what they don't want to hear in the way they least want to hear it, you'll have their undivided attention and they will become your most loyal readers. I owed every single 'success' of my journalistic career, if we can call it that, to people who would curse and swear when reading my pieces, who would screw up the newspaper and trample on it, only then to wait impatiently for my next article which would drive them around them bend all over again.

Over time, I developed a special style of my own – a kind of hybrid – mixing investigative journalism, cultural criticism and conspiracy theories. The 'investigative' bit shouldn't be taken literally. Naturally I didn't have any 'insider' sources, access to classified information or anything like that. I examined information which had already been published and drafted my articles in the margins. But I dissected these texts like a forensic scientist, and a whole host of things came to light. I discovered logical lapses, discrepancies and incongruities in the statements of the players. If you knew where to look and what to search for, an author's style provided ample information about masked intentions, hush-ups, and the toxic influence of editors and media barons. The lies of politicians overlapped with the lies of tycoons, who used their media to expose the former's skulduggery. I studied the ownership structures of the media and the ownership structures of firms. I learned to link what I read in the crime columns with the movements of stock-market indices, and I became skilled at recognising the jargon of party spokespeople in the words of academicians. In my articles, stories about crimes in village schools rubbed shoulders with the theory of the Frankfurt School, the names of bankers stood next to Brecht's, and the tragic fates of Bosnian refugees bore so many similarities to Walter Benjamin's final days. My speculations were no less truthful than supposedly objective information, and were far more interesting.

From the first day on, I felt the deepest disgust for the job I was doing. Journalism is not for the respectable. Which is to say, it should have been the ideal job for me. But there was too much lying and falsity even for my taste.

Today journalists not only play the role of committed thinkers, who communicate important realisations about human existence and work hard to unmask society's hypocrisy. Journalists today are also detectives, exposing what is hidden: it is they who visit criminals in their troubled dreams, where they dread what will be discovered and what dirty work the reporter's X-ray vision will alert the public about, and with the sensitivity about injustice being so great the public prosecutor and police are bound to react. It is a story about bold journalists who uproot society's weeds, a yarn intended for brains readily narcoticised with fairy tales. Journalists are like the animals in the story who band together, holding each other by the tail, and tug and tug until they finally pull a turnip out of the ground.

There is nothing noble in public activism, nothing enlightened or heroic. All the talk about incorruptible public intellectuals and their virtues is a naive fantasy. It's a simple, even trivial matter – a question of the market and the stock exchange, but not of the spirit.

Everyone who participates in 'public life' possesses a certain symbolic capital. The media are just a market for symbolic capital which can be enlarged by the action of the media. Or diminished. Like information, symbolic capital can be transformed into money in one way or another. And just like the dollar, the global currency, symbolic capital has no firm foundation.

The idea of free media flows from the idea of the free market. Both one and the other are pure ideological constructs. Neither one nor the other exist.

The media are a tool for achieving the interests of their owners. Those interests meld with the interests of other ownership structures and political groups, and together they form networks of interest groups.

Publishing in the papers means to serve one of the networks of power. Every communicable truth, however well hidden and dangerous, is a truth to the detriment of one person and the advantage of another, who probably, or rather certainly, has skeletons of their own in the closet. Such a truth is only a partial truth and therefore not the truth at all. Your most brilliant stroke is just the move of a pawn: you are lifted up and put down again on the board so as to keep playing your paltry role as a fighter for the truth, for which you will of course be paid and perhaps even recognised by society.

You'll be the hero of a game in which the media raise the symbolic capital of the interest groups behind them and undermine the symbolic capital of their rivals, who retaliate in kind.

The thought that anyone could consider me the conscience of society was frightening. I despised society as deeply as can be, and it choosing me to be a guardian of its conscience was irrefutable proof that I was right to do so.

One of my really top-notch pieces, or so I considered it at the time, set off a chain of events which saw me leave the safety of home and reject the precious rituals which had given my existence a degree of predictability and structure. The water flowed out of the narrow, concreted channel it had crept along, never to return.

6

Do you like anniversaries and find them meaningful? Do they give you a sense of security and continuity? People need something to keep them grounded, you think, and can't just let themselves be swept along by the floodwaters of time?

Then here's a good anniversary for you.

On Sunday it was four decades since Theodore Robert Bundy, nick-named Ted, killed Lynda Ann Healy and thus began his killing spree. All that remained of the girl were the bloodstained sheets in her basement flat in Seattle. Two and a half months later Ted killed Donna Gail Manson, who was not related to Charles or Marilyn Manson.

Bundy went on killing, absolutely unhindered, until September of the next year. He was one of the most infamous serial killers. When he was finally arrested, the American authorities were so inept that they allowed him to escape twice: once only briefly, but the second time, in January 1978, for long enough to break into an isolated house, where he raped two women and beat them to death with a wooden club. One hour later, Ted had moved on and bludgeoned a woman in another house. It was not until July 1979 that he was arrested again and condemned to death.

Ted diligently penned appeal after appeal and, as a God-fearing American, was able to have his execution postponed for ten whole years. He even acted as a police consultant in the case of the Green River serial killer. That slayer was never caught, but Bundy's public-private partnership with the police served as a model for the cooperation of the law-enforcement agencies and the maniac in the film we all love, *The Silence of the Lambs*. Before he was executed, he confessed twenty murders, although it's estimated that he left over one hundred victims in his path.

Apart from being a serial killer, Ted Bundy was a Republican Party activist.

John Wayne Gacy was … you know, different to Bundy. Teddy-boy raped and killed girls – Gacy preferred boys. Bundy was a handsome, char-ismatic killer, while the namesake of John 'The Duke' Wayne was a paunchy, nondescript boy from the block. Bundy behaved like a star, while Gacy did his best to be friendly to everyone and, if possible, to blend into the background.

Gacy hid the corpses of his victims under his house. When he ran out of space, he threw them in the nearby river. At his trial, he confessed thirty-three murders. He was sentenced to twenty-one life sentences and twelve death penalties.

For the next fourteen years the state needed to administer him the lethal injection, Gacy claimed he himself was 'the thirty-fourth victim', in other words that he was the victim of a conspiracy to frame him.

Apart from being a serial killer, John Wayne Gacy was a Democratic Party activist.

With a little luck and more caution, both men could have gone undetected. Two so cunning and capable guys could have achieved a lot if only they had concentrated on politics – if they had killed legally.

In a world just a bit more twisted and just a little further to the right, Ted Bundy and John Wayne Gacy could both have become American presidential candidates. This hypothesis is not as far-fetched as it might sound.

A serial killer is a perfect candidate for the presidency of any large country. He is already prepared for what awaits him: the sowing of death. Whoever becomes president of the USA – or Russia, France or Britain, it makes no difference – goes on to become a killer. It is not usual, as far as we know, for American presidents to cruise their country massacring young women and men before taking their oath of office. And yet, under their command, the armed forces and secret services will kill countless people throughout the world.

Bundy and Gacy mistreated their captives, just as the presidents' soldiers would do in Iraq, Guantanamo and CIA concentration camps in Europe. How many Bundys and Gacys are wearing American uniforms today? How many prisons are there where these maniacs torture their victims in the name of the Constitution and the American people?

A US president must also have a wife, of course.

Americans are fascinated by serial killers and presidents, and as he was waiting on death row, Ted Bundy received love letters every day from beautiful women, many of whom looked just like his victims – brunettes with long hair parted in the middle. Before he was executed, he chose one of them to be his bride and managed to ensure offspring. Thanks to artificial insemination, the lady bore Ted Bundy's child. It would have been a shame if those genes had been lost.

Gacy had an even more dynamic prison life, full of fine art and the proceeds from it. And despite being behind bars, he maintained a romantic involvement with a twice-divorced mother of eight. She used Gacy as a marketing tool and managed to get on several talk shows. 'John Wayne' himself took to painting in a big way. He produced self-portraits and pictures of clowns – before his time in jail he used to dress up as a clown at children's parties.

His social streak, after all, was why his neighbours couldn't believe someone as altruistic as Gacy was actually a killer. His paintings fetched prices of up to several hundred thousand dollars, and when the artist died he left behind a substantial endowment. The state was furious at him having acquired wealth through being a serial killer and sued Gacy's estate to recoup the costs of his fourteen years in prison.

The state was so furious because it jealously guards its exclusive right to kill with impunity. And even makes a profit from it. So if the state is a repressive, murderous machine, why couldn't it also be run by a killer – one who knows what the business is about?

I find that the whole debate about the abolition of the death penalty misses the mark. The nature of the state is not going to change if the state decides to stop frying murderers on the electric chair. Abolishing the death penalty does not do away with the state's right to kill, as is often misleadingly claimed, because the state will still have the right to wage war and to run secret services with all they death they sow. The state will kill for as long as it exists. And it will kill more, the bigger and more powerful it is.

But what a terrible, crying shame it was that we never saw a presidential debate between Ted Bundy and Wayne Gacy: their heated exchange on foreign policy or the issue of bringing American troops home from abroad; and both candidates swearing, although they were serial killers, that the life of American citizens was sacred to them. Gacy would probably have flirted with the gay community and had the sympathies of liberal commentators. Ted Bundy, as a Republican, would probably have opposed abortion from a 'pro-life' position.

A perfect crime is not one where all traces are removed, thus making it a mystery even for the cleverest investigator. A true perfect crime is one which is not even recognised as a crime, one which is legalised and becomes an integral part of society, tradition, civilisation and politics – such a crime, ultimately, serves as the basis of every state.

7

Ten days after the article was published, the phone rang. A warbly female voice announced that she was calling from the Ministry of the Interior and advised me that I had the honour of receiving a call from the minister himself: *The boss wants to speak to you.*

Minister Mandušić was most cordial. If anyone had listened to a recording of our conversation, they would have concluded we were old acquaintances who had gone through a lot together: a sackful of shared memories and, even more importantly, shared secrets. I assumed that Mandušić knew a lot about me – this may be a failed state, but the secret services in such states work with particular effectiveness. I also knew a thing or two about him, in a way. The assumption that one knew things about the other was his reason for inviting me to meet him, and it was mine for accepting the invitation.

Goran drove me to Podgorica. We took the long way, via the Petrovačka Gora mountain range, because it was a rainy day and Goran thought we had a good chance of meeting the Lady in White.

The Lady, people told me, was a spirit which had the habit of way-laying superstitious travellers in the deep of night, especially when mist and rain turned the winding road into a Gothic *mise-en-scène*. She didn't steal souls or make travellers pay a black toll: all she took was a tribute in fear. And fear is cheap and never runs out.

Goran knew several people who claimed to have seen the Lady. They said she came flying up to the car, clung to the bonnet and pressed her bloody, pock-marked face against the windscreen. However fast they drove and however much they jolted around the curves, they were never able to shake her off the car. When she went, it was because she wanted to. She left behind a trail of blood and pus on the bonnet, which stank for months afterwards and was impossible to clean off.

'Alright then,' I said to my friend, who, when he wasn't drinking with me, spent his free time watching horror films, being the owner of the largest collection of ghost, Gothic and zombie movies in Eastern Europe. 'What would you do if we met the Lady?'

'I'd say: "Hey sis, where ya been all this time?"' he shouted. He added that, for him, there was no difference between his Lady and the Lady of Međugorje. In searching for the Lady in White, he hoped for the same thing which takes fervent Catholics on pilgrimages to Međugorje in Herzegovina: a miracle to confirm his faith. Of course, even if he doesn't meet her, he believes – no, he *knows* – that vampires exist and that spirits can be seen by everyone who doesn't obstinately shut their eyes before them.

Passing through the wilds of the Petrovačka Gora range, we were caught unawares not by the Lady but by a police patrol. A dumpy policeman literally came rolling out of the forest and levelled his stop sign at us like Father Karras waved the cross above the body of possessed young Regan.

'How ya goin', boys?' he drawled, leaning in the car window. That was overly familiar for my taste. I replied coldly and officially, the way he ought to have addressed us. People like that take it as an insult if you don't go along with their chumminess. Nothing irritates them more than elementary decency, and it makes their hair stand on end like a wildcat's. Montenegro is full of characters like that. Here dirty old men you see for the first time in your life ask you, 'So what are you fucking, boys?' and reach for their shrivelled groin with gusto. And it's not a rhetorical question: they really do expect you to stop in the middle of the street or on the terrace of a café – wherever you've had the misfortune of running into them – and, whatever you've just been doing or intend to do afterwards, they insist that you scrap your plans and describe your last act of coitus for them in detail.

The policeman made no bones about being offended. If I had spat in his face it would have caused less affront than me being aloof.

'Alright, sir. Now, boys –,' he said and chuckled at his own joke, which eluded me, 'drive slowly, the boss is expecting you. Come on now, skedaddle,' he added and patted Goran's car like he might the flanks of a horse.

'And they say there's no functioning state here!' Goran sighed and put his foot to the floor.

Later, when I thought back to that day, I'd understand that it was then that I first noticed a sign of The Hand. As these things go, the terrible realisation did not hit me until afterwards, when it was too late: what if there's a hand guiding me through life? Not a Good Hand from above, nothing like that. More likely a Black Hand from below, from the police and intelligence-service underground. Nothing metaphysical or transcendental: no kind of god. But very much real and existing. The hand of some monstrous thing which only just comes into view, too big for me ever to see the whole of it, and large enough to block my view of everything else. In the years which followed, I would come to doubt that anything I did was of my own free will. I would see the volition of that Black Hand in my actions and would convince myself of its existence innumerable times. Yes, it was omnipresent, particularly when it seemed there was no one except me. Back then in Goran's car up in the Petrovačka Gora range, I would doubt that my article was the real reason for the minister's call. *What if he knows a lot more about me than I thought? What if I don't know anything about him, especially not what I thought I knew?* I asked myself.

We were in the grips of paranoia when we arrived in Podgorica. Goran was also troubled: what if that policeman had searched us and found the grass? What if the fatso had just been on patrol and a proper police ambush was waiting for us on the road into the city? My friend had decided to combine the pleasant with the useful, as they say, and had brought along a few little packets of Albanian ganja. There were buyers in Podgorica. I was convinced that the police weren't interested in small-time dealers, when not even the big ones interested them. But dark thoughts about what the minister could want of me whirled like a swarm of flies, whose persistent buzzing left me thinking just one thing: *this is not going to end well*.

We arrived at the Ministry of the Interior. A bay was reserved for us in the parking lot at the front. An officer pointed us the way and gave a conspiratorial nod. As we were entering the building, Goran remembered that he still had the grass on him. He admitted this to me in a whisper as we were waiting for security to search us.

'Perhaps this is the right moment to run out to the car,' I suggested.

'I forgot to lock the car, d'oh!' he groaned theatrically and smacked his forehead.

'Don't worry, it's in safe hands,' a seven-foot man said, who now introduced himself as head of security. 'There's no need for a search, they're with me,' he added for the police at the entrance.

The wall of men in blue opened wide before us like the gates of hell.

We went up the broad, marble stairs to the first floor, where the minister's office was.

'I'm leaving you now. You're in good hands,' the hulk said.

The door of the office opened. Red carpet, mahogany-panelled walls, photographs of the minister's meetings with foreign statesmen, glass cases of gifts he had been given at those meetings, among them a 1886 Winchester rifle from the director of the CIA. Then the secretary, whose birdlike voice I recognised. She ushered me in to see the minister. Goran waited in the front room, where the secretary promised to bring him coffee and a cold drink.

Massive leather furniture. On the floor a three-finger thick Persian rug, as soft as cotton wool, capable of defying gravity, which I couldn't restrain myself from taking a few steps on, as light as a moonwalk.

A Montenegrin flag in the corner. More mahogany, more showcases with gifts. A small library: the collected works of Marx and Lenin, several editions of the Letters of Petar I Petrović-Njegoš, the Montenegrin prince-bishop, a handful of titles on Russian-Montenegrin friendship, Catherine Albanese's *America: Religions and Religion*, a whole shelf of conspiracy-theory books on Freemasons and Illuminati. The room was dominated by a desk, a real masterpiece of the furniture of power. It plainly divided the world into the space in front of it and that behind it.

I cleared my throat discreetly a few times to try and announce my presence. There was no answer. I looked around the room searching for cameras. I thought I saw one above the bookshelves, but it was just a smoke detector.

Then I heard a toilet flush and the minister, smelling of soap, emerged from a room hidden behind the bookshelves.

'Ah, there you are,' he said in mock surprise. 'You caught me at an awkward moment. What can I say –,' eloquent Mandušić continued, 'the powerful have to shit too. We are also organic, very much so. Do you know the greatest desire of everyone in power? To escape the terror of nature and to overcome their biological limitations. That's why those in power hide away in monumental buildings, in temples of marble and steel. That's why they love monuments: they don't decay. And that's why the photograph is their favourite format: because it freezes time and turns it to stone. If we could command it, time would stop right here in the moment of our greatest triumph and our calm, firm rule. But to rule also means to await the moment when the mob will lynch us. That's not on the photo: it doesn't show the next episode with its arrests, public humiliation and perhaps even public execution. There's just the suspended light and suspended time of the moment before the fall.'

He threw his left arm over my shoulder. 'Come on, let's go into my study.'

He led me into a small room with piles of books and files on the floor. As I reclined in the armchair, I surveyed the titles: Melville, Auden, Dostoyevsky, Pound, Hegel, Benjamin…

'You know I have a PhD in literature from Zagreb,' he said. 'A lot of people wonder why I've ended up here, heading the police force. It's quite simple, actually: imagine the state as an enormous novel, a text which is continuously evolving and being written. My job, like that of a writer, is to have complete control over all the characters in the story. Who will understand them, with all their desires, hopes and ambitions, if not me? Who else can say what a character will do on the next page if not the writer, if not me? In society, as in a good novel, nothing happens spontaneously. Everything flows from the logic of the story and the nature of the characters. The ideal police officer doesn't solve crimes which have already happened but prevents future ones. It's not about interpreting the text but writing it.'

He took a bottle out of the cabinet – Aberlour single malt, twelve years old.

'Your favourite, if I'm not mistaken,' he winked. 'What can you do? People bring bottles. You know what we Montenegrins are like. It's a nice custom, if you ask me. Ultimately it's civilised, if we recall that they once used to bring dead animals, or even worse, children … Note the element of progress: it's better for them to offer a bottle of whisky than an ox's heart, isn't it? But now we're a candidate for joining the European Union and this custom, like so many others, will die out. Because it's corruption, you think? I'm rather an expert on corruption, believe you me, and this is not corruption,' he declared, raising his glass of whisky.

'You see, that's exactly why I've called you. Not because of corruption –,' he said through a laugh, 'but the European Union.

'The accession process "is under way", as they say, and I have to travel to conferences on security in Europe. Speeches are held, as you can imagine. We shepherds come together and talk to each other about the importance of properly supervising the flock.

'Now … I'm a proud man; that should come as no surprise. I'm not prepared to read out claptrap at those meetings. I have a horde of advisors, but I use them for just one thing: I ask them for their opinion, and then I do exactly the opposite of what they advise. Unfortunately I don't have time to devote to those speeches. So now we finally come to you, and I apologise for keeping you in suspense. I've been following your pieces for a long time. In fact, you could say I'm a devoted reader of yours. You remind me of myself when I was younger. Your delusions are charming and you argue them elegantly, with extraordinary zeal and conviction. That's what attracted me to your pieces. Don't get me wrong: I know very well you're not right, but still you almost convince me of your positions. That's a rare talent, and I could make good use of it. So I'm making you an offer. You can give up writing for the papers. Nothing really important is written about in the papers, nor are any problems resolved in newsprint. I'd like you to write for me. Be my ghost writer. There's no occupation like that within the system, of course, so you won't have to come in to work: your workplace will be your own study. If you want to move to Podgorica, we'll rent a flat for you. If not, we can deal with everything over the phone. There are no secrets here – everything is wire-tapped anyway, including this conversation. The pay isn't great, and government employees aren't rich, as you know, but it's certainly more than you earn now. That's it, that's all. There are no hidden conditions and no contract you have to sign in blood. It's a clean, strictly business relationship. What do you think?' he asked as he poured me another whisky.

'I need to think it over.'

'Just what I expected you to say,' he replied. 'I wouldn't employ a gutless yes-man.'

He saw me to the door, and before we parted he added:

'You know, after every meeting, however important it was, I don't think about what else I could have said. My only thought is what would best have been left *unsaid*. Remember that when you write for me.'

Goran later told me I came out of the minister's office *a different man* – that's how he put it.

I was silent all the way home, as if I was thinking about something important. Actually I had fallen into torpor, equally distant from all thought and all emotion, a state where I felt exceptionally at ease, so much so that I wanted it to last forever. I waited in the car until Goran had sold his weed, and then we travelled on home without a word. I invited him in for a drink, but he had promised to take his sister to the shops. He would see me that night, he said.

I went into my room and studied it: the rickety double bed with its stained blankets which cried out for a dry-cleaning; the threadbare plush armchair; the wooden desk; the ashtray full of cigarette butts; the glasses with the remains of the previous night's drink; the pictures on the spotty walls. Everything was in its place. Everything was the same.

But nothing was the same any more.

8

The newspapers reported on my appointment for weeks. Columnists wrote reams about the relationship between intellectuals and the system and about me betraying the principles of free journalism. NGO activists issued lengthy statements expressing abhorrence at the idea of a journalist working for the police. And one writer, wanting to explain the dimension of my fall, told an anecdote about Goethe and Beethoven. The two of them were walking along a forest track, he wrote, and a duke's coach was coming from the other direction. Goethe, if I remember correctly (or was it Beethoven?) stepped aside to avoid the horses which were bearing down on them with frightening speed. Beethoven (or was it Goethe?) refused to get out of the way. When the coach had passed, Beethoven (or perhaps it was Goethe after all?) blamed his friend for stepping aside to let the nobleman and his horses pass. The world is full of bigwigs, Goethe said (or was it Beethoven; one of them was definitely Goethe – or was one of them definitely Beethoven?). I sent that idiot an e-mail to thank him. I'm not sure if you consider me Goethe, or perhaps Beethoven, I wrote, but either way I'm eternally grateful: no one has ever made me a nicer compliment.

If I was able to see myself as a victim, if only for a moment, I would have called the whole thing a media lynch. But I refuse to be a victim, and there's nothing I dislike more than people who complain all day about their rights being threatened. That's why it's hard for me to live in this world, where everyone seems to just want to be a victim.

Since that's the way things are, I viewed the media's sudden concern for my humble self with utter contempt. It felt like a bucket of slops had been tipped over me by the two tycoons whose newspapers I wrote for before accepting Mandušić's offer. Whether they had nothing better to do or it was ordinary human malice, those two criminals acted as if they were offended by me no longer wanting to work for the pittance they paid. Minister Mandušić gave me more than just moral support – he furnished me with a list of people in the 'public eye' who were overtly or covertly in the pay of the two mentioned crooks. Interestingly, the names on the list coincided with names of the people who had disparaged me in the papers and, more importantly still, with the names on a list of public figures who were also on the payroll of Mandušić's secret police. Public intellectuals were secret agents and vice versa. Free journalists were spies, and vice versa. Independent media were secret-police bulletins and papers were edited by police officers, while newspaper editors did police work. Who on earth could make head or tail of this? I was ultimately glad about my decision to no longer participate in public life, which was nothing but the meanest brothel, where people careless enough to open the papers or turn on the television picked up deadly viruses and nasty contagions and carried them back to their homes.

If you have the misfortune to be written about in the papers, people descend on you like flies are drawn to shit. One day your name is mentioned in the press or on the TV news, and the next you won't be able to walk down the street for all the creeps who want to speak to you. Whether they criticise you or offer what they think is well-meaning advice, it leaves you feeling equally polluted and smelly. There is nothing which can remove that horrid, stinking aura from you except anonymity. And that is hard to regain, especially in a small country like Montenegro, where unfortunately people have good memories, are idle, and above all prone to malice. If you once become famous, or if you disgrace yourself, it doesn't matter which, you have to carry that stigma for the rest of your life.

But when that big, black blowfly came thumping on my door one morning at the crack of dawn, before the dustmen had even collected the rubbish, and introduced itself as *Great-uncle Tripko, your grand-mother's brother – don't you remember me?* things had really gone too far.

9

The night before, Goran, Maria and I had knocked off two bottles of Cardhu which Mandušić had sent me. The whisky ran out before midnight and unfortunately I didn't have anything else in the house except beer. The shops were closed at that hour in winter, so I had no choice but to call my neighbour Ramiz to help. He was someone you could rely on in an emergency. And we didn't need to wait a thousand years for our saviour: before five minutes had passed, Ramiz burst into the house with a box full of Rubin brandy.

'Let me give you young 'uns a word of advice –,' he said with a slur, 'whisky is good but always in short supply.'

Ramiz received a small Swedish pension or regular social-security payment, I never found out exactly what. He claimed to have 'earned' these means for a comfortable retirement simply by being in Stockholm: when he saw an open manhole, he seized the opportunity and jumped in, and later he sued the government. He wore a leather waistcoat all year round with two letters emblazoned on it: MR. That stood for Master of Rubin. He proudly bore that self-awarded title, and that was how he lived – and died – after having sent truckloads of Rubin brandy through his liver.

Anyway, where was I ... *Great-uncle Tripko, my grandmother's brother*, woke me from my drunken slumber. I had never seen the fellow in my life, and that's how things should have stayed. He burst into the house, demanded coffee, and, while a huge pneumatic hammer was pounding in my head, he began a monologue about why he had lugged his old arse all the way from Višegrad, Bosnia.

He blathered away for a good half hour, but it was clear from the first sentence, no, from the first word, no, from the first grim smile illuminated by a golden tooth (in place of the second left upper incisor, if I'm not mistaken), that Tripko wanted money.

Gruesome war crimes were committed in Višegrad. Anyone who's interested, although that's not many, can learn more or less everything about them today. But one thing is never mentioned when people talk about the war crimes, and I can't help but put it down to hypocrisy. The terrible thing to do with the war crimes is not just that some people were killed, but that some others weren't – Uncle Tripko for example – I thought that morning.

I bet he watched and applauded while Muslims were being butchered on the bridge over the River Drina, if he wasn't assisting the killers already. No doubt about it: that's the sort of mug he was. One look at Tripko and you could reconstruct his entire life with all the details of that worthless existence: a junior officer in the Yugoslav People's Army, who took early retirement and was now as fit as a fiddle at the age of seventy because he never had to work hard, his wife bore the load of the labour for him, and he beat her and cheated on her with waitresses and cashiers until she died of a heart attack. This beast had now read in the paper that a relation of his, 'a bosom relative' as he put it, had landed himself an important position, so now he came rocking up to get his share of the booty. 'Who can help each other if not family?' he philosophised as he slurped his coffee.

'Listen,' I finally said to him, 'I'm not sure we know each other, but that doesn't change a thing. Money is not an issue – there is no money. Even if I had any I wouldn't give it to you. If it makes things easier for you, take a look around. Do you see the hole I live in? Do you think some moneybags lives here?'

Then my uncle reared up and transfixed me with a gaze of primordial hatred.

'You little shit!' he thundered. 'Do you think you can get rid of me like you shake a tick off your trouser leg? No money, eh? A cushy position but no dough? Do you think Tripko's an old duffer? You don't know Tripko, sonny. Uncle Tripko will teach you to mess him around! This house you live in, this *hole*, as you call it – is mine. You think it was left to you by your grandmother, do you? But your grandmother wasn't your grandmother. My kind sister, bless her soul, brought you up like her own son because she had a heart as big as Russia, though you weren't kith or kin. But I won't have you loafing around here by the sea in my house while I rot away in a thirty-square metre hovel by the Drina. I go to sleep at night not knowing if I'll be kidnapped and wake up downstream! And to see you here like this!'

As strong as a bear, he grabbed me by the throat and pinned me against the wall: 'This is *my* house, *you're* the stranger here, and you dare to fuck me around!' he hissed. 'You think you're a clever Dick, don't you. You think you're better than me – you, a whore's little bastard, the son of that monster!'

Thus spoke Tripko, and he was a man of the old school: he honestly believed that every argumentation, however logical and rhetorically powerful, became even deadlier when backed up by a degree of brute physical force. Finally he threw me onto the bed like a stuffed toy and stormed out of the house like a huge, retarded boy in a huff, slamming the door behind him.

'You'll be hearing from me. Start packing and get out of my house quick smart!' he shouted from the terrace.

I lay on the bed and closed my eyes. All I could think of in the moment before sleep took me was what an utter scourge he was.

10

I never saw Uncle Tripko again. His solicitor didn't call me, and no letter with a court summons or eviction notice ever came.

Nor did Tripko ever arrive home in Višegrad.

It seems his neighbours alerted the police two weeks after he left for Montenegro, where, he told them in confidence, he had some important real-estate business to attend to. The papers reported that his car was found near Lake Piva, in front of a tunnel on the road from Plužine to the Bosnian border. Although divers were unable to locate his body, the investigation established that Tripko committed suicide by jumping into the lake. No farewell letter was found. The details of his visit to Montenegro were not known, the police announced.

Tripko disappeared, and with him the danger of me losing the house. What a lovely and apt happy ending, I thought at first. Alas, there is only one happy ending – the Apocalypse – even if it is only a promise. Everything else is just an open ending, a continuous series of open endings, whose resolution not only resolves nothing but further complicates already unbearably complicated things. Whenever someone says to me, 'That's simple', I think: Sure, mate, everything's simple if you've got no idea. To an ignoramus, everything seems self-explanatory, and 'obviously' is their favourite word.

In fact, everything which exists is complicated beyond our power of comprehension. If you think twice about things, if you re-examine your own assumptions and convictions, everything you think you know will turn out to be as enormous and mysterious as the Sphinx.

I tried my very hardest, but I couldn't forget Tripko's words. The fire belched by that ireful prophet of doom swept away the serenity of my world. All that remained of my peace and calm was the cold smoke rising from the scorched landscape I had lulled my existence into.

What the hell did he mean about me not being my grandmother's grandson? Was that undeniably vile man really such a rotter as to openly hate his sister's daughter? What could my unfortunate mother, whom my grandmother always spoke of as a saint and martyr, have done to offend him? Why did the papers write about the disappearance of Tripko Pavlović – not Hafner, but Pavlović? The man in the photos, which accompanied the articles, was Uncle Tripko. Right man, wrong surname.

Why did my grandmother never mention that she had a brother? Why the mix-up with surnames of close relatives? What else did that good woman keep secret from me?

11

After Tripko left *my* house and vanished into the void, I slept the whole day and the next night. I woke up beside my grandmother's grave. There were two lucratively paid, lazy gravediggers, whom I felt were taking absolutely ages to do the job. I hadn't informed anyone about grandmother's death. I remember I didn't have an obituary notice printed, and of course I didn't permit the outrageous perversion of announcing her death in the newspaper. Although the cemetery was unfamiliar, I knew I was in Bar. I didn't know anyone in that city and had her buried there so I could be sure nobody would come along and spoil things – those were my thoughts as I prepared the details of the funeral, I knew.

I had paid the workers well. They misunderstood the gesture and considered it their duty to pretend to be deeply touched by her death. When we'd buried her I couldn't make them leave the grave. They just stood there, crossing themselves ceaselessly in compensation for the lack of mourners. 'The poor woman: to die so alone and for no one to come to the burial,' one lamented. 'May the dark earth rest lightly on her after such martyrdom,' the other said. I desperately wanted to be alone but they refused to go. Instead, they came up with new and

The Olcinium Trilogy

ever more pathetic folkloric creations. This introduced an element of the ridiculous, which was superfluous because funerals are ridiculous as they are, in common with all situations where people feel obliged to be serious and dignified. I was reminded once again that the nicest thing we can say about a person is that one day they will die and cease to bother us. In the end, I had to pay the workers double before they finally agreed to leave. At a cemetery, surrounded by the dead, we're at the source of cognisance. At a cemetery we learn at first glance all we need to know about life: that we're going to die. I sat down on the dry stone wall by my grandmother's grave and lit a cigarette.

The wind blew several snowflakes into my face. I looked around and saw that I was alone at the cemetery, which extended out to all four corners of the world. Row upon row of stone crosses marched to the horizon, where threatening black clouds were mustering. War is the father of all things, I remember thinking: an army of dead against a heavenly army. Thunder rumbled through the valley. Both the cemetery and I witnessed those sound effects of nature in impassive silence. Wherever I looked, I saw graves mounted with crosses, upright and dignified, marking lives spent in humiliation and submission.

All around me, and as far as the eye could see, stretched the future in crystal-clear memory which was not mine.

When I finally saw the familiar world of my room, I quickly got dressed and ran out into the bright day. I rushed to the cemetery below the Old Town here in Ulcinj, where I had really buried my grandmother in the presence of two gravediggers and several of her old friends, who in the meantime had also died. Grandmother was buried here on 5 August, not in the winter and not in Bar; not on a squally day but in the suffocating heat; not with indifference but with all the pain I was capable of feeling. The old ladies, her friends, gave speeches and I cried all the way through, which they found touching. Even the gravediggers felt it appropriate to comfort me because I was crying so persistently. I remembered all that. But at the same time I wasn't sure about it all because the memory which gripped me that morning was suddenly purer and more powerful than my own.

I ran to the cemetery in the hope of finding out what I really did remember. I stood in front of my grandmother's grave and heaved a sigh of relief. The gravestone did give her name: *Olga Hafner, born 9 May 1930, died 5 August 2003. Erected by her loving grandson,* was carved in the marble.

12

When I got home, I tipped all the photos of my grandmother onto the floor and started looking through them again, searching for some detail to support the suspicion I was unable to shake off. I went through the family history for myself again and again, like as student preparing for a crucial exam.

Apparently, my mother had ignored my grandmother, who begged her not to go with that man. She fell in love with my father, a good-looking officer, who was a thrice-decorated piece of shit. It was his bravery which killed him. He went to Libya and died there in circumstances which were suspicious, to say the least. When he found out my mother was pregnant, he quit the army and vanished. He was a man who feared no enemy and saved two comrades from a burning tank (his first medal); who boldly intercepted assassins sent into the country by Croatian Ustashi émigrés (his second medal); and who shielded a general with his body when a crazed soldier from Kosovo fired at him (his third medal). And yet he fled head over heels from me, who wasn't even born. He heard I was due in five months' time and knew instantly what he had to do. He discarded everything – status, friends and the wife he claimed to love – and moved to Greece, where he enlisted in an American paramilitary outfit. They sent him to Libya, from where he never returned. His name was rarely mentioned in our house. Grandmother made sure of that. She told me terrible tales about that man, so I grew up grateful that I'd never have to meet him.

My mother was killed in a traffic accident in Germany soon after my birth. Grandmother then resigned from her job in the police force, where she worked as an office clerk, and devoted her entire life to me. From Visoko in Bosnia, where I was born, we moved to her family's house in Ulcinj. Her ancestors were originally from Izmir, she told me, and had come to Ulcinj following the Messiah – Sabbatai Zevi. They were in Zevi's company when he and his devotees put ashore at the quay, here at the end of the Ottoman Empire; for the Sultan had banished them when the Messiah's prophecies became too irrational, and the man himself too mad to be bought off and too famous to be executed – thus the danger to the throne. As Jews, this was just another station of exile for them. Zevi died ten years after coming to Ulcinj. His followers remained here to guard his grave, waiting for him to fulfil his prophecy that he would be resurrected. Grandmother told me that her distant ancestor, the one who first raised a house here, on whose ruins ours was built after the 1979 earthquake, was among the chosen ones who lowered Zevi into the earth, from where he had not yet arisen.

Grandmother and I lived together happily in Ulcinj – we needed no one else – until one searingly hot day when a dry sirocco was blowing, and her kind heart failed.

The sorrow I felt in the first few days after her departure and the funeral soon gave way to a sense of complete freedom. There was no one else I loved, and no one else loved me. I was no longer indebted to anyone or anything. My life belonged to me alone, and I didn't give a tuppence for it: there was nothing I desired in the future, and there was nothing in the past that others desired of me that would enslave me. Everything was here and now, doused with alcohol and filled with idleness and indifference. Why delve into the past, when all I would find there could only jeopardise the perfect freedom I lived in?

And then Uncle Tripko spoiled everything in just a few sentences. He seeded doubt in me which I couldn't root out. I had never cared about my background. I was brought up not to ask and not to think about my family. And yet here I was, examining the flimsy, perfunctory saga of a family which lurched from one misfortune to another, a story which suddenly revealed gaping holes and soon turned out to be a fairy tale, shabbily contrived and unconvincingly told. How could I have believed in it, I asked myself, aware of the answer: because I wanted to. That was enough; that is always enough. Everything we believe in are fairy tales. The firmness of our belief does not depend on the persuasiveness of the story but on our determination to remain blind for all evidence which could turn the story on its head. If we decide to seek the truth, everything collapses like a house of cards. Truth levels everything before it like an earthquake and carries it away like a flood. As soon as doubt arises, everything is doomed: nothing remains of all we believed in, happily relied on and made the foundation of our existence – only ruins covered in stinking sludge.

13

Here were the photos I had browsed through with grandmother hundreds of times: her and my mother drinking coffee beneath a cherry tree in the garden in Visoko one May; her and my mother in Ilica Street in Zagreb, arguing about my father (grandmother with her arm around my mother's shoulders, my mother looking through her, a tram passing by, and an elderly gentleman who had just come out of an ice-cream parlour bowing to them and raising his hat); her and my mother in front of Le Plaza Hotel in Brussels, where they spent two pleasant nights in long conversations about the Magritte exhibition they had seen, with coffee and Petit Beurre biscuits; her and my mother on Red Lion Square in London, searching for Cromwell's secret grave; her strolling beside Lake Ohrid in an elegant costume bought in Paris; her and friends at a festive lunch at the source of the River Bosna to mark the retirement of her colleague Milutin, who played the accordion and sang Bosnian ballads like a nightingale, and who died of a heart attack not long afterwards while singing like a nightingale to celebrate the birth of a grandson, an event he had waited a whole decade for, saying over and over again, 'I just want to have a grandson, then I can die in peace', meaning he died happy, like a man whose final wish has been granted; her and me strolling along the Stradun promenade in Dubrovnik, where she went with me for my seventh birthday (the bus from Ulcinj took five whole hours); her at the grave of her daughter in the town of Kronberg near Frankfurt, where she bought me a little sailor suit in a children's clothing boutique (I wore that suit obsessively until it fell to pieces – its process of disintegration was recorded in several photos); her at a Munich airport café drinking Julius Meinl coffee with milk and waiting for the clerks of the bank where my mother kept some hard cash she had willed to me (money my grandmother intended to spend on my education but which would be eaten up by the hyperinflation of the 1990s); and her by the sea in Oslo, where she travelled as if to fulfil the desire of one of her daughters, who died without having seen the northern ends of the earth, which she had dreamed of all her life. All these scenes were suddenly no more than illustrations of a tall story to lull a child to sleep. They documented nothing but lies.

But instead of telling myself to stop, I returned the photos to their places in the albums. Instead of shaking off all the questions I had and all that would necessarily follow, because questions are like misfortunes and never come alone, I crammed everything into my rucksack and raced off to Podgorica with the kind of determination which can only get you into trouble fast. Mandušić arranged for me to be received immediately at the forensic centre, where they promised to carry out a full analysis of the 'evidence', as they called it, as quickly as possible.

Needless to say, the findings confirmed my doubts: they are always confirmed.

All the photos were fakes. But very well done, I was told, the work of a master retoucher – a true professional. They were all produced in the same workshop in the space of a few days. It was as if someone had been given the task of fabricating a watertight family history. Grandmother hadn't been to Oslo, Germany, London or Brussels, at least not in those photos. She had never argued with my mother in Ilica Street or had a congenial coffee with her in Visoko. Who was that young woman in the photos with her? Who was my mother, Ida Hafner? And my grandmother? Was she really mine? And who the bloody hell am I? So many questions which couldn't be ignored once they had finally been asked …

14

What could I do? I sold the house and moved to Podgorica, where I used the money to buy a flat. The investigation which had been foisted upon me and I was now in the midst of could not be conducted from Ulcinj. I had to be physically close to the police, whose resources Mandušić generously placed at my disposal.

'What you're telling me requires serious organisation and means,' he said tersely and called Inspector Todorović, whom he instructed to assist me in any way I needed. 'Interesting, very interesting,' he muttered. 'You'll appreciate that this is now my problem too – having a man close to me with a past like this … '

I took a trip to Visoko, where I was supposedly born and had family roots. There was no proof of my birth there, nor any trace of Olga, Ida or me, David Hafner. But in the local archive I did find a birth certificate and a baptismal record for Tripko Pavlović, who had a sister named Olga.

I travelled on from Visoko to Višegrad and booked into a motel there. That same night, I sneaked out and broke into Tripko's house. I located his photo albums without much trouble. They were full of photos of him and Olga Pavlović, my grandmother.

The next day, already back in Podgorica, I met with Todorović on the terrace of Hotel Montenegro. He had promised to make enquiries with the Bosnian police about Olga Pavlović, and now he read out some of the notes the Sarajevo police had compiled. It turned out that she really had worked as a police clerk in the section which issued identity papers in Hrasno, a suburb of Sarajevo, where she had moved as a teenager and finished high school. Olga was reliable and popular with the other staff members. Her former colleagues stated that they had been surprised when she decided to take early retirement in August 1983, less than four months after I was born. Milutin Zec, who she shared an office with, said that it was 'as if the earth had swallowed her up'. As far as he knew, she never got in touch with any of her co-workers and friends again after she retired. He searched for her at her old address, 103 Lenin Street in the suburb of Grbavica, but the door of her flat was opened by a woman he had never seen before, who had come to the city from some godforsaken village. She wasn't sure, but she seemed to recall that Olga had mentioned moving to the coast. After that, Zec no longer searched for her, but he hoped for a long time that that kind and cheerful woman would get in touch again one day, when the unusual circumstances which had befallen her and forced her into such secrecy had changed; and he emphasised how 'out of character' her abrupt departure was.

15

Despite these revelations, it took months before I finally made a breakthrough in the investigation, which seemed to have run up against a tall, impenetrable wall separating me from myself.

Podgorica was sticky and slow. The months there passed like months in hell. Podgorica is a city of false poets, false academics, false journalists, false civil-society activists, false political leaders and false fathers of the nation. The city is a heap of lies and falsehoods on a patch of sun-scorched ground.

And all that is to do with the simple fact that Podgorica is a fake city. I had often mused about there apparently being cities without boulevards, but until I came to Podgorica I didn't know there could be boulevards without a city. To live amidst such haughty ugliness, as one is surrounded with in Podgorica, is unbearable for anyone with an ounce of good taste.

Old Podgorica was destroyed in Allied bombing raids in 1944. The only way to make the new Podgorica more beautiful would be to conduct a new and equally devastating bombardment.

But the greened terrace of Hotel Montenegro was a comfortable niche in that extremely unwelcoming city, and I had my weekly meetings with Todorović there. Over time, he was sounding increasingly like a scratched record: no progress, no progress, no progress ... In the end, he and I talked about everything: football, politics, alcohol – anything but the job he was meant to be doing for me. Todorović, like all policemen, had the talent of being inconspicuous when he wanted to be, and that is a quality I appreciate in people whose company I share. Our weekly stock of comments on current events would quickly be used up, so we drank our coffee and smoked in silence, watching the passers-by swarm along Saint Peter Cetinjski Boulevard, while liveried waiters darted to and fro around us. They looked like they had stepped out of a time machine which had come straight from the 1980s and the days following Tito's death.

Hotel Montenegro was supposedly a scaled-down replica of a hotel in Havana, so, sitting in the shade of the tall, massive Cuban columns during Podgorica's sweltering heat, you could imagine you were somewhere nicer. The hotel's furnishings were old and functional, in contrast to the leather armchairs and marble tables of Podgorica's other hotels and bars. Here they served strong Turkish coffee and perfect Jelačić cubes, confections named after the former Croatian viceroy which were rich yet refreshing, as well as caramelised-milk ice cream – a flavour full of childhood memories.

The city authorities were no different to the populace of Podgorica in feeling the greatest imaginable antipathy towards beauty and tradition of any kind, and ultimately they ordered that Hotel Montenegro be demolished and a chrome-and-glass Hilton raised in its place.

When they destroyed the only place in Podgorica where you could feel you weren't in Podgorica, my meetings with Todorović came to an end. They say that Guy de Maupassant vocally opposed the construction of the Eiffel Tower. He claimed it would irreparably destroy Paris. When the tower was built, because progress, particularly progress towards the worse, cannot be halted, journalists observed that Maupassant had the habit of dining in the Eiffel Tower's restaurant. Stupid as journalists always are, they reminded him that he had been the most vocal opponent of the construction of the Eiffel Tower and asked if it wasn't hypocritical for him to now be sitting in the tower every day. 'Not at all,' he allegedly replied, 'the Eiffel Tower is the only place in Paris where you cannot see the Eiffel Tower.'

In Podgorica, alas, you always knew you were in Podgorica: a city which, like all other urban abortions in the world, constantly and aggressively reminds you of its existence. I therefore kept my outings to a necessary minimum – although it was still unbearable – and received Todorović's empty reports by phone in the flat.

I am a person prone to nostalgia and who can enjoy sorrow. Few things in life have brought me as much happiness.

Cooped up in my flat in Podgorica, I missed the routine of my old life in Ulcinj: the security of repetition and the comfort of rituals. I missed the throng of the steep, narrow lanes, which always had water running down them from the nearby courtyards where women washed carpets and children yelled in a language I had never learned. I missed the old men in their white caps, like egg shells, sitting on stools in front of the pastry shops and smoking, the tinkle of bicycles on the worn-out cobblestones, and the voice of the muezzin from on high, calling the faithful to prayer. I missed the wall of sound on summer afternoons: the hysterical cicadas, the braying of thirsty donkeys and the stomp of horses left to wander the olive groves all summer (in the autumn they would be taken out to the scrub to cart firewood their owners gathered for sale). I missed the clear February days cleansed by the northeaster, the cold which the wind brings from the snow-covered Albanian hills, a freshness good for thinking and for sleeping. I missed my conversations with Goran, so much like confessions. And, most of all, I missed Maria.

16

She wrote to me. She sent long mails and brilliant essays imbued with her exquisite melancholy, which grew and grew, towering over her like the blue shadow of a tired, old oak, its branches like sonorous, silver gallows. Her thoughts about suicide, which at first frightened her and made her want to dispel them, merged into an idea which took control of her, and she became its fragile body. If I had been able to imagine myself as a knight, even for just one second, I would have raced off to Ulcinj to try and save her. But to love means to unconditionally accept. To love Maria meant to love the death which was approaching not timidly, like a thief in the night, but proudly and with dignity, like a matriarch with her retinue.

My mother hasn't come out of her room for years, she once wrote. *The servants bring food and alcohol to her chambers. Ever less food, ever more drink. They leave the trays at the door and run without looking back; fear drives them, and so they gossip about her in the kitchen. The only sign that she is still alive are the empty bottles and tins they discover from time to time in the corridor. One night I opened my eyes and saw her naked, still beautiful – terrifyingly beautiful – leaning over me in bed. She put her hand on my forehead: 'My poor child, my poor little me,' she whispered. Her hand was icy cold and as soft as a spiderweb. I wanted to speak, but I was only able to stare at her. Then sleep took me.*

17

At the time, Maria was reading Jacques Le Goff's *Your Money or Your Life: Economy and Religion in the Middle Ages*. Despite her nervous disorder and all the alcohol, her mails to me left no doubt that her intellect was still a fine instrument she played like a virtuoso:

William of Auxerre wrote on the cusp of the twelfth and thirteenth centuries: 'The usurer acts against the natural laws of the universe because he sells time, which is common to all creatures… nothing gives itself as naturally as time: willy-nilly, all things have time. Since the usurer sells what necessarily belongs to all creatures, he injures all creatures, even the stones; thus, if men were silent against the usurers, the stones would cry out if they could; this is another reason why the Church pursues the usurers.' The usurers misappropriate God's time, with terrible repercussions: earthly justice is curtailed. And, William adds against the usurers: 'God says: *When I take back possession of time, that is, when time is in My hands again and no usurer can sell it, I will judge in accord with justice.*' David, the accusation could not be more serious: the usurers prevent God from administering justice fairly! But if the usurers stole God's time, was the Church not a party to the crime?

The stakes in the conflict between the Church and the usurers were enormous: 'The whole of economic life at the dawn of mercantile capitalism was called into question,' Le Goff writes. An enduring ban on earning money based on time, which is the essence of usury, would have meant destroying the very precondition for credit transactions. It would have meant an alternative history. Can we imagine history without banks, without debt?

On one side stood the Church's time, which belonged to God and could not be sold. On the other there was that of the merchants, whose business rested on 'hypotheses around the concept of time – the accumulation of stockpiles in anticipation of scarcity, and buying and selling at favourable moments'.

Our world is at a crossroads. Concession by concession, each of which is more significant than the last, 'the aristocracy of money changers is

succeeding the aristocracy of money minters'. In the Middle Ages, 'a great indifference towards time' prevailed. But after Saint Bernard, who cursed money,
people soon arrived at the conviction that *time is money*: not just subject
to sale, but a firm currency which ensures prosperity and social prestige for
those who possess and distribute it. All this, Le Goff says, 'heralds the Stock
Exchange, where minutes and seconds would create and destroy fortunes'.

In 1355, the councillors in Aire-sur-la-Lys allowed entrepreneurs to erect
a belfry whose bells would not call to prayer but chime the hours of com-
mercial transactions and the working hours of the weavers. The workers
who came from the surrounding villages to work needed to be called. The
church bells lost their monopoly over the measurement of time. Many contemporaries were concerned and considered that Europe was beginning to
beat to 'infernal rhythms'.

Time therefore became secularised. It would no longer flow to the
cadence of divine service but to the rhythms of production and transaction.
The merchant who travels to open up opportunities for his business and thus
extends the market is living Aristotle's definition: *time is the number of motion*.

He is aware of the price of time: the duration of his journey can be clearly
expressed in terms of money.

For the merchant, professional time becomes the time he lives in, a
dimension fundamentally detached from petrified, supernatural, ecclesias-
tical time, whose demands he will ever more be obliged to ignore. But the
merchant will donate part of his profit to the Church and work on his own
personal salvation. Le Goff says, 'It is important to eliminate the suspicion
that the psychology of the medieval merchant was hypocritical.' He sincerely
hoped for salvation, but he prayed with equal sincerity for the success of
his transactions, in which he resold *God's time*.

Before long, the citizens of Aire would be calling the time given by the
working bell *reliable hours*, as opposed to the *unreliable hours* of the church
belfries. The decisive move towards the domination of working time came
with mechanical clocks, Le Goff writes. The foundations of that innova-
tion were laid in the thirteenth century, and by the second quarter of the
fourteenth century urban clocks had been installed across northern Italy,
Catalonia, Flanders, Germany, northern France and southern England. The

sixty-minute hour was introduced, which constituted one twenty-fourth of the day. Instead of the working day, which went from dawn till dusk, the so-called *nono*, the ninth hour, was introduced and the hour became the basic unit of work. The ninth hour was intended for rest. It began around what today is two in the afternoon and finished at three, only to be brought forward to today's *noon*. Did you know that that is the origin of the word noon? Despite these developments, time had not yet been standardised. In *Journey to Italy*, Michel de Montaigne describes the chaos a traveller finds himself in because time changes from one city to another: the zero hour is sometimes midnight, sometimes noon, and it could also be sunrise or sunset, Le Goff explains. The crucial shift towards the subjectivisation of time would only come with the invention of the wristwatch, which measures our personal time. It also marked the end of *God's time*.

18

In another mail, Le Goff's book fuelled her obsession with debt and guilt. She wrote to me:

Dear David,

If we've learned anything from Nietzsche, it's that the relationship of the debtor and the creditor is the foundation of society. It's like this: the morals of a community are a catalogue of what we owe others; tradition – of what we owe our ancestors; the family we were born into – what we owe our parents; the Church as steward – what we owe God; patriotism – what we owe the state and nation; the economy – what we owe the usurers; ecology – what we owe Mother Nature; life itself – what we owe God, Nature, providence and chance… or in my case my dear mother, who never fails to remind me of that.

And politics is a guardian of the system where everything can be changed except the fundamental debtor-creditor relationship, i.e. nothing. What then is the meaning of life other than damn repayment of debt? I mean, other than the production of even more debt to saddle our children with? Which you and I won't have, fortunately, because we're not villains like that.

I think I've already mentioned Benjamin's essay to you, the one where he claims capitalism is a pure religious cult – one of the most extreme in human history. A cult is something which turns our lives into an unrestricted celebration of the outwardly secular, but which is actually occult: a permanent liturgy, restless and merciless. It is a cult which, instead of repentance and absolution, offers an endless feeling of guilt which becomes stronger with every heartbeat, an endless accumulation of debt: both ethically and literally, expressed in money. I read in the paper this morning that every French baby comes into the world with 22,000 euros of debt. People are thus born in chains, while all around us, as far as the eye can see, flags of freedom proudly fly. Before the baby grows up and can begin working and repaying the debt, it needs an education. Which is not possible, of course, without incurring additional debt. The Federal Reserve estimates that the total sum of student loans in the USA amounts to one thousand billion dollars.

I know all this, and still *I can't do it*… I can't because I feel a debt to my mother, who had me so I would be her toy, and then kept me to be her slave. I can't, because that debt makes me feel guilty. Benjamin points out that the German word *Schuld* means both guilt and debt.

There is no mousehole for me to hide in, not when I'm surrounded by all those stewards of debt acting as agents of the creditor. The Church is only the most flagrant example. Jesus died for us on the cross to free us, after which we are indebted exclusively to the Church. It warns us that writing off the debt will not come cheaply – we are indebted to those who represent Him who relieved us of our debts. That is what has now become of La Nona Ora, the ninth hour…

At the ninth hour, Jesus cried out with a loud voice: 'Eloi, Eloi, lama sabachtani?' Father, Father why have you forsaken me? I yell and shout: Mother, Mother why will you not forsake me?

The Olcinium Trilogy

How was that woman able to implant the idea in me that I have no right to kill myself while she is alive? To begin with, she considered the pregnancy from which she bore me to be a greater sacrifice than Jesus's death. Jesus ultimately died at the ninth hour, while she had to carry me for a whole nine months. She preached at me about the pain of parents who lose their child. There was nothing more terrible, she said, and surely I wouldn't do that to my poor mother. She hammered that into my head, so now I hang from the gallows of life, bleeding and in pain, but there will be no relief for me until she dies. Which she refuses to do. The tankerloads of alcohol she's drunk would have killed an elephant, but she continues to drink and to rule this house with confidence, along with my life. She is the owner of my debt.

It's like that everywhere, the whole world over. The Academy of Arts and Sciences and other institutions of national culture present themselves as stewards of tradition. The army traditionally figures as a steward of the debt to the nation-state, while in peacetime that job is assumed by the class of political representatives. Not to mention the Superego, which is the most brutal debt collector: however much guilt people feel, and however much regret they pay off the interest with, the principal remains untouched (moreover: the more we regret, the greater the guilt), but the actual amount we owe is unknown, though obviously immeasurable. The issue of debt is evidently a keystone of society, but also of our personality.

The representatives of debt like to stress that we are free. My mother, too, says I should do as I like and tells me it's my life and mine alone. But before I take the final step, I should at least spare a thought for my mother and what it would mean for her… That's how it is. Not only did Jesus free us, but freedoms are guaranteed to us by the Constitution and the laws of the land, as well as the Charter of Human Rights, libertarian traditions, and ultimately the army, as our freedom's last line of defence. We are free, ultimately, to choose our usurer: the choice of bank where we will raise a loan is a luxury and ours alone.

Whenever I look at my watch, it's three o'clock – always the ninth hour. I wake up at night, drag myself to the kitchen because I'm burning with thirst, and the clock on the wall shows three in the afternoon. Has it stopped? I check, and I see that it's working. Then at dawn, when the mist has fled before the light and those stupid roosters are crowing their heads off, the clock in my mobile shows three in the afternoon. I check all the clocks in the house: they all say it's three. I tell Tereza, the cook, a *woman of the people* and an expert on the irrational. She crosses herself and offers me her rosary. 'You need protection: don't refuse the Saviour,' she says to me. 'I'll pray for you when I'm next at the monastery.' She's five months pregnant, but that doesn't stop her from going on a pilgrimage by bus to Ostrog Monastery every third week. What does she pray for there? For the return of her child's father, who bolted when he heard she was pregnant.

19

There were times she would ring at three in the morning, sometimes drunk, sometimes stoned. We'd talk until dawn, or until she fell asleep with the phone in her hand. Then I lay in bed and listened to her breathing. That was all I had of her. It was enough.

20

My days in Podgorica continued like that until Todorović knocked on my door one morning and announced jubilantly: 'We're onto something!'

Olga Hafner, actually Olga Pavlović, my grandmother who wasn't my grandmother, had signed a deed of adoption and taken me from an orphanage in September 1983. The manager of the orphanage was still alive. Todorović had found her in Dobrota near Kotor, where she had retired to a house inherited from her late husband. At first she refused to talk on the topic: 'It was so long ago. No one can remember things like that.' But Todorović was persistent, and in the end she told him that a secret-service agent had brought the boy to the orphanage. 'We'll send someone for him,' the gloomy man said before he left. Less than a month later, he visited again and gave her instructions: 'The woman will introduce herself as Olga Hafner. This is her photograph. You'll give her the child, and you won't ask any superfluous questions. Is that clear?'

She saw the agent once more – after the woman had taken the baby. He suddenly turned up in her office and sat down at the desk. He demanded all the documents which proved the child had been at the orphanage and then proceeded to burn them one by one. 'None of these ever existed,' he explained to her. 'None of this ever happened, especially not the child. Is that clear?'

She was a woman for whom orders were orders, particularly when they came from the state. She would have taken the secret with her to the grave if Todorović had not turned up and invoked the 'interests of the state'. *The system has come to claim its own, so I will give it its due,* she thought.

But the old woman didn't remember my mother's name. She couldn't have, because she had never known it. Neither the mother nor the child had a name, and none of their particulars had ever been revealed to her. She looked after the child in secrecy and passed it on to Olga Hafner under a cloak of silence. Everything to do with the child was a secret – one she never stopped thinking about and still remembered every detail of today, in advanced old age, when even the faces of her late husband and daughter were fading.

That's good for starters, I thought when I saw out Todorović, who had given me three kisses when he arrived, according to Orthodox custom, and gave me three more when he left, glowing with happiness at the idea that Mandušić might promote him for accomplishing the task so well. *I'm becoming a serious secret,* I thought – *something it's not beneath my dignity to deal with.*

I could forget about grandmother and everything she had told me about myself. Now I had to focus on my mother – the key to the story. Who was 'Ida Hafner' and what was her real name? What did that woman do to earn the dubious privilege of having the Yugoslav secret service take care of her child?

So many questions and not a single answer ... I'd think about it all tomorrow, I decided. I phoned Goran. As I expected, he accepted my invitation: a party at my place in Podgorica tonight. He promised to bring Maria. I had reason to celebrate. Todorović's discovery amounted to an ontological promotion. I wasn't actually a lazy, nihilistic alcoholic from a provincial backwater. Whatever I finally discovered myself to be would be more exciting than what I thought I knew about myself. The feeling which had accompanied me from the very beginning of my existence – a sense of absolute, cosmic cold and solitude – now seemed much more complex than a whim or a character flaw; it seemed understandable, justified and ultimately correct. Not only did I perceive all my fellow citizens as foreign, but I was foreign to myself. That's how it was and that's how it always would be, because that's how it was meant to be.

I opened a present from Mandušić – a bottle of eighteen-year-old Jura, poured myself three fingers of whisky (the closest I ever got to Orthodoxy and their three-finger salute) in a crystal glass of my grandmother's, stretched out on the couch and put on a Mono album at full blare: *For my Parents.*

21

The party was to my liking: lots of alcohol and not many people. I had a load of Mandušić's whisky all to myself because Maria and Goran were getting into a batch of rare Primitivo Barrique – no more and no less than ten bottles – which they had taken from Elletra's splendid wine cellar. Everything was great until Radovan turned up with two business partners and a prostitute in tow.

You could see straight way that he had succeeded in life. The lady of his heart had rags worth a good two thousand euros *on* her and at least twice that much *in* her, in implants. I congratulated Radovan on moving on from *The Second Chance* and those asylum seekers from undemocratic Eastern Bloc states, and I really meant it – I am someone who takes delight in others' good fortune. But that wasn't to the liking of his escort. She claimed she wasn't a prostitute; in any case she didn't feel like one. Seething with rage, she stepped up to me and hit me with her CV: she had earned a law degree and done a PhD in public relations; now she ran an NGO which 'worked to strengthen democratic institutions and control the work of the Montenegrin government in coordination with a number of foreign embassies in Podgorica' – those were her exact words; and she performed legal services for Radovan in connection with a site he had bought in Bar, where he planned to develop a five-star, luxury boutique hotel. She had come along because Radovan insisted and assured her I wasn't a bad guy, although she harboured the deepest contempt for me and all intellectuals who betrayed every principle they had ever stood for.

Radovan grabbed her by the hand and pulled her away to the other room, where, to my horror, he poured her a full glass of Mandušić's whisky. Then he came back to me and said with a wink: 'How about she blows you one afterwards? I'll pay.'

'No thanks,' I said. 'That bit about cooperating with foreign embassies hit me like a ton of bricks. I hate to think what that means and what repercussions it could have for the people of this country, and thus for me. Call it paranoia if you like, but after that I need a good stiff drink,' I remarked and walked away. I hoped I'd seen the last of him.

Throughout the evening, Radovan and his business partners took it in turns to perform legal consultations with the NGO activist in my toilet and showed absolutely no interest in mixing with me, Goran and Maria. The three of us went out onto the balcony and sat there, drinking. Maria and I were slagging off Radovan, who, ever since we'd known him, had succeeded in turning other people's money into his own and setting up a big construction firm which sold hundreds of flats along the coast. Like me, Maria had detested him from the very beginning but put up with him because he found it 'awesome' to socialise with us and was willing to be our free taxi service and drive us home when we were drunk, high or sick. Now Maria, like me, didn't have the nerves to cope with the animal any more. Goran, as usual, had to say a few words in his defence. That struck me as suspect.

'Hold on, you haven't become a "business partner" of Radovan's too, have you?'

He went red. The topic was clearly unpleasant for him. He decided to play the *I'm offended that you even thought of it* card. I didn't want to torment my friend, so I accepted his bluff:

'Forget it, I was just joking. They're all welcome. Cheers, and may our livers always be young … '

The peaceful coexistence between us and Radovan's crew lasted until Maria wanted to dance and put on 'Enola Gay' by Orchestral Manoeuvres in the Dark.

'Why the hell did ya put on those poofs?' the drunken Radovan yelled the moment he heard the word *gay*.

I opened the door and pointed to the corridor.

'Out!' I hissed. 'Or would you prefer leaving through the window?'

Those swine who had rooted their way to success in the new capitalist system figured I meant business. They were right: animals like that have a good sense of danger. They grabbed their things and made a move, leaving a few used condoms behind on my bathroom floor.

'You're making a mistake, mate,' Radovan whispered on the way out. 'Things have changed – you're not in a position to mess around Radovan any more.'

I slammed the door behind them.

'Good, let's start again,' I called, as if they had never been there. 'Put the song on again.'

That was just what Maria had been waiting for. I dropped into the armchair and watched as she danced with her eyes closed, so beautifully, with such dedication, as if that was her last will and testament, as if she had chosen it to be her life's final deed.

Later, when Maria had fallen asleep on the couch and Goran and I were pouring our third *one more and then it's off to bed* out on the balcony, I explained what had so infuriated me about Radovan's idiotic comment.

'What you don't know is that that song is my and Maria's little secret,' I told him. 'Once we were sitting on the terrace of my house in Ulcinj before dawn, after a drinking spree which makes this look tame, watching the calm sea and the currents coming up from Otranto, and she proposed a scenario for the end of the world. Imagine: shit happens and everything is obliterated in the flood. Only she and I survive. Nothing terrible, you might say: we are the new Adam and Eve, and everything can begin anew. But then we give the "up yours" salute to God, history and the human race. We live happily and not particularly long. But we never shag and make babies, so everything ends with us. The two of us reign over a world, finally globalised, where only two human beings still exist and there is only one state – ours. And its anthem is "Enola Gay".

'Why did Maria choose that of all songs? "Enola Gay" isn't a pro-gay hit from the 1980s, as Radovan thought, and as the former BBC1 editors also assumed when they banned it from being aired. Enola Gay was the name of the plane which dropped the atom bomb on Hiroshima. Enola Gay was also the name of the pilot's mother. Imagine: he named the B-29 *Superfortress* which would sow fire and death after his mother! "What dedication to the mother-destroyer! What a man! What a son!" Maria exclaimed in a rapture of delight,' I told him.

Goran patted me on the shoulder and trudged inside. I heard him crash onto the bed.

I poured myself another whisky and stared at the empty streets which Maria and I would reign over with composure one day when everything was finished, when the water receded and the sludge it left behind dried, and the bones of those it had purged from the world were crumbled by the sun and blown away by the wind. My queen slumbered in her chamber while I, the tired ruler, stood a lonely vigil over my kingdom.

22

Two years passed, and still I knew nothing more about my mother – and thus about myself. I was still cooped up in my hole in Podgorica. One time Mandušić tried to pull me out of there. An international meeting was being held in Budva, where the participants were to use lofty terms such as 'democracy', 'human rights' and 'united Europe' to explain why complete control of the population was necessary. Mandušić imagined *I* could attend as a speaker for the Montenegrin police.

I agreed because the meeting was to be held at Hotel Splendid, and I saw the opportunity for a free binge and for enjoying the luxurious rooms and bars.

I had planned to write my speech there, in Budva. But I stayed up late drinking on the first night of the conference, and the second as well. On the third day, I decided to talk without a prepared speech. I went up to the rostrum in front of around a hundred police, politicians and activists, and told them the following story.

Several years ago I met Peter, a Hungarian writer, in a beachside café in Ulcinj. I don't know what he was doing there. But, as usual when I run into a foreigner wandering our country and desperately searching for a way out of the labyrinth of ugliness and mindlessness they have voluntarily entered, I felt a sense of shame – as if I was somehow to blame for their misfortune.

Peter was a great guy. He was a misanthrope, but those are the only kind of people who should be allowed to enter Montenegro, where only misanthropes will feel at home and find everything they're looking for.

Before I could finish my first espresso, he let fire three politically incorrect, and therefore witty, remarks.

'Is it true that Russians have bought up half of Montenegro?' he asked.

'They do literally buy territory, and no one knows how much of the country they already own,' I told him. 'Montenegrins are satisfied for the time being. They sell land to the Russians, buy flats and big SUVs, and then drive along the coast and bellyache about the Russians having bought everything. On the way they tank up their fuel-guzzling jeeps at Russian-owned Lukoil petrol stations. Soon all the petrol stations are going to be Russian, people say, because allegedly Lukoil is going to purchase Jugopetrol. Montenegro previously sold it to the Greeks, but they're unable to make a buck even from selling petrol.'

'What's the solution then?' Peter asked me.

'The solution is universal and always the same,' I told him. 'In the end, the Montenegrins will stage a revolution, nationalise everything, and then things will start all over again. Or they won't. But that's always an option.'

Then Peter, who had now drunk four espressos and moved on to Jäger-meister, began a nostalgic colonial discourse.

'Hungary used to have access to the sea,' he told me. 'The Adriatic was our *mare nostrum* and Pula – the traditional summer resort for Hungarians. We built Rijeka, and even Naples was once ours.'

One of the effects of coffee consumption must be the annulment of colonial consciousness, it occurred to me.

Then our conversation moved on to suicide.

'The suicide rate in Hungary has always been high,' Peter told me. He was one of those people where you can't tell from their face if they're being deadly serious or lucidly sarcastic. 'People from elsewhere misinterpret the Hungarians' predilection for suicide. In Hungary, suicide isn't to do with depression. It's a culturological phenomenon, above all. Hungarians are a proud people who love their freedom. To die on your own terms, at a time of your choosing, is the only true freedom.'

'Listen, Peter, it looks to me as if you Hungarians are the ideal occupiers,' I confided in him. 'If you get into gear while we're driving out the Russians, you could occupy Montenegro. You'd come, build some roads and other infrastructure, and then simply vanish – by killing yourselves. We wouldn't even have to chase you out.'

It dawned on me that a true, mature democracy is not one which guar-antees a transition of power without civil war and insurrection, or where minorities are adequately represented in parliament through their own elected delegates. Nor is it one with a complete separation of powers, or where the full rule of law has been achieved, or which successfully uses all legal means of repression in the fight against corruption…

A true, mature democracy is one where the citizens confide responsible public functions solely to people prone to suicide.

To my mind, the story was short, clear and instructive: what else do you expect of a speech?

For some reason the audience didn't share my opinion. There was no applause, not even of the polite, half-hearted variety. People whom I had expected to have seen and heard everything, so that nothing could surprise them any more, looked at me in astonishment, as if I was standing there naked, at the very least. Unable to conceal her uneasiness, the moderator muttered something about it being democratic to listen, even to bizarre and extreme opinions, and hastily called up the next speaker.

I judged that my participation in the conference was no longer required, so I checked out at the hotel reception, gave a generous tip to the young fellow who drove the car up from the garage, and shot off to Podgorica and my flat, which I hated, but at least I wasn't surrounded by idiots there.

23

The media scandalised the whole thing, but two days later everyone forgot about it because a man in Nikšić killed a neighbour and his three small children, so the masses had a new incident to be horrified at. Mandušić didn't comment on the event. He didn't send me to any more meetings like that, though, or to any at all.

But he didn't sack me. It seemed that listeners liked the speeches I wrote for him more than they appreciated my ad-libbing in Budva.

He cut my pay by a third, but I didn't complain. It was easily earned money. After sending the first few speeches to Mandušić I realised it was pointless to invest any effort or inventiveness in the work. Everything politicians said and all they were expected to say was a pile of commonplaces and mind-numbing phrases. Therefore I prepared about fifty stock sentences: about parliamentary democracy, the inclusion of minority groups, the importance of a military deterrent for the stability of tolerant societies, the history of Montenegro with emphasis on the so-called Mediterranean foundations of its culture, about multiculturalism, a few quotes from Hegel and a little Plato from *The Republic*. I arranged all this on a large, B1 sheet of paper and pinned it to the wall of my study.

It resembled the magic squares the alchemists used to draw in the Middle Ages. A magic square enchanted the people of the time, just as they have always been fascinated by short sequences containing some pattern, which they like to believe proves the logical order of that large sequence, the biggest one of all, which they call the world. In an alchemist's magic square, the sum of the numbers along the vertical and the diagonal was always the same. In my magic square, however I arranged the hackneyed sentences and whatever order I assembled them in, the effect was the same: absolute bureaucratic dimness and liberal-democratic ideological blinkering. Applause for the thinker, please. That's the crux of it: people once strove for perfection. Now we're quite satisfied with the least bad of all systems, as its devotees describe democracy.

24

Maria and I started to fall out of touch. Like a nugget of gold thrown into water, she sank into melancholy. She went down wordlessly, without resistance, and accepted it as her destiny, if what we're frolicking towards can be called that. Maria's sorrow was more than just a state of mind – it was her own aesthetic choice. Sorrow is so beautiful, she used to tell me, and she only said what she meant. And did what she said.

Goran got a job at a bank. He became a loans officer and felt he had it good. He bought a new car, helped his father repair the roof and do up the front of the house, and generously supported his sister. Our drinking sprees became a rarity and later ceased altogether, because Goran decided that alcohol must not get in the way of his career. So his career got in the way of our friendship, which continued to be as sincere as before – except that we no longer practiced it.

As for my investigation, it really 'got off the ground', as the journos like to say, when I received a mail from an unknown address, woven-hand@gmail.com, drawing my attention to the unusual biography of Júlia Fazekas. I read the life-story of this serial killer with interest and enjoyment but then forgot about it. Two weeks later, from the same address, I received what was supposedly a scan of police records compiled by an Inspector Rešid Spahić from the Bosnian Centre for Public Security in Sarajevo.

Spahić claimed to have discovered irrefutable evidence that some of the atrocities committed in Višegrad during the war by a unit under the command of the cousins Milan and Sredoje Lukić had not actually been war crimes as qualified by the tribunal in The Hague but ritual killings. Spahić assumed there had been more such crimes in Bosnia, and he also suspected that the killers were still at large. And not only that: he maintained that because of the nature of the crimes, because occult killers don't stop until they're arrested, the investigation was bound to reveal a series of murders extending up until today. We were dealing with a well-organised group of psychopaths with influence in the state and police apparatus – influence sufficient to block the investigation and send it in the wrong direction – which had left a bloody trail and an unknown number of victims all through the country.

1,760 people were killed in Višegrad in the first months of the war. Hundreds of houses were burned down and the mosques demolished.

Almost two thirds of the population were forced to flee: long lines of Muslims left the town, and afterwards Višegrad was proclaimed Serbian. Day after day, for weeks, people were killed and their bodies thrown from the bridge into the Drina. On 18 June, a group under the command of Milan Lukić killed twenty-two people. They were tied to cars and dragged through the town, and parts of their bodies rolled along the streets. Survivors later testified that some of the victims had their throats cut, and then their internal organs removed. Spahić claimed he had discovered a house with a shrine, where those organs were offered to the devil. He claimed to have witnesses, whose identity he wasn't prepared to reveal, as well as photographs confirming his testimony.

On 28 June 1992 – St Vitus' Day and the anniversary of the Battle of Kosovo – Milan and Sredoje Lukić forced about sixty Muslims into a house in Pionirska Street and threw in grenades. Then they set the house on fire. Some people tried to escape by jumping out the windows, but the Lukićs were waiting outside, armed with automatic weapons, and mowed down the fugitives. They killed fifty-nine people that day. Seventeen of them were children, one of whom had been brought to the house after being born at the maternity hospital the day before. One of the survivors told Spahić that he had seen pentagrams painted in blood on the walls of the house when he was taken there. Later he managed to climb out through the bathroom window and run away before the Lukićs closed off that escape route, too, with a hail of bullets. Before his flight from the bathroom he had seen the dismembered bodies of three children and their hearts lying in the bath. He could still see those three little hearts before his eyes today and hear them beating, Spahić's witness said.

I called Todorović. I asked him to enquire about Spahić and try to confirm the authenticity of his report. He came to see me that same afternoon. Yes, Inspector Rešid Spahić did exist. And yes, he had presented his theory about occult crimes in wartime Višegrad to senior staff at the Bosnian Centre for Public Security. It was dismissed as being just another of the conspiracy theories, which Spahić, as it turned out, rather bombarded his superiors with. But he seems to have been particularly fond of this story because he threatened to 'go public' with it if the directors of the Centre didn't agree to open an investigation and grant him the extra powers he was requesting. He was suspended. He went for a long walk on the slopes of Mount Trebević near Sarajevo, from which he didn't return. His body was never found.

A person unknown to me was trying to tell me something. I assumed I would receive more messages from wovenhand@gmail.com in the days ahead. The sender obviously wanted to direct my attention to something. It was up to me to discover what.

What was the link between the biography of Júlia Fazekas and the satanists who masked their crime in Višegrad as a war crime?

Who could my mysterious benefactor be? Todorović hadn't been able to pick up his trail, although I explicitly demanded that of him. Police documents were not accessible to just anyone. If he was a member of the police, or someone who controlled its operations, he would be able to find out all the things I got Todorović to ask his friends from the Bosnian services. It could be someone with an interest in me finding out more. Or a person afraid I'd find out something I shouldn't, and who therefore set a trap for me and hoped I'd fall into it.

25

In my efforts to arrive at some answer to these questions, even an inconclusive one, I returned to the biography of Júlia Fazekas, which my mysterious friend had so kindly recommended to me.

Júlia Fazekas was vilified after her death. Today she would be glorified as a radical feminist.

Little is known about her life prior to 1911, when, like an angel of death, she appeared in the Hungarian village of Nagyrév, about a hundred kilometres from Budapest. She was a middle-aged widow.

The police first took an interest in Júlia in 1911, when an investigation into illegal abortions she had performed did not result in any conviction. Júlia would find herself in court nine more times over the next ten years, faced with the same charge. She was acquitted every time.

When the Great War began, the men of Nagyrév were drafted into the army. The women remained alone – that is, until a prison camp for Allied soldiers was set up near Nagyrév. How exactly they managed it is not known, but the women of Nagyrév arranged for prisoners to come and spend nights in their beds.

Problems began when the menfolk started coming home from the war. Their wives, who had got to know the charms of free love and life outside the fetters of patriarchy, were not willing to go back to the old ways. And that is where Júlia Fazekas helped them.

Júlia had a sizeable supply of arsenic and also of *know-how*, as people would say today. She selflessly shared both with her sisters.

The first victim was called Peter Hegedusz. No one remembers the names of the others who were killed – and it seems there were three hundred of them. This would allow us to conclude that the most important man in a woman's life is not the first one she sleeps with, as is mistakenly believed, but the first one she kills. To be fair, the sisters didn't just kill men. They also eliminated women who reminded them of their former lives of misery: mothers, sisters, aunts and others.

Júlia Fazekas was the informal village doctor, by fortunate circumstance, so it was she who carried out the post mortems, if they can be called that. And there was no end to the fortunate circumstances – her cousin was the local clerk in charge of issuing death certificates. In Júlia's opinion, the men of Nagyrév died a natural death. For fifteen years, the menfolk of that Hungarian village dropped like flies – the result of wartime stress, it seemed – before officials started to get suspicious.

When this brood of vipers had killed off their husbands and male relatives, the sisters got the urge to do a bit of killing in the neighbouring villages, too. In July 1929, a choirmaster from Tiszakürt accused the wife of a certain László Szabó of trying to poison him with wine. The authorities didn't react – where would they be if they had to follow up every case of intemperance followed by nausea and vomiting in Hungary? But when the fellow dragged himself to the police station more dead than alive and started shouting in a delirium that he had been poisoned by Mrs Szabó, they had no choice.

They arrested the lady, and she opened her soul to them. Her testimony led the police to Mrs Bukenoveski. She told them that Júlia Fazekas had provided the arsenic used to kill her seventy-year-old mother in 1924. She threw the body in the River Tisza, and Júlia Fazekas pronounced the old woman dead by drowning.

Eight women from Nagyrév were sentenced to death and seven to life imprisonment. Eleven more were sent to jail. One of these, Mária Szendi, declared in court that she killed her husband because she was fed up with everything always having to be his way. 'It's terrible that men have all the power,' she told the judge, who showed no understanding for her form of struggle for gender equality.

Júlia Fazekas eluded male power and its institutions. She drank a mug of wine laced with her own arsenic.

26

I drew a parallel between Júlia's killings and the 'Višegrad crimes' pointed out by Spahić. These, too, were committed in wartime and went undetected at first. For those with killing in mind, war is the best time. Submerged in a sea of blood and surrounded by so much other killing, crimes committed in wartime have a good chance of going unnoticed. Some set of statistics would show them in the end, but they would most likely be included in the long list of war crimes, just as Spahić claimed.

I needed to go for a walk to air my mind. I headed off along Saint Peter Cetinjski Boulevard towards Podgorica's Block 5, which I passed through without noticing the monstrosity of that Socialist-era estate built for teachers from the villages and the workers of the aluminium smelter. I cut through the leafy Tološi neighbourhood and continued on towards agreeable Mareza, only to find myself the very next moment in Oxford Street, London. I didn't feel a bit of surprise or slow my step. As if they had a will of their own, my legs led me on to Red Lion Square.

I sat down at one of the plastic tables at the small café at the entrance to the park. A Moroccan family – a father and his two teenage daughters – were serving couscous, tahini and soup with meatballs and cinnamon. I wasn't hungry. I ordered mint tea. Smoking cigarette after cigarette, I drank a whole pot of tea, and then ordered another. The head of the family came over to me and sat down at the table. He claimed to know me, and that I had been his guest once before. As far as he could remember, I had slept at the October Gallery, in a comfortably appointed apartment the size of a matchbox located just around the corner.

'You asked me to tell you about Cromwell, remember?' he asked. 'You were fascinated by the story about the publican, a follower of Cromwell's, who hid the leader's body from soldiers here on the square. When Cromwell was buried in Westminster Abbey in 1658, he gave them the body of an unknown man he had dug up at the paupers' cemetery. So when the Royalists decided to desecrate Cromwell's tomb in 1660 and take revenge on his remains, it was actually quite a farce for those who knew the secret: the body they dug out of the Westminster tomb, clapped in chains and posthumously beheaded wasn't Cromwell. Do you remember? You wrote down what I told you in a blue notebook with a golden emblem on the cover, just like the one poking out of your rucksack. That's how I remembered you – it's not every day that someone listens to the story about the hidden grave as if it was the greatest secret in the universe. More tea?' he asked as he shook my hand and apologised for having to leave me. 'Work calls.'

Feeling poisoned by all the nicotine, I walked to the other end of the square, passing a Korean, who must have been a singer and was posing in a white shirt for a photographer and his numerous assistants.

I jumped the fence and headed to the left. I strolled into Conway Hall as if I was a regular there, passing workers unloading old pianos from a truck. There was no one at the reception. Just like last time, I thought. I went up the winding stairs to the second floor, where, as I expected, I found the door of an office with the sign 'Istros Books. Independent Publishing House'. I went down to the first floor and sat on the balcony of the hall, where I remembered watching – or someone else remembered watching – Slavoj Žižek and Srećko Horvat talk about the future of the European Union. The hall was now full of pianos which would soon be sold by auction; a monthly event at Conway Hall.

I went down a badly lit corridor, passing the office where the person whose memory this was had spoken with an urbane old lady, an intimate friend of Lucian Freud's, and heard her story about the New Year's Eve party where she and Lucian danced. And then I left the building and bought a box of Walker's shortbread at the corner shop. Wandering aimlessly westwards and enjoying the sweet, buttery taste at the top of my mouth, I chanced upon the Wallace Collection.

The poster at the entrance announced that Dürer's *Melencolia I* was on exhibit. An anonymous buyer had apparently acquired the copperplate for 72,500 pounds at Christie's and later decided to donate it to the Wallace Collection, a museum which had played an important role in his life, he confided to the management.

Dürer was on show as 'Treasure of the Month'. Despite that pompous billing, the public didn't care much for the German genius. As in every other gallery or museum, they thronged in front of the Dutch Masters, who were more popular in England than all other painters except Turner, I was so bold as to presume, not knowing if I was presuming it now or back then. The Dutch Masters reminded people of gobelin tapestries with their quaint or bucolic scenes, except that gobelins were somehow more cheerful, without the unnecessary dark tones the Dutch plastered their canvases with.

I arrived in front of Melancholy in the middle of a presentation. I – for my memory tells me it was me – was now standing beside a curator and two old men, who were crying and holding each other's hands. What a brilliant curator, I thought (now, when I'm remembering this, or back in the gallery?). He was better, in fact, than most of the cultural commentators whose books I used to waste my time on. He spoke with a devotion and passion which are rare today, and which here in the Balkans are only found in zealots who elaborate to people with the same mindset the reasons for attacking a neighbouring village with murder in mind.

'As Klibansky, Panofsky and Saxl correctly emphasise,' the curator explained in a steady voice, 'Dürer develops the idea of Geometria succumbing to Melancholy and Melancholy inclined towards Geometria. He unites two figures in this picture: the brilliant mind of Geometria and the destructive seductiveness of Melancholy … Panofsky claims elsewhere that this is actually a spiritual self-portrait of Dürer himself.'

The curator then turned our attention to the magic square in the upper right-hand corner of the engraving. The artist's contemporaries, he explained, considered the harmony of the magic square, whose numbers always give the same result, regardless of their arrangement, to symbolise the harmony of the Creator's work.

To my mind, however, the key to understanding the picture was the scrawny dog lying sprawled at Melancholy's feet. In it, I saw the figure of the cynic, that dog among people. Surrounded by all manner of paraphernalia for measuring and discovering the laws of the universe, oppressed by numbers and geometric patterns, disillusioned by both people and angels, he no longer has the strength to warn about the madness of so-called wisdom. He lies there with indifference, waiting for everything to collapse and for that which he rationally warned about to be confirmed, which the others just heard as a bark.

But I didn't stop in front of Dürer for long because my attention was attracted to a pen-and-ink drawing to the left of Melancholy. It showed a barefoot man in tatters, accompanied by an old woman in rags. The figures were represented in a realistic manner. The burdens they carried on their backs clearly set their existence apart from the sublimeness of Melancholy. I forgot about Dürer and devoted all my attention to studying the symbols the artist had placed around his two sad heroes. The barren tree could represent winter, but I preferred to see it as a genealogical dead end: a withered and poisoned family tree, which all the names had fallen from like yellow leaves. The old woman warmed herself at a brazier, which revealed her vocation: it was an accessory for black magic. A piece of parchment with a hexagram and other magical symbols lay on the ground next to her. From that woman, his mother, there was no escape.

'The owl you see –,' I heard the curator's voice, and turned around towards him, noticing that we were now alone in the hall, with him standing unusually close to me, 'does not just symbolise night, solitude and ill omen. Here, too, we profit greatly from Klibansky, Panofsky and Saxl, without whose work no serious interpretation of *Melencolia I* and Dürer's imitators would be possible. They point out that the owl also stands for *studio d'una vana sapienza*, vain wisdom, which is precisely what the Church Fathers accused goddess Minerva's winged servant of. Now look at the cobweb. In the Renaissance, the spider's weaving was considered *opera vana*, labour in vain. That's right: all the labour of the man in the picture is in vain. He is totally under the power of this femme fatale, and that he will remain. All he can do is resign himself – to her and to melancholy.

'The author of this mid-sixteenth-century drawing was a German, perhaps from southern Germany, perhaps from Switzerland; some-times the work is mistakenly considered French. What attracted me to it, and the reason I devoted a considerable amount of effort to having it here in the complementary collection of Dürer's followers' works, is a seemingly minor detail: the hedgehog. Just look at the cute little creature, which has made its nest right in the barrel the melan-cholic person is sitting on. Did you know that the female hedgehog keeps putting off the birth of her babies for fear that their spines could tear open her womb? The longer she waits, of course, the bigger and sharper the spines will be, and the greater the pain – that's the price of procrastination. That's how it is with melancholic people, too. Whatever they intend to do, their inhibitions prevent them from doing it and they keep putting it off. But some things just need be done.

The melancholic person therefore has to do them in the agony which comes at the end, after all the delay. Think about that,' the curator said, patting me on the shoulder and then disappearing into the labyrinth of the Wallace Collection's rooms.

27

When I came round, it was night-time. I was sitting on a beer crate beside the main road to Nikšić with a circle of cigarette butts around me, ten or so kilometres from home. I felt a terrible weariness. With the greatest effort I raised my hand to hail a taxi.

After that, I snored away on the back seat. The angry driver woke me up when we arrived at the address I had managed to mutter. As if I was hauling a whole foreign life behind me, I trudged to the lift, which took me up to my flat. Instead of immediately going to bed, I sat down in front of the television and goggled at a horrendous political debate, where a pack of dim-witted reprobates in the studio were trying to convince the dim-witted viewers to vote for them. This concentrated idiocy shook me awake, and in that tired and irritable state I waited for morning.

My body ached as if someone had been thrashing me all night. Sluggish and half-asleep, I made coffee, sat down at the computer, opened the search engine and typed in 'murders at Red Lion Square'. Nothing. Then I typed 'death at Red Lion Square'. I opened a short newspaper article from 1980, which told me that a certain Jovan Plamenac, aged sixty, had fallen asleep at the wheel of his car, broken through the fence on Red Lion Square and crashed into a tree. He died at the scene of the accident. The report was accompanied by a small photo of the deceased.

Jovan Plamenac, I found out when I searched further, was a

prominent figure in Chetnik émigré circles in London. He had joined Draža Mihailović's Serbian quisling movement as a young man and was rapidly promoted, owing to his cruelty towards the enemy. After the war, he fled via Slovenia to London. The Yugoslav authorities tried Plamenac *in absentia* for the shooting of twelve Partisans in central Serbia, where he had been a commander. He was sentenced to life imprisonment. The British authorities refused to extradite him.

From the moment I began to doubt my origins up until that day, the only pattern in my investigation was that nothing was as it seemed. By the same logic, I could assume that Plamenac's death had not been an ordinary traffic accident, either.

Let's say Plamenac was killed. Poisoned, for example, like Júlia Fazekas's victims, and that his death was later attributed to the wrong cause, as with Júlia's victims and those Inspector Spahić wrote about in his report. How did that relate to me and my mother? The conclusion was improbable, alarming and unwelcome, but inescapable: what if Plamenac had been killed by my mother, and she did it in such a way to make it look like an accident? Why would she have done that? Why did the Yugoslav secret service take care of her child – me – then give me a false mother, the police clerk Olga Pavlović, and a false identity with the surname Hafner? Because my mother worked and killed for the Service? And the Service looked after its own people? That meant that, by my very birth, I had become part of the Service. Is that why Mandušić employed me and tolerated my frankly disgraceful behaviour?

I shared my doubts with Todorović. He looked visibly uneasy while I was speaking and could hardly wait for me to finish.

'You're crazy, quite crazy. Where you're heading is just madness,' he said. 'Stop before it's too late,' he added and left in a hurry.

Something told me my contact with Todorović had come to an end.

That was no longer important. The *crazy* story I had discovered, or constructed – I still had to find out which – needed to be resolved. I got myself an express British visa and took a plane to London, where the trail led.

28

Fuck this for a joke, I thought when I sat down at the Moroccan café on Red Lion Square. I ordered mint tea and lit a cigarette. I must have been really been staring at the Moroccan, because he came up to me.

'Do we know each other?' he asked politely.

'No, not at all,' I replied. 'Forgive me. You see, a friend told me about you.'

'Say hello to your friend,' he chuckled and was about to go back to the kitchen to make more food for the guests who were coming in droves now it was lunch hour. I decided to play the game to the end and beckoned him to take a seat.

'I see things are hectic –,' I apologised, 'but I have to ask: where exactly on this square was Cromwell buried?'

A minute or two later, I came across the piano carriers in front of Conway Hall. I followed the winding stairs up to the second floor and peeked into the office of Istros Books. A blonde woman was working at a computer: 'Hello, can I help you?' she asked. Then I went down one floor and took a photo of the pianos which had been brought to be auctioned.

It suddenly occurred to me that I could visit all the places I had seen in my visions and take photos. That way I could take control of my memory, and also of time: those photos would guarantee that it was *my* memory of *my* time. Later, by comparing my own memories with others' memories of the same places, I would try to discover some kind of trail to follow. Where would it

lead me? Probably nowhere, but what else could I do? In my situation, every move, however crack-brained it was, seemed an equally rational choice.

I stayed the night at the October Gallery. The rooms were indeed comfortably appointed and the size of a matchbox.

29

I travelled to London once more that year, too.

The trip came after the birth of an idea which was truly bizarre, but as such not far from the truth. And that idea, in turn, came after another mail from Wovenhand.

He had sent me a link to an article about the murder of Stjepan Djureković, one of the Croatian managers of the Yugoslav state oil company INA until he came into conflict with the country's Communist leadership. He fled to Germany and there, seeking safety from his powerful enemy, and any allies he could find, he joined up with the Ustashi émigrés. In Yugoslavia he was accused of plundering INA in league with the German secret police.

Djureković was killed in 1983 in the town of Wolfratshausen near Munich. The German media immediately blamed the Yugoslav secret service. They claimed the plan to kill him was code-named 'Operation Danube'. That brought an involuntary smile to my lips. I thought back to my school years and the Geography lessons with a senile teacher, whose name was Melisa; she had a habit of eating chocolate in class and ended every lesson with digressions on the Thracians and Illyians. The Thracians called the lower course of the Danube, which flows through the Balkans, Istros.

I gazed at the article I had been sent. It was old hat. I had already made the connection between my mother and political murders by the Yugoslav secret service without Wovenhand's assistance. So what was my secret friend trying to tell me? Maybe he didn't mean to tell me anything new. Perhaps he just wanted to confirm my doubts and encourage me to keep developing my conspiracy theory.

One mystery still begged to be solved: Olga Pavlović's photos. What was the point of all those trips she never went on? Why all those fake destinations? Why didn't they simply take a pile of photos in Ulcinj? Especially since it was rather unlikely that my make-believe grandmother, who lived modestly and taught me modesty, could have had the money for all those trips abroad. What if the Service itself had left a trail on those photos which they expected me to find, I suddenly thought?

What if I was expected to investigate the locations on those photos?

I sat down at the computer and started an extensive search. By evening I had linked all the places in Olga's photos with the bizarre deaths of members of the Yugoslav diaspora.

At the end of it, I believed Olga's photos were a secret map of the political murders ordered by the Yugoslav secret service. Murders which I now believed – couldn't *not* believe when faced with the evidence – had been committed by my mother.

Independent investigations in the different countries had declared that the deaths were due to 'natural causes' or 'accidents'. But I no longer had any doubt as to what Wovenhand wanted to tell me through those mails. By now I was able to recognise the murderous signature of my mother, who was evidently a virtuoso of death, a master assassin who went undetected, although the murders took place under the very nose of the police.

A pre-war banker and post-war financier of the Ustashi émigrés, who had returned to Zagreb in his old age when he thought he was no longer important to anyone and that no one would want to take revenge on him any more, who had hoped to spend the evening of his life in the city where he was born, was found dead in his flat in Ilica Street.

Then there was a Kosovar, the owner of several patisseries in Brussels, who died in a room of Le Plaza Hotel, where he had checked in accompanied by an eye-catching lady, whom the receptionist didn't doubt was a prostitute – a lady who disappeared without a trace before the police arrived. The investigation confirmed the obvious: that the gentleman had suffered a heart attack while having sex. It had been too much excitement for him. He should have borne that in mind, because his medical record card noted that he had had a serious heart condition for many years.

Then there was a poet who, after being translated into French, believed he was important and went on to complain to the Paris newspapers about the lack of democracy in his native country, after which he was recruited by the French secret service. Wordsmiths are naturally rapturous, and therefore careless, and it seems this fellow was pondering a new poem when he fell from Dubrovnik's walls in an ill-starred moment.

In another case, a former member of the Yugoslav parliament committed suicide in Oslo, where he had followed his male lover, leaving behind a wife and two children. Norwegian newspapers mentioned that the confidential documents he had brought with him from Yugoslavia and offered to the Norwegian secret service in exchange for citizenship were not found in the flat he had rented and where he put a small-calibre bullet through his own brain.

There was also a successful German businessman, the son of a Serbian Chetnik officer, who was not satisfied with producing quality shoes for an affordable price but wanted to sell weapons to Libya, where no wise man would do business because the Yugoslav state was already the exclusive supplier of military hardware. He died in a fatal accident in a Munich airport toilet – electrocuted when he plugged his shaver into a faulty socket. As a result, twenty workers at the airport were laid off.

And so on: the same story in every city on Olga's photos.

30

The only place where Olga supposedly had her photograph taken more than once was Queen Mary's Rose Garden in Regent's Park in London.

The faked photos showed Olga Pavlović standing next to a rose bush named Ingrid Bergman. I easily found that place: at the very entrance to the rose garden, where the first rose bush bears the actress's name. I stood in front of the little sign and wondered what this could possibly mean. The thought flashed through my mind that my mother's fate might have been in some way similar to that of the figure Bergman plays in Hitchcock's *Notorious*, but I had no time for that theory.

The rose garden has a small lake, and two photos showed Olga feeding the ducks. I stood on the bank and looked into the turbid water, but that told me nothing. The ducks were well fed.

Disappointed with my visit to Regent's Park, into which I had strolled full of optimism and came out of knowing even less than before, I decided to go back to the Moroccan's at Red Lion Square for some tea.

Tired and thirsty from the half-hour walk, I sat down at one of the familiar green plastic tables. A young couple next to me was loudly slurping the soup with meatballs and cinnamon. They were hungry, that was plain, for the daughters were constantly bringing them new dishes. I discreetly examined the pile of food on their table. He bolted down couscous, while she attacked bun after bun, licking her fingers and even managing to drag them through the tahini in her gluttony. I ordered another pot of mint tea, lit a cigarette and mused that few things are more repulsive than people who eat like voracious animals – perhaps only people who drink like a fish.

Freud's lady friend from Conway Hall crossed the square with a takeaway cup of Starbucks coffee. Then the Moroccan came up to me, smiling amiably.

'Ah, my favourite guest!' he said.

'You remember me?' I asked.

'Of course. You stayed here nearby, at the October Gallery,' he confirmed. 'Am I mistaken? "A comfortably appointed apartment the size of a matchbox", you said when you dropped in for coffee in the morning. You told me where you stayed the night and I asked what the accommodation was like. I was curious because I've had guests who have enquired about the place. Many of my guests ask me to tell them about Cromwell. But you're different to all the others – you were so completely fascinated by the story about the publican who hid Cromwell's body from the soldiers on the square! How could I forget? You wrote down what I told you in a blue notebook with a golden emblem just like the one poking out of your rucksack. That's how I remembered you: it's not every day that a man listens to the story about the hidden grave as if it was the greatest secret in the universe,' I said these very words to myself a second before he spoke them.

Then, as I knew he would, he asked *More tea?* as he shook my hand and apologised for having to leave me.

31

Mandušić sacked me. His secretary called and conveyed the threat in a sugar-sweet voice: the boss asks that you not try to contact him any more. He advises you not to talk to anyone about the details of your business relationship, and certainly not to write about it. The boss has been kind and approved a type of severance pay: you'll receive your pay as usual for one year more.

And so Mandušić vanished from my life, along with all those marvellous bottles of single malt he sent me while he believed I could be of use to him. The whisky was one thing, but otherwise I had no objections to his decision. Mandušić had already proved to be remarkably patient. I hadn't responded to calls from his office for weeks, and it had been months since I sent him a speech.

However, my dismissal meant that I lost my access to police information, without which the chances of discovering my mother's identity clearly became negligible. But I was not to be discouraged. I would have to think faster, differently and better.

Ultimately I still had help. Wovenhand hadn't forgotten me. His two mails – one in which he sent me details of the interrogation of David Richard Berkowitz, and the other a memo of Inspector Spahić about a conversation with one of the Višegrad killers – helped me fill in the gaps in the picture of my mother. But it wasn't particularly clear, and certainly no brighter. It felt like a bottomless pit gaping in front of me, and it was too threatening and too far beyond anything I had ever dared to imagine, even in my darkest fantasies, for me to look into it without fearing the worst. And that's why I knew I would continue to stare at that horrible mass, darker than the universe, heavier than lead and stickier than tar, which trickled from what was my mother after I had constantly handled it and squeezed it and bombarded it with questions. I would stare at it for as long and as persistently as I had to until I saw the bottom. That could destroy me, of course, and that made it all the more attractive. What other, pressing work did I have anyway? My investigation had brought passion to my life – be it for knowledge, truth, or something much more trivial – and I had become addicted.

32

David Richard Berkowitz was a serial killer who performed under the artistic name 'The Son of Sam'. I was familiar with his murderous opus but had never been particularly interested: I didn't care for the New York of the seventies, where he committed his murders, nor the way in which he killed. After studying truly inventive serial killers, why would I take an interest in one who shot his victims with a revolver? Still, I ended up writing an article or two about his life and work.

What made Berkowitz special is what I didn't know about him and was revealed to me by Wovenhand's mail. In a letter from prison, he claimed: 'There are more Sons out there – God help the world.' His prison correspondence contains descriptions of occult crimes committed by the 'Four-P Movement', a cult based in California. He claimed to have been part of its New York affiliate.

The two sons of his neighbour Sam Carr were also allegedly members of the cult, whose rituals involved shooting at innocent strangers and torturing dogs by flaying them alive.

The cult was based in New York's Untermyer Park. Bodies of skinned dogs were indeed discovered there on several occasions. Michael Newton's *Encyclopedia of Serial Killers*, which Wovenhand cited from abundantly in his mails, states:

Reporter Maury Terry, after six years on the case, believes there were at least five different gunners in the "Son of Sam" attacks, including Berkowitz, John Carr, and several suspects—one a woman—who have yet to be indicted. Terry also notes that six of the seven shootings fell in close proximity to recognized satanic holidays, the March 8 Voskerichian attack emerging as the sole exception to the pattern. In the journalist's opinion, Berkowitz was chosen as a scapegoat by the other members of his cult, who then set out to "decorate" his flat with weird graffiti, whipping up a bogus "arson ledger"—which includes peculiar out-of-date entries—to support a plea of innocent by reason of insanity.

In October 1979, Berkowitz wrote:

I really don't know how to begin this letter, but at one time I was a member of an occult group. Being sworn to secrecy or face death I cannot reveal the name of the group, nor do I wish to. This group followed a mixture of satanic practices, including the teachings of Aleister Crowley and Eliphas Levi. It was (and still is) totally blood-orientated and I am certain you know just what I mean. The Coven's doctrines are a blend of ancient Druidism, teachings of the secret order of the Golden Dawn, Black Magic, and a host of other unlawful and obnoxious practices.

As I said, I have no interest in revealing the Coven, especially because I have almost met sudden death on several occasions (once by half an inch) and several others have already perished under mysterious circumstances. These people will stop at nothing, including murder. They have no fear of man-made laws or the Ten Commandments.

A story similar to Berkowitz's confession was told by Spahić's witness. Spahić found him in Višegrad, where he was a highly esteemed member of the community, a kind of hero (the inspector writes that people passing him in the street greeted him with respect). He lived modestly and worked as a builder's labourer. He didn't mind talking about his crimes. After three mugs of beer at a local pub, he confided in Spahić that he knew he would *never be put on trial*.

'So you don't deny that the murders you committed were connected to certain rites?'

'No, but I can't talk about that. I really can't.'

'Can you at least give me a hint of what you believe in?'

'Listen, old man, thanks for the beer, but you're sounding like an idiot. "No" means "no", OK?'

'Alright. But is it some kind of Church?'

'Uh-huh. It's a Church, just like an inverted cross is still a cross. But I warn you: you're treading dangerously. Do you realise what power you're up against?'

'Can you at least tell me the name of your group?'

'*At least?* You'll never find that out.'

'Are there many of you?'

'Enough.'

'And where?'

'Wherever history is made. Wherever there is power.'

I knew what I had to do now. I sat down at the computer, and soon a new series of deaths opened up in front of me.

33

In each of the cities where I established that a member of Yugoslav émigré circles died under peculiar circumstances, an as-yet-unsolved occult murder also occurred.

A teenage boy died on Kaptol Hill in Zagreb. Street sweepers found him leaning up against the wall of the cathedral, his veins slashed. Judgement was passed: he had been listening to heavy metal, whose dark messages had driven him to suicide. Instead of searching for the killer, the police spent their efforts writing a communiqué about the harmfulness of the "obscure music our young people are exposed to".

In Brussels, in a lane behind Le Plaza Hotel, a bag of human organs and scraps of wax was found beside a rubbish skip.

In London, the bodies of a young man and a young woman were found on a houseboat moored in the canal near Camden Market. The investigation was quick to establish a heroin overdose. But what then was the explanation for the small, hidden shrine discovered on the boat, and the decapitated crows sacrificed to whatever power they (the killers or the killed?) believed in?

In Ohrid, Macedonia, the waters of the lake washed ashore the bloated, badly-decomposed corpse of an old woman with eyes and tongue missing. Had they been eaten by the fish because the body was in the water for so long?

Another teenage death was reported, this time from Oslo; the young man had been obsessed with the devil and listened to heavy metal.

In Dubrovnik, a girl committed suicide by hanging herself from a beam in her parents' high-ceilinged drawing room. No one was worried that there was no chair at the spot where she died. How did she get up high enough? And did she shove the crucifix into her vagina herself, in a moment of derangement before death?!

In Frankfurt, at the main cemetery, someone dug up the corpse of a child who had died of a rare tropical disease which made its body rot and its brain turn to mush. The disease left the doctors dumfounded, all the more so because, as far as they knew in their ignorance, there was no kind of insect in Frankfurt capable of transmitting such a disease. No one cared about the details: for example, the flayed dog skin which had been draped about the gravestone, a little angel spreading its wings above the child.

At Munich airport, on a remote part of the runway, a pool of human blood and the mutilated bodies of three dogs were found.

In some places, the ritual crime occurred just one week after the 'natural' death of the émigré, in others it was a whole year earlier or later. But the pattern was clear. I had marked the killings of émigrés on a map of Europe with blue dots, and now I designated the ritual crimes on it in red. Even when confused, our brain strives for some form of order, and then, after establishing order where there was none, we cause even more chaos ... I thought that the map, and with it the portrait of my mother, would only be complete when I was able to link the locations of all the killings and end up with a perfect circle. I took a felt-tip and began joining the locations of the crimes. It was far from being a circle. I moved back a few steps and tried to imagine what shape I would get if I traced the lines further, towards the margins of the map. And then, in my mind, I saw a number nine stretching across all of Europe.

34

I stood perplexed in front of the number, but it didn't mean anything to me. Still, it was a clear and unmistakable sign, and it was up to me to interpret it.

I sat down at the computer and set about searching for information about the number nine and its role in occult rites.

The first website I opened confronted me with a Protestant pastor: 'The number nine is important to the followers of occult teachings mainly because of their perverse enjoyment in Jesus' death, which was marked with the number nine,' he thundered.

The key to the interpretation he presented lay in the Gospel of Mark in the New Testament: "And at the ninth hour Jesus cried with a loud voice, *'Eloi, Eloi, lama sabachtani?'* – 'My God, my God, why hast thou forsaken me?' And some of the bystanders hearing it said, 'Behold, he is calling Elijah.' And one ran and, filling a sponge full of vinegar, put it on a reed and gave it to him to drink, saying, 'Wait, let us see whether Elijah will come to take him down.' And Jesus uttered a loud cry, and breathed his last."

Mark thus claims that Jesus died at the ninth hour. I asked myself when that was, by our reckoning. The answer was not easy to find. The more I looked into the issue, the less I knew – almost as little as the self-declared authorities on biblical matters. I read debates about whether Jesus was really crucified on a Friday, or if it was a Wednesday. And both sides, needless to say, were in possession of convincing arguments.

That strengthened my conviction that history is fiction, as is every confession, not to mention people's memoirs. It is just as dogmatic to interpret history from a history textbook as it is on the basis of conspiracy theories. Whether we read a printed page or search with a candle in the margins for what was written in lemon juice – we will ultimately make our own story anyway, becoming the narrator of what we believe in and hold to be the truth. Every one of our truths will be our own, and our own account. There is only one kind of storyteller: the unreliable. There is only one kind of authorship: the unreliable. Even God is unreliable as an author, so what do you expect of everyone else? In the end, poetry would seem to be the least fictional medium, since it was the very first to forsake any pretence of so-called objective truth. To learn about the First World War from Trakl, the holocaust from Celan, capitalism from Pound and communism from Brecht is the only thing which makes sense.

* * *

What caused people to doubt Mark's account? In Jesus's time, the Jewish day began at nightfall and lasted until the following night. The Roman day began at dawn, at six o'clock in the morning, and lasted twelve hours, until six in the afternoon. How did Mark calculate time: as a Jew or a Roman? I googled the text of the New Testament. It was clear from Mark's description that Jesus was crucified in the daylight.

I remembered Maria's mail and opened it again. *The ninth hour by the Church's reckoning of time, which would soon be replaced by the mercantile way, began at what we today call two in the afternoon and lasted until three,* she wrote.

I could rely on Maria and Le Goff, and felt that we had resolved that question satisfactorily.

So much for the Christians and their ninth hour. But more than that, I was interested in what the *occultists* thought about that hour. They evidently attached great significance to numbers and even had a special name for the discipline: Gematria. Also, as I was to learn, they considered nine to be a perfect number, one which *always returns to itself*. Nine, I read, 'is a snake which bites its own belly – a snake consuming itself'. It is the number of the full circle. The sum of the numbers denoting a full circle, 360 degrees, 3+6+0, is nine. The sum of all the numbers up to nine, I read further, 1+2+3+4+5+6+7+8, is thirty-six. 3+6=9. When we add the number nine itself to that sum, we get 45. Even the mathematically challenged with no feel for systems of numbers can see where this is heading: naturally, 4+5 equals 9.

Moreover, if we vertically arrange all the numbers gained by multiplying the number nine by the numbers 1 to 10, we end up with an unusual order: the column on the left consists of the numbers 1 to 9, while the column on the right is an inversion of it, made up of the numbers from 9 to 0 in descending order.

9

18

27

36

45

54

63

72

81

90

There are people, I discovered, who believe that a person's date of birth reveals the number in whose power they will live – the number which conceals the secret of their destiny. I decided to play the game. I was born on 1. 5. 1983. 1+5+1+9+8+3 make 27, which means that my dominant number is 2+7, i.e. 9.

Hang on, I thought, let me check if there are any other nines in my life. Olga was born on 9.5.1930, for example. I added up the numerals of her date of birth and ended up with the number 27 once more, i.e. 2+7, again nine. When did Olga die? 5. 8. 2003. Add up 5+8+2+0+0+3, and what do you get? Eighteen. 1+8, damn it, equals nine.

I visited the site unhypnotize.com and found out an interesting thing. The book *Numbers: Their Occult Power and Mystic Virtues* by WW Wescott apparently describes the importance of the number nine for the Freemasons – "There is a Masonic order of Nine Elected knights, in which nine roses, nine lights and nine knocks are used." The number nine, it says, is the number of the Earth "under the power of evil".

Looking through Google's results for the search string 'number 9 and the occult' then bought me back to my date of birth. The first of May, as it turned out, was the second day of Beltane, the great pagan festival (or satanic, depending on your source). Beltane is an old celebration of fertility and the Earth goddess. The Celts sacrificed animals in the Scottish highlands on Beltane, I read, but every fifth year they also sacrificed humans, usually condemned criminals and prisoners of war.

The Beltane revellers light a bonfire of nine different kinds of wood and dance around it naked. They drive a large shaft into the ground, which clearly has a phallic function. Then they dance around it in circles, the women clockwise and the men anticlockwise. It is as if their bodies form the two hands of a clock moving away from each other, until they meet again (at the point where the clock shows the number three – the ninth hour – I wondered?).

Later I came across a Christian blog where priests offered advice to survivors of ceremonies which involved ritual abuse.

The priests claimed that ritual abuse took place at three levels: as physical, spiritual and mental torture. As examples of physical torture they cited gang rape, the breaking of bones, hanging by the legs, the severing of body parts, burying a person alive, locking them in a cage, and lowering them into holes full of insects or snakes – basically the standard repertoire of horror and porno films.

Spiritual torture involved breaking the victim's will and making them believe there was no hope. The priests claimed they had come across cases where women were forced to bear children which the cult members took away from them at birth, or they were made to choose which other victims would be killed. During this abuse, their tormentors would read out from occult texts they believed in.

The aim of mental torture, in turn, was to ensure that victims remained members of the cult, even if they led a seemingly normal life or kept returning voluntarily to rites such as the Black Mass and Beltane; and, most importantly, that they never reported their tormenters to the authorities.

With most victims, ritual abuse became their lot at a very early age. Where did those children find comfort? In what we usually all too lightly call madness, the priests claimed on their blog. Those who managed to dissociate themselves from the horror would survive. They created a dissociative identity for themselves, I read – what psychiatrists used to call multiple personality disorder. I searched for a definition of dissociative identity disorder and felt a wrenching coldness, as if I had just opened a freezer where a gruesome secret was waiting for me. *Dissociative disorders or dissociative identity disorders,* it said on the screen, *are marked by changes in a person's sense of identity, their memory or consciousness. People with this disorder can forget important events from their past, or temporarily forget who they are, or even assume a new identity. They can leave their habitual environment and wander off. In an episode of depersonalisation, people quite suddenly lose the feeling of their own ego. They can feel they have left their own body and are observing themselves from the outside. Sometimes they move as if they are sleepwalking, in a world which has lost its reality. Similar, but more intensive episodes occasionally occur in schizophrenia. However, the experiences of the schizophrenic person do not have the 'quasi' quality which the person with depersonalisation reports.*

This site referred to a description of the satanic nature of Beltane taken from Beltane (2005) by the Joy of Satan Ministries, retrieved from http://www.angelfire.com/empire/serpentis666/Beltane.html.

I couldn't check it because the page was no longer active.

I read a heated debate on www.davidicke.com/forum/show-thread.php?t=168329 about whether Beltane was a satanist or just a pagan ritual. Someone mentioned the pentagram which the Beltane fires form when seen from a bird's-eye view (or God's?). Sceptics demanded photographs as proof.

So I entered 'beltane occult images' in the search engine. The photos from a festival somewhere in Scotland showed naked people painted red. They were yelling and running across a field with flaming torches. A woman knelt in front of a man and reached out for his penis, while a couple beside them had (or at least simulated) sex standing up.

I imagined I was in a forest, lying naked on the leaves. The air was cold, but I was enveloped in writhing, warm bodies. The smell of human flesh mingled with the smell of the earth. My fingers felt damp, but I couldn't tell if it was from the bodily fluids of the woman beneath me or the moisture of the ground.

I waited for the moment when the fire of the wooden phallus in the field nearby would throw its light on us.

35

Come on, you don't believe in the devil, I said to myself. But *me* not believing, *me* knowing that the devil doesn't exist, doesn't mean *they* or *she* didn't believe. When has the non-existence of something ever been a reason not to live one's life by it and to kill in its name? Things which don't exist, but which people believe in, produce consequences much more real than things which exist and no one believes in. What is world history if not a tale of bloodshed in the name of nation and religion – those ghosts of culture and identity?

Confronted with another of my mother's terrible secrets, I did what I normally did when I wanted to forget what I was struggling to understand, or didn't dare to try: I fled from the unbearably specific into the unbearably general. Thinking about the miserable state of the world is a real consolation compared to thinking about the poverty of one's own existence. A dirty little secret common to all initiatives and movements to make the world a better place is that people work towards bettering the world so as not to have to work on themselves. Few things are as relaxing as launching into a furious tirade about the miserable state of civilisation, the human race and the planet … Every critique of so-called objective reality has to end in a farce, and the proponent of a better world as a comedian. As far as I was concerned, the world was perfect: it only existed so I'd be able to complain about it. I walked in circles through the flat and recited the obvious: invoking reason in the face of their *convictions* is about as effective as invoking statistics about droughts when a flood is swallowing up whole cities and bearing down on your house and your library – your *temple of reason*.

Surrounded by people with such firm convictions and such weak reason, where can you run to?

In a country where expectant parents who find out the baby will be a girl say, 'let's hope she's pretty rather than clever', and where there's no greater joy for parents than to produce a dim-witted macho to continue the family line, where can you run to?

My fury grew, and with it my hunger. I opened the fridge, but there was nothing except ice and Coca-Cola. I called a taxi with the plan of going to a good restaurant near the airport, where I would be able to have a decent meal, knock back a few drinks and, so I hoped, at least briefly forget about my mother, the shepherds, the flock and their convictions.

I got in the back. So as to forestall any form of communication, I told the taxi driver I had a splitting headache and needed quiet.

On the road out of the city we were nearly killed by a bald idiot in a BMW, who came flying into the roundabout and cut across our path.

I exploded.

'What can you do but stop the animal and put a bullet in his brain, right here by the roadside?!' I raged. 'Shouldn't the police shoot drivers like him? I mean, seriously, having a police force only makes sense if they publically execute people like that. What else is the point of a repressive apparatus? That's how it is, and that's why I've never wanted any form of power for myself. Every attempt to make the world a better place necessarily demands mass executions, and I don't have the stomach for that. I would willingly applaud, but I couldn't order killings myself. That's how things are, especially in countries like Montenegro, where the brutishness in people can only be driven underground by the harshest repression. Montenegro, Serbia, Croatia, Bosnia, Macedonia, Albania and Kosovo aren't proper states, just like Montenegrins, Serbs, Croats, Bosnians, Macedonians, Albanians and Kosovars aren't civilised peoples, but herd-like populations. You can't even regulate the traffic here without summary trials, let alone make a fairer society.'

The driver followed my tirade in stunned silence. I saw the fear in his face via the rear-view mirror. Respecting all the traffic signs, he drove me to the restaurant, snatched the money I held out to him and fled as fast as he could.

I wolfed down a giant, rare steak and ordered a double black Johnnie. I kept drinking until closing time, and then the waiters joined me. When we finally left the place, I was too drunk even to get in a taxi. The good people took me to a nearby motel. On the way they removed all the money from my wallet: oh well, nobody's perfect. They were at least considerate enough to leave my credit cards. They had drunk all night on me – that's the sort of kindness which touches people's hearts – so they felt the need to return the favour.

36

Zonked out as I was, I missed four calls from Maria. When she realised she wasn't going to reach me, she sent a text message: Goran has killed himself.

It didn't fully hit me until I was in the taxi and we were driving past Lake Skadar. I needed that confrontation with the beauty of the landscape to make me register what had happened. Beauty is so difficult because it's always completely out of context and there's no place for it here. The cruelty of existence is only bearable because people are such pathetic creatures. Horrible things happen to us, and we deserve horrible things. Full stop. Whatever happens to us can be sad, but not unfair. And yet beings as pure and poorly equipped for the slaughter as Goran ought to be exempted from the logic of existence. When what is good and innocent is exposed to the laws of the world we live in, all reason and all consolation vanish. Since that's how it is, I calmly accepted all the torment and torture, the industry of death and all the atrocities people have done to others, but fell to my knees at news of children burning dogs alive. We've been taught to live with the history of our race, which is nothing other than a history of atrocities. But sometimes the madness of so-called normality becomes unbearable. That's why I think that when Nietzsche collapsed over the flogged horse in Via Carlo Alberto in Turin on 3 January 1889, it wasn't a moment of madness but one where his mind finally broke through all that had previously shackled it, an hour of the greatest lucidity and the purest cognition, so complete that afterwards there was no return – an hour of confrontation with horror, face to face, after which the only way of escape ledinto madness.

I called Maria. Through her weeping, she told me what had happened. Goran had taken her out to dinner the night before at the newly built hotel in the Old Town. It had been a real feast. One dish followed another, all of the very finest, accompanied by a connoisseur's choice of wines. What's the occasion, she asked him. Let that be a surprise, said Goran. She felt that he enjoyed every moment of the evening, talking about me and the three of us, reminiscing about our times together, and coming up with a host of old memories which had long since faded for Maria. They said goodbye heartily, with a hug. He stayed to finish off the bottle of Chilean red. He paid, gave the waiters an excessive tip worth as much as their Sunday pay, and asked them to bring another bottle while he smoked a cigar on the terrace: a good Primitivo, if you please. Then he went out and jumped.

37

I went by taxi to the cemetery below the Old Town. Goran's father could hardly wait to see the last of the body. He didn't want any condolences, ceremony or speeches, only for the corpse to be lowered into the earth as soon as possible. I found him at the gate of the cemetery. In spite of everything, I felt the need to say a few words and give him a firm handshake. He just stood there, visibly disturbed by the unpleasant obligations his son had foisted upon him. He didn't even look at me when I walked past to join Maria, who was standing at the open grave dressed in black and sobbing inconsolably.

Goran's father hurried the gravediggers until they had finished. At that moment, Goran's sister threw herself onto the mound. She crammed soil into her mouth, so we couldn't make out what she was trying to say, but it seemed she was begging him for forgiveness, promising she didn't know it would be like this, and swearing she had never imagined her husband was capable of doing what he did. Her father strode up, jerked her by the hair and dealt her a fierce slap in the face. He glanced at her full of contempt and then went up to Maria.

'Stop that whining,' he hissed. 'You should have jumped with him. You're going to do it sooner or later anyway. That weakling! As soon as he was born I knew he was weak and would bring shame on the family. I'm going now, to get away from all the disgusting things people are saying about us,' he said so that all could hear him. He was the first to leave the cemetery, like an offended guest who demonstratively leaves a gathering.

Later, Maria and I had coffee at the quay, and she read out sections of articles about Goran's death. It was devastating that we as his closest friends – his true brother and sister, as he used to call us – had not noticed the glaring signs of the coming tragedy. We learned about the reasons for our best friend's death from the morning papers. I had been busy with the troubles caused by my mother, Maria had woes with her own, and we had totally forgotten about Goran, it's true. His fall lasted for months, two whole years even, and that last night it just ended on the rocks below Kalaja. If one of us had reached him a hand it may not have saved him, but at least he wouldn't have died feeling totally alone, deserted and betrayed by those closest to him.

Goran approved loans to people he shouldn't have: to poor people, where it was obvious they wouldn't be able to pay it back, and to desperate people prepared to cry and grovel in his office, to kiss his hands and bless him when he gave them the money in breach of all the bank's guidelines. He approved dozens of loans like that to people who later didn't respond to his calls, avoided him in the street, and ultimately drove him from their doorstep, hurling insults when he came to ask them to repay their debt because otherwise it would fall on him. He gave a loan to his sister's husband, twenty thousand euros, for which she had been begging for weeks; the rat gambled away a third of the money that same night and lost the rest by the end of the month in failed black-market operations. Goran also gave an astronomical amount to Radovan. That swine had money and could have paid his debt, but he still didn't. That's how people have become rich and successful from time immemorial: by abusing the trust of a good person, screwing them over, and driving them to their death.

Finally, in imminent danger of imprisonment, Goran took out a loan in order to pay off part of the other people's debts, and then another to pay off the first loan. But then it was all over. They summoned him to the bank's central office in Podgorica and gave him one week to pay back all the money, otherwise they would hand him over to the prosecutor's office and impound all his family's assets. 'This has never happened to us before,' they told him at the end of the meeting.

'Embezzlement yes, we've had that, but a case such as yours, where *you* pay off the debts of the people you gave loans to … Do you realise how much this goes against the very principles of banking?' A clerk who had been at the meeting told journalists: '"How could you believe those people?" I asked him with disbelief as he was leaving. While he was waiting for the lift he just said, "They're good people, and in different circumstances they would have done the right thing."' She was rewarded for her confession with a little portrait at the bottom of the page – taken when she was younger and more attractive, I cynically presumed.

Maria and I sat in silence, smoking and watching night fall. She went off to the toilet. There was excitement at the next table: one of the teenagers claimed to have seen a pod of dolphins. The others unsuccessfully tried to take snapshots of the animals with their mobiles so as then to post them on social networks. The horde of juveniles gambolled around the café with their electronic gadgets pointed out to the sea. When they finally calmed down and went back to their seats, a boy with a piping voice said that dolphins ought to be killed because they were pests. His uncle was a fisherman, and dolphins ate fish out of his nets. The girls felt sorry for the dolphins at first – they're so cute! – but in the end they all agreed: if they needed to be killed, what could they do about it? The females of the species now opted out of the debate and decided to hang around on fashion websites until the males returned from the hunt. The males, indeed, were sharing their experience: what was the most effective way of killing a dolphin? They started with the individual animal: you throw a fish from the boat, and when the dolphin comes up you harpoon him. Later they thought of mass executions: you throw a few sticks of dynamite at the pod of dolphins. Within a minute, the boys had moved on to genocide: you fill an old fifty-litre tub of house paint with nails and twenty kilos of dynamite, attach a long fuse and lower it fifty metres down on a rope; dolphins are curious creatures, and the whole pod follows the tub. When it goes off, it's like a miniature atom bomb. Nothing is left alive down there.

When Maria came back from the toilet, I grabbed her by the arm and said, 'Take me away to where there are no people'.

38

She insisted I stay at her place for a few days.

'We have to visit the grave. We'll do up that gloomy mound a little,' she said. 'His father won't notice – that swine won't be going to the cemetery again until he dies himself.'

I had no objections. That was what I had secretly been hoping. I needed Maria's company.

We ate dinner in silence. Tereza had cooked swordfish, which was just perfect, and afterwards she served cake, although we didn't touch it. I couldn't take my eyes off her huge belly. She noticed, but it didn't bother her: she seemed to enjoy the attention it brought. It was only one more month until the baby was due, and Maria offered that she could move into the outhouse where her father had once lived. She could live there with the child, and her obligations at the villa would be reduced to a sensible minimum. 'You're a good worker, and it's hard to find the like of you,' Maria told her. Tereza gladly accepted and called Maria her patron. She was constantly giving her new crosses from Ostrog Monastery, which Maria put away in a drawer of her wardrobe.

'We haven't seen each other for such a long time,' I said to Maria when she had sent Tereza off to bed. 'There are so many things I've been meaning to tell you, but now I just want to sleep. My strength is giving way and my head is empty.'

'And your heart?' she teased. 'No, no, off you go. I'm tired myself. There's always tomorrow. Everything will be better in the morning.'

39

She lied so I wouldn't feel guilty. She didn't go to bed herself. When I came down for breakfast, I found her sleeping on the sofa in the drawing room with an empty bottle of wine beside her.

Tereza was waiting for me in the kitchen with an excellent espresso and freshly made croissants. She didn't stay for long because the bell with 'Mama Elletra' on it rang: the lady was awake and needed the assistance of the servants. Tereza darted off upstairs like a whirlwind.

Wovenhand wrote again. Like his previous mails, this one too concealed a real pearl inside a shell of worthless commonplaces. That morning, he wrote to me about Ed Gein. I skimmed over his biography, which I knew down to the last detail: after the death of his dominant mother, Gein tailored his world and his house in Plainfield, Wisconsin, to match his madness. There were just two murders, meaning he didn't fit into the FBI classification, which presumes that a serial killer has slain three or more people. He dug up graves, snatched the corpses and took them to his house. There he made furniture with the body parts, as well as dresses he wore, especially on the nights with a full moon. He peeled the skin off the faces of the dead women, covered his own body with it, and long stood gazing at *her*, at himself, in the mirror. Everything Gein ever wanted was to be a woman. One particular woman: his mother.

Together with Gein's biography, Wovenhand sent me an excerpt from an article by Aleksandar Bečanović, the Montenegrin film critic:

Paul Cronin's book Herzog on Herzog *mentions a less-known fact about Gein: Herzog filmed his depressing description of the 'American dream',* Stroszek *(1976), in Plainfield, of all places. 'What is exceptional about Plainfield,' he emphasises, 'is that five or six mass murderers emerged there in the space of just five years. There is no clear explanation for the phenomenon. It sounds crazy, I know, but that's the way it is. There's something very* bleak and evil about Plainfield, and even during the filming the police found two dead bodies just ten miles away from us.' One of Herzog's friends at the time was the director Errol Morris, a passionate researcher on everything to do with serial killers, who had even done an interview with Gein. Morris discovered that the graves the body-snatcher dug up formed a perfect circle, in the centre of which was the grave of his mother. Morris wondered if Gein had also dug up his mother's grave and Herzog, always prepared for an adventure on the verge of reason, suggested that he and Morris meet soon afterwards and dig up the grave. But when the time came around, Morris got cold feet and didn't turn up. Herzog's comment: 'Later I also realised it was better that way. Sometimes it's best to just have a question, not the answer.'

Clearly, my stay in Ulcinj was going to be shorter than I had planned. This time, the pointer I had received was unambiguous: *go and see, find your mother's grave*. I called the travel agency and bought a ticket for a flight from Podgorica to Frankfurt the next day.

It had been blatantly obvious the whole time, and yet I hadn't realised – the key to the mystery could be mother's grave and what I would find there. Or what I didn't find. Poe was right when he wrote, in 'The Purloined Letter': the best way to conceal a thing is to make it obvious.

40

The villa suddenly seemed as confined as a prison cell or even a grave, and I was too excited to wait for Maria to wake up. Especially since the chances of her getting up before the afternoon were negligible.

I decided to go for a walk through the Ulcinj olive groves where Goran and I used to go and hide from the unbearable crowds which gathered in the town in the summertime, during the tourist season.

I went down into town and then up through the suburb of Nova Mahala to the olive groves.

'People have told me – serious people, mind – that they've met spirits up here,' Goran once said. One of them, whose words he had no reason to doubt, told him what he had experienced late one evening while returning from a walk to Valdanos Bay. Night had more or less fallen, and even in the gentle settings of an olive grove the night can seem threatening out among the trees. He could hear the yapping of jackals in the distance, but what worried him were the sounds which came from closer at hand. Somewhere half way from Valdanos to town, he heard voices speaking Italian. There: in the clearing ahead of him a group of people dressed in the fashion of the 1930s were listening intently to two Italians who were demonstrating how best to prune olive trees, if his rudimentary grasp of the language was any guide. One of the instructors was sitting on a bulge in an olive tree and demonstrating how and where to cut it, while the other spread a net out on the ground, which the mature fruit were meant to drop onto. He fled head over heels and didn't stop until he reached the first lamp-posts, where he made sure he was safe.

I recalled the kindness and naivety of my friend, who himself seemed not to be of this world, as I walked deeper into the olive grove. I stopped next to a dry stone wall to light a cigarette. Turning, I happened to see an unusual tablet on the wall: a Star of David had been carved into a stone together with Latin letters which, to my mind, meant nothing.

The owner of the property, whom I hadn't noticed before, saw me taking photos on my phone. He greeted me amiably.

'Are you Olga's son?' he asked.

I nodded. There was no point denying it.

I offered him a cigarette.

He told me he had bought the property quite recently. It had once belonged to a family which moved away to Shkodër in Albania after the Montenegrins captured Ulcinj in 1878. Now he had fixed up the property, cleared the scrub and built walls. Here, behind the stone wall I photographed, he had discovered the narrow entrance to a cave. It had been covered with a stone slab, and when he scraped the moss off he saw an inscription he couldn't read and 'the Jewish symbol', as he called it.

He realised it had to be something sacred. Although he was a Muslim, he respected what was holy to others. He therefore decided to have the sign and the letters transcribed from the slab onto the tablet I had photographed.

I asked him what the inscription meant. He didn't know, and he didn't want to risk his luck by offending whatever the inscription at the cave's entrance was dedicated to.

'It's been here for centuries. Who am I to change things now?' he said.

I suspected that a poorly educated stonemason may have miscopied the inscription, so I asked him to show me the old slab.

'It broke,' he told me. 'It fell and crumbled to pieces when workers were moving it. But I remembered the inscription and noted it down on a piece of paper, which I later gave to the mason.

He took me to the cave's entrance – a shaft now sealed with a heavy metal plate and locked.

'Have you ever been into the cave?'

'God forbid, not for anything in world.'

'Would it bother you if I did?'

He looked at me as if I had taken leave of my senses.

'I'm serious,' I said to him. 'Who knows what might be inside. I'm amazed you were able to curb your curiosity.'

'I was never curious –,' he shuddered, 'just afraid.'

It took some time, but finally I managed to persuade him to open the shaft for me. He gave me a torch and a length of rope he found for me on the property. Before I descended into the cave, he called one of the workers who were earthing up the olive trees.

'This man is a witness,' he told me. 'If anything should happen to you, it was your own decision to go in. I tried to talk you out of it, but you wouldn't listen. Alright?'

'Of course,' I said.

What he called a cave was actually a tunnel, almost two metres high and one metre wide. At first I thought it was some kind of underground storeroom which had been dug for the tools needed for work in the olive grove. But the end of the tunnel could not be seen. I kept going deep underground, until I could no longer hear the voices calling me to come back. Soon the light from the tunnel entrance had disappeared too. A sensible person would turn back now, I thought. Where is this leading me? Whoever dug this subterranean passage did so for a good reason. Why else would they have invested so much effort? It must have taken years to dig. And above all: the stone with the inscription undoubtedly had religious significance …

I must have been going for a good hour when the torch began to flicker. Soon I'd run out of light, and there seemed to be no end to the tunnel. *What now?* I thought. In order to save the battery, I turned off the torch and went on, holding on to the wall of the tunnel with my right hand.

Soon I was sick of roaming through the dark, and yet I was completely indifferent to my own destiny. I felt that if this was to be my end, I would be entirely satisfied with it.

I sat down and leaned my back against the wall. I hunched up and hugged my knees to my chest. It was warm and cosy in the tunnel. The air smelt sweetish, like the caramelised milk Olga used to make for me as a child when I had a cold. You have your qualities, I said to myself, but bravery is not one of them. All your strength always came from indifference and the thought that you had nothing to lose. That's why you're not afraid even now, although you're in serious quandary. I felt my body flag and all the strength drain from me. The torch fell out of my hand and sleep came over me, quiet and comforting, like mist at the scene of a terrible crime.

When I woke up I was saved. Or doomed. In any case, I had a butt-end of life left to think about that.

A ray of light came from my right; it gradually spread until it blinded me and stabbed me in the brain. I screamed with pain. Tears welled up in my eyes, which soon saw that the way out was just an arm's length away.

The tunnel led to Balšić Tower, the tallest building in Kalaja. I crawled to the exit, which was hidden by an antique chest which I easily pushed aside. I found myself in the building which was raised in the fifteenth century, if I remember correctly, and today serves as a gallery.

Everything was clear now: the tunnel and the inscription at the exit were no longer a secret. On the wall of the narrow chamber in Balšić Tower, for those able to read it, lay the answer to all the questions I had asked myself while wandering along the tunnel.

I would later write several articles about it, and even an essay for Channel Three of the Croatian Radio: about the Star of David which was carved into the wall of Balšić Tower by Sabbatai Zevi, the self-proclaimed Messiah, whom Olga had told me about with so much passion. Or rather, it was her favourite of all the lies she used to tell me: the lies of a woman whose love I can't deny and which was all the more precious because she was *assigned*, not born, to the role of my grandmother. The anger I felt at having been lied to receded over time. In the end, I felt only love and respect for her. She played her role perfectly and died on stage without a single gesture giving away the fact that she was acting.

Zevi was born in Smyrna, now Izmir, on 9 August 1626, on the anniversary of the destruction of the Temple. That was a Sabbath. He died in Ulcinj on 30 September 1676. That was Yom Kippur. He was forced to change faiths and died as an exile, but he was not forgotten, as Olga used to say. Olga herself seemed ultimately to believe the lies she had been taught by the authors of my life story, and she cherished the tenderest sympathy for the false Messiah – she, the false Jew.

What else did I learn about Zevi from my former grandmother? There was the story about the grandiose promise he gave his many followers, who poured into Izmir from all over Europe, in anticipation of the great day: in 1666 he would lead his people back to Israel.

In the twenty-fifth year, Zevi announced he was the Messiah. He declared the abolition of God's Law. His followers grew more numerous by the day because people need hope in times of trouble – what time is not like that? – and now he called on them to eat the forbidden fruit. He publically wedded the Torah, only to later tear it up and trample on it.

In 1666, instead of fulfilling his prophecy, he converted to Islam under threat of death.

From then on, his name was Aziz Mehmed Efendi. The Sultan expelled him to Ulcinj, where he put ashore with several dozen devotees, and this was the foundation of the lie about my Jewish origins. (Or perhaps it was not a lie, for I had not learnt the truth of my background.) I have always been intrigued by Ulcinj's lack of a Jewish cemetery – and of any marked Jewish graves at all. But actually there is one: Zevi's. He was buried in the old bazaar, in the courtyard of an Albanian family home; the Manas. But can we be sure that it is really Zevi in that grave, I often asked myself, without having a proper answer.

Zevi spent the last years of his life in Kalaja, in Balšić Tower, where he set up a small shrine with the Star of David carved into the wall. That secret place of prayer is irrefutable proof that Zevi never really changed his faith. His spirit didn't leave Ulcinj: it was too great for the small town, which didn't want to remember him, to push away to the margins of its insignificant history.

Even today, the people of Ulcinj suspect one another of being descended from Zevi's Jews, who, like their master, only pretended to convert to Islam and secretly went on practicing their own religion. The townsfolk whisper about Russian Jews who have built houses in nearby Liman Cove, with a wonderful view of Balšić Tower. You can hear people arguing in the cafés that the Jews have settled in that part of town so as to be close to the Messiah, whom they still believe in, in spite of all that occurred. People in Ulcinj are dour and monosyllabic when asked about Zevi. The tourist guides and signs don't mention him, although he was the most important person ever to have lived in the town.

It was doubtlessly Zevi's followers who dug the secret tunnel from his final residence to the olive grove. Was the tunnel used by Zevi to leave the fortress without being noticed? Or by his devotees, in order to secretly visit him? Or was it not dug until after Zevi's death, for some unimaginable reason? Was my coincidental discovery in any way linked to my investigation about my mother and to the fact that Olga, and thus I, were given a rare Jewish surname?

The gallery was shut, so I jumped out through a window. A pack of dogs was standing there in front of me as if waiting for me. I picked up a stone and threw it at the big, black one which was the leader of the pack. It hit him on the back. The dog didn't growl or move but just stared at me, like the rest of his motley but disciplined army. To the left of me was a stone wall, a good two metres high. The dogs' jaws wouldn't reach me there, I reasoned, so I ran to the wall and climbed to the top. I looked back and saw that the dogs were still motionless and looking at where I had been a few moments earlier, as if I still lingered there. I jumped down on the other side of the wall, went through the narrow, urine-sprayed alley between two houses and made off into Ulcinj's labyrinth of steep lanes; so like a living organism, a creature constantly changing shape.

41

Maria was waiting for me in the garden. In her white summer dress, with her long black hair down, looking rested and fresh, and with her bare feet up on a chair, she looked like someone who had never known sorrow and had no way of knowing it because she had just come running out of the Garden of Eden. The illusion was broken when she spoke in a voice still heavy from the night's drinking spree and ordered Tereza to make us a carafe of mojito. That was the Maria I loved: wounded, wild and dangerous – allusions to innocence only detracted from her charm.

'Have you seen that Japan was hit by another earthquake last night?' she asked. 'Just a few hours after the ground had settled the social networks, already idiot-friendly, were hit by a tsunami of brain-dead comments, which boiled down to: "Look, Mother Nature has sent us another warning. What will be in store for us if we keep refusing to respect her and go on opposing her laws?"

'But Mother Nature is no less a tyrant than God the Father. And not only that: Mother Nature doesn't give a damn about us. Christian and Muslim fundamentalists who believe our cities will be fire-and-brimstoned because we tolerate homosexuals and their "unnatural" practices, and Mother's fundamentalists who believe we will be blotted out because we tolerate the disruption of the natural balance, are on the same ontological wavelength. Their vengeful Mother who destroys us is just a Dionysian version of their Apollonian, wrathful Old-Testament patriarch,' she sneered.

'To say that we ourselves are to blame for tragedies, whose dimensions are beyond our comprehension, because we offended Him or Her, the "One" who determines our destinies, is the most facile and therefore most commonly encountered answer. Any old balderdash which attributes "meaning" is obviously still more desirable than the absence of meaning. Meaning is highly overrated, to be sure. Never before has a higher price been paid for something which doesn't exist.

'What is in balance in the natural world? What harmony can those nutters see in the tyranny of Mother Nature? Wherever you look in this garden, some wild animal is preying on a thing smaller and weaker than itself. Everywhere creatures are dying in terror and agony, meeting a slow, painful death in the jaws of another which, *naturally*, sucks its blood and savours the head it crunches between its teeth. The harmony is just in our imagination when we watch that beauty from a safe distance. We only see the green and the waving treetops and are oblivious to the death and horror which actually reign there. So-called harmony is only visible to us standing outside, exempt from its laws. What we see is a garden to us, but for everything *inside* it is a battlefield, a slaughterhouse, where the universal code is to kill and be killed.

'And then there are all those botched-up creatures, whose design shows not only the absence of order, but also of reason. Take the hedgehog, for example. Its spines protect it against others, but the very same prickles cause it great pain. The hedgehog's strong point is also its tragic flaw. Did you know that the female hedgehog keeps putting off the birth of her babies in fear of the pain which their spines could cause when they leave the womb?' she asked.

42

The opportunity I had been waiting for to confide in Maria about all the disquieting and improbable but very real discoveries I had made about my mother came after dinner.

We withdrew into the drawing room. I sat on the divan, and she lay down, with her head on my lap and her right arm reaching down my legs.

'Don't I just look like the woman on Lucian Freud's painting *Standing by the Rags* ... Don't I just!' she repeated. The thought obviously amused her. Then, with the greatest attentiveness, she listened to what I had to tell her ...

'That's the way it all is, I believe,' I said at the end of my confession. She stroked my face, pulled my head down to hers and kissed me on the forehead.

'What a shame that's not all true,' she said. 'Because if it was – if you were her son – you would have saved me from misery. That would have been easy for you. You would have saved me, and I would finally have been able to love you: because I can only love that which can destroy me.

'That's why the bond between me and Elletra is so strong,' she continued, 'and that's why she can run this house and my life from her tower without giving a single order. Of all the things she's done and said which made me suffer, do you know what hurt the most? It was long ago, back when she still used to leave the house and I had just made it through my teenage years. One morning we went for a walk through the pine forest. It was early summer, when you can still get through town and feel relaxed. Among the few bathers we saw on the beaches were a young man and woman. He was reading a book, and she lay with her head on his lap, softly humming. And Elletra said, "If only I could feel the light-heartedness of the beginning again for just one second, if only I could turn back the clock to when my illusions and hopes were stronger than all the signs of inevitable doom."

'That morning, I had the terrible realisation that nothing of mine, not even my sorrow, is unique. We convince ourselves that our sorrow is exalted, that our pain makes us exceptional, and that when it hurts we are close to something authentic and significant. But sorrow is like the large intestine: everyone has one. Even in pain you're not alone or special. Realising that my mother had already been in the space I considered my very own sanctuary, that she thought and suffered the same way as me, yet became the picture of misery she was that morning and still is today, and that I'm no different to her – *that* was a blow I have never recovered from,' Maria said.

Then she went and sat at the piano. I don't know what it was she played, but it was slow and repetitive. I stared at her long, white fingers caressing the keys made from parts of a dead elephant and soon fell asleep, imagining my mother, with her eyes closed and a look of enjoyment on her face, kneeling over a victim and gently running her finger over his dead, clenched teeth.

43

The boat see-sawed on the water like a cradle. Loud music and the hubbub of the crowd jostling at Camden Market came from outside. Drunken boys sang fans' songs, and a cheerful Pakistani called out the specialties at his stall.

I stepped over the police 'do-not-cross' tape around the scene of the crime. Below deck there was a large red stain on a white rug and two chalk outlines next to it where the bodies were found. I could see a hole made by a knife in the wooden wall of the cabin. I was interested in the shelf with the DVDs and looked for a silver case with 'X' written on it in blue felt-tip, a Verbatim disc. It wasn't there. As I was heading to the kitchenette, I passed a cracked mirror in the corridor. Despite the dark, I saw a woman in the mirror: a pale face framed by golden hair, beautiful and terrible at the same time because the eyes were missing in her otherwise perfect, well-proportioned features.

When I opened my eyes, water was dripping from the ceiling. An unbearable clamour came from upstairs. It was Tereza's voice, and through her crying I could hear her shout: *Call the police! Call the police!* I propped myself up on the ottoman and realised it was like a boat in water: Maria's drawing room was flooded. I got up and made for the stairs but stopped beside the big window which looked out into the garden: water from the house was gushing out through it, turning the manicured lawn into a mire. Day was breaking. The first rays of sunlight were piercing the treetops. Tereza screamed again and I started running up the stairs.

Water was pouring in a torrent down the broad, winding stairs. The bathroom door stood wide open and I could see Tereza kneeling beside the huge old cast-iron bath, holding Maria's lifeless body. As I rushed in to help, I trod on something and slipped. I reached into the water with my left hand. It came out holding an empty jar of zolpidem sleeping tablets. Only then did I notice that my Patek Philippe watch, Maria's present for my eighteenth birthday, was broken and had stopped at the number three. When I saw Maria's naked body, as white as a sheet, I closed my eyes in shame and took a few steps back; now I could only see Tereza's back, with Maria's arms dangling down it and her fingertips playing in the water.

'Call a doctor, call the police, for God's sake call someone!' Tereza sobbed.

44

Inspector Kruti held a short, routine conversation with me.

'Were you close to the deceased?'

'You know I was.'

'I know, but please bear with me. It's the procedure. You're the last person to have seen her alive.'

'Possibly, but I fell asleep early and now I blame myself. If I'd stayed awake I would have been able to stop her.'

'I doubt it.'

'What makes you say that?'

'I'm thinking of her condition, of course. She went to see Dr Milić for years. He prescribed her antidepressants, but she didn't take them.'

'I would have thought a doctor's medical ethics would prevent him from giving you her record card.'

'Spare me that, please … So the last time you saw her alive was when she was playing the piano?'

'That's right.'

'That's all for now. Are you planning to leave Ulcinj?'

'Yes, actually. I'm flying to Germany this afternoon. Is that a problem?'

'Why should it be? I'll leave you now to your pain. I have a long day ahead of me: I have to question all the servants and try to somehow contact Madam Elletra …

'You're not staying for the funeral?' Tereza asked when she saw me on the stairs with my bag in hand. She didn't wait for an answer; she prodded the carpet in the corridor to check it was dry and went over the bathroom floor again with another cloth. Then she sat on the edge of the bath, stretched out her tired, swollen legs and stared at her belly. She gave a heavy sigh but was satisfied, like someone who has just cleansed the world of all its filth.

45

At least I think that's how it was.

Two days later, when I was sitting on the terrace of Hotel Catalonia Colombo in Manacor, I received a mail from Inspector Kruti. He complained that I hadn't been answering his calls. The autopsy confirmed that Maria had died of an overdose of sleeping tablets. Her death was still considered a suicide, but he'd like to have a word with me about one circumstance and kindly asked me to come to the Ulcinj police station to answer a few questions as soon as possible; he didn't like to think he might have to subpoena me. The tablets Maria took, zolpidem, were not sold in Montenegro; he had checked my bank account and established that I had recently bought a pack of those same tablets with my Visa card at a pharmacy in Oxford Street. He was sure we would soon be able to clear up this strange coincidence.

What should I tell the good inspector? That the big picture we try to piece together is never complete? That there always remains some detail which doesn't fit into the mosaic, some trifling little thing which overturns the system we thought we had seen, something which deletes all the answers we've arrived at and opens up a host of new questions?

Should I tell him about my investigation and the blank at the heart of it, marked with a question mark? Should I let him know that there is no grave of an Ida Hafner at the cemetery in Kronberg near Frankfurt? Should I share with him what Wovenhand had written the day before, which led me to Mallorca? Should I tell him that I already know this won't be the end, and that after my visit to the cemetery here everything will just keep on going, till kingdom come?

With these thoughts in my mind, I came across a curious news item in the copy of *The New York Times* which the friendly waiter brought me with my coffee:

Associated Press, London – The future will stop completely, claim Spanish scientists, who have devised a theory to explain why the universe appears to be expanding and accelerating continuously. Ultimately, they say, time will stop completely.

Observations of supernovae, or exploding stars, found the movement of light indicated they were moving faster than those nearer to the centre of the universe. But the scientists claimed the accepted theory of an opposite force to gravity, known as dark energy, was wrong, and said the reality was that the growth of the universe was slowing.

Professors Jose Senovilla, Marc Mars and Raul Vera said the deceleration of time was so gradual, it was imperceptible to humans. They claimed dark energy does not exist and that time was winding down to the point when it would finally grind to a halt long after the planet ceased to exist.

The slowing down of time will eventually mean everything will appear to take place faster and faster until it eventually disappears.

There was a final sentence, too, where the language of science, having reached an impasse, returned to the language of poetry. I lingered over it for a long time. Professor Senovilla made the statement in the *New Scientist* magazine, describing what would happen when time finally stood still, and I recited this sentence to myself like a prayer for the comforting outcome I want to believe in:

'Then everything will be frozen, like a snapshot of one instant, forever.'

Lightning Source UK Ltd.
Milton Keynes UK
UKHW012117080819
347643UK00005B/154/P